HARRY LOVE:
PRESCRIPTION FOR
MURDER

Daphne E Machon

ATHENA PRESS
LONDON

HARRY LOVE: PRESCRIPTION FOR MURDER
Copyright © Daphne E Machon 2003

ISBN 1 84401 146 1

First Published 2003 by
ATHENA PRESS
Queen's House, 2 Holly Road
Twickenham TW1 4EG
United Kingdom

Printed for Athena Press
Printed and Bound by Antony Rowe Ltd

HARRY LOVE: PRESCRIPTION FOR MURDER

*For the Nurses, Health Care Assistants and staff
Of Kettering General Hospital, especially on
Twywell and Harrowden C Wards.*

Acknowledgements

My thanks to Northampton CID for their invaluable help and patience. Thanks also to the officers of Market Harborough Police Station who so readily answered questions when accosted by me in the street, or when I telephoned the station sounding desperate.

Chapter One

Monday morning – and as usual Detective Sergeant Charlie Marlow and Detective Inspector Ed Harrington were dashing to Police Headquarters with only minutes to spare before they would be deemed late. Ed sometimes wished he had not agreed to collect his friend each morning, as he liked to be early for work, and for as long as he had known him Charlie had always found deadlines to be his failing. Now Ed regularly found himself having to urge his colleague into putting a spurt on; like today, as once again Charlie had kept him waiting. Ed drove his well-worn black Saab into the police car park and pulled into one of the spaces reserved for the CID team. 'One of these days you're going to make me late, Charlie,' he grumbled as he unfolded his long legs and lifted his 6' 4" frame from the car. 'Perhaps you should go back to using your motorbike. The Super might be an affable old boy most of the time, but his tongue is pretty sharp when he's put out and he *is* hot on timekeeping as you well know.'

'Stop fretting, Ed, we've always made it on time so far. But if you would prefer me to get the bike out, then I will.'

'No, no, I don't really mean it, I like your company in the morning. It's just that today is special, with the new Chief Inspector arriving. The Super wants to brief us before the new broom reports in.'

Charlie grinned and ran his hand through his short-cropped fair hair, his blue eyes sparkling, and said, 'We'll be there.' At thirty-six years of age he was just two years younger than his friend and the live wire of the partnership. He leaped from the car and turned to join Ed just as a smart little red Lotus Élite swept into the parking space beside them. The woman at the wheel braked smoothly as Charlie held up his hand in front of her car.

'Sorry, sweetie,' he smiled, eyeing the good-looking redhead with admiration, 'I'm afraid you can't park here.' He pointed to the area a few metres away. 'Over there if you don't mind.'

'But…'

'No buts, sweetie – over there, please.' Charlie smiled his usual disarming smile and the young woman, not wishing to become involved in an argument, reversed her car and moved away to where she had been directed. Charlie looked enviously at the red Lotus before hurrying off to catch up with Ed who was already on his way into the Station.

'Do you have to call all women "sweetie", Charlie?' asked Ed. 'One of these days you'll find yourself in hot water.'

Charlie chortled. 'I'm only being friendly. They don't really mind.'

From the window of the CID quarters at the top of the building, Superintendent George Hollyoak watched as the two men came across the tarmac. The tall, dark, broad-shouldered Harrington and the equally tall but fair and slightly built Marlow. They were two of his best men. The serious, conscientious Ed Harrington and the lively, energetic Charlie Marlow. They made an excellent combination, each complimenting the other, although he recognised that Marlow was more often than not kept in line by the solid Harrington. The two men entered the CID room to be greeted warmly by their colleagues. They were popular with the team and well regarded by the senior officers in the Station who knew them to be straightforward and incorruptible.

'Just made it, I see,' said Superintendent Hollyoak, glancing at his watch. 'The new DCI will be here any minute and I do want to give the right impression.'

'What impression is that then, sir?' quipped Charlie.

'The best, if you don't mind, Marlow,' replied the Superintendent. 'Chief Inspector Love is highly qualified, not only with a Cambridge Law degree, but a first at that.'

'Hmm! We'll see.' Jack Fuller, a plump, old-fashioned copper, muttered his disapproval. He was not too sure about these high-flying youngsters with their string of university qualifications. He'd been a policeman now for thirty-two years, the latter twelve as a sergeant, and he considered good policing to be all about knowing the area and the people and ordinary, down-to-earth hard work. Now this young chap was being thrust upon them and would no doubt throw his weight around and change things. He scratched his head and rearranged his thinning hair over the ever-increasing bald spot that he knew was appearing. Perhaps it was time he considered retirement; he had been thinking of it for some time.

Superintendent Hollyoak was speaking again. 'Now I want you all to welcome DCI Love into the department. We are a strong team and known for our loyalty to each other. I wish for that to continue. Chief Inspector Love is straight from the Met and very experienced. I think we are extremely lucky to have such a person joining us, so I'm relying on you to do your bit. Right!' he added, as there came a light knock on the door. 'Now don't let me down.'

The door opened and standing framed in the doorway was a tall, auburn-haired woman in her late thirties. She was strikingly handsome, her green eyes appearing as emeralds against her smooth olive skin. She smiled as she strode through the line of open-mouthed officers; the beautifully cut skirt of her navy suit moving with oiled precision across her long thighs. She reached Superintendent Hollyoak who took her hand in a warm grasp.

'Harry,' he said, 'we are delighted to have you join us. Team,' he went on, turning to the stunned group in front of him, 'may I introduce Detective Chief Inspector Harriet Love.'

You could have heard a pin drop in the CID room, and it was some seconds before people pulled themselves together and murmured their 'good mornings'. George Hollyoak walked with Harriet down the line of officers introducing her to each one in turn. She laughed a musical laugh as she was confronted with the numerous names thrown at her. 'I'll do my best to remember your names,' she said; her voice as musical as her laugh, 'but do bear with me, won't you, if I make mistakes?'

As the Superintendent and DCI Love drew near to Charlie and Ed, Charlie just wished that the ground would open and swallow him up as he recognised the driver of the red Lotus Élite from the car park. The Chief Inspector stood immediately in front of the two friends.

'Inspector Ed Harrington and Sergeant Charlie Marlow.' Said the Superintendent, introducing them.

Ed nodded as he was addressed and said, 'Good morning, Ma'am,' as positively as he could muster, trying hard to quell the feeling of jealousy that unexpectedly churned in the pit of his stomach. The woman in front of him must have been the same age as himself – possibly younger – and he suddenly remembered how close he had been to going to university. An unfamiliar feeling of envy gnawed at his insides. Fleetingly he felt sad, thinking of the death of his father that had prevented him studying for a degree. But that was all in the past, and now he must accept the new DCI with good grace and move on.

The soft voice was now acknowledging Charlie, but Charlie found that the muscles of his face appeared to be frozen and he was unable to speak. Chief Inspector Love looked him straight in the eye and said, 'Good morning, Sergeant Marlow.' Her voice was low, well educated and beautiful. Charlie finally managed to mutter something inaudible and followed this up with a sudden bout of coughing. As the new officer was about to move away, she turned to Charlie casually.

'Would you be a sweetie and move my car into the correct parking space?' She held up her car keys with two long fingers of her slender, beautifully manicured hand. 'I was unsure where to park when I arrived but I have no doubt you will know where I ought to be. It's a little red Lotus. You should have no difficulty finding it as it's the only vehicle in the visitors' area.' She dropped the keys into Charlie's outstretched hand before turning to follow Superintendent Hollyoak back up the room.

Charlie swallowed his embarrassment as he heard his colleagues chuckling. He hurried from the room to move the Élite into the space that he had forced the redhead to move from barely ten minutes earlier.

Superintendent Hollyoak took Chief Inspector Love to her office leaving the officers in the CID room to recover from the shock of having a woman, and a glamorous one at that, join the team as their senior officer.

Jack Fuller was the first one to speak. 'Don't know what the force is coming to. A bloody woman! Bad enough being a high-flying Cambridge graduate without her being a woman as well.' He snorted and turned back to his desk.

The room was alive with animated conversation about the new senior officer. Petite Narinder Pancholi turned to her friend, tall athletic Sally Pringle. 'Wow! That's a turn-up for the book.'

'And one in the eye for the chauvinists among us,' replied Sally, thinking of Charlie Marlow. The two women DCs had been friends for some time and shared a house together in the village of Wicken just outside Northampton. It was not too far from the police station here in the pretty market town of Torreston where they were based.

A sarcastic cheer went up on the return of Charlie and Sally nudged Narinder gleefully.

'Parked the car neatly, have we, sweetie?' asked Duncan McAllister, his unruly red hair standing on end as usual. Charlie pulled a face as he went over to join Ed. Only he and his friend understood the implication of being asked to re-park the red Lotus, although everyone else in the room recognising the term 'sweetie' had guessed that somewhere along the line Charlie had put his foot in it.

'Blimey,' muttered Charlie. 'How was I to know that the new DCI would be a film star!'

'Perhaps that will teach you to stop being condescending towards women,' replied Ed, shuffling through a file of papers and not looking up. 'Come on – we should be out and about. I'd like the investigation on this stolen car racket completed today.' He waved the sheaf of papers and turned towards the door. The two officers left the police station together.

In her office, Harriet turned to George Hollyoak. 'They had no idea I was a woman, had they?'

The Superintendent chuckled. 'Well, no. Everyone calls you Harry, so I thought I would go along with the idea that you were a man. I wouldn't have missed the looks on their faces when you walked in, for anything.' The big man rubbed his hands together gleefully.

Harriet was not so sure about the joke. 'I don't want to get off on the wrong foot, George. I need to be part of this team, and heaven knows it's difficult enough being a woman without treating it as humorous.'

'Come come, Harry! No one could ever consider you or your

work humorous. You are one of the force's brightest and most conscientious officers. I couldn't believe my luck when I was told that you were to be sent here.'

Harriet wrinkled her nose. 'I hope you didn't pull any strings on my behalf.'

'Certainly not.' George Hollyoak pulled himself up to his full 6' 2". 'There was no need for me to do that. The selection team was more than impressed with your CV.'

'Mmm.' Harriet hoped that it was true. The last thing she wanted was favours. She was determined to be successful due to her own abilities. She wanted no help from family friends.

George Hollyoak continued. 'I've known your parents for years and you since you were born, my dear. I was obliged to inform the selection board of my closeness to your family and I withdrew from the selection board immediately your name came up for this post. You need have no fear that you were favoured by me, I can assure you, and I promise you – you will receive no favours from me while you work here. Does that make you happy?'

Harriet smiled. 'Yes, thank you, George. It will be "Sir!" from now on, and I must be Chief Inspector Love.' She hugged the large man in front of her. 'Now show me the rest of the Department and tell me exactly what is going on at present.'

Superintendent Hollyoak happily showed Harriet around the police station and was not unaware of the stir he caused when he introduced her as the new Detective Chief Inspector to the uniformed division downstairs.

'Bloody hell, where did he find her?' gasped a young constable as he entered a room just as she and her escort were leaving.

'That, young man, is the new DCI,' said the Duty Sergeant. 'Now close your mouth and bring me those papers I sent you for.'

Harriet spent the whole day organising her new office and reading up on the on-going cases being handled by the CID at present. She was excited about this new position and had been told by Chief Superintendent Grayson that she would have a free hand in her investigations, with her immediate boss being George Hollyoak. Knowing George as she did, she knew there would be no interference on his part, although it was comforting to have his experience to hand should she need it. She left the police station at six that evening. It had felt like a long day even though she had done relatively little in the way of police work, but tomorrow she would throw herself into the real world of detection.

'Tomorrow' came earlier than expected when Harriet's bedside telephone screamed in her ear at the unearthly hour of ten minutes past four in the morning.

Awake in an instant, she grabbed the receiver.

'Ma'am, it's Sergeant Yates from the Station. The body of a woman has just been discovered by the refuse collectors behind the shops in Osborne Close. Uniform are at the scene in Cygnet Lane and an ambulance is on its way.' The calm voice of Sergeant Pete Yates gave Harriet directions and a few more details before informing her that he would call her assistants and Forensic and they would join her there. He wished her good luck on her first case and hung up.

Harriet realised that her heart was pounding furiously. How stupid, she thought, as she dressed swiftly, pulling on black jeans and sweater and grabbing a red jacket from behind the door. She had done this sort of thing dozens of times before in the Met, why should this be special? But she knew the answer to that. She needed to prove herself, for here in Torreston she was in charge of the division. She was no longer just another inspector in an enormous squad in London; she was now the Chief Inspector and the leader. She desperately needed to do well.

There was little traffic on the road as Harriet drove her little red Lotus to the address the Duty Sergeant had given her. She was glad that she had obtained authorisation to use her own car, it was so much nicer than the CID cars in the pool.

The area behind the lock-up shops where the body had been found backed onto Cygnet Lane, a pedestrianised area that ran beside the Cottage Hospital grounds. Harriet parked at the end of Osborne Road near the Close with the row of shops. Taking her torch from the glove compartment, she swung her long legs from her car and walked into Cygnet Lane as Sergeant Yates had advised her. The lane was narrow with a wooden fence in a dilapidated condition separating it from the backs of the shops.

The other side of the fence was cluttered with dustbins, skips and rubbish thrown out by the shopkeepers. The flashing blue light of the patrol car guided her to the murder scene. She hurried towards the group of people gathered by a gap in the fence, to be greeted by silence as the men standing there gaped at her. A young constable moved forwards with his hand raised, but before he could address her Harriet took her warrant card from her pocket and held it up for him to see. 'Detective Chief Inspector Love,' she said clearly. 'And you are?'

'Constable Stockwell, Ma'am,' said the young man swallowing hard, the look of complete amazement still on his face.

'Constable Harrison,' said the second officer coming forward hastily.

'Where is the body?' asked Harriet matter-of-factly.

'Er, over here, Ma'am,' answered PC Stockwell, pulling himself together with difficulty and pointing through the gap in the fence to the row of bins. 'Be careful, Ma'am, it's not very nice round there.'

Harriet smiled without turning round. What did these young men think she was, a china doll? She had been brought up on crime and investigation and had seen many a horrific scene. She did not have to enjoy all that she had witnessed but certainly one became used to it. DCI Love walked gingerly through the fence and went to the bins. She placed her feet carefully, shining her torch in front of her as she proceeded. She did not wish to destroy any possible evidence. As she directed the beam of light behind the foul-smelling bins, she was confronted by the lifeless body of a young woman lying among a pile of rubbish, a small black handbag beside her. The woman was wearing some kind of uniform. A red scarf was knotted tightly around her neck, her blue face and protruding tongue distorting her once good-looking features. Harriet caught her breath. It did not matter how many murder scenes you visited, death, and more accurately murder, was always horrendous.

She stood for a moment taking in the sordid scene in front of her. The young woman lying among the rubbish could have been resting had it not been for her discoloured face and grotesque expression and the fact that she would hardly have chosen such a disgusting place to retire. The dead woman's white flesh gleamed in Harriet's torchlight, the red scarf around her neck standing out like some kind of bizarre warning. The DCI walked back to the waiting men and turned to the two refuse collectors, who were obviously shaken by their discovery. 'Come and sit over here,' she said kindly, directing them to a bench.

The two men gratefully moved away from the gap in the fence and sat down just as they heard a car pulling up in Osborne Close at the front of the shops. Ed Harrington and Charlie Marlow walked down the alleyway between the buildings and cast an eye at the body before stepping over the broken fence and joining their boss, who was standing with the men who had made the sickening discovery. A second car edged its way along the narrow Cygnet Lane. This one contained a police photographer and two further officers, all clad in their white protective gear and as they joined the growing group of police officers, the SOCO team – Scene of Crime Officers – was complete.

Charlie and Ed greeted Harriet in unison.

'Morning, Ma'am.'

Charlie was now fully recovered from his humiliation of the previous day and was eager to start work on this new case. Ed nodded as he acknowledged the DCI, his face grim. He still found murder distasteful and was amazed at how some officers came to terms with gruesome situations so quickly.

'Good morning,' said Harriet, 'if you can call it that. Inspector, would you and Sergeant Marlow take statements from these two gentlemen who discovered the body, while I have a word with Forensic, who I think are just arriving.'

She left Ed and Charlie to question the two refuse collectors and moved away to greet a young woman dressed from head to toe in white protective gear who had just reached the scene. Her assistant was an older man who followed behind carrying a heavy-looking case. This he readily placed at his feet as Harriet joined them.

'I'm Detective Chief Inspector Love,' Harriet put to the woman in front of her, holding out her hand in greeting.

'Dr Stacey Boston,' replied the woman in white as she shook the proffered hand. 'This is John March,' she added, introducing her colleague.

'Not the most convivial of circumstances in which to meet for the first time,' sighed Harriet, 'but don't let me detain you. PC Stockwell will show you the body. Nothing has been disturbed, but I should like the handbag that's lying beside the body as soon as possible so that we can identify her.' The DCI beckoned one of the constables and he hurried over.

'Ma'am?'

Harriet placed a kindly hand on the arm of the anxious-faced young man and asked him to take Dr Boston to the murder scene. 'There's no need for you to stay with the body,' she added gently.

Luke Stockwell had never seen a murder victim before – and it had to be murder, as no one could strangle themselves with a scarf, could they? – and he was feeling decidedly queasy. He hoped that in the poor lighting no one would notice that he felt like vomiting, but certainly the DCI had spoken to him sympathetically, which he appreciated.

He wondered if she had guessed that he was not accustomed to dealing with dead bodies. He guided the doctor to the crime scene but did not go near the bins again. PC Stockwell returned to his colleague at the squad car, and as casually as possible he climbed into the passenger seat and leaned back against the headrest taking deep breaths of air.

Somewhere in the distance a clock struck five. People were now gathering behind the blue and white tape that cordoned off the area at the front of the shop. Two press reporters were making themselves particularly unwelcome by trying to force themselves through the crowd to obtain photographs. One in particular was being quite objectionable, by pushing his camera into Harriet's face and shouting questions at her. Harriet looked at him, noting his yellow teeth and piggy eyes and in a quiet, firm voice she asked him to move back behind the tape. She had instructed that Cygnet Lane be closed completely until it had been scoured for evidence. Many people used the lane as a short cut, and having discovered that it was closed because of a murder they were gathering like vultures. Incidents such as this attracted onlookers like bees to the honey pot. There was nothing that Harriet could do about the spectators but as long as they stayed well back she was content to leave things as they were for the time being. Stacey

Boston appeared from behind the refuse bins holding a small black handbag in her gloved hand and she handed it to DCI Love. 'It's been dusted for fingerprints.'

Harriet, who had taken her own latex gloves from her pocket and donned them in readiness, carefully accepted the handbag.

'The body can go to the morgue whenever you're ready,' said Dr Boston. 'I've done a preliminary examination and I'll carry out a detailed one at the post-mortem.'

'What can you tell me so far?' enquired Harriet carefully placing the handbag in a large plastic bag.

'Well, the victim is a young woman in her early twenties, and death as far as I can tell was from strangulation. No sexual assault. She has been dead for about six hours which puts her death at around ten thirty last night. She's wearing a nurse's uniform, so presumably she was coming off, or going on duty when she was attacked. The only skin break on the body appears to be a small cut on her left earlobe. She is not wearing earrings, although her ears are pierced, so perhaps she scratched her own ear when removing them. I don't know if nurses are allowed to wear earrings on duty these days,' she added.

Harriet nodded. 'Thank you, Dr Boston. SOCO are making a detailed search of the area and we'll see what turns up. I'll wait for your full report of the post-mortem.' She turned to speak to Ed Harrington as he came up beside her. 'Inspector, when the Scene of Crime Officers have completed their examination, would you ask uniform to remove the body and make sure the area remains cordoned off. Leave two constables on guard until you can summon support. The ambulance is waiting.' She then spoke to Charlie. 'Sergeant tell the spectators that the show is over and try and move them away.'

'Right, Ma'am,' Charlie replied. He went up the alley to Osborne Close. The crowd had grown in the last few minutes and he had to raise his voice to keep them back. The covered body was eventually brought up the alley and placed in the ambulance. A weird, calm, silence fell over the crowd. Only the flashing of the reporters' cameras' disturbed the atmosphere. The white vehicle drove away. No one in the crowd spoke. They just stood there mesmerised. Murders just did not happen in a place like Torreston.

Harriet turned to say goodbye to Stacey Boston and John March and as they departed she breathed in deeply and exhaled very slowly. A life had been taken. What a waste! A dangerous killer was at large and he needed catching.

A young, bespectacled, serious-looking man in white protective gear came up to her. 'You must be DCI Love.'

'I am. Are you in charge of the SOCO team?' Harriet looked at the man in front of her. He was in his late thirties and little more than five feet eight inches tall. He was very slight with wisps of sandy hair escaping from beneath his protective headgear and his dark brown eyes appeared enormous behind his large glasses. He had an intense expression on his face as he answered.

'Yes, Ma'am. Sergeant Phillip Hewitt at your service. We shall be here some time, but we shall be removing most of the rubbish and stuff from around the bins and taking it away for detailed examination. I don't want to miss anything.'

'Thank you, Sergeant, I'm sure you will be more than thorough.' Phillip Hewitt returned through the gap in the fence like a mole retreating into its burrow. He was eager to continue leading the search. Harriet turned to speak to DI Harrington and DS Marlow.

'Right! Let's see if the contents of the handbag can tell us who the dead woman is.' She handed Ed her torch as she removed the handbag from the plastic bag and carefully opened it, Ed shone the beam into the small opening. A driving licence and building society book were both in the name of Carol Young, and the address was 56 Cossington Road, Torreston.

'Cossington Road's only a few hundred metres away,' said the DI. 'If she worked at the Cottage Hospital, this would be a short cut home.'

'Pity she didn't take the car and go the long way round,' muttered Charlie, looking at the driving licence.

Harriet replaced the items in the handbag and spoke to Ed. 'I'm leaving you in charge here. Call the Station and ask for assistance in searching the area and keeping both Osborne Close and Cygnet Lane closed. I shall go with Charlie to Cossington Road. I don't yet know the area very well so I shall need to be directed.' She handed the bag to the DI. 'We'll meet back at the Station.'

'Right.' Ed was happy that at least his new boss had enough faith in him to leave him in charge. As he watched the DCI leave with Charlie he reached for his mobile phone to call in for reinforcements.

Charlie couldn't remember the last time he had been driven by a woman. It was true he was something of a chauvinist, and perhaps this was part of the cause of the break-up of his marriage; but that had happened over two years ago and now he was once again enjoying his freedom. He occasionally wondered if he was the marrying kind at all, as he was certainly happier living on his own. He noted how smoothly the DCI drove the Lotus. He was usually very critical of women drivers but today he was unable to find fault. The soft voice of his boss broke into his thoughts.

'You are supposed to be directing me, don't forget.'

'Sorry! Right at the next corner and first left.'

Cossington Road was made up of neat terraced houses with tidy gardens, shiny windows and pretty curtains. Number 56 was about halfway along and Harriet pulled up behind a black Golf that was parked directly in front of the house they wished to visit.

Charlie rang the doorbell. There was no reply. He repeated the action and they again waited. 'Let's look round the back,' suggested Harriet. They opened the side gate and walked to the rear of the premises. Like the front of the house it was neat and tidy with a narrow walled garden and numerous pots of flowers on a small terraced area outside the kitchen door. The house appeared deserted.

'She probably lives alone,' said Charlie, 'so she won't have been missed yet.'

'We'll try next door.' Harriet looked at her watch as she led the way from Number 56 to Number 54. 'It's nearly six and there's a light on in the bathroom.' She rang the doorbell. The door was eventually opened by a sleepy-eyed young man in a dressing gown.

'Good God! What do you want at this hour?'

'Sorry to disturb you,' Harriet began, holding up her warrant card, 'but could you tell me where Carol Young might be?'

The young man scratched his head still not fully awake. 'She works at the Cottage Hospital. She probably isn't up yet I don't think she goes on until later as we know she comes home at about ten thirty at night.'

Charlie spoke, holding up his warrant card as he did so. 'Does she live alone?'

'Yes.'

'Has she any relatives that you know of?'

'Not locally. Her family live in Leeds. She goes home on her days off, that's about all I know. Has anything happened—?'

'We're not sure,' Harriet interrupted. 'But should there be any news we will certainly inform you. Is that her car outside her house?'

'Yes, the black Golf, but she usually walks to work as it isn't far across the back.'

'Thank you for your help.'

The two officers moved away and Charlie jotted down the car number as they passed the Golf. They climbed into the Lotus and before driving off Harriet rang the Station to ask for a vehicle check on the young woman's car. Harriet put away her mobile phone and started the engine. With Charlie giving directions she set off for the Cottage Hospital, taking the longer route that, regrettably, Carol Young had not taken the previous night.

Chapter Two

Talking to the staff at the Cottage Hospital revealed that Nurse Carol Young had left the medical ward, on which she worked, at about ten fifteen the previous night.

'According to the duty book, she signed off with Maeve Cochran.' Sister Cheyney showed the entry to DCI Love and DS Marlow.

'Where does Nurse Cochran live?' asked Harriet.

'Plover Street,' came the reply, 'I can give you the number.' The sister fumbled through her desk drawer and produced a heavy folder, which she flicked through. 'Number 12,' she started looking anxious. 'Has something happened to Carol?'

'We're not sure at the moment but we will keep you informed.' As she was about to leave, Harriet added, 'I see that you are allowed to wear earrings on duty.'

Sister Cheyney fingered the gold studs in her ears and smiled. 'Only if they are small studs like these.'

Harriet nodded and she and Charlie left the ward together.

'So where is Plover Street?' asked Harriet once they were outside.

'Even closer than Cossington Road, so they could have walked part of the way together.' Charlie pointed in the direction of the murder scene. 'No need to take the car, we can walk.'

'Good idea, it might give us an idea of time and distance.' Harriet followed the sergeant across the hospital car park and out into the lane that ran beside the perimeter fence. Just metres along Cygnet Lane there was a left-hand turn into Plover Street.

'That took just seven minutes,' said Charlie looking at his watch. They carried on along Cygnet Lane, walking at a steady pace, and arrived at the refuse bins minutes later.

Harriet paused where two uniformed officers stood on guard at the gap in the fence. 'How long was that from the turn-off to Plover Street, Sergeant?' she asked.

'Barely four minutes,' replied Charlie. 'Forensic were spot on with their times.'

The two uniformed men knew Sergeant Marlow and guessed that the woman with him must be the new DCI that they had heard so much about. They showed no surprise therefore when she approached them for a few words. They informed Harriet that Inspector Harrington and his team had left about ten minutes previously. Harriet and Charlie retraced their steps to the turn-off to Plover Street, but this time they turned into it, looking for Number 12.

'Here we are,' said Charlie, stopping in front of a house displaying a large 12. He rang the bell. A middle-aged man who was dressed and ready for work opened the door.

'Detective Sergeant Marlow and Detective Chief Inspector Love,' said Charlie, holding up his warrant card.

Harriet did likewise. 'Mr Cochran?' she asked.

'Yes, what's happened?'

'Please don't be alarmed,' said Harriet, 'we need to ask Maeve Cochran a few questions regarding a colleague she was on duty with last night.'

'Is Maeve Cochran your wife?' asked Charlie.

'No, my daughter,' came the reply. 'She and my wife are not up yet, but you had better come in if it's urgent.'

'I'm afraid it is,' said Harriet. 'We should be obliged if you could call your daughter for us.'

Harriet and Charlie were taken into the front room and offered seats. Some minutes later a tired-looking young woman of about twenty-four or five appeared at the doorway in a dressing gown.

'What's happened?' she asked anxiously.

'We understand that you left the hospital last night with Carol Young. Could you tell us the time and where and when you parted company?' Harriet kept her voice low and as gentle as possible. There was never any easy way of delivering bad news.

Maeve sat down sharply. 'Has something happened to Carol?'

Harriet went over and sat beside her, placing an arm round her shoulders. 'The body of a young woman has been discovered in Cygnet Lane and her handbag contains items indicating that she could be Carol Young.'

The young nurse began to sob. 'Oh no! No, not Carol...'

Mrs Cochran appeared at the door. 'Please – come in,' said Harriet. She rose from her seat beside Maeve, allowing the mother to take over the comforting of her daughter.

Mr Cochran had to leave for work but promised he would do his best to return home as early as possible. When Maeve was calmer Sergeant Marlow took over the interviewing, but there was little that could be added to what the two officers had already learned. The two nurses had come off duty at about ten fifteen and walked together as far as the turn-off to Plover Road, where they parted company.

'We always did that when we were on the same late shift,' wept Maeve. 'It's such a short distance and reasonably well lit, we never gave it a second thought.'

'And you saw no one in the vicinity at all last night?' For all his 'attitude' Harriet observed that Charlie was conducting the interview with a gentleness and sympathy that hitherto she wouldn't have looked for in the sergeant. She felt a new regard for him. George had told her that he was a commendable officer, and George Hollyoak did not make comments such as that without sound evidence.

Charlie spoke again. 'Do you by any chance know the address in Leeds of Carol's parents?' And as Maeve shook her head, he added, 'Or perhaps their first names?'

'Her father is called Ken, and I think her mother is Mary or Marjorie. I'm not absolutely sure.'

'That's a great help,' smiled Charlie. 'I'm sure we shall find them from that.'

'Just one more question,' said Harriet, as Charlie concluded his questioning. 'Was Carol wearing earrings last night?'

Maeve thought only for a second. 'Yes. Her tiny pearl studs. She always wears...wore' – her voice broke – 'them on duty.'

'Thank you, we will leave you in peace. We're only sorry that we had to bring you such terrible news, but until we have contacted her parents and she has been officially identified, we should be grateful if you say nothing to anyone.'

Maeve nodded and the officers left the house to return to Torreston Police Station.

Back at the Station, Harriet met up with Inspector Harrington and the rest of the team. Ed had already set up the Incident Room with the usual assortment of white-boards, pens and maps, the material they had gathered so far and diagrams of the murder scene. Harriet took over the briefing and added to the equation, the information that she and Charlie had gleaned from their enquiries at the hospital and from Maeve Cochran.

'Nurse Cochran is adamant that there was no one in the lane as they walked home and she is positive that there was no one in the vicinity as she and Carol Young left the hospital.' Harriet cast her eyes around the room at the solemn faces absorbing her every work. 'Now does that mean the attacker was lying in wait for just Carol, knowing that she and her friend parted at Plover Street? Or was it simply a fluke that he was already in the lane and met his victim by chance? Either way we need door-to-door enquiries in the roads where the houses back onto the lane and a close search of the lane itself. I'll leave you to organise that, Inspector Harrington,' she said, turning to Ed, 'while I speak to West Yorkshire Police to see if they can trace Mr and Mrs Young.'

'Right, Ma'am.' Ed moved to the front of the room and began organising the team into groups.

Harriet went to her office to telephone, and having spoken to the Duty Sergeant in Yorkshire, she sat at her desk to mull over the happenings of the morning. It was still only eight thirty but it felt as if she had done a full day's work. She covered her mouth with her hand as she yawned widely.

There came a light knock on the door, and in response to her calling, 'Come in,' the slight figure of DC Duncan McAllister entered.

'Could I have a word, Ma'am?' he asked almost shyly. 'I have spoken to DI Harrington and he's told me to come to you.'

'Of course. Duncan isn't it?'

'Yes, Ma'am.'

'Sit down.' Harriet indicated a chair by her desk, and the young officer, whose mop of red hair was particularly unruly this morning, cautiously sat down.

'Now! What can I do for you?'

Duncan McAllister took a deep breath. 'I hope you don't think

I'm stupid,' he began, 'and I hope I am not out of line coming to you, but last year a nurse from Motherwell Infirmary was murdered. I remember it well for two reasons. One, my sister is a nurse and was working at the infirmary at the time, and they were all very shaken by the incident. Secondly, the victim was strangled by a scarf. A red, pure wool scarf.' He waited, searching the face of the DCI tentatively.

'Really!' Harriet was now very alert. 'Well done, Duncan. You're certainly not out of line bringing me this information. Thank you, we will check with the National Computer link to see if there have been any similar cases over the years and I will also get in touch with the Motherwell Police. Do you remember the outcome of the murder?'

'No one was ever charged, Ma'am, as far as I know. Although suspicion fell on a boyfriend that she had fallen out with, no evidence was ever produced that might incriminate him.'

'Thank you, anyway Duncan, you've done really well. I'll let you know what we turn up from HOLMES.' She smiled at the young officer, who was thinking how amazingly beautiful she was. He left the room in somewhat of a daze. He had never been praised like that before.

HOLMES stood for Home Office Large Major Enquiry System and linked all information regarding murders and other serious incidents from around the country. Harriet would have to send a fax to all other forces requesting information on similar murders in their area. She decided to detail Jack Fuller to the task of searching for the relevant information.

Within the hour West Yorkshire returned Harriet's call, informing her that they had located Mr and Mrs Young, and a car had already been despatched to collect them and drive them to Torreston for the identification of their daughter. Harriet sighed as she replaced the telephone receiver. This afternoon she would have the harrowing task of escorting the Youngs to the mortuary, but before that happened she needed to search the murdered woman's house to look for anything that might implicate a boyfriend or others associated in her murder.

She telephoned the CID room for DS Marlow and minutes later they once again set off in the little red Lotus. At Cossington

Street, Harriet pulled on her latex gloves, glancing at Charlie as he did the same. Using the keys from Nurse Young's handbag she let them into Number 56. The small house felt cold and surprisingly empty. Or was it just that Harriet and Charlie had the knowledge that its owner was dead? The rooms were small, sparsely furnished and painted in pale colours to give them the appearance of being larger than they were. The curtains and cushions were bright and cheerful, and magazines were scattered on the floor. In the kitchen the remnants of a meal from the previous night remained on a tray on the breakfast bar, but other than that the place was spotlessly clean and still bore the smell of a cleansing disinfectant. There was a small bathroom and two bedrooms upstairs. One bedroom was quite large, which Carol Young obviously occupied, and the smaller appeared to be a guest room. The only photograph on display was that of a middle-aged couple in a silver frame on the bedside table, which Harriet took to be the woman's parents.

DCI Love turned to DS Marlow. 'I'll check up here, Charlie, if you would search downstairs. Quite honestly I have the feeling that this murder is a case of this poor soul being in the wrong place at the wrong time, and this visit won't turn up anything that might indicate who the killer is.'

'Right, Ma'am.'

As Charlie left the room to return downstairs Harriet started opening drawers. Suddenly she had felt vulnerable, standing in the bedroom of a dead female whom she had never met. She had no desire to see her male colleague searching through this woman's underwear, and gently she slid her hands beneath the nearly folded garments drawer by drawer.

The search revealed nothing, as Harriet had suspected and within the hour she and DS Marlow returned to the police station.

Sergeant Jack Fuller was delighted to have been asked to request information from the rest of the country, and he immediately set about sending the all-important fax, detailing the murder of Nurse Carol Young and the murder weapon, a red scarf. He asked that all forces check back at least four years for any murders of nurses and most particularly any strangled by a scarf.

The forces with an interest in the Torreston case would send him the computer disc that their force had compiled, by registered post. This would take a day at least and he was eager to commence searching the National Police Computer link for comparable murders. He really did not want to wait a whole day now that his appetite had been whetted. Sergeant Jack Fuller was feeling quite jubilant.

Just before twelve, West Yorkshire Police contacted Harriet to inform her that the car carrying Mr and Mrs Young was almost at Torreston and would be arriving at the Station in ten minutes. Harriet contacted the Duty Sergeant and asked him to send an officer and car to the front entrance to drive herself and the Youngs to the mortuary. Ten minutes later she was standing at the Station door as the West Yorkshire Police car pulled up. Harriet greeted the two officers, introducing herself and shaking their hands. The two young men tried to hide their amazement at the cordial reception given them by this handsome woman and hastily opened the rear doors of the car for Mr and Mrs Young to alight.

Harriet greeted the couple with compassion, saying how sorry she was that they had to face the ordeal of identifying the body of their daughter. She then turned to the two officers who had brought them to the Midlands.

'You men go to the canteen and have a coffee and some refreshments before you think about the return journey. I will take Mr and Mrs Young to the mortuary.' She guided the couple over to the division car that was waiting for her and the sombre party left for the mortuary.

The murder victim was indeed Carol Young and on returning to the Station, Harriet escorted the dead woman's devastated parents to a quiet room and asked a constable to organise tea for them. Neither of them wanted to eat anything, and this did not surprise Harriet. Who would ever wish to eat again on learning that their daughter had just been murdered?

The two Constables from West Yorkshire sat drinking coffee in the police canteen and munching their way through an enormous plate of sandwiches. They acknowledged Jack Fuller and his friend, Sergeant Graham Collins from Uniform, as they sat down at the same table.

'And who are the lucky ones having Mother Love to look after them?' quipped the first constable grinning over his sandwich.

'Some mother,' laughed the second. 'Bet she doesn't get her hands dirty if she can help it!'

'Might damage one of those beautifully manicured nails,' agreed the first young man.

'She might also be able to teach you a thing or two you ungrateful youths.' Jack Fuller found himself leaping to his boss's defence. 'What other chief would give you time off to lounge around here while she takes over from you?' he continued, not knowing why he felt suddenly so protective towards DCI Love.

The two constables were quite taken aback. Senor officers were always good for a bit of sniping at and they were not ready for the onslaught from the sergeant in front of them. They looked at each other and shuffled their feet uncomfortably. The Chief Inspector must be something special if the men at the station were prepared to fight her corner like this.

Sergeant Fuller rose and left the table taking his coffee with him, feeling somewhat abashed. He had no idea why he was so fervent in his defence of DCI Love, but he did know he was not going to have two spotty-faced upstarts from another force having a dig at *his* boss. Heaven forbid, what was happening to him? He always moaned about young graduate officers, and as for women in charge… well! Now here he was jumping in with both feet to support an officer who was not only a graduate but also a woman. He must be going soft. Mind you, he told himself, this is what you have to expect when women high-flyers are put in charge of men. He knew there would be problems, he'd said so only yesterday. He gulped down the remains of his coffee and left the canteen. Jack Fuller was feeling restless; he wanted to get cracking on that computer. He was excited at the thought of sifting through the information, if any, that should start arriving tomorrow.

The rest of the team returned to the Station at lunchtime but none of the officers had any information that could possibly help in the murder investigation. The lane had undergone a fingertip search to no avail, and the rubbish immediately around the bins where the body had lain had been collected and taken to Forensic for a microscopic search. To-date they had no clues. There had been no footprints near the refuse bins or in the alleyway between the shops, but this was not surprising as there had been no rain for weeks and everywhere was as dry as a bone. Unlike most films and television plays, no vital object had been dropped by the killer, although the one thing they did have of course was the scarf. DI Harrington had sent this for forensic examination and by the middle of the afternoon the red scarf and typed report of its examination arrived in his office. Disappointingly, this too revealed little. The scarf was pure cashmere and expensive, and the only hairs to be found in its fibres were those of Carol Young herself. Did the scarf belong to the victim? But it was July. Who would wear a scarf in July? Ed Harrington asked DCs Sally Pringle and Duncan McAllister to return to Maeve Cochran's house to ask her if the murdered woman had been wearing a scarf the night she was killed. 'At least Ms Cochran should be up at this hour,' he said as he handed Sally the address.

Ed sat down for a moment gazing at the scarf in his hand. Everything was moving so swiftly that he had barely found time to consider the new DCI. She was certainly calm and composed and not the slightest bit ruffled at having a murder thrown in her lap on her very first day in charge. The feeling of envy crept over him again. Perhaps he would have been a graduate officer and in charge at this moment if his father had not died. He jumped to his feet as the door opened to admit DCI Love.

'Catching your thoughts?' she said with a smile.

'Sort of… we just don't have any clues at present, but door-to-door enquiries are still going on and we shall have to see if anything turns up there.'

Harriet nodded. 'I understand that Duncan told you about the nurse who was murdered in Motherwell. I have asked Jack Fuller to check with the Home Office to request details from the Motherwell Police, and to request all forces in Scotland for any information on similar cases on their patch during the past few years.'

'Right,' said Ed. 'We should receive the first replies by tomorrow.' He handed Harriet the forensic report on the red scarf. 'Not a great deal there, I'm afraid.'

Harriet read the report. 'Who would be wandering around with an expensive cashmere scarf in July? And if the killer is the same person who murdered the nurse in Scotland, does that mean he has several such scarves?'

'We *are* trying to trace the scarf, Ma'am, but all the labels have been removed, which makes it a rather long-winded process.' Ed folded the evidence and replaced it in its plastic bag before locking it in the safe.

The DCI walked to the door. 'Let's hope we get a break tomorrow, Ed. I'm just going along to Superintendent Hollyoak's office to report on the day, should you need me.' She smiled her disarming smile as she opened the door. 'Oh and do call me Harry,' she said, 'all my friends do.'

'Er, thank you, Ma'am, I...' but Harriet had gone.

Harriet managed to get away from the Station by eight o'clock that evening. It had been an extremely long day and she was now exhausted. She drove to her pretty little cottage on the edge of Torreston and parked her car on the drive. She had owned the cottage for three years but only ever managed to escape there infrequently due to her busy life in London. The property had belonged to her great-aunt, her grandfather's sister, and had been left to her on the old lady's death. Harriet's desire to live in the cottage permanently was the main reason for her applying to Torreston for the DCI post. She was overjoyed when offered the position she now held, not only because of the cottage but also by the fact that her parents lived in the Midlands, and she would be able to visit them more often.

The front of the cottage was screened by a high laurel hedge and the gravel drive ran like a horseshoe up to the front door, in one gateway and exiting through another. The drive circled a small but very green lawn with a beautiful magnolia tree standing proudly in its centre. The flower borders were in full bloom and were a mass of vibrant colours, the smell of which wafted delicately in the evening air. The cottage itself was about three hundred years old. It was painted white and had small leaded windows and an original oak door with a large brass lion knocker. Although central heating had been added to the oak-beamed cottage to bring it in line with modern living, little else had been forced upon the property to spoil its charm. A board hung above the front door, creaking slightly in the breeze and displaying the name – Magnolia Cottage.

Harriet yawned as she unlocked the door and immediately her large, fluffy Maine Coon tabby appeared beside her rubbing his head against her legs. Harriet gathered him up in her arms and held him close, burying her head in his fur.

'Hello Toastie, have you missed me?' The cat purred loudly, knowing that now at last he would be given food. Kicking off her shoes, Harriet headed for the kitchen where she fed her ravenous pet before she uncorked a bottle of claret and placed it on the side to breathe while she took a bath. She was too tired to cook potatoes to go with her salad, but she was grateful for the wine, which she always found comforting. She slept soundly that night and struggled to rise next morning when the alarm sounded at seven.

As Harriet drove into the Station car park she was closely followed by the black Saab of Ed Harrington. Ed had been amazed to discover Charlie Marlow actually standing on the doorstep as he drove up to collect him. What a turn-up for the book – Charlie on time! Ed parked beside the red Lotus Élite. Harriet climbed from her car at the same time as Charlie.

'Am I all right to park here, Sergeant?' she said with a serious face.

Charlie, always the good sport, grinned and was rewarded with a dazzling smile in return.

'Good morning Ed,' Harriet called across to the driver of the Saab.

'Good Morning, Ma'am,' replied the DI, as solemn as ever.

Harriet ignored the fact that he had not accepted her offer to call her Harry. She supposed that as yet he did not consider her a friend, and for now at any rate he was wary of her. She would not push things but let them take their own course. They walked into the Station together.

George Hollyoak always arrived at the Station early and his mouth fell open on this particular morning when he realised that all the CID team were on the premises ahead of him. He popped into Harriet's office. 'What have you done to muster everyone so early?'

'It's not me,' she laughed, 'it's this murder case. Everyone is very involved and eager to secure a result. We're hoping to receive some computer discs from other parts of the country today. Certainly information is arriving by registered post from Scotland, with the details of the Motherwell murder and those of another nurse's death in Stirling that was never solved. The Scottish Police have been very helpful and are faxing their own forces and collating information for us.'

'Good, good,' responded Superintendent Hollyoak as he left her office. He was pleased with how well the team was working and so far none of the regular officers seemed to be finding it difficult to work under the new DCI. Even Jack Fuller appeared motivated and relaxed. Things couldn't be better.

A postal delivery arrived at the Station at nine that morning and the DCI was asked to sign for two registered envelopes. On seeing the contents of the envelopes she sent for Sergeant Fuller.

'Here you are, Jack, the first of the discs you asked for.' She held out the two discs and eagerly DS Fuller grasped them as if his life depended upon them.

'Thank you, Ma'am. I shall get on with it immediately.' He almost ran from the room, clutching his prize like a small boy not wanting anyone to wrestle them from him. In the CID room he inserted the first disc.

Some time later Jack Fuller leaned back in his chair and wiped his perspiring brow. What he had discovered made the hairs on the back of his neck rise, and with mounting excitement he started to write down incidents, with dates and locations. With his findings in his hand he walked down the corridor and knocked on the DCI's door.

Harriet looked at the information handed to her by Sergeant Fuller. 'A strangled nurse in Newcastle in January, but no mention of a scarf, and another in Northallerton in March and yes, a red scarf was used.' She looked up at Sergeant Fuller. 'That's interesting. And we know the nurse in Motherwell was murdered with a red scarf because Duncan told us so. That makes three, possibly four, if the Stirling murder matches. Too much of a coincidence, wouldn't you say, Jack?'

'Indeed I would, Ma'am.'

There was a knock at the door at that moment and Harriet called out, 'Come in!'

DI Harrington appeared in the doorway. 'A courier has just delivered this package, Ma'am. I have signed for it.' He handed the delivery to Harriet, who opened it immediately. 'Another disc, Jack. This is from Sheffield. If it's a "scarf murder" it means they are getting nearer to us.' She handed the disc to DS Fuller.

'I'll scan it straight away and get back to you, Ma'am.' He hurried off.

'Sit down, Ed,' said Harriet, placing Jack's notes on the desk in front of him. 'This is what has turned up on the computer so far. You will need it to update your information in the incident room.'

DI Harrington sat at the DCI's desk and read the details of the previous murders. 'They all have the same hallmarks, except that in the Newcastle murder there is no mention of a scarf.'

'There's no mention of *any* murder weapon,' agreed Harriet, 'although the post-mortem confirms that death was due to strangulation.'

'Nasty business,' said Ed rising to his feet. 'I'll go and add this to what we already know.'

'One thing, Ed.' Harriet looked up at the tall figure beside her. 'Can you get someone to check if any of the dead nurses were wearing earrings – and if they weren't, were their ears pierced?'

'Will do, Ma'am,' answered the DI, and he left the room. He strode down the corridor to the Incident Room wishing he could bring himself to be friendlier towards the new DCI. She was doing her job efficiently and she was more than professional but something was holding him back. That tiny bit of resentment was still biting at his insides, and a small part of him was suggesting that this woman was too good to be true. Back in the Incident Room Ed added the latest information to the notice boards.

The note accompanying the package from Sheffield pointed out that the information on the disc showed details of an attack on a young nurse in Nurcroft, a suburb of the city, and although it was not a murder the sergeant who sent the disc felt that the similarities matched those of the murder which the Torreston Police were investigating. Jack Fuller scanned through the information on the screen in front of him. The nurse who was attacked had managed to fight off her assailant after he had put something soft around her neck and tried to strangle her. She had been going on duty at the local hospital when she had been attacked just outside the hospital gates. There was no mention of a scarf, but again the similarities to their own case were too close to ignore.

Sergeant Fuller presented DCI Love with this latest information. Harriet was pleased with the progress they were making. 'Well done, Jack. Take it all to Inspector Harrington in the Incident Room. The discs from Scotland should be here this afternoon so you will be kept pretty busy for the rest of the day.'

The Sergeant puffed out his chest as he left the DCI's office. He was really enjoying himself. There was nothing like getting your teeth into a bit of real police work to make you feel useful. He hurried down the corridor to hand over his notes to Dl Harrington.

Chapter Three

The door-to-door enquires had revealed little. It appeared that none of the residents of the streets in the vicinity of the murder had heard anything unusual on that night. Narinder Pancholi and Bob Finch had trudged along the whole of Plover Street and were now halfway along Osborne Road, the road off which Osborne Close ran. They had discovered nothing that would throw any light on the murder, but methodically they wrote everything down that was of the slightest relevance.

Narinder knocked at the next door. A plump middle-aged woman opened the door and the two officers held up their warrant cards. The woman gave her name as Mrs Lord.

'Dreadful business,' she said. 'I help out in the kitchens at the Cottage Hospital and always take the short cut down Cygnet Lane. I certainly won't any more.' Like the previous occupants of Osborne Road, Mrs Lord had seen and heard nothing on the night of the murder.

The next house drew a blank also. The couple who lived there were away on holiday. 'Spain, I think,' they were informed by the woman in the house beyond. 'They left a week ago and I don't expect them back until the weekend. They both teach and it's school holidays.'

'Bully for them,' muttered DC Finch as they closed the gate and moved to the next house, 'Wish I could have eight weeks' holiday.'

'You'd hate teaching,' chided Narinder. 'You're a born policeman.'

They moved on up the road. They spoke to young couples, elderly couples, pregnant women, divorced women, divorced men and young single working people. None were able to throw any light on their enquiries. Many of the large Victorian terrace houses had been converted into flats, and several of these were occupied by young working couples. It was in one of these divided houses that that the two DCs found something a little more tangible. The steps up to the front doors of these houses were relatively steep and at this property, Number 113, there was also a ramp running alongside the steps. The officers chose to walk up the steps where Narinder read the two nameplates on the wall in the entrance porch. 'Another house divided into two flats,' she observed, pressing the top bell.

A female voice came through the intercom. 'Who is it?'

'Torreston Police,' replied DC Pancholi. 'We should like to ask you a few questions, please.'

'Is it about the murder?'

'Yes it is,' replied Narinder.

A buzz came from the speaker. 'Come up, the door's open.'

DC Finch opened the door and the two officers stood in the hallway. Facing them was a staircase and on the right of the hallway was another door with a Yale lock.

'That must be the downstairs flat,' observed DC Finch.

They climbed the stairs to find that the door of the top was already open and a young woman sporting a very painful-looking black eye was standing there waiting for them. She touched her bruised face in embarrassment when she saw the officers looking at it. 'Fell down the last few stairs,' she explained self-consciously.

'Mrs Caldwell?' asked Narinder, having read the name on the plate downstairs.

'Yes. Come on in.'

'Is Mr Caldwell at work?' asked Bob Finch, as the officers followed her into the sitting room.

The young woman in front of them hesitated. 'I suppose so. We're not exactly on speaking terms at the moment.'

'When did you last see him?' Narinder looked at the black eye and wondered.

Mrs Caldwell hesitated again. 'Day before yesterday. He went off in a huff and is staying with his brother over in Betchley Road.'

'When do you expect him back?' Bob Finch was warming to the questioning.

'Oh, he'll be back when he's cooled down, don't you worry. He often has spells like this, but he'll come round, he always does.

But anyway he wasn't here on the night of the murder so he can't help you. What was it you wanted to ask me?'

DCs Finch and Pancholi spent nearly half an hour with Mrs Caldwell and left the upstairs flat of Number 113 feeling that the husband warranted further investigation. In the hallway downstairs Narinder read the name on the second door before pressing the bell. They heard noises from within and it was some time before the door was cautiously opened by a young man in a wheelchair. The man had a pale, sallow complexion and the deepest blue eyes Narinder had ever seen, looking almost out of place in the wax-like countenance. The wheelchair explained the reason for the ramp. 'Sorry to keep you waiting,' smiled the man, 'but I'm not exactly Michael Schumacher in this thing.' His breathing was strident and rapid and Narinder smiled sympathetically.

'We're sorry to disturb you, Mr Ainsley,' she apologised, showing her warrant card. 'But we are making enquiries about the murder that occurred on Monday night behind the lock-up shops in Osborne Close?'

'I heard about it,' replied the young man, his face clouding, 'please come in.'

The two officers followed the wheelchair into the front room where the young man invited them to sit down. Narinder obliged and promptly began coughing. Bob Finch remained standing and looking at his colleague, asked her what was wrong.

'I'm sorry. It's those joss sticks, they always affect me.'

The smell of incense was strong in the small room and the man in the wheelchair was apologetic. 'I'm so sorry, officer, but I nearly always have one on the go as I find them so calming – and in my position every little thing helps.'

It was Narinder's turn to be apologetic. 'Please don't apologise, Mr Ainsley. This is your home and if the sticks are a help to you then of course you must light them. Now let's get the questions over with.' She put her hankie up to her nose in an attempt to mask the sickly smell.

Mark Ainsley turned to Bob. 'I was at the hospital on Tuesday afternoon for my physio and the murder was the topic of conversation on everyone's lips. I was quite devastated. The nurses there are wonderful.'

'Did you know Carol Young?' asked Bob Finch.

'Was that the name of the nurse who was murdered?' The young man appeared genuinely upset.

'Yes,' answered Narinder gently, pretending to blow her nose.

'No, I didn't know her. I really only know the people in the Physiotherapy Department.' His voice broke a little. 'They are all so kind. I don't know how I would cope if it were not for them. How could anyone harm one of the nurses?'

'How do you get to the hospital for your treatment?' Bob Finch too softened his voice, noting how distressed the young man in the wheelchair had become.

'The hospital car picks me up and brings me back.'

'I don't suppose you saw anybody hanging around the hospital grounds on Monday afternoon? Anybody who looked out of place, that is,' added DC Finch.

'I'm sorry, no. I left the Outpatients at four thirty and was brought straight back here. Garry Hobbs was on car duty and he wheeled me through the front door and left me. He sometimes stays for a cup of tea if he hasn't to dash off somewhere, but on Monday he had another pickup and left immediately.'

Bob Finch spoke again, 'Can you tell us anything about Mr Caldwell from upstairs?'

The pale-faced young man pulled a face. 'Nasty piece of work, and a bully. He's always shouting at his wife and I know he hits her. I can hear them fighting through the ceiling when I go to bed.'

'Does he often go away?' asked Narinder.

'He's always running to his brother. I don't know why Veronica puts up with it. She should have left him months ago.'

'How long has the bullying been going on?' Bob Finch had already decided that Mr Caldwell needed interviewing.

'Well, I've lived here nearly a year and it's been going on as long as I can remember.'

Narinder smiled at the young man and thanked him for his help. 'We can see ourselves out, thank you. You stay here.'

The two police officers left the ground floor flat a few minutes later and continued down Osborne Road. 'Phew!' gasped Narinder. 'I'm glad to be out of there – the smell was choking me.'

They headed for the row of shops, and in the flats above them they were again confronted by an assortment of residents. Not all were at home, which meant more names to be added to the list for their return visits. At a scruffy-looking flat, where the paintwork was peeling on the front door and the net curtains were decidedly drab, they had a substantial wait while someone inside grunted and grumbled before finally opening the door.

'Now what?' demanded a sour-looking man leaning on crutches in the doorway. He was in his early fifties but looked older because of his scowling face and thinning hair. His grey eyes were dull and lifeless and he squinted as he peered at the two officers standing in the doorway.

'Sorry to disturb you,' said Narinder politely. 'We are making enquiries about the murder of the nurse whose body was found behind these flats.'

Bob Finch stepped forward. 'Could we come in, Sir? We are asking everybody the same questions, it's purely routine. Could you give us your name?'

The man's scowl deepened. 'Preston Skinner. I've only just got back from the hospital and I'm tired. Come in if you have to.' He stood to one side and as they entered he kicked the door shut with his foot.

'Do you attend the hospital often?' asked Narinder.

'Every week for my physio.'

'Does Garry Hobbs take you?' Narinder was not too impressed with the attitude of the man but she forced herself to stay polite.

'Yes, and brings me back.'

Bob Finch eyed the sharp-featured man and posed the next question. 'How did you damage your legs?'

'Fell down these bloody stairs and broke them both. I'm going to sue. The lighting is bloody awful, I could have been killed.'

Bob looked across at Narinder, remembering how Mr Skinner had viciously slammed the door shut with his foot. 'Still painful, are they?'

'Can hardly walk sometimes, and the people at the hospital don't seem to care. The nurses are damn condescending. *More physio, Mr Skinner*! That's all they suggest, but it don't work and I'm fed up with it.'

DCs Finch and Pancholi continued with the questioning and were more than glad to leave the dirty flat and the aggressive Mr Skinner. By five thirty they had completed their allocated roads and returned to the Station to hand in their notes to DI Harrington. They would have to return at a later date to interview those who had been away or at work. DC Finch made a point of mentioning Mrs Caldwell and her black eye and suggested that perhaps the husband should be interviewed. 'He wasn't at home on the night of the murder, Sir,' he said, 'but I… we think he gave Mrs Caldwell the black eye. He sounds a nasty piece of work.'

'Right – thanks, you two. Have you got the address where he's staying at the moment?'

'Yes, Sir,' answered Narinder, handing over a piece of paper. 'This is his brother's address where he's been for the past three nights.'

DI Harrington took the address. He would pay Mr Vince Caldwell a visit himself tomorrow.

The computer disc from the Scottish Police had arrived and Sergeant Fuller was busy scanning the information they contained. 'Looks as though we have a serial killer on our hands,' he announced.

DI Harrington came across and looked over his shoulder. 'What have you found, Jack?'

'The murdered nurse in Stirling was strangled by a red scarf, and here's another in Airdrie. Duncan was right about the Motherwell murder, and again with a red scarf and – heaven forbid! – there's a fourth. This one in a place called Annan, right on the Scottish border. That's four in Scotland last year.' Jack ran his hand through his thinning hair and puffed out his cheeks. 'Now it appears he's moved down over the border.'

DI Harrington jotted down the dates and places of the Scottish murders. 'You carry on here, Jack, while I take this information to the DCI. I've got some other information that she asked for.' He left the room and went down the corridor to Harriet's office, where he knocked lightly and entered on invitation.

Harriet smiled as Ed walked in and he responded with his usual nod.

'I have the details of the murders matching ours, which have occurred in Scotland, Ma'am.'

'Sit down, Ed.' Harriet indicated the chair in front of her desk. 'So how many have there been besides the Motherwell one that Duncan told us about?'

'I'm afraid it's not good.' The serious-faced DI Harrington placed the list in front of Chief Inspector Love.

'Good God!' She read through the list. 'Four starting in February of last year, to November. Then we go to Newcastle in January of this year, followed by the nurse attacked in Northallerton in March.'

'Then we have another failed attempt in Sheffield last month, and now Carol Young this week here in Torreston.' Ed Harrington, for all his six feet four and outwardly tough appearance, was in fact a gentle soul at heart. He loathed violence in all forms, and as for murder, he found it quite harrowing.

The DCI looked up from the paper. 'I'd like to speak to the nurses who were attacked and survived Ed. They are the only witnesses we have in this catalogue of events. Are you able to come with me tomorrow morning?'

'I was going to visit Vincent Caldwell tomorrow, but if you're happy with DS Marlow conducting the interview, then I should be able to accompany you, Ma'am.'

'Right!' Harriet rose from her chair. 'That's what we'll do. All right if we go in your car?'

'Absolutely.' Ed tried hard not to show his relief at not having to be the passenger in his boss's car. He stood. 'What time would you want to leave?'

'Pick me up in the car park at eight. That will give us a reasonably decent start. I'll go and tell the Super what we're doing and leave you to organise Charlie and the rest of the team for tomorrow.'

Ed walked towards the door. 'By the way, Ma'am, I checked out the earrings on the other dead nurses and none was wearing any; but in answer to your other question, yes, they all had pierced ears. Is there some significance in that?'

'I'm not sure,' Harriet wrinkled her nose. 'I only made enquiries about earrings after Dr Boston mentioned that there was blood on the dead woman's left ear. I asked Maeve Cochran whether her colleague had been wearing earrings on the night of her death and she assured me that she was. There *were* no earrings on the body. Strange isn't it?'

'Certainly is,' agreed Ed. 'But surely no one would go around murdering women just for their earrings.'

'I wouldn't think so.' Harriet wrinkled her nose again and fleetingly Ed felt admiration for this handsome woman. The DCI was speaking again, 'Perhaps the stealing of the earrings is just the killer taking a trophy of his achievement.'

'Perhaps,' Ed agreed. 'But the fact that they are all nurses is definitely significant. If he takes earrings after each murder, what happens when a victim isn't wearing any?'

'I just don't know, unless of course he knows his victims in advance and is aware of them wearing earrings,' suggested Harriet.

'Could be. Perhaps our talk with the women tomorrow will throw some light on the affair.' Ed moved towards the door. 'I'll see you at eight tomorrow, Ma'am.' He left the office.

Harriet respected the tall DI but felt a little saddened that he was so reserved. Perhaps he would soften tomorrow when they were forced to spend the day together.

The following morning, DCI Love and DI Harrington set off for Sheffield at eight o'clock. Harriet had deliberately not suggested going in her car, deciding that perhaps Ed would feel less inhibited if he were the driver. The journey was uneventful and took just over two hours. Arriving in Sheffield they had no difficulty in finding Nurcroft and the address of Sheila Werrington. She had been advised by the Sheffield Police that two CID officers from Northamptonshire would be calling that morning and as she was not on duty until 6pm she was at home and awaiting their visit.

Sheila was a tall, well-built young woman of twenty-eight. She showed Harriet and Ed into her sitting room and offered them coffee.

'I'd love some,' smiled Harriet. 'Travelling always leaves me gasping for an injection of caffeine.'

Ed too accepted the offer, and while they were waiting for the coffee to arrive, Harriet opened her file containing all the information on the murders.

'This attack took place in June of this year and was the fifth involving a nurse. No mention of a scarf though.'

'If it's the same assailant, then she's lucky to have got away,' replied Ed. Sheila returned with the coffee and placed it on the low table in front of them. 'Help yourselves to milk and sugar.'

'Thank you,' said Harriet, relieved to see that it was served in a cafetière and obviously not of the instant variety. 'We understand that you were attacked a month ago right near the hospital. We do have a copy of your statement but we'd be grateful if you could go over the story again for us.'

Sheila Werrington shuddered as she remembered the attack. 'I was going on duty, it was about ten to ten and not even dark. As I came up to the gates I was pounced on from behind and someone threw something soft over my head and round my neck and started dragging me towards the bushes. I was choking and couldn't cry out for help. As the grip on my throat tightened I lashed out with my elbow and made contact. I heard a painful grunt and the pressure on my neck lessened. That was my opportunity. I kicked my foot backwards and upwards and again made contact, hopefully in his groin – the bastard!' She half smiled at this, but her pained expression indicated the fear that had gripped her that night.

'Go on, Sheila,' said DCI Love gently.

'Well, his grip on my arms relaxed and I fell forward onto my knees, gasping for breath. As I struggled to my feet I heard footsteps running away and I realised that he had bolted through the bushes.' Tears came into her eyes. 'Someone was coming up the drive. I couldn't believe my luck; I really thought that I was going to die.' She wiped her eyes with the back of her hand.

'You were very brave,' said DI Harrington, leaning forward and offering the young woman a spotless white handkerchief. 'Is there anything at all that you can tell us about your attacker? You obviously didn't see him as he kept behind you all the time, but is there anything that strikes a chord?'

'Well, I got the impression he was no bigger than me and probably no stronger than I am. I'm an athlete and work out practically every day at the gym.' She smiled at last. 'He bit off more than he could chew when he picked on me.'

Harriet put down her coffee cup. 'Anything else that might help us?'

Sheila thought hard. 'He had a smell about him.'

'What sort of smell?' asked Ed.

'Stupid, really.' Sheila hesitated. 'It was a hospital smell. Sort of antiseptic.'

'This was not in your statement.' Harriet sifted through the papers she had placed on the coffee table.

'I didn't really think about it at the time. Being a nurse I'm surrounded by hospital smells, they're with me all the time and I suppose it didn't dawn on me that my attacker was the one with the hospital smell and not me.'

'Could he have been a colleague? Is there anyone on the staff you can think of who might have done this?' Ed posed the question carefully.

Sheila shook her head. 'Heavens no! Everyone at the hospital is beyond suspicion. Maybe I just imagined the smell and it was me all the time. My friends say I always smell like a hospital when I go out with them.'

Ed spoke again. 'I don't suppose you could identify what it was that was tied around your neck?'

'Not really, but it was soft like a tie or scarf. He used it to drag me backwards into the bushes.' She paused. 'Why have you come all the way from Northamptonshire to question me?'

DCI Love answered her. 'A young nurse was strangled by a scarf in Torreston a couple of nights ago. Since then we have discovered that there have been other murders where a scarf was used to strangle the victim. The similarities to your attack are very strong and as you are the only witness, we were hoping that your evidence might help us in our enquiries.'

'I see,' whispered Sheila. 'It appears that I'm lucky to be alive.'

'Possibly,' said Ed. 'Just be on your guard and try not to be on your own at quiet times of the day. Mind you,' he added, 'if it is the same chap who has committed all the murders, we think he's now on our patch and no longer in Sheffield.'

'Thank you for your time,' smiled Harriet, rising. 'And the coffee. If you think of anything else at all, however silly it might appear to you, please get in touch.' She handed her card to the young woman. 'Just one more thing. Do you always wear studs in your ears on duty?'

Sheila Werrington frowned. 'Yes I do. Why?'

'It's a long story, but thank you again.' The two officers left the house and returned to the car.

The person who had been coming down the road on the night Sheila Werrington had been attacked was a male nurse called Clifford Jarvis, and he was their next port of call. Although well into his forties, he still lived with his mother. When Harriet and Ed explained who they were and what they required, Mrs Jarvis, a thin, scraggy woman with grey hair scraped back with an elastic band, allowed them into the house. She eyed Harriet up and down suspiciously. 'You're a policewoman then?' she asked in disbelief.

'I'm afraid so,' replied Harried putting away her ID card. 'Is your son Clifford at home?'

'He's upstairs getting ready to go on duty. I don't want you making him late. He's never late for duty, you know.'

'Very commendable,' said DI Harrington. 'Would you tell him we're here please.'

'Very well.' She left the room and could be heard screeching up the stairs. 'Clifford, Clifford, you've got visitors! It's the police about that attack on the nurse last month.'

She returned to the sitting room and addressed Ed. She could not be doing with women in what she considered a man's world. This tall man must surely be the one in charge. 'He's coming. You'd better sit down.' Mrs Jarvis sniffed and plonked herself down in a chair opposite.

'We'd like to speak to your son alone, if you don't mind,' said Harriet, thinking the poor man would be intimidated by the presence of his mother.

'We have no secrets. I'll be all right here.' She looked at Ed totally ignoring Harriet.

DI Harrington spoke firmly. 'We wish to interview your son alone, Mrs Jarvis.'

The woman sniffed and rose from her seat. 'If you must.' And as Clifford entered, 'I shall be in the kitchen if you need me, Cliff.' Then she left the room.

Clifford was a small wiry man with a long, somewhat sad face. The result of living with his domineering mother, thought Harriet eyeing him up and down. He lowered himself into the chair that his mother had vacated. 'Sorry about my mother,' he almost whispered. 'But she's a good sort really.'

'I'm sure she is,' said Harriet, generously. 'Now could you tell us exactly what you saw on the night that Sheila Werrington was attacked near the hospital gates.'

Clifford Jarvis quietly and precisely ran through the happenings of that night. He had been coming to work when he saw a struggle ahead of him just outside the hospital gates. 'At first I thought it was a couple larking about, but then I realised that the woman was trying to fight off the man. I ran towards them, at which point the woman fell forwards onto her knees and the man, without turning I must add, ran off into the bushes. He obviously heard my footsteps, and not wishing to be recognised ran off without showing his face.'

'It was definitely a man, then?' asked DI Harrington.

'Oh yes indeed,' came the immediate reply. 'Not of any great size, but definitely a man.'

'Is there anything at all that you can tell us about him?' enquired Harriet.

'Not really.' Clifford looked thoughtful. 'It was getting dark and quite honestly I couldn't really tell you what he was wearing. Except for the hat, that is. He had on a close-fitting hat pulled well down over his ears.'

'If it was difficult to see that night, how sure are you that the assailant was a man?' Ed was writing carefully in his notebook.

'It wasn't that dark, but it was not as clear as it could be to see colours and exact details. But I know it was a man because of his stance and mannerisms and the way his body moved as he ran off, even though he obviously had some deformity of his lower limbs.' Clifford sat up proudly in his chair. 'I wrote a thesis on the human body and the relationships between the male and female body, so in a way I am something of an expert on the subject.'

Harriet did not doubt for a moment that this little man would be correct in his assumptions. He might be henpecked by his domineering mother but he was certainly confident in his statement. Clifford Jarvis was not the sort to overlook any point, however small; he was a demon for detail and a master in his delivery. Harriet glanced across at Ed and nodded.

'What exactly do you mean by a deformity of his lower limbs?' asked Ed.

'The way he ran indicated to me that this man had either some congenital deformity of his legs or had, in later life, acquired some damage due to an accident or weakness of his muscles due to illness. Either way the attacker most certainly had something wrong with his legs.'

'Thank you, Mr Jarvis,' said Harriet. 'You have been most helpful and more than precise in your evidence.'

'You have to be exact in my line of work,' said Clifford with a smile. 'One mistake could cost a life.'

The two officers asked one or two more questions before leaving the house and returning to the car. Harriet turned to Ed. 'I'd just like a quick look at the spot where the attack took place. It always helps to give you a clearer picture of an incident if you can visualise the scene.'

Ed drove his Saab to the hospital, which was only minutes from Clifford's house. He parked at the bottom of the drive beside what appeared to be a gatehouse. There was no one in the small building and so they walked up the gravelled path together. 'No wonder the attacker heard Clifford coming,' said Ed. 'On this gravel you could hardly be silent.'

'The attacker must have already been in the bushes, waiting,' mused Harriet. 'Sheila didn't mention anything about hearing him. She just said he sprang at her from the bushes.'

Ed ran his fingers through his dark hair. 'Wonder if he was waiting for her specifically, or was she just unlucky to be the one that came along at that moment?'

'As in the Carol Young case,' agreed Harriet.

They reached the top of the drive and paused at the second gateway. Harriet walked to the bushes at the side of the entrance where the attacker had been waiting.

'He'd be well hidden if he was lurking here.'

'The local police did a fingertip search of this area,' said Ed, 'but nothing was uncovered.'

A voice from down the drive hailed them loudly and the crunching on the gravel indicated that someone was approaching. They turned to see the figure of a plump, bald-headed man in a blue uniform running – or at least trying to run – up the drive. 'Hi there!' The shout came again. 'What are you doing in those bushes, and what exactly are you doing here at all?'

As the man drew close, the words HOSPITAL SECURITY could be seen on the front of his jacket.

Simultaneously DCI Love and DI Harrington produced their warrant cards and held them out to the fat man, who was red in the face and panting from the exertion of running.

'You're supposed to check in at the gatehouse,' he puffed.

'We might have done,' replied Harriet quite coldly, 'had there been anyone on duty there.'

'Ah well,' said the security man. 'I just had to nip somewhere. But I wasn't gone for many minutes. You could have waited.'

'We're far too busy to wait,' chipped in Ed. 'But you being absent from your post doesn't say a great deal for the security here.'

'Especially as you recently had a nurse attacked on the premises,' added Harriet. 'What's your name?'

'You're not going to report me, are you?'

'No. But we do need names so that we are able to check later who we have interviewed.' Harriet felt an instant dislike for this man. But it was not really her place to check up on hospital security men.

'Sid Blaine. And I wasn't on duty the night the nurse was attacked.' The fat man showed his indignation and mopped his perspiring brow.

'Who was?' asked Ed.

'Fred Weatherburn,' said Sid. 'He lives in the cottages over there.' He pointed to a row of cottages that were visible in the distance. 'Number 2, Cherley Street.'

Harriet wrote this down and said, 'thank you.' Glancing at the DI, she raised an eyebrow before turning to walk back down the drive closely followed by her colleague. They returned to the car and DI Harrington drove the short distance to Cherley Street.

Fred Weatherburn was unable to throw any light on the

investigation either. He had certainly not heard anyone moving up the gravel drive after Nurse Werrington had passed by the gatehouse, so whoever attacked her must have come over the wall further round the grounds and slipped into the bushes. He confirmed that Clifford Jarvis had spoken to him as he came on duty minutes after the nurse, and it was his shouting that had caused him to run up the drive to discover what had happened. He had called the police on his mobile telephone instantly. The officers thanked Fred Weatherburn and left.

As they climbed back into the Saab Harriet spoke. 'I'm starving. I hadn't realised the time. We'll find a quiet pub for a bite to eat and we can go over all the evidence we have so far. Is that okay with you?'

'Sounds fine,' agreed Ed, pulling away from the curb. 'But if we're to move on to Northallerton we'd better not take too long over lunch.'

'Agreed.' Harriet was keeping a look out for a decent pub and, spotting one, called out. 'That one looks reasonable.'

They stopped at the Black Bull and enjoyed freshly made sandwiches and a cafetière of coffee.

'Real coffee,' sighed Harriet as she poured. 'I'm afraid I'm addicted to it. I can't stand that instant stuff.'

They discussed the evidence that they had gathered so far and Harriet was relieved to see that DI Harrington appeared relaxed and forthcoming in his conversation as they compared notes. 'Still no real lead from anything we've heard today,' he said. 'The attacker was slight and not overly strong and smelled of hospitals. Not a great deal to go on.'

'Perhaps the woman in Northallerton will be more enlightening.' suggested Harriet.

'Let's hope so,' said Ed, rising. 'We'd better make a move. It will take at least another two hours to get there and it's already five past one.' He insisted on paying and graciously Harriet accepted. 'But my turn next time,' she insisted as they left the pub.

They returned to the Saab and Ed started the engine. 'You can navigate, Ma'am,' he said almost light-heartedly as he drove off.

They reached Northallerton before three o'clock and Harriet

opened her *A to Z* of the town in order to guide the Inspector to Friar Lane. 'Number 3,' she muttered, peering at the numbers on the gates. 'Must be the other end – that one was one hundred and something.'

Ed cruised down the lane and pulled up smoothly outside a small house displaying the number three. Together they walked to the front door where Harriet rang the bell. There was no reply. The DCI went next door. DI Harrington leaned against his car and watched as his boss rang the bell. A young woman with a squalling baby on her hip opened the door on a safety chain. Harriet held up her warrant card and the woman released the chain. 'Could you tell me where I might find Miss Pawlett?' she asked.

'At the hospital,' came the reply. 'She's on the day shift. She'll be home at six.'

'Where is the hospital?' asked Harriet.

The young woman rocked the screaming child up and down and raised her voice. 'Penfold Road. Back up this lane and onto the main road. Head for the town centre, but at the second roundabout you will see the hospital sign directing you to the left. From then on you can't miss it.'

Harriet thanked her and returned to the car. 'You probably heard all that,' she smiled. 'Shall we go?'

Detective Inspector Harrington nodded. 'Right, Ma'am.' He started the car and pulled away.

He had found the day surprisingly enjoyable so far. The Chief Inspector was more than easy to work with, and not once had she pulled rank on him. Not even when Clifford Jarvis's mother had gone over her head and addressed him instead of her. Perhaps he was being unfair in his opinion of her. He would make the effort to be less frosty, but no way could he bring himself to call her Harry. He returned to the main road and at the second roundabout turned left into Penfold Road where the hospital sign was clearly showing the way. Hopefully Nurse Pawlett might be able to give them a few more clues as to who this maniac might be, as up to now clues were decidedly thin on the ground.

Chapter Four

The hospital where Nurse Pawlett worked was also a Cottage Hospital and DI Harrington parked in the visitors' area. Together he and DCI Love reported to the Enquiries desk where they showed their warrant cards and asked to see June Pawlett. They were taken to a small sitting room and offered coffee, which turned out to be instant and was immediately rejected by Harriet. 'I'm sorry,' she said, looking at Ed apologetically. 'But I just cannot drink that disgusting stuff.'

Ed poured a cup for himself. 'I can drink any liquid that's brown and hot and smells something like coffee.'

A young woman in a nurse's uniform appeared in the doorway and DI Harrington rose to his feet. She was petite and dark-haired and was, Harriet noticed, wearing small gold studs in her ears. 'You wanted to speak to me about the attack in March,' she said in a quiet voice.

'Yes, if you don't mind,' replied Harriet. 'Do sit down.' And as June Pawlett complied Harriet said, 'Just tell us exactly what happened in your own words.'

'I have told all this to the local police.'

Ed nodded as he sat down beside her. 'We know and we're sorry to put you through it again but it would be very helpful to our enquiries about a similar incident in Northamptonshire.'

'I see.' The young woman wrung her hands together. 'I haven't been able to sleep since the attack. I'll do anything if it means he'll be caught.'

'We'll catch him,' said Harriet, gently. 'Tell us your story.'

'I was on the late shift and had parked my car in the staff car park when someone grabbed me from behind. A scarf was put round my neck and I grabbed at it and managed to get my fingers underneath it as it tightened. I was being dragged backwards towards the hedge when I stumbled and sat down. My attacker tried to drag me to my feet but I pulled forward with my grip on the scarf and he started toppling forwards too, sort of over my bent back. He was not very steady on his feet and I thought he was probably drunk. When he realised that he was not going to be able to drag me any further, and the fact that he couldn't pull the scarf any tighter because I was holding on to it, he let go and ran off. I was left terrified and holding the scarf. I just sat on the tarmac and cried.'

'You didn't see him at all?' asked DI Harrington.

'Not close up. He stayed behind me the whole time. But I looked round as he ran off through the parked cars. He was wearing a dark-coloured anorak and a close-fitting hat. That's really all the description I could give the police. But there was one other thing. He certainly ran in a strange manner. That's what convinced me that he was drunk.'

Harriet asked the next question. 'Did he smell of alcohol?'

'Well, he certainly had a smell about him and yes, it was like alcohol, but more like antiseptic.'

'Did you hear a car drive off after the attack?' Ed was busy taking notes and looked up as he spoke.

'I don't think so. Frankly I was so scared, I was intent on getting to the hospital for safety. My legs were shaking and I just ran as fast as I could. Fear is weird. I couldn't even scream.' June Pawlett covered her face with her hands as she remembered. 'It's like in nightmares – your legs just won't move fast enough and the big bad guy chasing you is getting nearer and nearer.'

Harriet put a comforting hand on her shoulder. 'You're safe now, June.'

DI Harrington added, 'He doesn't appear to strike in the same place twice, and at present we think he's in the Midlands, so try and take comfort from that. But of course be on your guard, as we are advising all nurses at the present time.'

It was now four in the afternoon and they still had to visit the police station where Harriet had requested that they see the scarf used in the attack on Nurse Pawlett. They thanked the young woman, who returned to her duties and the two officers headed back to the car park. Once again Harriet navigated from her *A to Z* and ten minutes later they arrived at their next destination.

As they entered Durston Police Station the Duty Sergeant

looked up. On seeing the two tall, imposing figures he smiled. 'You've just got to be the coppers from the Midlands that we've been told to expect.' He pushed a button under the reception window and the door beside them opened. 'Go through.'

DCI Love and DI Harrington entered the main foyer of the police station. Harriet immediately knocked on the door of the Duty Sergeant's room and the door opened. The Sergeant greeted them with the same smile, 'Just hang on there for a bit love. I'll tell Geoff you're here.'

Ed Harrington suddenly saw a totally different side to his senior officer as he heard DCI Love speak in a quiet, firm voice.

'Do you normally allow visitors onto the premises without asking for identification, Sergeant?'

For a moment the smile faltered on the sergeant's face. 'Come on, love, tell me you're not from the Midlands Force.' His smile had returned.

Ed wanted to shout out to the man to shut up as he dug a deeper and deeper hole for himself.

'We are indeed,' replied Harriet, producing her warrant card. 'And Love is correct. DCI Love and DI Harrington. And your name is?'

The Sergeant stood up straight and pulled his tunic jacket down where it had rumpled at the waist. 'Sergeant Remshore, Ma'am. And my apologies. I had no idea—'

'It makes no difference who I am, Sergeant. You check everyone before allowing them through that door. Why do you think it has a concealed lock?' Her steady green eyes fixed on the man in front of her and he swallowed hard.

'Yes, Ma'am. It won't happen again. Er, here's Sergeant Roberts.' With relief he saw his colleague coming down the corridor and thankfully he introduced the visitors. 'This is DCI Love and this is DI Harrington. Sergeant Geoff Roberts, Ma'am.'

'Thank you, Sergeant.'

Gordon Remshore returned to his room and wiped his brow. He felt such a fool. Who would have thought that such a stunner was in fact a DCI. He hoped she would not report him. He certainly wouldn't make that mistake again.

Sergeant Roberts showed them into a side room and produced

the red scarf from a plastic bag. Harriet gave it to the DI. 'Is it the same, Ed?'

'Looks exactly the same. What did forensic turn up?' he asked.

'Absolutely nothing on it from anyone else other than the victim.'

'May we take the scarf with us?' asked Harriet.

'Sure, why not. We have it on our records and we've done all the test that are feasible. It will just sit in the evidence box from now on.'

'Thank you,' said Harriet, turning to leave.

Ed replaced the red scarf in its plastic bag and followed the DCI out of the room. At the locked outer door Harriet turned to Sergeant Roberts. 'Where do I sign?'

'Sign?' queried the officer.

'For the scarf.'

DI Harrington noticed that DCI Love's voice had once again become quiet and cold. 'I am removing evidence from your Station and you need a signature for it.' The green eyes were fixed again and the sergeant hastily got the message.

'I'll get the book, Ma'am.' He vanished into the office and Harriet met Ed's eyes. She shook here head. 'We're not as lax as this, are we, Ed?'

'Certainly not, Ma'am. I can't imagine Sergeant Yates or Fisher letting anyone within a hair's breadth of the door handle of the Station without identification, and as for removing anything from the building... Well, I can assure you, Pete Yates would want a signature in triplicate.'

'That's reassuring.' smiled Harriet just as the sergeant returned with a thick blue book.

The red scarf was duly entered and signed for and the two officers from the Midlands left the police station. As the outer door closed behind them Sergeant Roberts joined Sergeant Remshore in his office. 'Blimey!' he gasped. 'You wouldn't want to work with her, would you?'

'Cold as steel, these senior women,' agreed Gordon Remshore.

'And no sense of humour.' Geoff Roberts sat down and blew his nose loudly. 'You're turn to make the coffee I think, Gordon.'

DCI Love and DI Harrington returned to the car. 'Home, Ma'am?' asked Ed.

'And don't spare the horses,' smiled Harriet her green eyes once again sparkling.

It was after nine by the time Harriet and DI Harrington arrived back at Torreston Station. As they entered the door, the eagle eyes of Pete Yates peered at them through the enquiries window.

'Evening, Ma'am, Sir,' he said. He unlocked the door into the Station proper and the two went through.

Harriet turned to Ed. 'You're right. I think Pete would secretly like even us to produce our warrant cards when we arrive. He most certainly would not allow strangers in without them.'

'He certainly wouldn't,' agreed Ed. 'I'll lock this evidence away and I'll be off if that's all right with you, Ma'am.'

'Yes, of course. And thank you for today, Ed, it's been most enlightening. We'll meet up in my office tomorrow after briefing and go over all that we have found out and see if we can make any sense of it. It's also Carol Young's funeral tomorrow and we should attend.'

'Of course, I'll see you tomorrow. Good night, Ma'am.'

DI Harrington walked down the corridor to the Incident Room where he locked the red scarf in the wall safe. He left the building and returned to his car, sliding his long form behind the wheel. The delicate perfume that the DCI always wore filled the interior and he breathed in deeply as he started the engine. He had enjoyed the day. DCI Love was certainly different. She was not just glamorous but highly sagacious. She was generous, and had a keen sense of humour with it. As Ed drove towards his house on the edge of Torreston, he wondered. Was this all just too good to be true?

Harriet went to her office to collect any messages that might have arrived during her time away from base. She too had enjoyed her day. DI Harrington was an excellent officer and easy to work with, but why was he being so cold towards her. Perhaps he did not approve of women as senior officers. If that was the case she must be even more single-minded at solving this murder. She closed her office door and left for home.

Detective Sergeant Charlie Marlow and Detective Constable Sally Pringle had been assigned by Inspector Harrington to interview Vincent Caldwell, husband of the woman with the black eye, and Garry Hobbs the hospital car driver. Ed had dropped Charlie off at the police station car park as usual and Sergeant Marlow had watched as the elegant DCI Love appeared in the doorway and walked over to his friend's Saab. She lowered herself into the passenger seat as if she were royalty and DI Harrington slipped the car into gear and drove out of the car park.

Lucky sod, thought Charlie, as Ed acknowledged him with a lift of his hand from the driving wheel as the Saab swept passed. Charlie headed for the car pool to collect his vehicle for the day. He picked up Sally at the Station entrance and together they set off for Betchley Road. Charlie looked across at the young constable and grinned. She was more than competent and Charlie had worked with her before and found her very able. She stood no nonsense from the male officers and they in return respected her. Sally was five feet nine and a County sprint champion over 100 and 200 metres. She belonged to the Starburst Athletic Club where she attended regularly, fitting her training in to coincide with her police duties. She was also a member of the local Leisure Centre where she worked out at some time of every day. Sally was certainly attractive with short fair hair and the brightest blue eyes…but, thought Charlie she was in no way a Harry Love.

Torreston was a popular market town with its centre dating back to medieval times. The murder had certainly stirred the sleepy community and the news boards all displayed similar headings referring to the dead nurse and the fact that a killer was at large. Betchley Road was on one of the new estates, and Charlie, knowing the town well, drove straight there. As it was still relatively early, Vincent Caldwell had not left for work at the local garage where he was a mechanic. He looked surprised at the visit from the CID but nevertheless reluctantly allowed them into the house. In answer to the enquires about the murder he exploded.

'I've been here for three bloody days! I know nothing at all about the happenings in Osborne Close or Cygnet Lane or wherever the murder happened.' His voice was harsh and aggressive. 'For God's sake, what has that bitch been telling you?'

'If you are referring to your wife,' said Charlie coldly, 'then the answer is, nothing. But we couldn't help noticing her black eye when we called on her yesterday.'

'Is she pressing charges?' sneered the obnoxious man in front of them.

'Not that I know of,' responded Charlie. 'But she might change her mind.'

Vincent Caldwell was a big man with a shaved head, making his appearance too much like a thug. Sally could image him at a football match giving hell to the opposing supporters. She knew she should not let appearances prejudice her opinions and tried hard to think positively.

She looked at the man and spoke quietly and calmly. 'Could you tell us where you were on Monday night between ten and midnight?'

The big man looked down at the fresh-faced DC. 'Using schoolgirls in the Force now, are we?' he sneered. Charlie went to speak in his colleague's defence but there was no need. Sally answered swiftly.

'We all know what they say about big men who are bullies,' she smiled sweetly. 'Now answer the question please before I demonstrate that brains will always overthrow brawn.'

Vincent was not sure what all that meant but felt he would not push his luck and make himself look foolish. He curled his lip. 'I was here with Bill all night. We'd got some beer in and spent the night in front of the telly. You can ask him if you don't believe me.'

'Why ever shouldn't we believe you?' smiled Sally sweetly.

'You just go and ask him,' scowled Vincent Caldwell.

'Thank you, Sir, we will.' Sally gave another sickly smile.

Charlie spoke. 'Where will we find your brother?'

'He's on the early shift at Garratts warehouse on the Harborough Industrial Estate.' The words were spoken in a sullen voice.

Charlie thanked him and stood to one side to allow Sally to leave the room. Once outside the young DC blew out her cheeks. 'Phew! Now that *is* a nasty piece of work, Sarge!'

'Doesn't make him a murderer, though. Come on, we'd better speak to his brother – even if only to convince that bully that we mean business.'

They drove to the Industrial Estate and circled the outer road. 'There it is,' called Sally as she spotted the sign GARRATTS WHOLESALERS OF MEDICAL SUPPLIES. Charlie pulled into the car park at the front of the main building. Together they entered the side door and reported to the desk displaying the sign 'All Enquiries' and rang the bell.

'Smells more like a hospital than a warehouse,' remarked Sally. 'And it's all very clean.'

'It does deal with medical supplies,' replied Charlie. 'And I suppose bottles get broken while being despatched. Still, I can think of worse smells than disinfectant.'

A woman appeared at the window of the office, and after showing her their warrant cards DS Marlow explained the reason for their visit. They were directed to a small room where they were offered seats and told that Bill Caldwell would be sent for.

Bill Caldwell was quite the opposite to his aggressive brother. He was only five feet six or seven, sandy-haired and bespectacled with a flat, bland face. When he spoke his voice was light and reasonably well educated.

Charlie began. 'We are making enquiries regarding the murder of Nurse Carol Young in Cygnet Lane on Monday night. I understand that your brother, Vincent Caldwell, was staying with you that night and we need to eliminate him from our enquiries if you can confirm his whereabouts.'

Bill Caldwell's expressionless face briefly showed anxiety. 'Why is Vince being suspected?'

'He is not necessarily a suspect,' replied Charlie. 'We are checking everyone who lives in the vicinity of Cygnet Lane, and your brother does live in Osborne Road.'

The man relaxed. 'Oh, I see. Well, we were together all that night watching TV. Vince had had a fight with his wife. They're always fighting, and he's always clearing out and coming to me.' The small man turned his attention to DC Pringle and he eyed her up and down. Sally was not sure that this quiet man with the deadpan face was not more threatening than his big, loud-mouthed brother.

'Are you not married, Sir?' asked DC Pringle desperate to say something to break the uneasy pause.

'Widower, I'm afraid.' Sally thought she detected a smirk on that pasty face.

'I'm sorry,' said the young woman.

'Is your brother in the habit of striking his wife?' Charlie looked steadily at the man in front of him.

'Well,' Bill Caldwell hesitated. 'He has got a bit of a temper, I admit, and they do go at it hammer and tongs sometimes, but quite honesty Vince would never do her any real harm. He always goes back when he's calmed down, and then they're all lovey-dovey again for months.' The soft voice droned in Sally's ears and something about the tone made Sally shiver.

'I see.' Charlie raised an eyebrow. 'Well, I think that's all we need to ask you for the time being. We'll let you get on with your work. Do you always do the early shift?'

'No, the shifts vary depending on the deliveries we have to make.'

'Do you supply all the hospitals in the Midlands?' asked Sally as they walked towards the door.

'The whole country,' came the silvery reply.

'And Scotland?'

'Absolutely. Wales and Northern Ireland.'

They had reached the warehouse entrance. 'Thank you once again,' said Charlie. 'Before we leave I need to speak to the manager, if you could direct us to him.'

'That's Granville Smith, he'll be over in the despatch office.' Bill Caldwell leaned arrogantly on the doorpost and pointed to a newly painted green door, which at this moment was firmly closed. DS Marlow and DC Pringle walked across the yard and Charlie knocked on the door. A middle-aged man, tall and thin in heavy rimmed glasses, opened the door and frowned.

'I' d heard the police were on the premises.'

'Mr Smith?' enquired Sergeant Marlow.

'Yes. Who's in trouble then?'

'No one at the moment,' said Charlie displaying his warrant card. 'It's more like eliminating people from our enquiries at present. Could we have the worksheet showing all your deliveries in the last twelve months, please.'

'Good God! Whatever for?'

'Sorry, I'm unable to disclose that at the moment, but I can assure you it has nothing to do with the company.'

'That's something, I suppose. You'd better come in.'

The small office was packed from floor to ceiling with boxes and papers. There were piles of papers on every surface and the desk surface likewise was cluttered beyond all comprehension. How anyone could work in an environment such as this Charlie could not contemplate. He thought he was untidy, but compared to this he was decidedly neat and methodical.

Granville Smith swept a pile of papers from his desk before standing on a stool and peering at the labels on the boxes on one of the shelves. 'Here we are!' he cried triumphantly. 'You may think this office looks chaotic but believe me, I know where everything is.'

'I'm glad to hear it,' smiled Sally, secretly wondering if that were true.

Granville blew a thick cloud of dust from the box and climbed from the stool. He placed the cardboard box on the table in the space that he had cleared. He opened it and began shuffling through the documents that it contained. He held out two sheets of paper to Charlie. 'That shows all our deliveries so far this year and this one shows the whole of last year. Is that what you want?'

'Absolutely,' said Charlie. 'Can I borrow these?'

'Better not,' replied Mr Smith, 'But I can copy them for you.' He moved across the office and uncovered the photocopier that was hidden by yet more boxes and documents. He handed the results to the sergeant. 'Is that it then?'

'Just one other thing. I need a list of the drivers who delivered these supplies.'

'Ah, now let me see.' Granville scratched his head. 'They're in a different place. You'd better sit down while I have a look.'

Sally looked around for a place to sit. There was no chair that did not have a pile of papers or boxes on it. She remained standing. As she did so she looked at the pictures on the wall. These were framed photographs of groups of men standing in front of lorries which all displayed the words 'Garratts Medical Supplies'. Her gaze moved along the rows of photographs. Each one was dated and went back twenty or so years. In the photograph dated last year, DC Pringle noticed that in the front row stood Bill Caldwell and beside him was his brother Vincent Caldwell.

She spoke to Granville Smith. 'I see Bill Caldwell's brother worked here last year.'

'He worked in the garage. Best mechanic we ever had. I was sorry to see him go, but he does still help out with deliveries if we get desperate.'

'Why did he leave?' asked Sally.

'The usual reason,' came the reply. 'More money somewhere else. Here's what I was looking for,' he added, climbing off the stool. He banged another dusty box down on the desk. Sally coughed as the dust flew in all directions. Another two sheets of paper were produced and again photocopied and handed to Sergeant Marlow.

Charlie and Sally left the building a few minutes later and walked towards the car.

'Well, one of the Caldwells does deliver supplies to hospitals,' Charlie began.

'And all over the country, including Scotland,' added Sally.

'Perhaps bully boy accompanies his brother on his travels when he's helping out.' Charlie scratched his head. 'It's all a bit too simple, though, isn't it?'

Sally agreed. 'We'll hand over our findings to the DI and let him decide. The new DCI will certainly have an opinion.'

'What do you think of her then?' Charlie cast a sly, sidelong look at his colleague.

'Apart from being stunning looking you mean?' Sally smiled at the sergeant. 'Well, she's very efficient and terribly cool and calm and quite frankly just what we need at the Station. What do you think?'

Charlie grinned. 'So far so good. She certainly knows her job, but let's see the outcome of this case.' They climbed into the car and set off for the Cottage Hospital, where they were to interview Garry Hobbs.

Garry Hobbs was at the hospital garage checking over the hospital car. The car was in fact a small minibus and the driver was in the process of filling the windscreen wiper's water bottle.

'Mr Hobbs?' Charlie stepped forward with his warrant card in his hand.

'Police! What can I do for you?'

Sergeant Marlow replaced his ID card in his breast pocket. 'As you to and fro a great deal from the hospital, we wondered if you might have seen anything or anyone looking out of place on the day of the murder of Nurse Carol Young.'

'Nasty business.' The young man shook his head. 'I didn't see anything out of the ordinary. I just ship patients up and down all day.'

'You took Mark Ainsley to Osborne Road, which is very near the murder spot. Nothing strange there?'

'No,' came the reply. 'I was particularly busy that Monday. Couldn't even stop for a cuppa with Mark, not that I was overly sorry. He can be a bit demanding sometimes and I spend most of the time at his place fetching and carrying for him. Still it makes you grateful that your own body is whole and you can walk on your own, so I don't really mind. I had to get back to the hospital after dropping Mark as I had to collect grumpy-guts – pardon my language, I mean Preston Skinner. Now he really is a nasty customer. Never has a good word to say about anyone, especially the nurses and hospital staff.' The young man gave a wistful grin. 'But I like my job. You meet loads of different people and many of them are jolly interesting. I should have liked to have been a nurse but didn't have the GCSE grades.'

'Did you know Carol Young?' asked Sally.

'Well, enough to say hi to, but then I speak to all the staff here. They all know me even if I don't know all *their* names.'

'That's strange,' said Sally. 'According to her friends on the ward you and she have dated.'

Garry looked uncomfortable and shifted his feet. 'For heaven's sake, I only ever went out with her twice.'

'But why deny knowing her?' asked Charlie.

Garry ran his hand through his hair in an agitated manner. 'I don't know, that was stupid. We went to the pub for a drink on two occasions only but on that Monday we had words and I thought you might misconstrue what had happened and put me in the frame.'

'We're more likely to consider you a suspect if you go around lying,' said Sally. 'What did you row about?'

'Oh, something stupid. She couldn't swap her duty for the coming weekend and I made a fuss because I wanted us to go out for the evening.'

Charlie sniffed. 'I would have thought that you of all people could understand about nurses duties and the difficulty they have in getting time off.'

Garry Hobbs bowed his head. 'I know, I know – don't you think I regret it and feel absolutely dreadful about her murder? I might have walked her home had we not had that row, and now I shall have to live with that thought for ever.' He choked and pulled out a large handkerchief and blew his nose loudly.

Charlie and Sally left Garry Hobbs a few minutes later and made their way to the security office. Here they collected the CCTV tape that DI Harrington had requested. They were to spend the rest of the morning in front of a television screen scrutinising this tape. Not knowing exactly what they were looking for, this activity was somewhat ad hoc. There were nurses coming and going, people who appeared to be patients, ambulances pulling up and depositing cases, and there was Garry Hobbs wheeling out patients at regular intervals and assisting them into his vehicle. Nothing strange or abnormal in any of the goings-on that Monday. They rewound the tape and placed it in the 'evidence' box in the Incident Room.

The following day the investigating team gathered for briefing at eight thirty. DCI Love entered the Incident Room looking particularly striking in a black trouser suit and emerald green silk blouse which accentuated the green of her eyes. She leaned her tall, slender body against the desk at the front of the room and carefully pushed her auburn hair back from her eyes before speaking. She told them of the outcome of the visit to Sheffield before asking the officers for any feedback that they might have.

DC Narinder Pancholi spoke first. 'We talked to Carol Young's colleague, Maeve Cochran, and she's adamant that Carol was not wearing a scarf the night she was murdered, and as we said at the last briefing, no one *would* be wearing a scarf in this weather.'

'Unless of course they needed it for ulterior motives,' added her colleague, DC Bob Finch.

Harriet spoke. 'We need to find the source of these red scarves. Anything to report on them yet, Inspector?' She turned to Ed.

'Not yet. We've circulated the description to all police forces and all shops and department stores that retail such things. We can only hope and wait to see if this produces anything.'

'Fine,' said Harriet. 'Wait until the end of the week and then start pressing. You know what people are like, they put such requests in a tray and it sits there for weeks on end.'

'I'll give it a day or so and then chase it up,' responded Ed. 'In the meantime the local press would like a statement.'

DCI Love pursed her lips. 'I'll have a word with them after this meeting Inspector. In fact, I'll write the statement, that way they'll be unable to twist my words to give them a totally different meaning. Has anyone anything more to throw into the melting pot?'

Sergeant Marlow stood up. 'You say that the woman assaulted in Sheffield smelt a hospital smell on her attacker, Ma'am. Interestingly, Vincent Caldwell's brother works at a medical supplies warehouse and the entire place smelt of antiseptics. Bill Caldwell smelt the same.'

'Where was he on the night of the Young murder?' DI Harrington asked.

'At home with his brother watching TV. They each alibi the other.'

'Check out their whereabouts on the other murder dates,' instructed the DCI to Sergeant Marlow in a voice that she might use to invite a friend to dinner. 'Everything, however small or apparently innocuous, that has the slightest connection with this case, needs checking so that it might be eliminated. This killer may well strike again. I see no reason why his heinous activities should cease now that he has reached the Midlands.' The briefing ended and the officers left to pursue their various investigations.

Harriet and Ed went to the DCI's office where they sat sifting through all the evidence they had gleaned so far. The DCI leaned back in her chair. 'It will take some time, Ed, but we'll have to check the staff list of every hospital where a nurse has been murdered, or attacked in the cases of Sheila Werrington and June Pawlett. We need to discover if there are any names that crop up in more than one of them. I understand you've already set up a team checking times and dates of delivery vehicles at these hospitals.'

'Sergeant Fuller is onto that,' replied the DI. 'He enjoyed the computer search so much that I thought it would be a good idea to keep him happy and put him in charge of this group.'

Was that a vestige of a smile? wondered Harriet watching Ed's face. Perhaps not. 'Good,' she said. 'I'm pleased Jack is engrossed the way he is. I'd heard rumours that he might retire.'

'I think he's put that idea on hold for the present, Ma'am.' Not that Ed was going to add that Jack had decided that working under the new DCI was more than satisfactory. Instead he added, 'Jack's of the old school. He's hard working and straight as a die, but he does have his ups and downs, and when he's on a down he always announces that he's going to retire.'

'So he's on an up at the moment, is he?' smiled Harriet.

'You could say that, Ma'am. This investigation has inspired him.'

'This is the fourth day of the case,' frowned the DCI. 'I was hoping we might be a little further on than we are.'

'It's always difficult when there are no obvious leads,' said Ed. 'And there doesn't appear to be any motive. We can only be persistent and keep searching. We'll get him in the end, don't worry, Ma'am.'

Harriet looked up sharply. There was almost compassion in Inspector Harrington's voice, as if he was doing his best to reassure her. But the same solemn expression greeted her and she just nodded.

'You're right. We'll catch him, but let's hope it's soon.' She rose from her chair. 'Are you able to accompany me to the funeral this morning, Ed? Afterwards I'd like to return to Cygnet Lane. Don't ask me why,' she added, 'I just don't want us to have missed anything.'

'I'll be ready in ten minutes,' said Ed. 'Everything is moving satisfactorily here, and the rest of the team know exactly what they are doing.' He left the room and Harriet gathered together her notebook, a packet of new latex gloves, just in case, and packed her black bag. She met Ed coming back down the corridor and together they left the Station for the church.

Chapter Five

Superintendent George Hollyoak was standing at the window of his office as the two senior officers left the building. He watched as the tall lean Harrington strode across the car park with the slender, immaculately dressed Harriet at his side. He so wanted his godchild to do well. She was one of the brightest young ladies he knew, but apart from her keen brain and exceptional qualifications she had beauty and personality as well. He had had no children of his own, his dear wife being unable to conceive, but although disappointed about this, he bore no bitterness. He and Nancy had been happy together, there was no doubt about that, and having known Harriet's parents for over forty years a strong bond had developed between the two families. He had been delighted when asked to be the child's godparent and he had undertaken these duties very seriously, carrying them out with great dedication. He had never forgotten her birthday, even though more often than not it was Nancy who remembered and bought the card, and at Christmas the two families always had a festive gathering where he presented Harriet with a special gift. Superintendent Hollyoak watched as he saw the pair get into Harrington's Saab.

He smiled. How like Harriet! No way would she undermine her male colleagues by expecting to drive them in her own car. The little red Lotus Élite had been a present from her parents on gaining her Cambridge 'First' and it was her pride and joy, but for today at least she would be the passenger in the black Saab. The car drove out of the car park and vanished down the road. The big man returned to his desk; another tedious day of paperwork in front of him.

At the church they could hear that the service was under way, so they made their way round to the graveyard where a freshly dug grave stood out cold and stark like an open wound. Although it was a warm morning Harriet shivered as she gazed at the bleak hole in the ground. Together she and Ed moved back and stood at a respectable distance. The mourners appeared soon afterwards, following the coffin to the graveside. Harriet and Ed searched the group for any face that might not fit, or one that they might recognise. But nothing and no one appeared out of place. After the burial Mr and Mrs Young came over to thank them for being there. 'It was good of you to come Chief Inspector,' said Mrs Young.

Harriet shook Mrs Young's hand. 'This is Inspector Harrington. We are working on this case together and we promise that we shall do all that is in our power to bring this criminal to justice.'

'I'm sure you will.' Mr Young stepped forward and put his arm around his wife. 'Thank you both for coming.' He guided his wife away.

Harriet and Ed returned to the car and left the church.

DI Harrington parked his car in Osborne Road quite near to the spot where Harriet had parked on first being summoned to the murder scene. Side by side the two officers walked to Osborne Close and paused outside the shops. The blue and white tape still cordoned off the alleyway between the shops but trade had once more commenced on the parade. A lone constable stood at the entrance between the shops and he stood to attention as Harriet and Ed drew near.

'Good morning, Ma'am, Sir.'

DI Harrington nodded. 'Good morning, Bond.'

Harriet smiled at the young man. 'Not James, I suppose?' The Constable grinned in return. 'No, Ma'am, Dean.'

Walking down the narrow opening between the shops, Harriet wrinkled her nose at the obnoxious smells. Another constable stood guard at the gap in the fence and on hearing footsteps he quickly turned and came towards them. 'It's all right, Constable,' said the DCI, 'we just want to take a final look before we call off the guard.'

'Right, Ma'am.' Luke Stockwell gave a broad smile and hoped that DCI Love recognised him from when he had been on duty the morning of the murder.

At the back of the premises the smells were no better. Apart from garbage and rotting vegetation there was a distinct odour of urine. Harriet trod warily as she moved to the spot which, last time she had visited, had been occupied by the lifeless form of Carol Young. Here all the rubbish had been collected and removed for a detailed inspection. Looking around the area Harriet sighed. 'Not the most pleasant of places, and not quite where you would choose to end your days.'

DI Harrington scuffed his feet around in the damp ground now void of litter. 'We should know today if anything of interest was found by the bins. How long do you want the guard to remain here?'

'I think we can call it off now. I'd like to walk back to the car along Cygnet Lane.'

She led the way through the gap in the fence and spoke to the constable. 'You can remove the tape now, Luke. Do the same at the other end of the alley and tell your colleague there's nothing more to do here.'

'Yes, Ma'am.' The smile widened. Not many senior officers knew your first name let alone ever called you by it. He started to roll up the blue and white tape. His ambition was to be in CID and he was determined to work as hard as he could to achieve that aim. Some of the blokes were anti-women bosses but he reckoned that DCI Love was okay. He would certainly be prepared to work for her. With the bundle of blue and white tape in his arms he hurried up the alleyway to speak to PC Bond.

Walking along Cygnet Lane some minutes later, Harriet thought how peaceful it was. How could anything as horrendous as the murder of a young woman occur here? The tall trees waved gently in the breeze and the birds were in abundance and cheerfully vocal. Vehicles were not allowed in the lane, and since the murder there had been few pedestrians. But the public would soon forget. They always did. Within weeks this path would be heaving again with couples, children and young mothers with prams. The two officers reached Osborne Road and walked slowly back to the car to return to the Station.

On arriving back at her office DCI Love produced a cafetière and tin of ground coffee from her desk and went to the kitchen to heat water. A voice behind her made her jump.

'Ah, there you are, my dear… er sorry, Chief Inspector.'

'George,' smiled Harriet. 'I think the kitchen is secluded enough for us to use first names.'

'I wanted to know how you got on yesterday up North.'

'It was all very interesting, and we did manage to speak to the people we needed to.' Harriet sighed. 'I'm not sure we learned anything that we didn't already know but some of the information obtained did confirm points which will inevitably strengthen our investigation.'

Superintendent Hollyoak placed a kindly hand on his goddaughter's arm. 'You'll get there, Harry, this case won't beat you. Stick at it and just keep me in the picture.'

'I will, and thank you for your faith in me.' She flashed a smile as the big man left the kitchen. DI Harrington appeared in the doorway.

'I smelt the strong coffee and gathered this is where you would be, Ma'am.'

'It's just made. Would you like a cup?'

'Thanks, I would. I've just received some exciting news from the detailed search of the rubbish at the murder scene. Sergeant Hewitt has just dropped it off. I'll show you over coffee.'

Once in the office, Ed produced a small plastic envelope and placed it on the desk in front of DCI Love. Harriet put down the coffee and picked it up. She held it up to the light and peered at it closely. 'Ed! It's a backing to an earring,' she exclaimed excitedly. 'A butterfly.'

'It is indeed, Ma'am.'

Harriet sat behind her desk. She put her hands up to one of her ears and carefully removed the pearl stud that she was wearing. She placed both the stud and the butterfly clip on the desk. 'It's not easy to remove studs from your ear, and certainly not if you are in a hurry. You have to be jolly careful or you drop the back. I can only presume that our killer is not overly bothered about the backs. He just pulls out the studs.'

Ed nodded. 'In the case of Carol Young he actually tore her ear whilst doing just that and dropped the backs. Forensic are carrying out DNA tests to confirm that the one found does belong to the victim.'

'Good – but the second one is still missing, I see,' said Harriet.

'I'm afraid so. Perhaps he did keep the other one.'

Harriet did her nose-wrinkling act. 'Hmm. I'd like to try something, Ed. Which women DCs are in the building?'

'Sally Pringle and Narinder Pancholi.'

'Which men?'

'Duncan McAllister, Bob Finch, Jack Fuller—'

Harriet interrupted the Inspector. 'That's fine, ask all of them to come to the Incident Room in ten minutes.' As Ed began to rise she added, 'Have your coffee first.'

Harriet produced two elegant china mugs from her cupboard and pressed the plunger of the cafetière into the hot brown liquid. She caught Ed watching her and she smiled. 'I can live without food, but coffee…no way.'

DI Harrington could not remember any senior officer ever making him coffee before and he gratefully accepted the mug that DCI Love handed him. He slyly looked at her as he drank. She was certainly good-looking but he was still unsure about this gracious behaviour to everybody. Perhaps it was he who was being unjust and this was the true Harriet Love that he was seeing. If that were the case then they were all most fortunate to be working with a real human being rather than some overbearing, arrogant senior officer intent on terrorising all those with lesser rank. DI Harrington finished his coffee and thanked his boss. He left the office to despatch the DCI's message to the team.

Later, as they gathered in the Incident Room, a buzz rippled round the room as to why they had been summoned. DCI Love entered, and in eager anticipation the group fell silent. Somehow this tall elegant woman demanded attention. She was friendly to all and smiled readily. She knew all their names and spoke to them as equals, never raising her voice or trying to undermine them, and yet in her presence they knew who was boss. They already respected her and in a strange way were in awe of her. There had never been such a handsome woman at the Station and secretly they were proud of the new Detective Chief Inspector. The men certainly were astounded by her beauty and in a strange way felt that the entire situation was unreal and that perhaps it would end at any moment. A trace of her expensive perfume lingered in the corridors and the rooms that she visited and at this moment it hung in the air of the Incident Room. Harriet gazed around the room, her green eyes alive.

'Would one of you ladies volunteer to be the guinea pig? I am going to ask one of the men to try and remove your earrings if you feel you could allow that.'

Sally and Narinder looked at each other. They were both wearing small gold studs. Sally was first to speak. 'I'm game, Ma'am.' She stepped forward.

Harriet spoke again. 'Thank you, Sally. Now if our killer is removing earrings, he most certainly must have great difficulty if he's wearing gloves. The clips at the back of the ear are not only small but poisonous to pull off unless you know what you are doing. Agreed?' She faced her audience.

'Absolutely,' agreed Sally. 'I've dropped more earring backs onto the bathroom floor than I care to count.'

'Right!' Harriet beckoned to Duncan McAllister. 'You can be our attacker, Duncan. Do you mind lying on the floor, Sally?'

'No.' Sally grinned as she lay down. 'Luckily I'm not wearing my Nicole Farhi outfit today.'

'Do your bit, Duncan,' said the DCI, 'and remember Sally you are dead so don't move.'

DC McAllister knelt beside DC Pringle and began to fumble with her earrings. Sally cried out. 'Hey! That pinches.'

Duncan gave Harriet an appealing look. 'This is really difficult, Ma'am. To get the backs off the earrings I have to get my nails behind the clips, and that will probably hurt Sally.'

'No it won't – she's dead,' giggled Narinder.

'This is actually serious.' The quiet voice of the DCI intervened. Perhaps you would like to be the corpse, Narinder?'

'Right, Ma'am.' She changed places with Sally.

'Bob would you be the attacker please,' said Harriet, turning to DC Finch.

'I'll have a go.' The young constable bent down beside his colleague.

'You most certainly couldn't get this type of earring off wearing gloves that's for sure. Sorry, Narinder,' he said, as

Narinder winced. 'Got one, though, but I've lost the back I'm afraid.' He rose to his feet holding up the small gold stud triumphantly. His colleague sat up on the floor and felt around for the butterfly back, which she soon found lying beside her.

DCI Love turned to DI Harrington. 'You see, tearing out the earrings – and our killer would be in a hurry – he's almost certain to lose the backs. Hence the one we found at the murder scene of Carol Young.'

'The other one either bounced a long way off or was just missed in the search.' Ed Harrington pondered. 'Or of course, did he manage to hold onto it and take it with the earrings?'

'There's always that,' agreed Harriet. She turned to the group of men and women in front of her. 'He kills and takes his victims' earrings but in all the cases there has never been any sexual assault.'

'Probably can't manage it,' said Duncan, hastily adding 'Sorry, Ma'am.'

'No, that's all right, Duncan. You could be correct. That's something we might remember. Anyway, thank you all for your, help. We still have a mammoth task ahead of us but stick at it and we'll get him in the end.' She flashed her dazzling smile before turning to thank DI Harrington. Then she left the room and returned to her office. Immediately animated chatter broke out in the Incident Room. Narinder turned to her friend Sally.

'I nearly choked when you said you weren't wearing your Nicole Farhi outfit today, because I reckon the suit the DCI has on is just that.'

'Do you really? Her clothes are fabulous, aren't they. Perhaps when I'm a DCI I shall be able to afford gorgeous clothes.'

'And drive a Lotus Élite?' said Duncan leaning over her shoulder.

'None of you will have any money to buy anything,' chipped in DI Harrington, 'because you will all be out of work. Now let's get on with this investigation, we have hours of checking to do. Every hospital where a nurse was killed or attacked has to have the staff list checked, so let's get cracking.'

'*Yes Sir,*' chorused Sally and Narinder as they returned to their desks and the pile of papers yet to be ploughed through.

The local paper had made the murder of Carol Young headlines, which was not surprising, and they had included the statement made by DCI Love. In it she stated that the investigation was in full swing and although the police had so far made no arrest they were hopeful of developments in the near future.

Harriet sat in her cottage that evening and read the report, '...Hopeful of developments in the near future,' she read aloud. If only...! What was she missing here? Was it under her nose? The connection was obviously nurses, but what about the earrings, and why a red scarf? Please let something turn up soon. This murder was her big break, she must not fall at the very first hurdle. This case had to be solved and solved it would be. Perhaps those developments she was hoping for would turn up tomorrow.

Developments certainly took them by surprise the next day. As Harriet sat in her office drinking her first coffee of the working day, a knock on the door announced the arrival of DI Harrington.

'Bad news, I'm afraid, Ma'am, there's been another murder of a nurse.'

Harriet rose to her feet. 'Where?'

'Harbourne.'

'That's still on our patch.' Harriet was astounded. 'He's never killed twice in the same area before. What is he playing at Ed?'

'Heaven knows,' replied DI Harrington. 'My car is ready if you are, Ma'am. The SOCO team is already on its way.'

'I'm ready.' DCI Love grabbed her jacket from the back of her chair and followed DI Harrington from the room. On the way down the corridor they met DS Marlow.

'I've just heard about the murder,' said Charlie. 'What do you want me to do, Ma'am?'

Harriet stopped. 'Look Ed, you take Charlie in your car and I'll follow in mine. It will give us greater flexibility if we have two cars at the murder scene. And don't lose me,' she added. 'I'm still learning the area.'

The three officers left the police station, and with DCI Love in her red Lotus, the two cars left the car park.

Ed Harrington glanced in his rear-view mirror to check that

his boss was close behind. Charlie watched his friend closely. 'How are you getting on with her, then?'

'Well enough.'

'She is a stunner though.' Charlie grinned.

'Can't say that I'd noticed,' replied Ed casually.

'You must be blind then. Everybody else thinks she's amazing.'

Ed blew out his cheeks. 'Charlie, the woman has not come to Torreston to be judged like a beauty queen. She's here as the DCI and has a job to do. And a damn difficult one, it seems.'

'You can still have an opinion about her,' persisted Charlie.

'Well!' Ed thought for a moment. 'She's efficient, professional, hard working and has a memory like a computer. Is that what you wanted to hear?'

Charlie sniffed. 'I was thinking more along personal lines.'

'Okay. She can't tolerate instant coffee, and she's the first senior officer who hasn't demanded that coffee and tea be made for her every ten minutes of the day. In fact, instead she makes coffee for others. Even me. How about that, Charlie?'

Charlie glanced across at Ed. 'Why are you so stodgy about her?'

'I'm not. But I shall wait a bit longer before I make up my mind.' Again that nagging tore at his stomach. He wished he could relax about DCI Love but somehow that feeling of jealousy and suspicion hovered in the background. He noted the red Lotus behind him as he swung through the park gates, and seeing two patrol cars in the distance with blue lights flashing, he drove across the grass to join them. An area of bushes and thick undergrowth had been cordoned off with the recognisable blue and white tape and he pulled up a few metres from the gathering.

The body of a young black woman had been discovered by a man taking his dog for a walk in the park in Harbourne. Harbourne was little more than a village on the west side of Torreston. Although not very large, it did support a small shop, a public house and a village school.

The white-overalled Scene of Crime Officers were already busy inside the cordoned off area when Harriet and her colleagues arrived. They showed their warrant cards and donning their latex gloves and plastic overshoes, DCI Love joined the group in the bushes with Ed and Charlie just behind her. Dr Stacey Boston was kneeling beside the body and she looked up as Harriet arrived.

'Same pattern, Chief Inspector. Strangled with a red scarf with no other injury or sign of a sexual assault. The body has been here all night. At a guess I should say she has been dead for at least ten hours.'

'Is she wearing earrings?' asked Harriet.

'No,' replied Stacey Boston. 'And in answer to your next query, yes she does have pierced ears.'

Harriet half smiled. 'Thanks. Do we know where she worked?'

One of the SOCO team spoke, 'There's no hospital near here but The Poplars is just outside the village.'

'What is The Poplars?' asked Harriet.

'An old people's nursing home, Ma'am.'

'Do we know the dead woman's name?' The DCI looked at the pathetic form lying on the damp grass behind the bushes. Her white uniform was wet and crumpled with streaks of mud defacing it, the red scarf around her neck standing out starkly.

Harriet looked away, feeling sick. She would never be able to accept the horrors of murder.

The SOCO spoke again. 'According to items in her handbag her name is Monica Meyers, Ma'am. She appears to live at One hundred and two Chaucer Street.'

'Thank you.' Harriet looked at the man who was speaking to her. 'I remember you from the Carol Young murder. Sergeant Hewitt, isn't it?'

'Yes, Ma'am.' Phillip Hewitt was amazed that the DCI remembered his name. No one ever seemed to know who he was let alone know his name. He had been in charge of the Scene of Crime Officers for the past four years and took the position very seriously. Nothing slipped by him and no search was ever performed by his men without one hundred per cent concentration. He took a deep breath. 'I'd better get on, Ma'am. We still have much to do.' Sergeant Hewitt returned to his task of scouring the ground for clues.

'One thing, Sergeant.' Harriet leaned over the crouched form. 'The earring back you found at the last murder scene was exactly what I'm after. Congratulations on finding it. I think the killer is removing earrings from his victims, so I'd be grateful if you could be on the lookout for the same here.'

'If there is an earring or an earring back here, Ma'am, then I shall find it, if I stay here all night.' Phillip Hewitt did not even look up, and Harriet was convinced that this quiet, owl-like officer would be as good as his word. She nodded briefly to DI Harrington and DS Marlow and retreated from the bushes.

'If that's the officer who discovered the back of the earring in the rubbish over at Cygnet Lane, then I am full of admiration for him.' Harriet pushed her hair from her eyes. 'That really is finding a needle in a haystack.'

Charlie chuckled. 'He's known as Toowitt Hewitt. He's just like an owl, Ma'am. Sharp eyes and all that. He doesn't miss much.'

DI Harrington spoke. 'He's reckoned to be the best SOCO member in the business. Never gives up and sifts through all the evidence with a fine toothcomb. If there *is* an earring back in the bushes, then I wouldn't be surprised if he found it.'

'I'm heading for Chaucer Street,' said Harriet. 'I'll take Charlie with me, Ed, if you would visit The Poplars. We still don't know for sure if that is where she worked.'

'Right, Ma'am. I'll meet you back at the Station.' Ed moved off to collect his car and Harriet and Charlie climbed into the Lotus.

Harriet paused before starting the engine. 'None of the murdered women have been sexually assaulted, Charlie. Just strangled and left.'

'Perhaps he's not capable, Ma'am, as Duncan suggested.'

'That's one line of thought. Or perhaps he's just doesn't fancy women as sexual beings...'

'A woman-hater, Ma'am?'

'Maybe. Let's get over to Chaucer Street and see what we can discover.' Harriet fired the engine and drove off.

Chaucer Street was a row of small terraced houses, fronting directly on to the pavement. At Number 102 Harriet paused.

'This is the part of the job that you could do without, Charlie.'

Her colleague nodded. 'The radio's on, so at least someone is up.'

Harriet rang the doorbell. A woman's cheerful voice called out. 'Coming, my darlin', you forgotten your key again?'

The door was opened by a large West Indian lady with a round face and sunny smile.

'Oh, sorry, my lovely,' she smiled. 'I thought you were my daughter. She is always forgetting her key.'

DCI Love held up her warrant card. 'Mrs Meyers?'

The smile vanished from the woman's face as she nodded. She held her hands to her cheeks. 'Don't tell me. Please don't tell me! Somethin' has happened to my little Monica.'

'May we come in?' Harriet's voice was soft and gentle.

They followed Mrs Meyers into the front room which was spic and span and decorated with brilliant colours. The bright orange three-piece suite was dotted with green and yellow cushions, and the pictures on the wall were a blaze of reds and orange. Even the carpet was a mixture of vivid colours, suggesting that the household was a lively and warm place to live. The once happy-go-lucky woman sat down heavily, her head in her hands. 'Tell me the worst.'

Harriet spoke in her quiet voice. 'A young West Indian nurse has been found dead on the park, Mrs Meyers. Could you tell us if your daughter goes to work that way?'

The woman nodded. 'She works at The Poplars and went on duty at nine last night I was expecting her home at any moment That's why I thought it was her when you rang the doorbell just now.'

Charlie spoke. 'Do you have a photograph of Monica?' The woman rose and with laboured steps she went to the sideboard and took out a biscuit tin which she placed on the coffee table. She removed the lid and took out a handful of photographs lying them gently on the polished surface. Harriet picked up a picture of a smiling young woman, the similarities to the woman in front of her being obvious. The round cheerful face, the sparkling white teeth and the happy persona. It was definitely the murdered nurse in the park, but she was now no longer smiling and carefree. Someone had certainly put paid to that.

Harriet took the woman's hand. 'I'm so very sorry, Mrs Meyers. Is there a Mr Meyers or someone else we can call for you so that you are not alone at this time?'

The tears began to trickle down the face of Mrs Meyers. 'I only have Monica. My husband died three years ago. She was such a lovely girl, everyone loved her. Nothing was ever too much trouble for Monica. She would do anything for anyone.' She began to sob and Harriet put her arms about her and let her cry on her shoulder.

Charlie looked on and a feeling of admiration crept over him as he watched DCI Love with her arms around the big West Indian woman. His boss really did care about people. This was no show. She was genuinely concerned about the misery this woman was suffering and she was oblivious to whatever he, or anyone else thought, she just needed to comfort this grief-stricken human being. He got up.

'I'll make some tea, Ma'am.'

Over the shoulder of Mrs Meyers, Harriet nodded and Charlie was not sure that there weren't tears glistening in those green eyes. He went to the kitchen to make the tea.

It was over an hour later that DCI Love and DS Marlow left 102 Chaucer Street. DCI Love had arranged to collect Mrs Meyers later that afternoon to take her to the mortuary to identify her daughter. She did not relish the task but knew that it had to be her that accompanied the distressed woman. Sitting in her car, Harriet spoke to Charlie. 'We need to get this killer, and sooner rather than later. Are we missing something, Charlie?'

'We've done everything possible so far, Ma'am. We just haven't had a break that would give us a suspect. But he's out there somewhere and we *will* get him, don't you worry.'

'I *am* worrying, Charlie. How many other murders must there be before we nail him? Let's get back to the Station and see what Ed has to reveal.' She started the engine and headed back to Torreston.

At The Poplars old people's nursing home, DI Harrington introduced himself and asked to see the person in charge. This turned out to be a Mrs Childers, a woman in her mid-fifties who bustled forward in a gleaming white overall.

'Now what do the police want with me?' she asked briskly.

'Does Monica Meyers work here?'

'She does indeed, but I'm afraid she is not here at present. She should have been on duty last night and didn't turn up for her shift. Left us in rather a mess but as this isn't at all like Monica I can only presume she had an emergency at home. She's not on the phone or I would have called her. But she'll be in touch I have no doubt.'

'I'm sorry to say that she will not be contacting you. A body has been discovered in the park and the handbag contains items indicating that the young woman is Monica Meyers. Until she has been formerly identified no name will be released and I should be grateful if you would say nothing of this at present. I'm quite sure that if the body is that of Miss Meyers then you will be swamped with reporters, so I advise you to be prepared.'

Mrs Childers was visibly shaken with the news of the murder. She gave Ed all the information she could which might help in the enquiry, but there was little in her statement that the Inspector thought was of any value. The Home had no CCTV system so there would be no way of checking the comings and goings of staff and visitors. He closed his notebook and returned to his car. He almost missed the presence of the DCI at his side. She was certainly easy to work with and extremely good company. But he was being foolish. He enjoyed working with Charlie and he had no cause to prefer working with his new boss. He and his friend went back many years. He'd been best man at Charlie's wedding, and three and a half years later had been there for him when he decided that it was all over. Charlie's wife, Claudia, was an actress and had still wanted to lead the life of a single woman. She told her new husband in no uncertain terms that having him around all the time spoiled her image. She needed to be desirable for her fans and to be able to respond to them. To begin with Charlie had forgiven her, knowing that people of the theatre tended to be passionate about friends; but being passionate was one thing, sleeping with them was another. Charlie wanted his wife to be at home, being passionate about only him. He forgave her for her affairs several times but as the months passed and nothing improved he decided he was unable to live in this way, sharing his wife with her many admirers and putting up with the snide remarks from Claudia's crowd. He realised that he had made a big mistake. Ed had warned him months before he tied the knot, but he had been besotted by the glamorous actress, and had blindly gone ahead with the marriage regardless.

Ed headed back to the Station. He remembered the nights that Charlie has slept on his settee and how his usually confident, outgoing friend had wept on his shoulder. Now with the divorce behind him Charlie was back to his old self, but it had certainly left him cynical and somewhat bitter about marriage. Ed gave a wry smile. At thirty-eight years of age, he himself was still a bachelor and so far had not met a woman that he wished to spend the rest of his life with. Since his father's death, when he was just nineteen, he had looked after his mother and was devoted to her. With a place waiting for him at Nottingham University he had not hesitated in turning it down so that he could remain with her. He had felt that he was unable to rob this slight, gentle, woman of both the men in her life. Ed had followed in his father's footsteps and joined the police. He had had no regrets and soon moved up the ranks to Detective Inspector. It was only now, with the arrival of the new Chief Inspector, that he was feeling pangs of regret. But it was no ones fault. Life was full of ups and downs and he had done pretty well in the Force. He thought of the murdered women and felt guilty that he should be thinking of himself at such a time. Their deaths were the issue here and it was up to him to help catch the killer. He would put his personal anxieties out of his mind. They were trivial in comparison to the misery being felt by the families of the dead nurses.

He drove into the police station car park and noted that the red Lotus had not yet returned. He sat where he was for a moment, reflecting. DCI Love was an excellent officer and he was quite sure that her appointment to Torreston had nothing to do with Superintendent Hollyoak knowing her. George Hollyoak was above corruption – everyone knew that – and as for DCI Love, she too appeared as straight as a die. DI Harrington left his car and made his way to the Incident Room.

Chapter Six

DCI Love and DS Marlow returned to Torreston police station and joined DI Harrington in the Incident Room. The Inspector handed Harriet a sheet of paper. 'The DNA report from the earring back. It definitely came from Carol Young.'

'As we thought,' replied Harriet. 'So this madman *is* taking his victim's earrings.' She sat on the edge of the desk. 'The dead women are all nurses, all young, single and wear earrings. What else have we got?' She looked at Ed and Charlie.

DI Harrington went to the board where the information collected so far, was displayed. He pointed to the map of Britain. 'The first murder was here in Stirling and then they moved down the country stopping with us. Why stop here?'

'Why start in Scotland?' added DS Marlow.

'And why more than one murder on our patch?' Harriet wrinkled her nose. 'I'll make a pot of coffee and while we drink it, we'll go over every single detail and see if anything adds up.' She rose but Charlie stepped forward.

'Let me make it, Ma'am.'

Harriet smiled. 'Only if you use my ground coffee. You'll find the cafetière and coffee in the right-hand cupboard of my desk together with a collection of mugs. Thank you, Charlie.'

Sergeant Marlow left the room and Harriet turned to Inspector Harrington. 'There must be a link here somewhere, Ed, but I'm blowed if I can see it at present.' They sat down at the table and Ed spread an assortment of papers in front of them.

Charlie returned carrying the cafetière and mugs on a tray. 'Does anyone take sugar?' he asked. Harriet and Ed both shook their heads and Charlie placed the tray on the table. The three began the task of sifting through all the evidence they had at their disposal, to see if there was anything that might implicate someone in their murder enquiry.

Three hours later, and the equivalent number of pots of

coffee, the colleagues were still poring over the piles of paper spread out in front of them. There appeared to be no apparent reason for the murders to be spread down the country and at present no one in any of the hospitals was linked to anyone else. The delivery dates of the drivers from Garratts Medical Supplies did not match with any of the murder dates and in fact, for most of them, both Vincent Caldwell and his brother Bill had alibis. Garry Hobbs the hospital car driver, and all the other staff members who had been interviewed by the police also came up with alibis. The staff lists from the hospitals so far scrutinised, showed nothing unusual. Nothing matched. Nothing linked the hospitals and no member of staff had worked in more than one of them during the past two years. The murdered nurses had not worked in any of the other hospitals where a nurse had been murdered, and as far as could be checked, none of them knew any of the other victims. Patient lists were now being checked by a team of officers. It would be a long and tedious job, but if the same name appeared at more than one of the hospitals then it would be worthwhile. There was a knock on the door that opened to admit the slight, bespectacled figure of Phillip Hewitt.

'Sorry to intrude, Ma'am, but I thought you might like to have what I discovered at the murder scene.' He held up a small plastic packet and Harriet leaped to her feet.

'I don't believe it! Sergeant, you're amazing.' She took the small packet and focused her eyes on the two gold earring backs that it contained.

Phillip Hewitt shuffled his feet. He was not used to exuberant praise from his seniors. 'All in a day's work, Ma'am. Nothing had been disturbed around the body and they were quite easy to see really.'

'Well done, Hewitt.' DI Harrington came over to the sergeant. 'I knew if the earring backs were there, you would find them.'

'Great work, Phil.' Charlie too was on his feet 'How about a coffee? We're awash with the stuff and there's loads still in the pot.'

'I won't say no. This searching lark certainly makes you thirsty and I haven't moved from the bushes since first thing this morning.'

'Good heavens!' exclaimed DCI Love. 'Are you telling us that you have been on your hands and knees in those bushes for nearly four hours?'

'Yes, Ma'am. You can't stop once you get started or you lose track of where you have and have not searched. I found the first back within the first hour but the second one took quite a bit longer. It was some way away from the spot where the body lay. It must have sprung off. They do, you know, if the earring is yanked out from the front with no regard for the back clip.'

Harriet hugged the plastic bag close to her. 'Thank you, Phillip. This is just wonderful.'

Sergeant Hewitt was beginning to enjoy the limelight. Usually his work was taken for granted. He was always thorough and as far as he knew nothing escaped his keen eyes when he was called to a crime scene. He smiled. 'I could see that you were convinced that the earring backs would be left at the spot, Ma'am, so I just persevered. You are very motivating when you make a request such as you did.'

Harriet gave the sergeant one of her wide smiles. 'I shall remember that, Phillip, when I need another favour. I presume these butterflies have been swabbed for DNA testing and I may keep them?'

'Yes. They're all yours now.' Sergeant Hewitt nodded as he gratefully gulped down the coffee that Charlie had handed him. 'Good coffee, Charlie. Not like the usual muck you serve up here…'

Charlie chortled. 'It's the Chief Inspector's special ground coffee. We're being educated in the finer things of life.'

DCI Love decided that the team needed a lunch break and it was agreed that the three would meet back at the Incident Room in an hour. Harriet carefully locked the earring backs in the safe before leaving the building for a breath of fresh air. She walked the short distance to the park where she sat on a bench, leaned back and closed her eyes. She turned the happenings of the last few days over in her mind. Why nurses? Why take their earrings? Why kill these young women in so many different parts of the country?

'Chief Inspector Love?' A voice broke into her muddled

thoughts and she opened her eyes to find Stacey Boston, the pathologist, standing in front of her.

'I thought it was you walking through the park,' continued Dr Boston. 'I wondered if you might like some company?'

Harriet sighed. 'I thought a walk in the fresh air might sharpen my brain. This case is a real puzzle.'

Stacey sat down beside the Chief Inspector. 'I've just dropped off the pathology report on Carol Young. As the first examination indicated, there is no other injury on the body apart from the scratch on the ear. Death was by strangulation.'

'Is it the same with Monica Meyers?'

'First impression is that she was strangled. No sign of any other injury or assault. I'm doing the post-mortem this afternoon and I'll get the report to you tomorrow. I don't suppose there will be any other injuries on the body.'

'Thanks. But you're right, Stacey – do you mind if I call you Stacey?' As Dr Boston nodded, she continued, 'There will be no other injuries. He just strangles his victims using these red scarves and takes their earrings. For heaven's sake, why take their earrings? And where is he buying all these red scarves?'

'He'll be deranged in some way, won't he? They nearly always are.' Stacey Boston touched Harriet's arm. 'Come on, let's go and have some lunch at the Red Lion. They make excellent pasta dishes and,' she grinned, 'the coffee is always *real* coffee.'

'How did you know I prefer the real thing?'

'Word gets around, Chief Inspector.'

'For goodness' sake call me Harry. Let's go then, I could murder some decent pasta.'

The two women walked across the park to the Red Lion public house on the other side. As they entered the busy lounge, heads turned in their direction; the tall strikingly handsome redhead with alert green eyes and the slightly shorter attractive blonde with dark blue eyes. They moved to the bar oblivious of the stir they had caused. None of the men who frequented the Red Lion would have guessed for one moment that these two women held such important posts and were at this moment involved in the solving of two distasteful murders.

Two young men leaning on the bar eyed them up and down. 'Now I call this very tasty,' said one young man.

'Very tasty indeed,' agreed the second. 'And what a pair.'

'What a pair indeed. Mmm!'

Harriet stopped in her tracks and fixed her green eyes coldly on the two men. Something in her look made the men hesitate. But they brazenly continued.

'I like big women.'

Stacey looked at them and turned up her nose in a disdainful manner. 'I don't suppose for a single moment that either of you have anything that you could remotely describe as big.'

'Apart from your mouths,' added Harriet.

The two women turned and went to the bar. Without another word the two men practically crawled away from them and sat down at a table by the door feeling extremely foolish. An older man standing at the far end of the room roared with laughter. 'That'll teach you whippersnappers to keep your place. You can't speak to women like that any more. They ask for respect these days.' He turned back to his glass of beer and raised it in the direction of Harriet and Stacey. 'Good on yer, ladies,' he said.

Harriet winked at Stacey. 'Men can be pretty pathetic at times. Why do they feel they have to be witty all the time. By the way, I trust you were referring to their brains when you insinuated that they had nothing that was very big?'

Stacey chuckled. 'I left that for them to work out. Some men can be so condescending, that's what annoys me. But don't let them spoil our lunch, I can't remember when I last had a pub meal with decent company.'

The two women ordered their pasta and took their soft drinks to a table at the opposite side of the room to the young men. Stacey sipped her lime and lemonade. 'I never dare drink when I'm working, in case it dulls my senses when I'm performing a post-mortem.'

'I'm the same,' smiled Harriet. 'I love wine but I forgo the pleasure when I'm on duty.'

Harriet found the hour with Stacey Boston most enjoyable. Stacey was thirty-five and, like Harriet, still single. 'I think that most men are scared off when they discover that I'm a pathologist,' she smiled.

'My job does the same to men, I'm afraid,' agreed Harriet.

Stacey put down her fork. 'Mind you, when the right guy comes along he won't care what we do for a living, will he?'

'I'm sure you're right. I just wonder where this "right guy" is hiding at present. I'm thirty-seven and I think my parents have given up all hope of me ever marrying.'

'Oh come on, Harry, women are marrying later and later these days. Thirty-seven is no age. Mr Right is out there somewhere, and in the meantime you have a very high-powered job to contend with.'

'Same with you,' replied Harriet. 'You're very young to be Senior Pathologist.'

'We'd better drink to us, then.' Stacey raised her glass in a mock salute.

They touched glasses and drank the toast. The barman came over to their table with the coffees that they had ordered and Harriet smiled at her new friend as she poured each of them a cup.

'Told you it was real,' said Stacey and as they drank their coffee, adding, 'Now I have to get back to the morgue to start that PM. I'll get the result to you as soon as possible.'

The women left the Red Lion. Dr Boston heading for the Mortuary and Harriet returning to the police station.

DI Harrington and DS Marlow were already in the Incident Room as she entered. 'I feel better for that break,' she smiled. 'Now back to the drawing board.'

They sat at the table once again. Harriet turned to Ed and said, 'Have we received CCTV tapes from all the hospitals where a nurse was murdered?'

'All but two,' came the reply. 'Those we have got are being viewed at this moment. We've assigned a team to that task and hopefully something might turn up.'

Harriet continued, 'It makes you wonder, if it's not a staff member and not a patient, is it a visitor? There wouldn't be a check on visitors, would there? They don't have to sign in or anything, do they?' The DCI wrinkled her nose. 'It has to be someone with connections to the hospitals.'

'Well, you can certainly walk into these establishments without any bother,' said Charlie. 'And when you think of the hundreds who must pass through the doors every day it will be some task to check every single one of them.'

Harriet rested her chin on her hands. 'Except for the nursing home where Monica worked. It really isn't that large and I'm sure they don't have that many visitors.'

'They also don't have a CCTV system,' added Ed. 'I asked for it when I was there making my enquiry about Monica.'

'But do they have someone on the desk?' asked Harriet.

'Yes. There was a nurse on duty when I called and the owner, a Mrs Childers appeared like lightning when I asked for her.'

Harriet stood up. 'Right! I'd like a word with the staff at The Poplars. It's a small place and visitors will be remembered.' She turned to DI Harrington. 'I have to take Mrs Meyers to the mortuary to identify her daughter later but we have time to make our enquiries. You come with me, Ed. Charlie, you take Sally or Narinder with you and return to the Cottage Hospital. See if anyone remembers incidents in the last few weeks that were strange or unexplained. You know the sort of thing. Anyone looking out of place or loitering without good reason.'

'Right, Ma'am.' Charlie leaped to his feet. He much preferred action to sitting round a table talking. He left the room to collect DC Pringle, who was in the smaller CID room busily sifting through the list of staff names that they had received from the hospitals. 'Are you fit, Sally? We have action!'

Sally looked up. 'Great. I think I'm getting blurred vision reading all this small print and not a single name has turned up in more than one hospital. It gets a bit tedious after a time.'

'We're going to the Cottage Hospital to talk to as many staff members as possible to see if we can trigger something in their memory that might give us a small lead.'

Sally grabbed her jacket from the back of the chair and they left for the car pool to collect a vehicle for the afternoon.

DCI Love and DI Harrington were already on their way to The Poplars in the black Saab. Ed had the sneaking feeling that his boss was being generous in allowing him to take his car, but he said nothing when she made the suggestion that he drove; just nodded and accepted the offer gratefully. At The Poplars they discovered a young woman sitting at the reception desk, and on showing her their warrant cards they asked to see Mrs Childers. The owner of the Home readily gave them permission to interview her staff and informed them that she would be in her office should they need her presence.

Harriet turned to the nurse on duty. 'Do you take it in turns to be at the desk?' she enquired.

'Yes, we do,' she answered. 'Mrs Childers does a roster for the whole week and pins it on the duty notice board. It shows which shift we are on and where we are to work.'

Ed stepped forward. 'Could you get us the duty rosters for the past five or six weeks, please?'

'No problem,' smiled the nurse. 'Mrs Childers always keeps them so that if anyone complains about unfair duties she produces the rosters as proof that we all take a fair share of the unpopular shifts.' She left the desk and vanished down the corridor to the Proprietor's office.

Harriet gazed around the entrance hall. 'No one would get into this place unseen would they?'

'No way, if someone was on duty at the desk,' replied Ed.

If our killer needed to suss out his victims – you know, to find out if they are single and wear earrings – he could hardly do that from a distance could he?'

'I doubt it. So what you're saying is that he must always have access to the hospital in some way to get close enough to his victim, before he attacks them.'

'Absolutely.' Harriet nodded vigorously. 'And coming into a small place like this might just be his undoing.'

The nurse returned with a sheaf of papers. 'Here you are,' she smiled. 'They go back months.'

Harriet took the rosters and held them so that DI Harrington could read them as well. The name Nurse Meyers sprang out at them. She had been on reception duty on two mornings of the previous week. One other name appeared on the list twice in that week. A Nurse Belford.

Harriet spoke. 'Could we speak to Nurse Belford, please.'

The nurse ran her finger down the current list. 'Pauline is on ward three. I'll go and fetch her for you.' She left the desk once again to return minutes later with a tall, dark-haired older woman.

'I'm Pauline Belford, how can I help you?'

'Please sit down.' Harriet indicated the chairs in the hallway and as the woman obliged, Harriet did likewise, sitting in the chair facing her. Ed remained standing and posed the first question.

'We notice that you were on desk duty on two occasions last week. Your shift followed on from Monica Meyers', and we wondered if you saw anyone in the building at that time who would not normally be here.'

Nurse Belford thought for a moment. 'We were surprisingly busy last week. We had several enquiries about beds and several prospective clients did call to view rooms.'

'Any male on his own?' asked Harriet.

'One elderly gentleman who was pretty distressed. His wife is suffering from dementia and getting too much for him at home. He was here on the Monday when I was on duty, and in fact because he was so impressed with the Home, his wife joined us the following Monday. She's still with us if you need to see her.'

'No need for that,' said Harriet.

'Any other male been asking questions?' persisted Ed.

'Not that I can remember,' frowned Pauline Belford. 'A youngish man did come to visit his grandmother, but she wasn't registered with us and Monica directed him to the Cottage Hospital.'

'How do you remember this man if it was Monica who was on duty?' Ed was now very interested in the discussion.

'We were just changing shifts. Monica was taking over from me when this man walked in. She told me to go on home and she would sort it out.'

Harriet too was excited. 'Can you describe this man?'

'We-ell, he wasn't very tall and wore an anorak and a woolly hat. That's why I remember him because of the woolly hat. I thought it strange on such a warm day.'

'Think hard, Pauline, this could be vital. Can you remember anything else about him?' DI Harrington spoke in a calm voice, trying hard not to appear over eager.

Harriet chipped in, 'Don't worry if it seems trivial to you. Any small thing that you can remember might help us.'

'He was very polite. *Over*-polite, now that I come to think of it. Sort of oily. You know the sort of thing, when men are trying to chat you up.'

'Did he talk to you or just Monica?' Harriet too kept her voice low and encouraging.

'He took no notice of me. I was getting my things together to go home. I heard Monica suggest that he tried looking for his grandma at the Cottage Hospital but that she was definitely not at The Poplars.'

'Can you remember his grandmother's name?' asked Harriet.

'Now let me think. I'm good at remembering names. Mitchell, it was Mitchell, Daisy or Dorothy Mitchell.'

'Well done!' said Ed. 'What did he do then?'

'I actually nipped to the loo at that point and when I came out he had gone. He was walking to the car park as I walked out of the front door.'

Harriet stood up. 'What a pity there's no CCTV coverage here.' She turned to Pauline Belford. 'Do you think you would recognise this man again?'

'I'm not sure. I wasn't really taking that much notice of him. You know how it is. I could hear him talking to Monica, but I wasn't particularly interested. Mind you, I'd probably remember his walk if I ever saw it again.'

'*Walk?*' Both Ed and Harriet spoke together.

'He had a strange walk.' Pauline pondered. 'A very strange walk. Not exactly a limp, but a dragging action of both legs. It was very slight but noticeable to me.'

'That's very useful,' said Ed. 'But he didn't use a stick, did he?'

'No. There was no stick.'

'Did you see what sort of car he had?' Harriet was beginning to think they had at last found their breakthrough.

Pauline half smiled. 'I'm not very good with cars but it was an old, ordinary looking thing, square rather than round, and a pale colour; blue or green. Could have been a Ford, but don't take my word for that.'

DCI Love thanked Nurse Belford for her help and left her card in case the nurse remembered anything else. She and DI Harrington left The Poplars and returned to the car.

'Something at last, Ed.' Harriet turned to her colleague as they sat in the car.

DI Harrington agreed. 'This chap really does sound fishy. Why wouldn't he know which institute his grandmother had been taken to?'

'And the woolly hat was mentioned by Nurse Pawlett and Clifford Jarvis.' Harriet made a fist. 'Back to the CCTV tapes, Ed, to see if we can glimpse a man in an anorak and wearing a woolly hat. No one in their right mind would dress like that at this time of year, would they?'

'Well, it is July.' Ed started the car. 'But people do wear strange apparel for no good reason.'

'True,' replied Harriet. 'But I still bet there aren't many people wearing woolly hats at the moment.'

'I expect you're right.' DI Harrington moved the car forward.

'Before we return to the Station, Ed, let's call at the Cottage Hospital to see if they have admitted an elderly patient by the name of Mitchell in the last week.'

At the Cottage Hospital DS Marlow and DC Pringle were moving between the departments asking the staff if they could recollect any males in the hospital during the past two or three weeks who were hanging around or just sitting in one of the waiting areas without an apparent appointment. Charlie spotted an attractive Sister sifting through papers on a desk at the Nurse's Station and he was transfixed. He was unsure as to why he felt so attracted to her, but he was. He sidled up to her. 'Could you spare a few moments to answer some questions?'

'Certainly not,' she replied somewhat sharply. 'You shouldn't be in here without an official tag. We don't allow researchers, or whatever you are, in the hospital so I should be grateful if you left.'

Charlie grinned. 'Sorry, sweetie, but I'm here on official business.' He produced his warrant card and held it up to her face.

'Well, Sergeant, that might well be, but would you please go to the office and obtain your tag. Then you might like to return, and if you address me in an appropriate manner, I might consider answering your questions.' She turned on her heel and strode away.

DS Marlow stroked his chin. 'Frosty or what,' he said turning to Sally as she came up to him.

'You deserved that, Sarge. We women don't appreciate your condescending attitude. I'd have thought you'd have learned your lesson after the way the DCI put you down the other day.'

'Who told you about that?' Charlie's smile faded momentarily.

'We all heard what she said to you. It was obvious you'd been stupid enough to call her "sweetie" before you found out who she was. You're the only officer that I know of who calls women "sweetie" and it's pretty sickening.'

'Sorry, Sally. From now on I shall turn over a new leaf and never again call any woman sweetie.' Charlie held his hand to the left side of his chest. 'Scout's honour,' he smiled.

Sally smiled in return. 'We shall see. Now we'd better go to the reception and collect our visitor tags before we get thrown out.'

They collected their passes and Sally went off to ask more questions while DS Marlow walked back to the nurses' station in pursuit of the frosty Sister. As he approached the desk the woman he was seeking came towards him. 'Now, officer, what can I do for you?'

Sister Jacques was of average height with dark hair and brown eyes that at this moment had a hint of amusement in them. Charlie noted that there was no ring on the left hand and decided that he would bide his time before introducing the soft line of chat-up. He was not sure about the less intimidating glint in the brown eyes but, determined not to offend the woman further, he graciously smiled at her. 'Sorry about that, Sister, we rather got off on the wrong foot. Shall we start again? I'm Charlie Marlow and I should be grateful if you could spare me a few moments.'

Sister Jaques played along. 'Good afternoon, Sergeant. I'm Liz Jaques. How can I help you?'

Charlie's familiar grin returned and he commenced asking questions regarding strangers in the hospital over the last few weeks.

Liz Jaques frowned. 'You can see how difficult it is to screen every single visitor to the building. We do our best and do insist that visitors report to reception where they are given a badge to wear; but as for patients and their relatives, well, we're fighting a losing battle.'

Charlie continued the discussion of unwelcome visitors on the premises before taking his life in his hands and asking the question that he had been dying to ask ever since meeting this attractive woman. 'Are you free for dinner tonight?'

Liz Jaques lifted her brown eyes to look at the tall, fair-haired Sergeant in front of her. Charlie's heart sank. He'd done it again. Been too pushy and messed up his chances of a date. Sister Jaques spoke. 'As luck would have it I'm off duty tonight, and I'd love a night out for a change.'

Charlie's pulse raced. He had no idea why this should happen. He chatted up females all the time. This was possibly a reaction to his divorce resulting in his new feeling of freedom. Since the break-up he was always casual about his relationships with women and never really took any dates seriously. Suddenly he was feeling different. He badly wanted this woman to like him, and on hearing her reply to his invitation to dinner he glowed. 'Can I pick you up at seven thirty?' He found it difficult to control his voice and he desperately tried to sound casual.

'That would be fine. I'll write down my address for you.' She went to the desk and scribbled on a piece of paper. She handed it to Charlie with a whimsical smile. 'I hope this isn't how you behave with all women?'

'Absolutely not.' Charlie spoke with conviction but for once in his life he felt a twinge of conscience. 'I'll be there on the dot of seven thirty,' he grinned. 'How about eating at La Tosca in Leicester? Do you like Italian?'

'I love it,' replied Liz, 'but now I really must go, I'm already late with the drug round.' She turned and walked up the corridor to the ward.

As Charlie turned to leave he came face to face with DCI Love. 'And might you also be late, Sergeant Marlow?' she asked. 'Or have you perhaps concluded your inquiries here?'

Charlie was momentarily flustered but he quickly gathered himself together. 'Yes, Ma'am I think we have finished here. I'll just go and collect DC Pringle and we'll be off back to the Station.'

'It's been a satisfactory afternoon, has it?' asked Harriet her face completely passive.

'Er… yes, yes. I've er… we've done everything we set out to do.'

'I'm sure you have, Charlie,' responded the DCI. Sergeant Marlow, not at all sure that she was not toying with him, quickly walked away to find Sally Pringle.

DI Harrington came up to Harriet. 'There is no elderly female in the hospital by the name of Mitchell. Daisy or otherwise. What has DS Marlow turned up?'

'Just a date, I think,' said the Chief Inspector, and Ed was convinced that she was smiling.

Sally walked beside Charlie. 'I have the name of someone who was dating Carol Young, Sarge. He too works at the hospital here.'

'Good work, Sally, we'll add it to the information in the Incident Room and interview him later.'

They returned to the police station where DCI Love and DI Harrington parted company. Ed went to the Incident Room and joined Charlie and Sally to bring the enquiry up to date by adding the latest information to the board. Ed was looking forward to having time off the following day. Harriet collected her own car and drove off to collect Mrs Meyers to take her to the mortuary. She was again to face the unenviable task of supporting a mother during the identification of her daughter. Harriet would then return home to her cottage, disappointed and weary after a day where she felt little progress in the murder investigation had been made.

Chapter Seven

On Sunday Harriet was able to steal a lie-in. She lay in bed with the fluffy bundle of her cat beside her, turning the events of the past week over and over in her mind. She was delighted with her first week in charge and with the support she had received from the team. Even the reserved attitude of DI Harrington could not dampen her spirits. It was the impenetrable core of the murder that made her subdued and she decided to spend the morning at home going over the evidence quietly on her own. She had one or two planned excursions that she intended to carry out later in the day, but for now it was coffee and toast and a concentrated effort in detection work.

Ed Harrington as always visited his mother on Sunday morning. She lived in a small modern house on a pleasant housing estate on the edge of Northampton, and at ten thirty he duly arrived, armed with a large bouquet of flowers. Mrs Harrington, like her son, was tall and slender. She had short, dark but greying hair, and at sixty-five years of age still displayed a youthfulness that the hardships of the past years had failed to erase. Ellen Harrington had been devastated by the death of her husband and the events of that fateful day, when a Chief Superintendent had called with the harrowing news, were still indelibly printed on her mind. Over the years she had slowly and with great determination put her life back together. Edward had been a great strength, and although she had tried desperately to make her son accept his university place, he had been adamant that he would remain at home and become the breadwinner. Mrs Harrington had received a substantial police pension, but nevertheless she was grateful for the support she had received from Edward, not only financially, but emotionally.

She welcomed her only son with a warm hug. 'The coffee is on and I've made some of those savoury scones that you like. I'm sure you don't eat properly living on your own.'

Ed kissed his mother on the cheek. 'Stop fussing, Mother. I live better than you suppose. Mind you, I have to admit I do miss your home baking.' He sat in the familiar sitting room where for years he had sat with his father and discussed law and politics. He looked at the photograph on the mantelpiece. His father was a striking figure in police uniform. Superintendent Frank Harrington had made headlines nineteen years ago when he had single-handedly prevented an armed bank raid. The gang had already shot the bank manager, who had pressed the alarm bell in defiance, and Frank Harrington swiftly placed himself between the robbers and the customers and staff, calling out to them to move into a back room. He then faced the gang and warned them that reinforcements were on the way. The three men had panicked and bolted, but not before one crazed youth had opened fire at the officer with a sawn-off shotgun at point-blank range. Frank Harrington died at the scene and was deemed a hero. He was awarded the George Medal posthumously, the medal now holding pride of place on Ellen Harrington's bedside table.

She came into the sitting room carrying the tray of coffee and hot cheese-and-herb scones, which she placed carefully on the low table in front of her son. Ed looked up and smiled. 'Instant coffee, Mother? I'm afraid I'm getting used to the real thing these days. Our new Chief Inspector has impeccable taste and only drinks ground coffee.'

Mrs Harrington poured the coffee. 'Does he now.'

'She,' contradicted Ed and as his mother looked up surprised he added. 'Yes! Our new Chief Inspector is a woman.'

'Good heavens, things are certainly changing. What would your father have made of that, I wonder?' An expression of thoughtfulness clouded her gentle face as she remembered her husband. 'What is she like?'

'Tall, auburn-haired, very glamorous and wears beautiful clothes. Hardly what you would expect in a Senior Officer.'

'Is she any good at her job, though?' Ellen Harrington eyed her son quizzically noting the tone of envy in his voice.

'So far she's doing okay. We have a particularly nasty case of murder on our hands at present and she seems to be on the ball.'

'I read about it in the paper,' said Mrs Harrington. 'Two

nurses have been strangled, both with a scarf. I presume both were done by the same person?'

'We think so. Too much of a coincidence otherwise. But don't let's talk about work. How are you keeping?' Ed tactfully turned the conversation towards other topics while he eagerly sampled his mothers baking. He stayed for two hours before leaving with the promise of joining her for Sunday lunch the following weekend. 'I'll have a go at the garden when I come next Sunday,' he said as he was going.

'The lawn needs cutting and I think it's time that the old elm came down. It's looking pretty dangerous to me. One sudden gust on a windy night and that will be that.'

He climbed into his car and started the engine. His mother stood on the step and waved him goodbye. She sighed as she returned in doors. How like his father he was! Please God protect him from harm…

Ed had arranged to meet Charlie at one o'clock for lunch at the pub. Charlie would be full of the date he had had last night with the nurse from the Cottage Hospital and Ed secretly wished that he could be as confident and forthcoming as his friend was when talking to women.

Charlie was already leaning on the bar when Ed arrived at the Red Lion and as he had predicted his friend was bubbling over with news of his outing with Liz Jaques.

'She's a real charmer, Ed! It's a long time since I've met someone as wonderful as her.'

'I hope you didn't try anything on then, Charlie.'

'Absolutely not. She kept me at arm's length, but you could tell she was interested in me.'

Ed smiled at his friend. He must be pleased for him. Charlie had had a rough three and a half years of marriage with the self-centred, flirtatious Claudia, and the break-up had all but crucified him at the time. 'Good for you, mate,' he said. 'When are you seeing her again?'

'Next Tuesday on her evening off. I've booked a table at the Three Swans in Market Harborough for an exotic dinner. The food there is pretty special, you know. Ever been there?'

'We celebrated Dad's fiftieth there.'

'Sorry, Ed.' Charlie touched his friend's arm. 'Am I going on a bit?'

Ed laughed. 'Of course you're not, Charlie. I'm really happy for you. Now, what are you having to eat? It won't be in the same league as the Three Swans, but it's decent food all the same.'

After lunch Ed and Charlie drove to Northampton where Ed needed to pick up a new set of number plates for the Saab from a garage owned by an ex-policeman. As they were walking down Cranbourne Avenue, Charlie suddenly grabbed Ed by the arm and pulled him into a doorway.

'What is it?' asked Ed.

'Shh! Look over there in the doorway of the Trelawny Hotel.'

Ed looked to where Charlie was pointing. Standing on the steps of the hotel, looking amazing in a dark green dress, stood Harriet Love. It was not the fact that she looked beautiful that made Ed gasp, but the fact that she was holding the arm of a familiar, distinguished figure.

'That's Sir Richard Fitzwilliam, for God's sake.' He turned to Charlie, who was grinning.

'So our boss is not so sweet and innocent after all,' he smirked. 'She has clandestine meetings with one of the most prominent judges in the country.'

Ed watched with dismay as Ms Love looked up at the judge. There was obvious feeling in the woman's face, and he felt bitter as he saw the affectionate way the judge put his arm about her shoulders. She in return put her arms about the big man and hugged him before kissing him on the cheek and turning to walk away from the hotel. Mr Justice Fitzwilliam returned inside and Ed turned to Charlie.

'You can't trust anyone these days,' he said shaking his head. 'The judge's wife is a delightful lady. I've met her at Police dinners when her husband was the after dinner speaker, and she really is charming. How could he do this to her?'

'It's none of our business,' replied Charlie pulling at his friend's arm. 'Come on let's get to Paddy's place before he thinks you're not coming and closes up shop.' They continued walking down the road. Ed was deep in thought about the revelation that DCI Love might be having an affair with Sir Richard Fitzwilliam, and remembering how hurt Charlie had been on discovering his own wife's infidelity.

Paddy Lynch was still at his garage. 'I'd just about given you up, Ed. I don't particularly want to work the whole of Sunday. Hi Charlie.'

'Sorry we're late, Paddy.'

'You look tired, mate.' The big Irishman wiped his oily hands on what appeared to be a pair of his underpants before shaking hands with both men. He turned to the bench where he picked up the new set of number plates and handed them to Ed. 'Is your new lady boss keeping your nose to the grindstone?' he grinned.

Charlie laughed. 'You've heard about our new boss then, have you?'

'News travels fast. I was informed that the DCI is a woman.'

Ed joined in the conversation not much wishing to discuss DCI Love, 'She is indeed. But to us she is just another senior officer and we make no distinction because she's female.'

'Ah!' Paddy pulled a face. 'Do I sense a little bitterness in your tone, Ed?'

'Certainly not. Now, what do I owe you?'

Paddy winked at Charlie as he produced the invoice from the clip on the wall. Ed wrote a cheque and handed it over. 'How's Barbara?'

'Just fine. More than a little bit happy that I'm no longer on the Force.'

'And the children?' asked Ed.

'Both fine thanks,' replied Paddy. 'Patrick will be taking his GCSEs next year.'

'Wow!' said Charlie. 'It seems like only weeks since you were dashing off duty to be at the hospital when he was born. Time certainly does fly.'

'Time you two were married and settled,' smiled Paddy. 'Anyone in the pipeline for either of you?'

Ed looked at his friend. 'I think Charlie has just become smitten. But time will tell. Now we must be off, Paddy. Thanks for the plates – and give our love to Barbara and the kids.'

They left the garage and retraced their steps down Cranbourne Avenue. They passed the Trelawny Hotel. There was no sign of

DCI Love or of Sir Richard Fitzwilliam. Ed looked away, unable to explain to himself the feeling of bitter disappointment he felt on discovering that his boss was, after all, like so many other disloyal people. He was more than surprised at the judge and yes, surprised at Ms Love also.

On Monday morning DI Harrington found great difficulty in meeting the eyes of DCI Love as he faced her across her desk. She was as bright and cheerful as ever and eager to get the murder investigation under way again. 'How close are we to completing the name checks from all the hospitals?' she asked.

'Today should see the conclusion of that investigation and then we are going back over the CCTV videos to look for a man in an anorak and a woolly hat.'

'Good,' replied Harriet. 'On your way back to the Incident Room could you ask Jack to come and see me. I'm going to ask him to get the poster campaign under way. It's a week today that Carol Young's body was discovered and since we've had a second nurse murdered on our patch I think we should send warning posters round to all the hospitals in the area.'

'How far afield do you intend spreading this campaign?' asked DI Harrington.

'As far as our own investigation is concerned, I suggest all hospitals in Northants and Leicestershire. If we then inform all other forces through the Internet, it's up to them to take the initiative and follow our lead. What do you think, Ed?'

'That sounds positive, Ma'am. I'll inform Jack.' Again he found it difficult to meet the steady gaze of DCI Love, and as he turned to leave he heard her cool voice addressing him.

'Are you all right this morning, Ed? You look decidedly seedy to me. Are you coming down with something nasty or have you just had a hectic weekend?' She laughed her musical laugh and Ed was forced to look at her.

'No, no, Ma'am. I didn't sleep too well last night, that's all.' Ed was somewhat disconcerted by the DCI's questions. It was true he had not slept well the previous night. He had tossed and turned in bed thinking of DCI Love with Mr Justice Fitzwilliam and he was angry with himself for being concerned. After all, as Charlie had said, it was none of their business.

'Well, try and get an early night tonight, we can't have you falling by the wayside or I don't know what I should do.' The soft melodic voice penetrated his thoughts and he nodded before leaving the room.

Harriet sat at her desk. The DCI was certainly a complex character. Always so serious and rarely able to laugh or even smile. She took a deep breath and busied herself with writing the report that she had promised George Hollyoak. DI Harrington's personal attributes were of no concern to her but secretly she hoped that his attitude towards her would soften soon.

Two hours later Harriet leaned back in her chair and read over the lengthy report she had written on the investigations carried out so far in the murder case. She signed the bottom of the last page just as the telephone on her desk rang. The voice at the other end greeted her in the usual formal manner. 'Good morning, Ma'am. It's Sergeant Fisher from the front desk. I have a gentleman here asking to see the person in charge of the scarf murders case. Says he might have some information for you.'

Harriers heart leaped. How she could do with some helpful information at this moment. 'Please bring him up to my office, Carl.'

She replaced the receiver and jumped to her feet. She grabbed the cafetière and tin of coffee from her cupboard and dashed to the kitchen. Sally was already there boiling the kettle. 'Sally, I hate to ask you this, but would you be so kind as to make me a pot of coffee and bring it to my office.'

Sally Pringle smiled. 'Of course I will, Ma'am. How many spoonfuls of coffee?'

'Two heaped ones, please, and then fill it up. I have sugar in my room and here's my little jug for some milk.' She turned and hurried back to her office just as Sergeant Carl Fisher appeared in the corridor.

'This is Simon Townsend from Leicester, Ma'am.'

'Thank you, Sergeant. Please come into my office, Mr Townsend.' Harriet smiled at Carl Fisher and mouthed, 'Thank you,' as she closed the door.

'Do sit down.' DCI Love indicated the chair at her desk as she sat down on the other side facing him. 'Now what is this information you have?'

The big man with a red face and thinning hair must have been in his sixties. As he sat down he produced a paper bag from his pocket. From the bag he drew a blue scarf placing it on the desk in front of Harriet.

'Might this be the same sort of scarf that you have been asking about in the papers? I know it isn't red, but it's pure cashmere, and not many places manufacture such things in this area.'

Harriet picked up the soft blue scarf. 'Where did you get it, Mr Townsend?'

'I worked at the factory where we made them. Bought it for my wife. We were allowed a discount, so I thought I'd treat her to a bit of real cashmere. They retailed at £48 and you wouldn't spend that on a scarf, would you? We made them in red as well, and when I read about the pure wool scarves used to kill those poor lassies, it just made me wonder. Then I saw that no one had come forward to say that they had sold such scarves so I thought a bit harder and decided to come and see you.'

Sally knocked on the door and entered carrying a tray with the coffee.

'Thank you, Sally.' DCI Love took the tray. 'Would you go to the Incident Room and ask DI Harrington to come here, and would he bring the red scarves, please.'

'Yes, Ma'am. Oh, and by the way, I discovered yesterday that Garry Hobbs, the hospital driver, had dated Carol Young. He was very reluctant to admit it so I have reported it to Inspector Harrington. He's added the information to the crime board just in case it's significant.'

'That's an interesting piece of news, Sally. Hobbs was certainly not forthcoming with that bit of news in his statement. We'll look into it.'

DC Pringle hurried from the room and Harriet turned her attention back to Simon Townsend.

'Now! Where is this factory, Mr Townsend?'

'Leicester, Ma'am. I worked there for thirty-five years and packed up work when the factory burned down nearly three years ago.'

'How did that happen?' Harriet leaned forward in her chair.

'It was a dreadful business.' Simon Townsend shook his head.

'It was near the end of the day in February when there came this almighty explosion and the building started to fall on our heads. Then came the fire. There were flames everywhere and real panic.' He shuddered as he remembered what had happened and Harriet quickly intervened.

'Have some coffee and start again in a moment when my colleague arrives.' She poured a mug of coffee and handed it across the desk. A knock on the door revealed DI Harrington carrying the plastic bag containing the scarves. Harriet poured two more mugs of coffee and indicated to Ed to sit down beside her. She handed the coffee to him.

'Thank you. Here are the scarves you asked for.' He put them on the table and Harriet took them from the bag placing them beside the blue one.

'What do you think, Inspector?'

Ed picked up the blue scarf and held it beside one of the red ones. 'They look identical,' he said.

Harriet explained who Simon Townsend was and related the story that he had just told her. Ed handed the scarves to the man sitting in front of them. 'Are they the same?' he asked Simon Townsend.

The big man picked up the scarves and scrutinised them. 'I'd know them anywhere,' he said. 'The double-knotted fringe was a speciality of ours. They're definitely from the Perfect Factory. The blue one I brought you has the label on it. Look.' He pulled out the white label which said 'PERFECT Pure Cashmere'. He continued speaking, 'The red ones have had the labels cut off. But apart from that they are the same. Definitely from the Perfect factory.'

'Why has no one come forward to say that they sell them, I wonder?' said Harriet and wrinkled her nose.

'That's easy to explain.' Simon Townsend sat up sharply. 'Apart from some of the workers who bought them as a luxury, they were for export only. None went to any shops or department stores in this country.'

'Our killer seems to have a good supply of them.' Ed took back the red scarves and returned them to the plastic bag. They were evidence, and he had no intention of letting them out of his sight.

'You'd have thought that the factory boss would have spotted his own goods though, wouldn't you. Unless of course he's involved in this case.'

Simon Townsend gave a hollow laugh. 'The owners of the factory were Raymond and Ralph Prefect – PERFECT, as you can see, is a twist on their name. They were both killed in the accident. That's probably why no one bothered to rebuild the place. Four other men were killed and dozens were injured. I was one of the lucky ones. I had gone outside to despatch a delivery when the blast occurred or I may well have been killed or injured myself.'

'What caused the explosion?' asked Harriet. 'If the owners were killed it was obviously not an insurance scam.'

'There was not a great deal of money floating about in the business, but the Prefects were straight up and very hard working. The boilers were pretty old and there wasn't enough money to replace them. One of them just blew. Sad thing was that this big assignment of scarves that was being exported might have been the turning point financially, but it all came too late.'

'What's the chance of obtaining a list of names of employees at the factory?' asked Harriet.

Simon Townsend was thoughtful. 'The entire place was destroyed. That includes records and all documents in the office. The only way to collect the names, is from me or anyone else who survived and can remember who worked there.'

DI Harrington like DCI Love was beginning to feel hopeful. 'Could you do that for us?' he asked.

'I'll try. My mate Griff can help me. He worked at the factory when I did. Got away with just burns, but he still has the scars. We meet regularly for a drink every week. I'll ask him to lend a hand. Between us we'll come up with a list of names, don't you worry.'

'We're very grateful,' Harriet stood up. 'Thank you so much for coming in. Do you have transport back to Leicester?'

'Yes, thank you, Ma'am.'

DI Harrington produced a pad and pencil. 'Could you give us your name and address before you leave, and that of your friend Griff.'

Simon Townsend did as he was asked and included his telephone number.

DCI Love was thoughtful. 'Supposing we send a car for you and your friend tomorrow and bring you here. You could sit in a quiet room with an officer while you recall the names of the factory workers. Would you be happy to do that?' She turned to DI Harrington. 'We need this information as soon as possible. We have a lead at last and can't afford to let another day go by.'

'I agree.' Ed turned to the witness. 'Are you prepared to come here tomorrow morning?'

'Course I am. I told you I'm retired now, so is Griff, and I'll do anything that will help catch that bastard.'

'Excellent,' replied Ed and turning to Harriet. 'Shall I sort that out, Ma'am?'

'Please do, Inspector. This could be the first real breakthrough that we've had.' DI Harrington nodded to Simon Townsend. 'If you come with me now I'll arrange transport for tomorrow. And even if your friend is unable to join you we would still like you to be here.' Ed guided the man from the room and took him down to the front office.

Harriet leaned on her desk. They had found the source of the scarves, but what was the connection to the murdered nurses and their earrings? Was the link the fact that many of the men at the factory were injured and taken to hospital? At least this put them in contact with nurses. Tomorrow they would hopefully have a list of names from the factory to work from, and depending on which hospitals the injured men were taken to another check would have to be made. Somewhere along the line a name would crop up that would start ringing alarm bells. She finished her now cold coffee and carried the tray to the kitchen.

On DI Harrington's return Harriet suggested to him that they visit the local newspaper offices in Leicester in order to read up on the fire that devastated the Perfect factory three years ago. It was agreed that DI Harrington would take DS Marlow in his car and Harriet would travel in her Lotus. 'I shan't be returning to Torreston at the end of the afternoon as I should like to visit my parents,' she explained. 'This is an obvious time to see them as they live in the area and I don't manage to get over very often, which is crazy when I now live so close.'

'I understand, Ma'am.'

Harriet picked up her shoulder bag and jacket. 'Sally tells me that Garry Hobbs had dated Carol Young. He didn't mention that to us, did he?'

'He certainly did not,' replied Ed. 'I shall be following that up, don't worry.'

'Good,' said Harriet. 'Are we ready then? The Mercury office is in St George's Street, do you know where that is?'

'I do,' replied Ed. 'We'll meet you there.' He left the room and strode down the corridor to collect Charlie. He secretly wondered if DCI Love was indeed meeting her parents or was she arranging another clandestine liaison with the judge.

At the Mercury office Harriet found Ed and Charlie already sifting through old newspapers of February three years ago. 'Something like that will be headlines,' said Charlie. 'It was probably the highlight of the year for the local reporters.'

'Here it is.' Ed pointed to the paper he had laid out on the table. The whole of the front page was given over to the explosion and devastating fire that ensued, which killed both Prefect brothers and four workmen. The three officers crowded over the paper and read the report.

'Simon Townsend was pretty accurate when he described the explosion and fire,' remarked Harriet gazing intently at the large picture on the front page. 'I wonder if somewhere in front of us is our killer?'

'Well, if he worked at the factory, then the answer is probably yes,' said Charlie. 'But exactly who he is remains a mystery.'

'Six killed including the owners.' Ed turned to the inside pages where other photographs showed more destruction and pictures of ambulance men carrying stretchers from the scene. There were pictures of the fire brigade tackling the blaze and groups of concerned onlookers being pushed back by the local police.

DCI Love looked at the pictures of the fire, the blazing factory and the crowds of people standing around. 'Can you get copies of all these photographs, Charlie, and any others that were taken. We'll take them back with us to look at in more detail. They may be of some help in the future, who knows. Then I should like to pay a visit to the factory site – it was over on Eastern Boulevard by the canal wasn't it?' Harriet looked at her colleagues.

DI Harrington nodded. 'Yes. If you think visiting the site might help, Ma'am, we'll go.'

'I'm sure we won't learn anything new to help our investigation,' said Harriet, as she rose. 'But somehow seeing the actual surroundings of the place you are discussing, gives you a sense of reality.'

'Certainly does,' agreed Charlie, folding the newspapers. 'I'll go to the office and sort out the photographs. Won't be long.' He vanished across the carpeted foyer to the news desk.

'I was about to offer to fetch coffee,' said DI Harrington. 'But seeing that they only have dispensing machines I thought better of it.'

Harriet looked up quickly. Was that amusement in his voice? Was that polished veneer beginning to crack at last? But no, Ed Harrington was as serious as ever. She smiled. 'Don't let my dislike of instant coffee stop you from having one.'

'I think I'll last, thanks.'

DS Marlow returned with a fistful of photographs and a copy of the newspaper they had just been looking at. 'We were in luck. These were stuffed in a box in the photographic room. I actually spoke to the guy who took them and he was able to put his hand right on them. Many of them are shots he took that were never published. We can keep these. He said we were lucky he had not already slung them out as he doesn't usually keep prints for as long as three years.'

'Excellent.' said Harriet. 'That's saved us a bit of time. Are we ready to go?'

'I know roughly where Eastern Boulevard is,' said Charlie, 'and I've got an *A to Z* of Leicester if I get lost. Shall I navigate, Ed?'

Ed nodded, and Harriet said, 'Fine, Charlie, I'll follow Ed's car. The factory was down by the canal so it shouldn't be too difficult to find.'

They left the Mercury offices and returned to their cars. The place where the factory had once stood was only a short distance away and Ed drove along the road by the canal, making sure that the DCI was close behind, until he spotted the old board displaying the Perfect sign. It was askew slightly and somewhat the worse for wear but it was still standing defiantly. He pulled onto the grass verge with the red Lotus drawing up alongside. The three officers walked to the fenced-off site and peered through the wire.

Chapter Eight

DCI Love was silent as she stood beside DI Harrington and DS Marlow outside the wire enclosure surrounding the derelict site of the once industrious knitwear factory. Even though the accident had occurred three years ago there was still that atmosphere of tragedy hanging in the air. It was particularly quiet here by the canal. Traffic could be heard somewhere away to their left, but considering that it was a Monday afternoon there appeared to be little activity.

Charlie broke the silence. 'I understand that the whole area is now earmarked for redevelopment so I suppose that's why no one bothered to do anything about rebuilding the factory.'

'Were the brother's married?' enquired Harriet.

'No,' replied Ed. 'They weren't that old mind. Only in their thirties.'

'Who claimed the insurance?' asked Harriet.

'That I don't know,' replied Ed. 'But I'll find out.' He took out his notebook and jotted down one or two things that he would need to follow up later.

Harriet looked around. 'The injured would have been taken to the Infirmary. It's only minutes away. We came past it on the way over.' She turned to DI Harrington. 'We didn't do a staff check of this hospital, did we, Ed?'

'No, Ma'am. Only the hospitals where the murdered nurses had worked.'

'Right! Can you see that a check on the staff at the Royal Infirmary is carried out. I think that perhaps the murder trail is a little warmer, but there's still a considerable amount of work to be done.'

It was beginning to rain and Harriet decided that they had spent enough time at the derelict site and should call it a day. 'We'll return tomorrow,' she said. 'If you and Charlie would like to go to the hospital in the morning, I should like to have a word with the officers who dealt with the fire. I'll make an appointment when we get back. I don't think you need an appointment to visit the Infirmary, Ed.' She went to her car. 'I'm off to visit my parents. I'll see you both at the Station tomorrow morning. Thanks for your work today.' She flashed a smile and climbed into the Lotus. The engine fired into life and the car swept away in a cloud of dust.

Charlie looked at Ed. 'Well, is she really going to visit her parents?'

'Nothing to do with us!' snapped Ed somewhat sharply. He got into his car and slammed the door. Charlie followed suit and sat in silence beside his friend as he swung the car round and headed back to Torreston. Charlie was conscious of Ed's coolness towards the new boss but he was not sure as to the reason. So far, DCI Love had proved to be more than professional in her work and very capable in running the department. Although she was friendly, she was certainly not familiar with the team and you definitely knew who was in charge. No one would dream of stepping out of line. Even the obstinate Jack Fuller was toeing the line these days, and he hadn't once mentioned that he might be thinking of retiring. What the problem was that Ed was having with DCI Love, was a mystery as far as Charlie was concerned. He turned his thoughts to his new girlfriend, Liz Jaques. He would be seeing her tomorrow night. He had already booked a table at the Three Swans, and Tuesday couldn't come soon enough for him. It was some time since he had felt so happy about a relationship, and remembering his married life with Claudia he puckered his brow and sighed. Ed's voice broke into his thoughts,

'Sorry I snapped. It's just been a long day, I don't know what came over me.'

'Forget it, Ed. I know you well enough not to take offence.'

'Good old Charlie.' Ed gave a wry smile. 'Perhaps our visit to the Infirmary tomorrow will turn up a name that we recognise. Do you fancy a pint before we go home?'

'I never say no to a pint,' grinned Charlie, 'and it had better be tonight as I'm out with Liz tomorrow night.'

'So you are, you lucky dog.' Ed glanced across at the jubilant Charlie. 'She seems a great person.'

'She sure is. You know, I'd forgotten that feeling you get in the pit of your stomach when you fancy a woman, Ed.'

'I hope it works out, Charlie. You deserve a break...' Ed was genuine in his comments, but he did wonder if he himself would ever find the woman of his dreams. He had had a close relationship with a woman once, but after nearly two years of her complaining about his demanding job, the romance finally fizzled out. If she had really loved him she would have accepted his work as part of the package; well that's what his mother had said at the time of the break-up. Since then Ed had dated one or two women, but none had really inspired him; and at the moment this murder was keeping him too busy to even contemplate a female companion.

It was seven o'clock when Ed and Charlie arrived at the Red Lion and after a pleasant couple of hours they parted company. Ed drove to his modern house on the edge of Torreston. The house was neat and tidy and far too big for just one person but Ed had decided to buy the 'larger than needed' house as an investment. He certainly had no need of four bedrooms, and even if the time came when he might have to have his mother live with him, he would still have much more room than he really required.

Charlie returned to his Victorian terraced house not far from Ed. His home was far less tidy than his friend's and he had to sweep dirty dishes and a coffee mug to one side of the coffee table to allow him to place his mail down. There was nothing very exciting in the post. Most of it, as always, was pure junk mail. He put his head back on the chair and closed his eyes. He hoped that Liz would take care going to and from the hospital. He had advised her to be careful and not to go anywhere on her own if the route was secluded. The warning posters that Jack Fuller had organised were now displayed on the notice boards of all the hospitals and residential homes in the area, and nurses were taking every precaution to safeguard themselves against this maniac who was still at large.

On Tuesday morning DCI Love held a short briefing in the Incident Room. She informed the team that they had discovered the manufacturers of the red scarves and explained about the destruction of the factory. 'We have obtained several photographs taken at the scene of the factory fire which Inspector Harrington has placed on the board.' Harriet indicated the display board. 'Please look at these photographs closely and see if you are able to identify anyone. I am returning to Leicester to speak to the officers who dealt with the accident, and Inspector Harrington and Sergeant Marlow are going to visit the Royal Infirmary where the injured staff from the factory were taken.' She turned to Ed. 'Perhaps Duncan could look after Mr Townsend when he arrives to try and sort out the list of factory workers' names for us. If you would like to organise today's duties and investigations,' she smiled widely, 'I'll go and make coffee before we leave. You and Charlie join me in my office when you have completed organising the workload.'

She left the Incident Room and minutes later the smell of coffee filled the corridors. DI Harrington sorted out the day's tasks for the team and some minutes later he and DS Marlow joined DCI Love in her office. Harriet already had the coffee mugs on her desk and on their arrival pushed down the plunger of her cafetière.

'You're spoiling us, Ma'am,' grinned Charlie. 'I have difficulty drinking the instant stuff these days.'

'Glad you like it, Charlie,' smiled Harriet. 'Have a biscuit, we may well have a long day ahead of us.' She pushed the plate of biscuits across the desk. Charlie accepted the offer but Ed shook his head.

Harriet looked at her watch. 'An hour or so to get to Leicester, and the rest of the morning for our interviews. Shall we meet up for lunch at one?'

'Sounds fine to me,' said Charlie, still munching a biscuit.'

'Ed?' Harriet looked at the Inspector.

'That leaves us only about two and a half hours for our enquiries.'

'I envisage returning for a further session after lunch,' said Harriet. 'But I thought it might help if we were able to have a quick discussion together before continuing in the afternoon.'

'Right, Ma'am, if you think that will be beneficial. Where shall we meet?' Ed finished his coffee and placed his mug carefully on the tray.

'There's a pub near the hospital if I remember correctly,' said Harriet. 'The something and Spatula. Do you know the one I mean?'

'I do, Ma'am.' Charlie wiped the crumbs from his mouth. 'There aren't many pubs I haven't heard of. Not that I've been in them all you understand,' he grinned.

'Fine,' said Harriet, 'I'll see you there at one.'

She picked up the tray and left her office. Ed and Charlie followed but carried on down the corridor past the kitchen where DCI Love was washing the coffee mugs, and out to the car park. Ten minutes later Harriet left the building and climbed into her Lotus to drive to Leicester. It was still raining and she was pleased to have remembered her umbrella. She had telephoned ahead to ask permission to speak to the officer concerned with the Perfect factory disaster of three years ago and the man she was due to meet was a Chief Inspector Raymond Fallows.

Harriet pulled into the car park at Leicester Police Headquarters and reported to the desk Sergeant. 'I have an appointment with Chief Inspector Raymond Fallows,' she said displaying her warrant card.

'Yes, Ma'am, you are expected.'

DCI Love was shown to an interview room where she was joined by a tall, well-built man in his early fifties. His hair was dark and cropped short and his brown eyes were piercing as he eyed her up and down.

'We didn't have senior officers like you when I was a young bobby,' he smiled.

Harriet was relieved to see that there was no resentment in his voice and no disapproval in his expression. 'Things are changing,' she said in return and smiled as she put out her hand. It was shaken warmly.

'I'm Ray,' said the big man.

'I'm Harriet, but my friends call me Harry.'

'Right – sit down, Harry, and tell me what it is you want to know.'

'I'm interested in the Perfect factory fire that occurred three years ago. What caused the fire and what was the outcome of the investigation?'

Raymond Fallows stroked his chin. 'It was a nasty fire, started by an explosion in the boiler room. There was no indication what so ever that foul play was involved. The trouble was, the building was old and money was tight and the boilers needed replacing. The explosion not only started the fire but caused the whole place to collapse. The brothers were together on the factory floor with the sales manager at the time, right above the boiler room. They and the immediate workers took the full blast and weight of the collapse. Both brothers were killed instantly, although I understand that the sales manager lived, even though he was badly injured. The heavy old beams crushed some of the men and many of those who survived got out with extensive burns and broken limbs.'

'What actually caused the explosion?' asked Harriet.

'There was nothing suspicious about the blast, as I said. It was put down to old and badly maintained boilers. The brothers had set themselves up in business on a shoestring and I think that some corners had been cut.'

'But surely the factory had to be passed by the Health and Safety people?'

Inspector Fallows nodded. 'They certainly had a safety certificate, but sometimes these are easily obtained.' He shrugged his shoulders.

'Someone must have claimed the insurance?' Harriet still had several questions she needed to ask. 'As neither man was married, who made the claim?'

'I presume it would have been the mother, Mrs Amy Prefect.'

'Could I have her address, please, Ray?'

'I have the relevant file with me,' smiled the Chief Inspector. 'I knew there would be names and addresses that you would need.'

By twelve forty-five Harriet had the answers to all the questions that she had brought with her. She glanced at her watch and Raymond Fallows, noticing the gesture spoke, 'Can I take you to lunch, Harry?'

'That's very kind of you, but I'm meeting my colleagues at one. Perhaps you would care to join us? They may well have questions to ask that I have forgotten.'

'I'd like that very much,' replied the Chief Inspector. 'It's not often one has the opportunity to speak with colleagues from another force.' He rose from his seat. 'I'll just be a minute and we'll be off. Oh, and there's a ladies' just down the corridor on the right.' He left the room.

Harriet found the ladies, room. She ran a comb briefly through her thick auburn hair and straightened the jacket of her navy trouser suit before leaving the room. Raymond Fallows was waiting for her in the corridor and together they left Police Headquarters.

'We'll go in my car,' said the Chief Inspector. 'I can bring you back here after lunch and we can continue where we left off. I'll show you the actual report from the fire brigade and the list of casualties, together with the names of those killed.' He guided Harriet over to his car.

DI Harrington and DS Marlow reported to the visitors' desk on arrival at the Infirmary and showed their warrant cards. Ed explained what they required and they were both given Visitor badges and directed to Accident and Emergency. Here the Sister on duty was the same person who had been at the hospital three years ago when the accident at the factory had occurred. Sister June Mapperly, buxom and in her forties, remembered the incident well.

'It was late afternoon on a Friday. It was my weekend off and I should have left early. When news came in that there had been a major disaster in the city I obviously stayed on to help with the dozens of casualties. A and E had been reasonably quiet for a change up until then, but things really did change. Some of the injuries were horrific. One of the senior men of the factory was still alive when he was brought in, but we were unable to save him. A large main beam had crushed him. Both owners were killed instantly. It was the burns that were so grim. Most of the men who survived were burned and many of them were in here for months after the accident.'

'Which ward were they taken to?' asked Ed.

'In cases like that they go on to a casualty ward initially and are transferred to the appropriate department once they have been assessed. Some were taken to the burns unit and some to Orthopaedics.'

'Where would we get a list of staff who nursed these men?' asked Charlie.

'Personnel, but the casualties were not all men,' replied Sister Mapperly. 'Two were women. One was the young secretary and the other the cashier. The cashier was unlucky, she only worked part-time to do the wages and she was in on that day because it was Friday, pay day.'

'Did they survive?' queried Ed.

'Yes they did, although the young secretary was dreadfully burned. The awful thing was, it was her face.' June Mapperly remembered vividly the horror of seeing the young woman brought into casualty with her face blistered and red raw and her hair burned away. 'I remember her name because it's the same as mine, June. She was in the burns unit on and off for over two years having skin grafts. She was devastated over the disaster and very, very bitter.'

'Was she dreadfully scarred?' asked Charlie.

'Yes, she was. Even with the skin grafts she was pretty unsightly and the worse thing was that where her hair had been burned off, her scalp was badly scarred and of course the hair doesn't grow there again. It went from worse to worse for June. Her fiancé deserted her. It wasn't really his fault. I spoke to him about it and he confessed that he was just repulsed by her appearance and couldn't see her any more. It was all a terrible tragedy.'

'That's pretty sad,' said Ed. 'Do you know if she ever worked again?'

'That I don't know. Her ribs were broken as well as one leg by the falling beams, and I do know she was having to attend physio classes to strengthen the mending leg. Makes you realise how lucky you are, doesn't it?' she added.

'It does indeed,' replied Ed feeling a twinge of guilt knowing that he was behaving in a less than cordial manner towards his boss. 'Thank you, Sister,' he said. 'We'll go to Personnel to collect the names of the staff. Where do we get the names of patients?'

'The records department. The hospital is well signposted. If you go back to the main entrance you will see where both the personnel department and the records office are situated.'

'Right, and our thanks once again. We might be in touch at some later date, but now at least we have a name to ask for.' DI Harrington gave one of his rare smiles which made his chiselled features, which were more often that not solemn, light up.

'Come on, Charlie,' he said to his colleague. They left Sister Mapperly to track down the list of staff members of three years ago and then to pursue the names of the workers from the Perfect factory.

At exactly one o'clock DI Harrington and DS Marlow arrived at the Spigot and Spatula just down the road from the Royal Infirmary. The rain had ceased but it was still very grey and gloomy. There was no sign of DCI Love. They waited a good ten minutes before Charlie became restless and started grumbling. 'Do we have to wait for the good lady boss before we can order a pint? I'm gasping for a beer.' He looked at Ed in desperation.

'Go and get one then, but make mine an orange juice as I'm driving.'

Charlie went to the bar to order the drinks and just as he was returning with the glasses in his hands DCI Love appeared accompanied by a large man who was a stranger to both Ed and Charlie.

DCI Love introduced her companion. 'This is Chief Inspector Fallows.' She indicated to Ed. 'DI Ed Harrington,' she said, turning as Charlie came up and adding, 'and this is DS Charlie Marlow.'

'Nice to meet you both,' said Ray Fallows. Turning to Ed, he said, 'Are you Frank Harrington's son?' When Ed nodded he added, 'I knew your father. One of the best, a great man and a brilliant officer. I was at his funeral but you won't remember me. How's your mother?'

'She's well, thank you.' Ed was unsure about this conversation and he certainly did not know the man in front of him. People rarely dug up the past and he suddenly felt very uncomfortable.

Chief Inspector Fallows looked at Harriet. 'Did you know that Harrington's father was a hero? He was awarded the George Medal.'

'No, I didn't,' replied Harriet. 'You must be very proud of him Ed.'

'I am,' answered Ed, 'but medals and fine words won't bring him back, and the work has to go on.'

Harriet felt a flood of compassion for her colleague. Was this family tragedy the reason for the chip on his shoulder? she wondered. Noting that Ed obviously had no desire to continue the conversation about his father, she rapidly changed the subject. 'Did you discover anything positive at the hospital?'

'There are one or two interesting lines of enquiry to follow up,' said Ed relieved that DCI Love had veered off the subject of his father. 'Not all the victims of the fire were men. Two were women, and one in particular is very bitter about the whole thing. She had ribs and a leg broken and was badly burned. The worst burns being to the head and face, which resulted in her fiancé leaving her.'

'That's interesting,' replied Harriet. 'Do you have her address?'

'Not yet, but we're returning to the Infirmary this afternoon to collect the names of the victims of the disaster. The woman in the records office promised to hunt them down while we were at lunch. We did manage to obtain the names of the staff for that period though.'

'Good work.' Harriet was beginning to think that perhaps at last they were seeing the light at the end of the tunnel. 'I'm returning to Police Headquarters with Chief Inspector Fallows. When you have the information about this woman, give me a ring and I'll join you at her address.'

'Right, Ma'am.'

Raymond Fallows stood up. 'Harry, how rude of me, what will you have to drink?'

'Just an orange juice, thank you, Ray, and will you order a large plate of assorted sandwiches for us all – on me,' she added with her usual musical laugh.

Ed looked away. All this familiarity and they had only known each other five minutes. The rat gnawing at his insides had returned!

Lunch lasted forty-five minutes, after which Harriet and Raymond Fallows left for Police Headquarters and Ed and Charlie returned to the Royal Infirmary to collect the list of names of the people injured at the factory fire. At the records office they were handed a sheet of paper containing the list of names that they were so desperate to obtain. Ed ran his finger down the page, stopping at the name June McFarland. 'Here we are. Aged twenty-five. Extensive burns to head and face and both hands. Multiple fractures of the ribs and fractured right leg.'

'And her address?' asked Charlie.

'Clarendon Park. I'd better ring the DCI.'

Charlie consulted his *A to Z*. 'Clarendon Park is a stone's throw away. What's the name of the road?'

'Sixty-six Ambleton Road,' replied Ed as he dialled the number of DCI Love's mobile telephone.

Her soft voice answered immediately, and having been advised by Ed that he and Charlie were off to Clarendon Park she agreed to meet them there as soon as possible. 'Don't wait for me before you start talking to this woman, Ed. We don't want to waste time. I'll join in when I get there.'

Ed and Charlie drove the short distance to June McFarland's terraced house. They rang the doorbell and waited. There was no movement from inside the house and Ed rang the bell again. Charlie stood back and viewed the premises and as he did so he saw the curtains of an upstairs window move. He nudged Ed. 'There's someone upstairs. I just saw the curtains move.'

Ed bent down and lifted the letter-box flap. 'Miss McFarland,' he called, 'it's the police! Sorry to disturb you but we do need your help.' He rang the bell once again. A shuffling sound was heard from inside the house and minutes later the front door was slowly opened.

Standing on the threshold was a young woman wearing a soft floppy hat and displaying the red shrivelled evidence of severe burns to the right hand side of her face. One eyelid had obviously been completely destroyed and the plastic surgery that had rebuilt it was less than attractive. Her eyebrow on that side of her face was missing and had been pencilled in over the puckered scar. She held the door open with hands covered with shrunken skin.

Ed had no need to ask her name. He held out his warrant card. 'Detective Inspector Harrington,' he said 'and this is Detective Sergeant Marlow. May we come in, please?'

'What's it about?' the woman asked.

'The fire at the Perfect factory three years ago,' replied Ed.

The woman, who was about five feet five inches tall, visibly winced. 'Come in,' she said in a quiet voice, opening the door wider to allow them to enter. In the front room she pointed to the settee. 'You'd better sit down.' As they complied she asked, 'What exactly do you need to know? The fire was three years ago and I was asked plenty of questions at the time. The police decided it was an accident and I'm still fighting for compensation.'

Charlie was amazed. 'Are you saying that you received no money for your injuries?'

'Not a penny, and I haven't worked since. Who would want to look at this face across the office?'

'I'm very sorry about your misfortune.' Ed was genuine in his remarks. The poor young woman in front of him was certainly grotesquely disfigured and she was correct when she said that people would not be happy looking at her. He continued in a gentle voice, 'I understand that you and your fiancé parted after the accident.'

June McFarland's eyes clouded and she hung her head. 'Would you want to marry someone looking like me?' She rose and walked across to a bureau. She opened a drawer and took out some photographs, handing them to Ed. Ed looked through them before handing them to Charlie. The young woman in the photograph was smiling out at them. Her long fair hair fell down onto her shoulders and it was easy to see that June McFarland was radiantly happy. In another photograph she was standing arm in arm with a sandy-haired young man who was holding onto her arm with both hands as if he would never let her go.

Charlie handed the photographs back to June. 'Life can be very cruel,' he muttered. 'Did he visit you in hospital for long?'

June smiled ruefully. 'Everyday to begin with. It seemed all right while my face was covered but when the bandages were removed he was just repulsed.' A tear ran down her scarred cheek. 'You can't really blame him. I know I look horrendous.'

The doorbell rang and Ed put out his hand to check June from rising. 'That will be Chief Inspector Love, DS Marlow will let her in.'

Charlie rose and went to the front door, returning seconds later with Harriet, whom he introduced to June. June McFarland glanced at the good-looking woman standing in front of her and burst into tears. 'I was pretty like you once,' she sobbed. 'Men used to ask me out and then when I did find the man I loved, this had to happen.' She touched her cheek and wept uncontrollably.

DCI Love walked across the room and knelt beside the young woman placing a hand on her knee 'Your face is scarred, but you are the same person inside. There is someone out there who will love you for just being you. You mustn't hide away, you're still beautiful underneath the scars.'

June McFarland lifted her tear-stained face. 'What about this?' she said bitterly. She snatched the hat from her head showing her hairless scalp and further ugly scars.

Harriet had to catch her breath before speaking again. 'Do you wear a wig when you go out, June?' she said quietly.

'I don't go out. I have got a wig but I don't bother wearing it.'

'Have you had counselling?' asked Ed.

'Oh yes!' came the reply, 'but what does that do to help you? I told them to stop coming after some months.'

Harriet's gentle voice came again, 'Why don't you try another spell? It would be beneficial, I'm sure.'

'I don't know, I really don't know.'

'Will you think about it?' asked Harriet.

'Perhaps.' June looked up at DCI Love. 'You're the first people who have visited me since the enquiry was closed.'

'What happened to your friends?' asked Charlie.

'They gradually stopped coming. I wasn't the nicest of people to talk to, I have to admit.'

'Tell us about your fiancé.' Harriet risked asking the question.

'Huh! Dave! Well, as I said, he visited me regularly to begin with but once he had seen what I looked like under the bandages, the visits became less frequent until he finally vanished from the scene. He was very generous, mind,' she added sarcastically. 'He did leave me a letter.'

Harriet wrinkled her nose. 'You poor thing. What you must have been through.'

'What was your fiancé's surname?' asked Ed.

'Spalding. Dave Spalding.' She spoke in a wistful voice and Ed felt guilty as he asked the next question. 'Could we have his address please?'

'One hundred and two College Street, Knighton. Why do you need to know that?'

Harriet patted June McFarland's knee as she stood up. 'We are interviewing everyone who had any connection to people involved in the accident. There's nothing for you to worry about.'

June's face tightened. 'Perhaps you had better interview the nurse that he ran off with then.'

'What do you mean?' Harriet turned quickly. The officers were suddenly very alert.

'Dave began chatting up one of the nurses who was looking after me. When he dumped me, she disappeared too and I presume they went off together. She was always smiling at him when he came to visit. Great, isn't it! Here she was, supposedly caring for me, and then ups and offs with my fiancé.' Her eyes glowered and she slammed the hat back on her head.

'Can you remember this nurse's name?' asked Ed gently.

'Could I ever forget it? Sam, everyone called her, I don't know her surname.'

Ed wrote this down in his notebook.

'We'll leave you now, June,' said Harriet, 'Please consider having another go with the counsellor. It will help, you know... and why not try wearing the wig, and at least walking in the garden?'

'I'll think about it,' promised the woman as she saw them to the door and said goodbye. June walked slowly back to her front room and picked up the photographs that had been left on the coffee table. She tore them into shreds, flung them on the floor and sat down and sobbed.

Chapter Nine

The three officers left 66 Ambleton Road and stood on the pavement beside Harriet's red Lotus. 'Well, that's a turn-up for the book,' said Charlie. 'The fiancé dumped her for one of the nurses and she's very, very bitter and twisted.'

Harriet looked at Charlie. 'You'd be pretty bitter if you'd been in an accident such as she was. Not only did she lose her fiancé but she lost her good looks and received no compensation for her pain and injuries. You don't really think that poor woman is capable of killing nurses for revenge, do you?'

'It's happened before,' remarked Ed.

'True, but she doesn't leave the house, let alone travel distances,' persisted the DCI.

'So she says.' Ed was not convinced that the woman they had just interviewed was not bitter enough to be able to commit murder, however sorry they might feel about her tragedy.

'What about her damaged leg? She did limp, and we have witnesses who state that their attacker had a strange walking action.' Charlie was now fired up. 'And didn't the attacker wear a woolly hat? You'd only wear a hat like that in July if you needed to hide something and her head was pretty unsightly, you have to admit. This *must* be the link we're looking for.'

Harriet pursed her lips. 'It's certainly a link and we haven't had a definite link before. But we mustn't jump to conclusions about the killer being June McFarland. Anyway, Nurse Belford said the person making enquiries at The Poplars was a man, and she made no mention of a scarred face – and she could hardly have missed the disfigurement of June.'

'You're right,' said Charlie, and Ed nodded in agreement.

'Mind you,' added Harriet thoughtfully, 'that's if this man seen at The Poplars is the man we're after.'

'He's the first likely customer we've had who has acted in a strange manner and been in the vicinity prior to a murder,' said Charlie.

'Let's go and speak to this Dave Spalding and see what he has to say,' said Harriet.

Charlie was checking his *A to Z*. 'Here's College Street. One hundred and two wasn't it?' As Ed nodded, he added, 'Follow us then, Ma'am, it's not that far away.'

They found Number 102 halfway along the tree-lined street and both cars pulled up outside. Ed rang the doorbell. No one answered the door and the DI rang again. After a long pause he said, 'Mr Spalding doesn't appear to be at home.'

'It's only five,' said Harriet. 'He must work, so let's hope he'll be home soon.' Charlie looked anxiously at his watch. He had arranged to pick Liz up at eight and he did not want to be late.

DCI Love was speaking again, 'We'll hang on for a while. It's beginning to rain again. May we sit in your car and wait, Ed? It would be a bit of a squash in mine.' She smiled widely.

Charlie chortled. 'Could be fun, though.'

DCI Love glanced across at the sergeant with a raised eyebrow indicating to him that he had transgressed. DCI Love always knew where to draw the line and her team was learning to observed this limit without question.

'Sorry, Ma'am.' Charlie wished he could keep his big mouth shut, and refrain from making inappropriate, banal comments, but he was on a bit of a high today thinking about his date.

DI Harrington held the rear car door open for DCI Love and he and Charlie sat in the front. They went over the information they had collected during the day and agreed that at last they had some significant data to get their teeth into. 'Now we have the name of the nurse that Dave Spalding became friendly with, we need to check whether or not she has any connection with the other hospitals.' Harriet was wrinkling her nose again. 'This spread of incidents is just so confusing.'

'From Stirling to the Midlands,' said Charlie.

'And then supposedly the murders stop here.' Ed flicked through his notebook. 'We have the names of all the injured from the factory, and hopefully by now we shall have the names of the rest of the workers from Simon Townsend and his pal Griff.'

'Then the checking starts again,' said Charlie.

A middle-aged woman, loaded down with shopping bags and

trying to hold an umbrella over her head at the same time, struggled through the gate of Number 104.

'Quick, Charlie,' said DCI Love. 'Have a word with Spalding's neighbour and see if she has any inkling as to how long he might be.'

Charlie was out of the car like lightning. He wanted this interview over so that he could return home to get ready for his dinner date. 'Excuse me, Madam,' he said as he reached the woman just before she could close the front door. He showed his warrant card. 'Could you tell us at what time Mr Spalding might return home?'

The woman peered closely at the warrant card that Charlie held under her nose. 'He won't be home for another two days. He's a commercial traveller and he's up in Yorkshire on business. I'm feeding his cat while he's away. There's nothing wrong, is there?'

'No, no,' replied Charlie. 'We were hoping that he might be able to answer a few questions for us. Is he away from home often?'

'Quite a bit. Look, come in – you're getting wet standing there. Let me dump my shopping, my arms are breaking, then I'll be happy to answer your questions.' She went into the hall and Charlie followed her as she entered the small kitchen and put the bags on the table. She placed her umbrella in the sink and turned to face the sergeant. 'Now young man what else do you need to know?'

'Does Mr Spalding live alone?'

'Yes, he does. He was engaged once but it all fell through due to her accident.'

'Hasn't he had another girlfriend since then?' Charlie waited for the reply while the woman filled the kettle and switched it on.

'No. There has been no woman in his life since that nice girl, June. It was all very sad. I liked June and thought they were very well suited. But fate plays strange tricks, doesn't it?'

'I suppose so,' said Charlie wondering what had happened to the nurse he had supposedly run off with. 'Does he travel all over the country in his work?'

'Oh yes. He's very well travelled. Goes abroad sometimes as well.'

'And Scotland?'

'All over the British Isles. Now, what's this all about?' The woman warmed the teapot and put in the teabags before looking at Charlie with suspicion. 'Is Dave in trouble?'

'I'm afraid I can't discuss the matter with you, Mrs…? sorry I didn't catch your name.'

'Mrs Charteris. But Dave is a nice young man and wouldn't hurt a fly. Keeps himself to himself and minds his own business. He'll be back on Thursday, and I think you should save the rest of your questions for him.'

She placed the teapot down heavily on the kitchen table and Charlie considered himself dismissed. He thanked her for her help and left the house.

Back in the car he eagerly related his findings to his seniors. 'Dave Spalding is a commercial traveller and goes all over the country, including Scotland. He's away in Yorkshire at the moment and won't be back until Thursday. According to his next-door neighbour, Mrs Charteris, he hasn't had a girlfriend since he broke up with his fiancée June.'

'Well done, Charlie,' said DCI Love. 'It looks as if we shall have to return to Leicester on Thursday. Also I'd like to visit Mrs Prefect and ask her what happened to all the insurance money.' She opened the car door and climbed out. She bent down and looked at DI Harrington. 'I'll inform DCI Fallows that we shall be returning to Leicester. Just out of courtesy.' She smiled, as she always did and Ed nodded.

'If you think it necessary, Ma'am.' A feeling akin to jealousy pulled at his stomach. She had certainly struck up a very swift friendship with this officer whom she had never met before. It wasn't usual for them to grovel to another force if they needed to cross the boundary to interview a suspect. He put the Saab in gear.

'We'll see you tomorrow then,' he said, and drove off without looking in the rear mirror to see if DCI Love was following. The day was over and like Charlie he was eager to get home. Charlie looked at his watch.

'You were a bit terse there, weren't you?' he suggested glancing across at his friend.

'What makes you say that?'

'You almost snapped her head off about informing Fallows that she needed to return to interview Spalding.'

'It's not something we're obliged to do.'

Charlie was not prepared to let his friend off the hook. 'No, but you know how the DCI operates. She's a lady and everything she does is gracious.'

'Oh, for heaven's sake, Charlie. *Gracious*! This is the police. We don't purport to be gracious.'

Charlie was not deterred. 'Okay then, courteous. She's always courteous and there's no harm in being courteous.'

Ed was now somewhat rattled. 'Come off it, Charlie, you've changed! I don't know what's come over you lately. I'll just put it down to the new woman in your life.'

Charlie grinned and decided it was time to change the subject. 'Talking of the new woman in my life, thank goodness Spalding was not at home. I was beginning to think that I'd miss my date with Liz.'

'We'll be back in loads of time. Stop fretting, Charlie.'

'Ooh! There's that tone in the voice again,' grinned Charlie. 'What *has* the DCI done to upset you?'

'Leave it, Charlie I'm not even thinking about what the woman said. I'm just tired. It's been a long day and I want it to be over.'

'Okay! Okay.' Charlie decided to clam up. He knew when Ed didn't want to talk further. During the rest of the return journey to Torreston, Charlie avoided bringing DCI Love into the conversation. They discussed the case they were investigating but Charlie found it difficult to concentrate, as his mind was elsewhere most of the time. He was relieved when at last Ed pulled up outside his house and he was able to escape.

'Thanks, Ed. See you tomorrow,' he said, and bounded up the rain-soaked steps to his house, eager to bath and change in readiness for his meeting with Liz.

The next day, Wednesday, was sunny and warm. The rain had cleared and the sky was cloudless. It looked as if it might be a hot day. Ed picked Charlie up at the usual time, noting that he was once again on time. Charlie had not kept him waiting now for over a week. He was unsure as to whether this was due to the presence of the new DCI or the fact the he now had a flourishing love life.

Charlie ran down the steps of his house and scrambled into the seat beside his friend. 'Good morning Ed. And my word it certainly is that.'

'You obviously had a good night last night.'

'Certainly did, Ed. Liz is just wonderful. I can't believe that I've met someone as great as her.'

'Well just don't blow it, Charlie. Take things easy and let things happen naturally. Now for the rest of the day, I should be grateful if you would concentrate your mind on this murder case we have yet to solve.'

Charlie chuckled. 'I'm raring to go. I reckon that when your personal life is settled, you're able to show more enthusiasm for your work.'

'Is that so?' muttered Ed as he pulled into the police station car park. The red Lotus Élite was already in its usual place and Ed drew up alongside. As they climbed the stairs to the CID rooms, the Inspector was hailed by DC Sally Pringle, who was hurrying along the corridor behind him.

'Inspector Harrington! Sir, can I have a word?'

'Of course, Sally, what is it?' Ed and Charlie stopped to meet the young DC who was obviously in an excited state.

'After you and the DCI had gone yesterday we all did as we had been asked and looked at the photographs that you had put on the board. And guess what?'

'What Sally?'

'Garry Hobbs is standing by the blazing factory watching the proceedings.' And as DI Harrington frowned trying to place the name, DC Pringle rushed on. 'He works at the Cottage Hospital here. He's the hospital car driver. Sergeant Marlow and I interviewed him when we did the routine checks after the Carol Young murder. You remember him, Sarge, don't you?'

'Yes, I remember Garry Hobbs,' answered, Charlie. 'I'll come and have a look at the photo.'

The three of them hurried to the Incident Room where

Charlie peered at the black and white photograph that DC Pringle pointed out to him.

'You're right, Sally. That's Garry Hobbs.'

DI Harrington stroked his chin. 'Now that is interesting. Well done, Sally.'

The photograph showed the factory blaze at its height. Standing in the foreground was a group of spectators about to be moved back by an officer in uniform who was bearing down on them with arms outstretched. Sally pointed to a young man clearly visible in the front of the crowd. DI Harrington also, looked at the print. 'Now are you both adamant that it's Hobbs?'

'Absolutely,' said Sally, and Charlie nodded vigorously in agreement.

'Yes, Sir, there is no doubt in my mind,' said Charlie. 'I wonder what he was doing in Leicester?'

'We'll soon discover the answer to that question,' said Ed, and he left the room to inform DCI Love of the discovery. He could smell the pungent aroma of strong coffee as soon as he reached the corridor where her office was situated. He was unsure as to which odour dominated the corridors these days, strong French coffee or her fragrant perfume. He knocked on the door and entered on command. Harriet looked up from the notes that she was reading and smiled.

'Good morning, Ed. I thought your arrival was imminent so I've made a large pot of coffee. Sit down, won't you.'

Ed obliged and accepted the china mug of strong coffee that was handed to him. 'Thank you, Ma'am.'

'I've been going through all the evidence that we've gathered so far,' said the DCI. 'I'll leave you to get the ball rolling on today's investigations but at the moment I'm waiting for Jack to bring me the list of factory workers that Simon Townsend produced for us yesterday.' As if by telepathy a knock on the door announced the arrival of Sergeant Fuller.

'Good morning, Ma'am, Sir.' He placed a sheet of paper on the desk. 'Mr Townsend and his mate were in their element yesterday reminiscing about their days at the factory, but they did come up with a full list of names of the workers.'

'Thank you, Jack, can we leave you to sift through them for any matches with our other lists?'

'Certainly, Ma'am I'll get on to it straight away.'

'Would you like to join us for coffee?' The green eyes looked up at the portly Sergeant.

Jack Fuller could not remember having ever being offered coffee by his superiors before and he was quite taken aback. He coughed. 'Er, thank you, Ma'am but no thank you,' he replied and added hastily, 'I've just had one, but I think I would have been wiser to have waited and had a cup of yours, it smells like the real stuff.'

He left the room still feeling overwhelmed by his new boss. She was not just prepossessing, but elegant, composed and more than capable. He couldn't understand how it was that the police station these days always felt so calm – and when was the last time he had heard scurrilous language in the CID room? Colleagues were behaving in an amazingly civil manner towards each other, and even Charlie had refrained from calling all the females 'sweetie'. The place had certainly not become namby-pamby; far from it, everyone was totally engrossed in this murder case and all the stops had been pulled out as far as the investigation was concerned. The work was still getting done, and in record time; in fact interviews and the collecting of evidence were running as smoothly as ever. It just appeared that all the cogs of the establishment had been fully oiled and there was no grating or sticking of the wheels as the machinery operated. The working environment was just – pleasant. Jack returned to the CID Room and sat down at his computer. He had another list of names to check and he did not want to make any mistakes. Secretly Jack regretted not being brave enough to accept the DCI's offer of coffee, but he had no wish to become over-familiar with the new boss. It was still early days.

In her office DCI Love turned to DI Harrington. 'Will you go and organise what you have to for the team today, Ed, while I give my report to Superintendent Hollyoak, then I'll be ready to come with you to speak to Mrs Prefect.'

'Yes, Ma'am but just one thing before I do. In one of the photographs of the factory fire, there's a man watching the activities who at the present time is a hospital driver here at the Cottage Hospital.'

'Do we have his name?'

'Garry Hobbs. He was interviewed by Charlie and DC Pringle following the Carol Young murder.'

'Does he live near the hospital?'

'Very close, Ma'am.'

Harriet wrinkled her nose, as she was in the habit of doing when thoughtful. 'Isn't he the driver who was reluctant to admit he had dated Carol?'

'Yes, he's the one.'

'Could you get me the report of his interview and the others who were spoken to that day, please, Ed.'

DI Harrington left the office and returned in minutes. He handed a sheaf of papers to DCI Love, who quickly scanned what was written there. She looked up at Ed.

'This man was never asked to give the whereabouts of his own movements on the nights of the murders,' she said quietly. 'I suppose that as he was not a suspect the question was not really appropriate.' She picked up her telephone and Ed heard her precise voice ask to see DS Marlow. As she replaced the receiver, she asked Ed, 'Are the two brothers who work at the Garratts Warehouse the only people on the "suspect" list?' She returned her gaze to the paper in front of her. 'It seems that the brothers have not been spoken to since Monica's murder, so we don't have details about where they were on the night of her death. For the time of Carol's murder each brother is an alibi for the other, so perhaps we should have delved a little deeper here.' Harriet looked up at Ed. 'Don't you think we should have checked out both brothers as they each alibi the other?' Harriet frowned very slightly.

'Yes, Ma'am. I'm sorry, I'll look into that.'

'It's not your fault, Ed. You don't have time to check every little detail in every single report. We do have to rely on our officers heavily in a situation such as this, and I'm surprised at Charlie.'

A knock on the door announced the arrival of Charlie Marlow. Harriet's voice did not change as she asked the question why both brothers had not been asked to give an alibi for the night of the second murder, and why Garry Hobbs had not been questioned also.

Charlie looked uncomfortable as he replied, 'I'm sorry, Ma'am I hadn't considered Bill Caldwell or Garry Hobbs suspects.'

'They may well not be, Charlie, but Vincent Caldwell is, and it was his brother Bill who gave him an alibi, so I think he should be checked out. As for Garry Hobbs, he has just turned up on a photograph of the factory fire in Leicester, which certainly puts him in the frame. Everyone with connections to the case must be treated in the same manner, Charlie, and checked carefully. Until they are cleared, they are all on our suspect list – and this includes both the Caldwells.' Her green eyes looked at the sergeant earnestly. 'Now we have to interview him again, and this all takes up time. We have a killer out there somewhere and he needs to be caught, and time is precious.'

'Sorry, Ma'am. Shall I revisit him today?'

'No, that won't be necessary. Inspector Harrington and I will do the honours this time. I think DI Harrington has another assignment for you.' She looked across at Ed, who nodded. 'But do take care in future, Charlie. Presume that everyone that you interview could be capable of killing these nurses and then you won't miss out on any searching questions.' She smiled at the officer in front of her. 'We're going to catch him, but we all need to be on the ball.'

Charlie felt relieved and gratefully made his escape from the DCI's office. Outside he leaned against the corridor wall. How could he have been so stupid as to not ask the all important question about an alibi to both brothers and Hobbs the driver? Wow! He exhaled loudly. He had thought he was going to be in serious trouble, but instead DCI Love had been her usual gracious self. He felt so stupid. Her polite, calm words had made him feel far worse. She was a very clever woman. She knew exactly how to handle people. Raised voices of aggression only made people feel resentful and provoked retaliation, whereas the calm almost reproachful attitude that was DCI Love's hallmark was very humbling. Charlie would never forget to ask even the most simple of questions in the future. He returned to the Incident Room to await details of his day's task from DI Harrington.

DCI Love looked at Ed. 'Charlie won't slip up again. He was very remorseful. Now this changes things, Ed. Would you organise Charlie and a WDC to go to Leicester to see Mrs Prefect so that we can visit this Garry Hobbs. We will still have time to attend Monica's funeral.'

'No problem,' replied DI Harrington. 'I'll sort that out and be ready to leave in about fifteen minutes. Do we go in my car?'

'If that's all right with you. It's a pleasure having a chauffeur.' This was only partly the truth, as Harriet loved driving her Lotus. At the moment, however, not knowing the area too well, being driven by someone else enabled her to get her bearings. She had excellent recall; she had always been aware that her memory was photographic, and having visited a place once she was able to repeat the drive without problem.

DCI Love put a quick call through to Chief Inspector Fallows in Leicester to inform him that she would not be visiting Leicester that day. She gave him the name of DS Marlow just in case Charlie needed any information while he was in that city. Harriet replaced the telephone receiver and picked up her report for Superintendent Hollyoak.

DI Harrington was already waiting in his Saab when Harriet came out of the Station. George Hollyoak had wanted to have a lengthy discussion about the case and Harriet had had difficulty in making her escape from his office. 'It's all in my report, George,' she said as she impatiently moved from foot to foot. 'DI Harrington is waiting in the car park and we have a great deal to sort out today. Let's try and find an evening soon when I can pop over and see both you and Nancy. It must be four or five months since I last visited.'

'Good idea, my dear. Nancy would love that, but we won't be allowed to talk shop.'

'We'll find a way, George. Now I really must fly. I'll try and have a word with you when I get back to the Station tonight.' And she was gone.

George Hollyoak sighed as he peered from his office window. How well he remembered active investigations. He missed the liveliness of working with a team and having companionship. Promotion was all very well, but being 'in the field' was what the job was all about. Now here were these youngsters running the show and he was left to sit and push a pen and attend boring meetings. He watched as the Saab drove from the car park and then returned to his desk to read Harriet's report.

Sally Pringle had been assigned as Sergeant Marlow's assistant for the day. She enjoyed working with, Charlie; he was always good for a laugh and these days he was surprisingly courteous. He had certainly been a different man lately. She had heard that he had a new woman in his life, so this must be the explanation, although she also realised that the new DCI was keeping him in line. What was it about Chief Inspector Love? She seemed to have the whole team under a hypnotic influence. No one wished to offend her or not come up to her expectations. Was this why everyone was working to capacity these days? Certainly no one ever tried to sneak off duty early and she had not heard a single snide remark about the elegant new boss. Even Sergeant Fuller was keeping quiet about having a woman in charge and hadn't mentioned retirement once. That was a first!

DC Pringle joined Charlie at the car pool. He grinned as she arrived. 'Not exactly a Lotus Élite, Madam,' he said, 'but in the circumstances it's the best I can do.' He opened the car door of the standard Vauxhall with a flourish and bowed as Sally got in.

Mrs Prefect lived relatively close to where the factory had once stood. Her address was an end-of-terrace house and Charlie wondered what she had done with all the insurance money from the factory fire if this was where she was still living. He rang the doorbell. A thin, dour-looking woman of about sixty-five opened the door. Her grey hair was drawn back severely from her sharp, sallow face and her steely grey eyes bore a hard glint as she frowned upon the two visitors standing on the doorstep.

'Well?' she asked.

Charlie produced his warrant card and held it for her to see. 'Sergeant Marlow,' he said, 'and this is Detective Constable Pringle.' He indicated his colleague who in turn held up her warrant card. 'Are you Mrs Pamela Prefect?'

'I am.'

'We should like to ask you a few questions regarding the fire at your sons' factory three years ago.'

'Why?' came the terse response.

'Just some loose ends we need to clear up regarding one of the employees.' Charlie was equally evasive.

The woman hesitated before standing to one side and reluctantly inviting them in. They were shown into the front room where Charlie and Sally looked around the sparse furnishings before accepting the offer of a seat. Charlie sat in the large armchair and Sally perched on a small stool to allow Mrs Prefect to take the only other chair in the room. As she sat down Pamela Prefect narrowed her eyes and addressed Charlie.

'Now what's all this about? The fire happened over three years ago and I just want to be left alone to forget the horrors of that day.'

Sally felt some compassion for the woman in front of them. To lose two sons in one accident must have been hard to cope with. She spoke gently. 'We're so sorry to open old wounds, Mrs Prefect, but we understand that June McFarland, who was badly burned in the fire, never received any compensation over the accident. Could you tell us why?'

The woman's face saddened. 'There was no insurance. That's the whole problem. The premium payment was two months overdue and the company refused to pay out. I never got a penny, so nor did any of the workers. It ruined my life. I put everything I had into the business to help the boys, and look at me now. I had to declare bankruptcy and now I'm living on the poverty line.' She buried her head in her hands. 'And I've lost both my sons.' A strange wailing noise erupted from her thin body.

'Do you live alone?' asked Charlie.

'Yes, my husband died some years ago. Thank God he wasn't alive to see his boys die like they did.'

'Mrs Prefect,' Sally Pringle said, leaning forwards. 'Can you think of any way that the cashmere scarves made at the factory might be in circulation in Britain? We understand that they were made for export only but some have turned up in this country.'

The woman raised a tear-stained face. 'The staff were allowed to purchase them for their families. And of course the sales staff would have had samples in their cars or at home. Why do you ask?'

'A scarf like the ones you manufactured has turned up at a crime scene,' said Charlie quickly. 'Have you seen any of the injured workers since the fire?' he asked.

Pamela Prefect shook her head. 'I was very ill for about a year after the fire. The shock nearly killed me. When I recovered I just couldn't face anyone from the business. They didn't know me. I was a sleeping partner and never visited the factory, so I left well alone.'

Sergeant Marlow realised that this pathetic woman had no bearing whatsoever on the case and was unable to give them any assistance in their enquiries. After a few more words, mostly of sympathy for her suffering, the two officers left the premises to return to Torreston.

Chapter Ten

DCI Love and DI Harrington arrived at Torreston Cottage Hospital and reported to Reception where they explained who they were and asked to see Garry Hobbs. The woman at the desk handed them Visitor badges and informed them that the driver they were seeking should be collecting patients from Outpatients to return them to their homes or other clinics in the area. The two officers followed the signs to Outpatients where they stood quietly in the doorway watching the activities in front of them. As a nurse walked past, Harriet spoke to her. 'Could you point out Garry Hobbs to me please.'

The woman pointed to a young man wearing a light blue overall. 'That's Garry. He's jut wheeling a patient to the minibus.'

Harriet and Ed made their way across the room to the man, who was carefully tucking a blanket around the knees of a pale-faced individual sitting in a wheelchair.

'Mr Hobbs?' asked, Ed.

'That's me.' The young man turned.

DI Harrington showed his warrant card and Harriet did likewise. 'Could we have a few words with you, please,' said Ed.

'Sure,' grinned Garry. 'What's it about?' he continued to wheel his patient towards the specially converted minibus that was parked a few metres from the entrance.

Harriet walked beside him. 'Wouldn't you prefer to go somewhere a little more private, Mr Hobbs?'

'Call me Garry, everyone else does. You can talk to me here. I've got no secrets – and certainly not from Mark.'

The young man in the wheelchair smiled a weak smile. 'Garry has been carrying me around for nearly two years. We know each other pretty well. I don't know what I'd do without his support and kindness.' He leaned over and dug his helper in the ribs. 'He's my legs and my soul.'

Garry Hobbs patted the young man's arm. 'You're okay, Mark.

I can't imagine what I would be like if I was unable to walk and had to stay in a wheelchair for the rest of my life.'

Harriet looked at the huddled figure in the wheelchair and thought the same. 'What's your name?' she asked kindly.

'Mark Ainsley.'

'What happened?'

'Car accident,' replied Mark.

'I'm sorry.' Turning to Garry, she said, 'Well, if you are happy with us speaking to you here we'll get it over with.' They had now stopped beside the bus.

Ed, his notebook in his hand, stepped forward. 'I see that you were on duty during Sunday, the day before Carol Young's body was discovered in Cygnet Lane. Could you tell us where you were Sunday night between the hours of nine and ten thirty?'

Garry Hobbs let out a stiff laugh. 'My God you don't think that I had anything to do with the murder, do you?'

'It's more a case of eliminating people from our enquiries at this stage,' replied Ed.

It was the young man in the wheelchair who spoke. 'You had something very important on that night, Garry. I remember, because I asked you to spend the evening with me but you said you couldn't because you had to do something urgently.'

Garry Hobbs looked decidedly uncomfortable and began to fidget.

'Would you care to explain your whereabouts?' asked Harriet.

Garry looked from the two police officers to Mark, an expression of dismay on his face. 'I was at home alone,' he muttered. 'I'm sorry, Mark, I just wanted a night in on my own and didn't want to hurt your feelings. I'd had a hell of a week and was really bushed. I just wanted to do nothing except sit in front of the telly and unwind.'

'So no one can vouch for you?' said Ed.

'No! I did pop down to the off-licence about seven thirty for a pack of six, but then I stayed in for the rest of the night and went to bed about eleven thirty.'

'What did you watch on television,' asked Harriet almost casually.

Garry did not hesitate. '*Monarch of the Glen*. I just got back in time for the start and then I watched the late film, *Rear Window*.'

DI Harrington wrote all this down before addressing the still embarrassed young man in front of them. 'Thank you, and could you tell us where you were on the night of Friday the tenth?'

'That's easy.' Garry almost smiled with relief. 'I was in the pub most of the night. It was John Howard's stag night and dozens of mates will tell you I was there.' He gave Ed several names and addresses, which the Inspector would check later.

They were interrupted by a shout. Another young man in a wheelchair was making his own way across from the Outpatients doorway. 'How much longer am I to wait?' he called.

'Sorry!' answered Garry running to meet him. 'These are police officers and they needed to speak to me.' He grabbed the chair and wheeled it towards the vehicle.

Harriet and Ed watched as Garry Hobbs manipulated the electric platform that lifted the chair into the bus. Having made sure that the chair was secure he turned to speak to them again.

'That's Mike Epsom, the Rugby player who broke his back during play. He gets pretty angry at times, but who can blame him. Played for the Tigers and was on target for an England place before the accident. Now look at him – permanently in a wheelchair.'

'Rotten luck,' agreed, Ed.

Harriet nodded in sympathy. 'Before we leave,' she said. 'Could you tell us what you were doing at the fire at the Perfect factory in Leicester about three years ago?' Garry Hobbs looked surprised. 'How did you know I was there?'

'That doesn't really matter,' said Ed. 'Please answer the question.'

'I was a porter at the Royal Infirmary and when we heard about the fire a group of us ran over to see if we could help. The factory was just at the back of the hospital, just minutes away.'

Ed nodded as he wrote. 'Thank you,' he said.

'Why did you leave the Royal Infirmary?' asked Harriet.

'I got this job. Better hours and more money.'

Minutes later DCI Love and DI Harrington left Garry Hobbs as he prepared to lift Mark Ainsley into the van. Once out of earshot, Harriet turned to Ed. 'What do you think?'

Ed shrugged his broad shoulders. 'He was certainly on edge, but probably he was embarrassed because of his lie to Mr Ainsley.'

'Well, he does have an alibi for Monica's murder, if it holds up. Get back to me, Ed when someone has spoken to the people who were at the stag night. They began walking to the visitors' car park. Garry Hobbs ran after them. He called out, 'Could you hang on a minute? I'd like another word with you.'

Harriet and Ed stood where they were and waited. Garry approached them looking somewhat subdued. 'I feel so mean,' he said in a hushed voice. 'Mark is always asking me to visit him in the evenings, and although I feel really sorry for him, he can be a dreadful drag. I frequently stay on at his place when I drop him off after physio, but quite honestly all I do is fetch and carry for him. He's very wearing, and so when he asked me to call round on Sunday night, I made up the excuse of having something important to do.' He looked appealingly at Harriet.

'If you have nothing to hide, Mr Hobbs, then you have nothing to fear,' she said.

'We shall check your alibi for the night of Monica Meyers' murder,' added, Ed, 'and if your friends are able to collaborate your story then you will be in the clear.'

'Oh, they will,' said Garry in a low voice. 'I promise you, I've never hurt anyone in my entire life. I've pledged to care for people, not harm them.'

'You'd better deliver your patients to their houses then,' said Harriet, not unkindly. 'We'll be in touch.'

Garry Hobbs walked back to the bus. He thought of all the times he had sat with Mark, listening to his idle chatter and wishing he could be in his own home. The dozens of cups of tea that he had made for his invalid friend and the numerous times he had carried him from place to place without complaint. The one night he had wanted an alibi he had chosen to duck out and stay at home. Now look where it had landed him; desperately trying to prove he had no part in a murder. He climbed into the minibus and started the engine.

Back at Torreston police station, DCI Love and DI Harrington were in Harriet's office when DS Fuller arrived to inform them that he had found a name on his lists that matched.

'Garry Hobbs,' he said excitedly. 'He was a hospital porter at the Royal Infirmary a couple of years ago and is now working here at the Cottage Hospital where Carol Young was murdered.'

Harriet smiled at Jack. 'Thank you, Jack, well done. Keep looking though, will you, we think there might be another link hidden in there somewhere. The computer discs are an invaluable help, aren't they.'

'They're amazing,' agreed Jack Fuller. 'I tell you what, Ma'am, if they'd had DNA and computers in the 1800s they'd have caught Jack the Ripper.'

'I bet they would, Jack!' laughed Harriet. 'But at this moment I would just like to hunt down our own Beast of the Night.'

Sergeant Fuller left the office and DI Harrington spoke, 'You didn't tell him we already knew about Garry Hobbs.'

'No need to,' smiled Harriet. 'Jack's doing a marvellous job. He's searching those lists with such dedication that I have no wish to dampen his enthusiasm.' She rose from behind her desk. 'First we have a funeral to attend, Ed, and then we shall visit Bill Caldwell.' She took her cafetière and tin of ground coffee from her desk cupboard. 'I'm getting withdrawal symptoms,' she explained with a smile.

Ed leaned forward and took the pot and tin. 'I'll make it, Ma'am.'

'Thank you, Ed. But do you have to call me, Ma'am all the time?'

'Force of habit, sorry.' Ed left the room to make the coffee wishing that he could snap out of this maladroit behaviour. He filled the kettle with water and snapped on the switch. What had this woman ever done to offend him? He was certainly not a misogynist. But that was the way he was acting, and he needed to remedy this ill-disposed, negative feeling towards DCI Love, and the sooner the better.

DS Marlow and DC Pringle arrived back at the Station and reported to Harriet. Charlie related all that had been said at the interview and concluded by saying, 'Mrs Prefect is a complete wreck. The death of her sons has devastated her, and having not received a penny in insurance she just lives like a hermit in her small terrace house.'

Harriet had no cause to doubt that Charlie was correct in his judgement of Pamela Prefect and she thanked him and Sally before suggesting that they add this latest information to the Incident Room data. Charlie and Sally withdrew from the office and DCI Love and DI Harrington left soon afterwards, setting off in the Saab once again.

Their visit to the medical supplies warehouse was unannounced but they were in luck as the man they had called to see, Bill Caldwell, was still on the premises. Harriet called in at the despatch office and asked Granville Smith if she might ask Caldwell a few questions. The warehouse manager looked at the warrant card held up for him to read and then his eyes fixed on the slender figure dressed in an immaculate navy trouser suit standing in front of him. The crisp white shirt that the woman was wearing beneath her jacket, accentuated the smooth, olive skin of her handsome face.

'Are you really a police officer?' he asked.

'I'm afraid I am.'

Granville Smith huffed before replying. 'Things are certainly changing. What's a nice young woman like yourself doing in this job?'

Harriet gave a half smile. 'I actually enjoy it. Now could you direct us to Mr Caldwell, please.'

Ed had been standing a few paces behind DCI Love while she had been talking, but on hearing the last question from Smith he too wondered what this elegant woman was doing running a team of detectives in a profession that could hardly be considered glamorous.

Granville Smith shrugged his thin shoulders. 'I thought you'd done all the questioning of him days ago.'

'Just a few loose ends,' said Ed stepping forward, 'if you wouldn't mind showing us the way.'

The thin man pointed in the direction of the main warehouse. 'He's loading his lorry ready to leave for Sheffield and I'd be grateful if you wouldn't delay him for longer than you have to.'

Harriet and Ed thanked the manager and walked to the warehouse. The smell of antiseptic met them as they entered the massive building through the large double doors.

'I see what Sally means when she says the place smells like a hospital,' said Ed.

At one side of the store they saw a slight, sandy-haired man tossing boxes into the back of a covered lorry. 'No wonder things get broken,' whispered Harriet as they advanced towards him.

Bill Caldwell turned as he heard the approaching feet. 'Well?' he said. 'What do you want? You shouldn't be in here.'

'Police.' Ed showed his card. 'Inspector Harrington and Chief Inspector Love. We need to ask you a few questions, if you don't mind.'

'I've already been spoken to if it's about the nurse's murder.'

'We're sorry to bother you again,' said Harriet, 'but we do have to eliminate everyone who is remotely connected to a case.'

The man fixed his eyes on the DCI and she felt a slight chill run down her spine as she realised the coldness in the look. 'What connection do I have?' he asked sharply.

'Your brother,' replied Ed almost as sharply. 'He lives near the first murder scene and he is known to be a wife-beater.'

'Doesn't make him a murderer,' came the surly response.

For all the near-educated voice, Harriet detected a hardness in the light tone and a snideness in his replies. 'Could we ask you to give us details of your movements on the night of the twentieth, between the hours of eight thirty and ten, and on the night of Friday the twenty-fourth.' Her own voice was now deliberately cool and direct.

Bill Caldwell pulled down the tarpaulin at the back of the lorry and proceeded to secure it. He spoke slowly and precisely. 'On the twentieth I was at home all night with my brother and on the twenty-fourth I was on a long haul job in Cornwall and stayed overnight in Truro. I have handed in the receipt for my stay at a B and B there, which is in the hands of the manager in the despatch office. Does that satisfy you?' His cold eyes were now triumphant and Harriet took an instinctive dislike to him.

Ed moved closer. 'So no one apart from your brother can account for your movements on the Monday night?'

'If that's how you want to put it.'

'Thank you for your help,' said Harriet, with great charm. 'We shall be happy to confirm your alibi for the Friday and hope to eliminate you from our enquiries.' She turned and with Ed at her side they left the warehouse.

'You'd like to pin these murders on him, wouldn't you?' growled Ed as they retraced their steps to the despatch office.

'You certainly would. He's not exactly edifying, is he? But unfortunately, as we well know, the killer would not expose himself by being aggressive towards us. He'll be far more obliging and helpful. We'll just check out Caldwell's alibi for the night of Monica's murder. It will be sound, you can bet your life on it. At the moment we will have to leave the Monday night on hold.'

Bill Caldwell's overnight stay in Truro was genuine, as Harriet knew it would be. Nevertheless when the DCI returned to her office she re-read his earlier statement where he had backed his brother's alibi for the night of Carol Young's murder. Having done so she rang through to ask DC Sally Pringle to come to her room.

'Sally, you say that Bill Caldwell is a widower. Do we know anything about his late wife?'

'Actually, Ma'am he has been widowed twice. I obtained these facts from the files in the manger's office at the warehouse.' Sally's earnest face generated genuine enthusiasm and DCI Love remembered her own early days as a young constable when she too was eager to throw herself into every incident that came her way. Not that she felt she had lost any of her own drive as she had risen through the ranks; far from it. The job still excited her and aroused her natural instincts of facing a challenge.

She addressed the young DC. 'I'd like you to do something for me, Sally. Find out all you can about the deaths of Bill Caldwell's wives. Don't ask me why, but there was something about this man that disturbed me. I don't think he had anything to do with the murders we are presently investigating, but something about his persona makes me curious.'

Sally's face lit up. 'Right, Ma'am. I shall enjoy doing this. I agree with you about Bill Caldwell. He was quietly... er what's the word I want?'

'Threatening?' suggested DCI Love.

'Absolutely, Ma'am. I actually felt very uneasy about his soft voice and deadpan face.'

'I had the same feeling.' Harriet frowned. 'Perhaps it's just a woman's intuition. See what you can uncover, Sally.'

Sally left the DCI's office to delve into the deaths of the two Mrs Caldwells. She would telephone Granville Smith for the dates of the deaths before paying a visit to the local newspaper to hunt down the reports that may or may not have been written about the deaths. Granville Smith was able to give Sally the information she required over the telephone. Bill Caldwell's first wife had died after seven years of marriage. 'November, thirteen years ago,' said Granville. 'He remarried only a few months after that, but his second wife was killed in a car accident five years later. Some people certainly are unlucky; you wonder how they cope with such tragedies in their life. Now Sarah was killed, let me see, it was summer because they were on holiday at Lands End. Yes, it was late August just a year ago next month.'

Sally thanked Mr Smith for his time and help and, collecting her car from the car park, she set off for the news office of the *Torreston Gazette*. Once at the office she made her way to the reading room where she settled down to search through the papers of November, thirteen years ago, and August last year. With her pad beside her on the table, Sally began to take notes. It was nearly an hour later that DC Pringle returned to Torreston police station to go through the police files where the reports of the two accidents were tucked away. Some time later she knocked on the door of the DCI's office.

Harriet was writing her report for George Hollyoak when she heard the light but eager knock on her door. On calling 'Come in' she smiled at the flushed face of the tall, athletic Sally Pringle as she swept into the room, obviously bursting with excitement.

'Sit down, Sally,' said DCI Love. 'I can see that something you've uncovered has got you going.'

Sally sat in the chair across the desk from Harriet and produced her notes. She informed the DCI of the death of Jenny Caldwell thirteen years ago and of Sarah Caldwell almost a year ago. 'Jenny fell down the stairs and broke her neck and Bill married Sarah just eight months later. Sarah was killed when the car she was in, rolled over the cliff at Lands End. According to the police report she was sitting in the car while her husband was off along the cliffs somewhere, supposedly bird watching, and she must have dozed off. The car just rolled over the cliffs. Very convenient, don't you think, Ma'am?'

'There must have been more in the police report than that, Sally.'

'I have a copy of it here, Ma'am. They pulled the car from the sea with Mrs Caldwell's body still seat-belted in it and an inspection of the vehicle didn't reveal anything suspicious.' She handed the report to Chief Inspector Love.

Harriet took the report and was silent as she read it. 'Strange that the second wife made no attempt to undo her seat belt or open the door as the car went over the cliff,' she said. 'And according to this report the handbrake was not on. Wouldn't you at least grab the handbrake if you found yourself in a car that was moving forwards towards the cliff edge?'

'She must have been very sound asleep,' replied Sally.

Harriet was still looking at the papers in her hand. 'The report states that the first wife was disorientated during the night when she got up to go to the bathroom. The Caldwells were sleeping in the spare room while their bedroom was being decorated, and in the dark she turned the wrong way at the top of the stairs and fell head first down them.'

'Sounds plausible,' muttered Sally. 'How do you prove it happened any other way? Pity she was cremated.'

'Difficult!' Harriet wrinkled her nose. 'But we can have a word with the interviewing officer on the second death. Interestingly, she was buried.' She read the name of the interviewing officer at the bottom of the page: Gordon Pettigrew of the Cornwall Force. 'But then the report was sent to us and handled by DS Paddy Lynch,' she went on. 'Do we know him?'

'Sergeant Lynch left the force about a year ago, Ma'am.'

'Damn.'

'But I understand he was, and probably still is, a friend of DI Harrington's. Shall I ask him where we might find him, Ma'am?' Sally was still eager to proceed with this probing of Bill Caldwell's affairs.

'It had better be me, thank you, Sally, but I will keep you informed.'

When DC Pringle had left her office, Harriet rang through to ask to speak to Ed who appeared at her door minutes later. Harriet asked him about Paddy Lynch and Bill Caldwell's second wife.

'I don't recall the case, Ma'am. Paddy and I didn't work as a regular pair; although in the early days we were both beat bobbies together and both made Sergeant in the same year. We just stayed friends over the years. He became disillusioned with the job and left the force to take on a garage. Many of us use his services when our cars need servicing or repairing because we know we can trust him.'

'Could you visit him, Ed, and ask about the death of Sarah Caldwell? See if he feels if there was anything at all suspicious about the way the car went over the cliff. Or indeed why apparently the woman inside made no attempt to get out of the car or pull on the handbrake? It's a long drop from the cliff top to the sea, and yet she amazingly didn't wake up.'

'Right. I'll visit Paddy at the end of the day before I go home. His garage is down Cranbourne Avenue in Northampton. Funnily enough I was over there only last Sunday.' He carefully watched the DCI's face as he spoke, watching for any flicker of embarrassment, but her expression did not alter.

'Take Sally with you if she can make it. She's quite fired up over Bill Caldwell.'

Ed nodded. 'I'll speak to her now.' He left the room wondering how it was that the DCI, having been informed that one of her officers had been close to where she was having a clandestine meeting with a judge just days ago, was able to show no flicker of emotion. Charlie was probably right; it was none of his business. He entered the Incident Room to seek out DC Pringle.

Sally was extremely excited to be asked to accompany DI Harrington on an enquiry. 'I should be at training this evening but I'll cancel. I rarely miss a session, I'm sure my coach will forgive me. What time shall I be ready to leave, Inspector?' she asked almost breathlessly.

'I can't leave before six,' replied Ed. 'I'm up to my eyes with work here. I'll telephone Paddy to see if he will be at the garage late, otherwise we shall be obliged to impinge on his home life. But knowing Paddy, he won't object.'

'I'll be ready at six unless I hear otherwise,' said Sally, already wishing the day would go faster.

Paddy Lynch agreed to speak to Ed at his workplace. 'I shall be here at the garage until at least seven thirty, Ed. I can work as we talk. What bee have you got in your bonnet over the Caldwell case?'

'I won't discuss it over the phone, Paddy, but I'll be with you around six thirty.' He hung up and turned his attention to the murder investigation at hand. Tomorrow he and DCI Love were going to Leicester to interview the elusive Dave Spalding. They would then be in possession of the full name of the nurse whom he had supposedly left his fiancée for. He wondered where the nurse could be at this moment.

Sergeant Jack Fuller handed Harriet a copy of the list of names of the employees from the Perfect factory fire. She read through them. Apart from the two brothers who owned the premises and the unfortunate young woman they had interviewed, no name sprang out at her that she recognised.

'I've checked and re-checked every name, Ma'am,' said Jack. 'The badly injured were eventually discharged from the infirmary but none of their names appear on any of the other lists that we have. They don't seem to have a connection with the other hospitals or the places where the murders were committed.'

The DCI thought for a moment. 'Are you able to do a follow up on where these injured people are now Jack?'

'I certainly can, Ma'am.'

'You can eliminate those we know about, such as June McFarland, because we have been to her address. Just collect information on the ones who were sent to hospital, Jack. I'd like to know where they all went after their discharge from the Infirmary and where they now live. Will you do that for me?'

Jack Fuller puffed out his chest. 'My pleasure, Ma'am. I'll be as quick as I can.'

After Sergeant Fuller had left her office, Harriet called on George Hollyoak. 'Here's my report on the investigation so far, George. For the first time I actually feel that we have a lead and things are beginning to shape up.'

'I'm glad to hear that, my dear. I've had the Deputy Chief

Constable on my back the last couple of days asking questions.'

'I'm sure you were able to fend him off, George. He's only hounding you because the press are on his back.'

'Don't worry, Harry, I've been in your shoes many a time in the past. You learn to grow a thick skin and ignore the criticisms. Once you have a result they soon change their tune and then they can't praise you enough.' He stood tall and pretended to read out a statement. 'For the hard work and dedicated persistence of Detective Chief Inspector Love and her team in tracking down this cunning criminal.' He handed her a sheet of paper.

Harriet laughed as she accepted the paper. 'Let's hope that is in the very near future. But seriously, George, I can't bear the thought of this murderer being out there somewhere and not knowing his motive for killing nurses.'

'You say you have a lead?'

Harriet explained the connection with the scarves and the factory. She told him about the young secretary whose fiancé had left her for one of the nurses, and Garry Hobbs and the two Caldwell brothers. 'Somewhere in there I am convinced we have the killer,' she concluded. 'It's all in the report, George, you can read it at your leisure.'

'Well done, Harry, the investigation seems to be in full swing. Now, when are you able to visit Nancy and myself?'

'How about Sunday lunch?' replied Harriet.

'Excellent, excellent. Nancy will be delighted. Shall we say twelve thirty for one?'

'I'll be there,' smiled Harriet.

'And you will accompany us to the Gala Dinner on Saturday evening, won't you, Harry?'

'I'd almost forgotten that,' said Harriet. 'I suppose I'm expected to attend.'

'You are indeed my dear. All senior officers will be attending; after all it is in support of the Police Benevolent Fund. It does a splendid job for our widows and orphans.'

'Right. I'll make sure the date is in my diary. When exactly is it?'

'This Saturday, my dear, at the Guildhall – seven thirty for eight. We'll pick you up at seven fifteen.'

Harriet smiled and nodded. 'I won't forget, George.'

As she left his office, George Hollyoak thought how beautiful, she was. She was not just beautiful though, she was gracious, kind and highly intelligent. He prayed that the outcome of this case would be acclaimed as a brilliant result for her. He did so want her to succeed.

Chapter Eleven

Detective Constable Sally Pringle was ready and waiting for Detective Inspector Harrington as he came out of the front door of the police station a little after six. His serious face broke into a half-smile as he was confronted with the enthusiastic young woman. Sally came across to him, trying hard to conceal her excitement. She had never been on an investigation with such a senior officer and she held DI Harrington in very high regard.

They arrived at the garage to be greeted by an oily Paddy Lynch. Paddy wiped his hands on an equally oily rag and his smudged face broke into a grin as he welcomed his friend. 'I won't shake your hand, Ed. But nice to see you anyway.'

Ed introduced Sally before getting straight down to business. 'DCI Love is interested in the deaths of Bill Caldwell's wives. What can you tell us about them, Paddy?'

Paddy frowned slightly. 'I wasn't involved in the investigation into the first death, but I did handle the second after the car and report was brought back to us from Cornwall. I have to say that I was curious about two sudden deaths and indicated my doubts to my senior officer. The first wife broke her neck when she fell down the stairs. There were no other marks on the body, according to the examining doctor, and it was recorded as an accident. Certainly nothing suspicious was turned up. As to the death of Sarah Caldwell, I was more than unhappy about the circumstances. The garage couldn't find any abnormalities in the structure of the car that might raise suspicion, although it was badly smashed up when it hit the rocks below and this must have made a detailed examination difficult. However, nothing was obvious about the wreck that could make us consider foul play, although I still had my doubts, and again, I did mention this in my report.'

Ed nodded. 'Yes, I saw what you wrote. Was a post-mortem done on either woman?'

'Not as far as I know. The doctor in Lands End was apparently satisfied as to the causes of death in Sarah's case and the doctor up here had never once mentioned anything suspicious in the death of the first wife.'

Sally was itching to speak and now bravely interrupted. 'Mr Lynch, I suppose the cause of death of Sarah Caldwell *was* drowning. Er, I mean, she wasn't dead before the car went over the cliff...'

Paddy smiled at the young DC. 'The doctor definitely gave drowning as the cause of death, young lady, and you can call me Paddy.'

Sally felt herself blush but did not back off. 'I just wondered why no one asked for a post-mortem in either case. I thought it was usual in a sudden death.'

'Only if the doctor is unable to give a cause of death,' said Paddy.

'But surely if you were suspicious you could have made the suggestion to your superior officer?'

Paddy wiped his hands vigorously. 'I have to say that since hearing of your DCI's interest in the Caldwell case I have thought about it, and yes, I have had a twinge of conscience. I did suggest it tentatively to the Chief Inspector at the time but it didn't materialise. I suppose on looking back, I was close to leaving the Force and he was coming up to retirement and no one bothered to pursue the matter. Anyway, in the death of Sarah Caldwell the investigation was carried out by the Cornwall Force.'

Sally turned her eager face to DCI Harrington. 'Is it too late to have an exhumation of the body, Sir?'

'It's never too late, Sally – if DCI Love demands it. She would have to put the request to the Coroner and have the Super's backing, but knowing our boss and her contacts, I don't think it would be a problem.'

Sally thought she noted a definite 'tone' to the Inspector's voice and glanced at him enquiringly, but his face had not changed and she decided that she must have imagined it. Paddy Lynch, who knew Ed well, spotted the bitterness in his voice but thought better than to discuss DCI Love in front of a junior member of his team. He would question Ed on the subject some other time.

Ed refused Paddy's offer of coffee, saying it was late and he would like to get home. 'We must get together some time, Paddy,' he added. 'I'd like to see Barbara and the boys again. It's been too long.'

'We'll arrange dinner one night. Give me a ring, Ed, when you're not rushed off your feet.'

Ed and Sally left the garage to return to Torreston. Sally was bubbling over. 'Do you think DCI Love will ask for an exhumation of Sarah Caldwell?' she asked breathlessly.

'I can't say, Sally, but if she really is suspicious abut Bill Caldwell, then it's quite possible.'

The next day was the day when Harriet had planned to interview Dave Spalding. According to Mrs Charteris, he was due to return from his commercial travels at two in the afternoon. As Ed drove his Saab to Leicester he relayed his conversation with Paddy Lynch. Harriet listened intently.

'It's interesting that the examination of the car didn't turn up anything criminal. But when you think about the accident in depth, you begin to have doubts. The report stated that car was badly smashed up at the front, and although the hydraulic brake pipe was severed it was not surprising due to the impact on the rocks. That in itself is pretty weird, don't you think, Ed? *Could* the hydraulic pipe sever like that?'

Ed shrugged. 'The chaps at the police garage seemed to think the damage was caused by the smash and certainly not cut. No one queried the damage.'

'Mind you,' persisted Harriet, 'isn't the brother, Vincent, a brilliant mechanic? And the Caldwell brothers are as thick as thieves, aren't they?'

'True,' agreed, Ed. 'Are you going to apply for an exhumation order, then?'

'I'll put it to Superintendent Hollyoak and see what he thinks.'

They pulled up outside Dave Spalding's house and Harriet was pleased to see a car parked in the driveway. 'Thank goodness he's back,' she said.

The door was opened by a thin man of average height. He had light brown hair and a long, pasty face with the palest grey eyes that Harriet had ever seen. The washed-out eyes were none the less compelling and for some seconds Harriet held their gaze before speaking.

'Chief Inspector Love and Inspector Harrington,' she said. 'Are you Dave Spalding?'

'I am.'

'We should like to ask you a few questions with regard to your fiancée and the accident at the Perfect factory three years ago.'

'Good God! I'd almost forgotten about that.' The voice was low, educated and precise.

'I'm surprised you are able to forget such a horrific incident that disfigured your fiancée so dreadfully.' Ed's voice was icy. 'May we come in, please?'

'Of course, of course.' Dave Spalding held open the door to allow Harriet and Ed to enter. The interior of the house was chaotic. There were papers and magazines on every surface and piles of laundry awaiting ironing dumped on the chairs. The furniture was cheap and uninviting and there was a definite musty smell about the place. A long-haired, black cat pushed its way into the room to rub itself up against his master's legs, and having done so he turned his attention to Harriet. Being a cat lover, Harriet instinctively bent down and stroked the loudly purring creature. 'Hello, puss! You're a lovely fellow. What's his name?'

'Lucy.'

'Oh' said Harriet.

'Short for Lucifer.'

'My word, such a name for a lovely cat.' Harriet stroked the furry animal again as it stretched its back legs and arched its back before curling up on a pile of washing and closing his eyes.

Dave Spalding hastily moved piles of clothes from two of the armchairs. 'Sorry about the mess,' he said, 'but I've only just got back and haven't had time to clear up yet. Here, now you can sit down.'

Gingerly Harriet obliged and Ed perched on the arm of the settee on the other side of the room. 'Now,' said Ed, 'could you tell us the name of the nurse to whom you were attracted whilst June McFarland was in hospital.'

The pale eyes narrowed. 'What's that got to do with anything?'

'Just answer the question please,' interrupted Harriet.

The man scowled. 'My private life is up to me,' he said. 'I tried hard to sustain my feelings for June after the accident but gradually I knew it was no good. I could barely look at her after they removed the bandages, and each day I visited I found it more and more difficult to speak to her, let alone sit at her bedside. In the end I told the nurses I couldn't face her any more. I wrote a letter explaining my feelings and left it for one of the nurses to give to her. I know it was cowardly, but you didn't see the raw flesh and extensive burns that I was having to look at.' He sat down on a pile of magazines on the floor and held his head in his hands. Harriet felt a twinge of sympathy as she remembered the face and head of June McFarland.

'June tells us that you were seeing one of the nurses during your visits to the hospital.' Harriet kept her voice placid.

'Samanntha gave me sympathy and allowed me to talk about my feelings for June. I did try and date her after I'd ended my engagement to June, but she didn't want to know. That was the last straw; I was in a terrible state. I tried several times to get her to go out with me but she was adamant that she didn't date patients or their visitors.'

'Could you give us the name and address of this Samanntha, please?' Ed took his notebook from his pocket and waited.

Dave Spalding lifted his head and focused his pale eyes on DI Harrington. 'What for?'

Ed felt that the emotion shown by this man a few minutes earlier had vanished rather rapidly and he had difficulty in keeping his voice calm. 'We need to ask her a few questions about the injured workers. Now, her name, please.'

'Samanntha – that's with two "n"s – Farndon.'

'That's an unusual spelling of her name,' remarked Harriet.

'Her mother was called Ann, so her father wanted his wife's name incorporated in the spelling of his daughter's name, as they didn't give her a middle one.'

'You seem to know a great deal about Nurse Farndon,' said Ed, writing everything down.

'She talked to me a lot during the time I was visiting June. She was a great help to me.'

'And where does she live?' asked Ed cutting him short.

'She used to live at Flat three, fifty-four Clipston Road, but she moved and I don't know where she went.' His voice dropped and his eyes glazed over. 'I tried to trace her but no one would help me. In the end I gave up.'

'One last thing,' said Harriet, 'could you tell us where you were on the nights of Monday the twentieth and Friday the twenty-fourth.'

'Am I being accused of something?' The long face dropped even further and the pale eyes narrowed.

'Not at the moment, Sir,' said Ed. 'Would you answer the question please.'

Dave Spalding scowled. He turned and went over to a briefcase that had been dropped carelessly on the floor and opened it fiercely. He took out a large book and flicked through the pages. 'Monday the twentieth. I was in South Wales and stayed at the Red Dragon hotel in Monmouth.' He snatched a piece of paper from the pages and held it under DI Harrington's nose. 'The receipt from the hotel,' he snapped. 'On the twenty-fourth I was working at head office in Nottingham and arrived home at about eight thirty in the evening. I had a bath followed by supper on my own and settled down to watch television before going to bed at about eleven thirty. I have no receipt for that evening, Officer.'

'So no one can vouch for your movements on that Friday night?' Ed was not deterred by the bitterness of Dave Spalding.

'Mrs Charteris spoke to me when I arrived home, and offered to bring me round some supper. I accepted, and she appeared again at about nine. But that's about it. I didn't go out again.'

'Thank you, Sir,' said Ed in an over-polite voice.

Minutes later Harriet and Ed left the home of Dave Spalding. 'Nice chap,' commented Ed sarcastically.

'We'll check his Wales alibi and have a word with his boss in Nottingham, Ed. But could he have reached Torreston to kill Monica at nine if he was still here at eight thirty?'

'No, more's the pity,' replied Ed. 'But nine was an estimated time of death, wasn't it? It could have occurred a bit later. I'll get someone to check with Mrs Charteris to make sure that she did speak to him at the time he said. Mind you, he could also have left

Monmouth and murdered Carol before returning to the hotel. Monmouth isn't that far away.'

'His treatment of June McFarland seems terribly callous, I know,' replied Harriet. 'but he too suffered a traumatic experience. Imagine suddenly seeing the woman you love transformed from a lovely-looking young woman to the person we saw the other day. Not easy for him, Ed.'

'Hmm.' Ed was unconvinced. He had already decided that Dave Spalding was a less than likeable person.

'We'll try the address that Samanntha used to live at,' said Harriet. 'Possibly a neighbour might know where she moved to.'

Ed grunted again. 'She was probably hiding from Spalding and told the neighbours not to reveal her new address to him.'

'Quite probably, but they will be obliged to tell us. Charlie isn't with us, so I had better consult the *A to Z*.' She smiled at her solemn-faced colleague. One day, she thought, he might smile back!

Harriet and Ed found Clipston Road easily enough and Harriet rang the bell of Flat 3 at Number 54. A woman's voice came over the intercom.

'Who is it?'

Harriet answered: 'Police. Could we have a word, please.'

'Hang on a mo.' A window above their heads opened and a young woman leaned out. She grinned at them. 'Have to be careful, you know. Can I see your identity cards?'

Harriet smiled back in return. 'Quite right,' she said, holding up her warrant card. 'Are you able to see it from there?'

'Well enough,' came the chirpy reply. There was a click from the front door. 'Come up the stairs. I'll be waiting,'

DCI Love and DI Harrington entered the hallway, which smelled strongly of incense and was lavishly arrayed with vases of flowers. They climbed the narrow stairs to find a dark-haired young woman, dressed flamboyantly in a sort of caftan, leaning on the doorpost of flat Number 3. She thrust out her hand. 'I'm Fiona West. I'm an art student, do come in.'

Harriet and Ed entered the brightly decorated flat, which had paintings all over the walls. An easel stood in one corner holding a large sketch of a nude young man reclining on a couch. The young woman saw Harriet looking at her work. 'We're doing life studies at the moment. Not bad, is it?'

'Very good,' replied Harriet, 'although I'm more of a landscape person myself.' She cast her eyes around the room taking in the other paintings on display.

'Could we get down to business?' Ed's voice broke into her thoughts.

'Of course.' Harriet turned to, Ed. 'Do carry on Inspector.'

Ed took over the interview. 'Miss West, we are trying to trace Samanntha Farndon, who used to live here. Do you know where she moved to?'

Fiona pulled a face. 'Yes, I do have a forwarding address. Sam was being hounded by this bloke and eventually had to get away. She made me promise not to give the address to anyone, but I suppose the police are a different matter. Is anything wrong?'

'We hope not,' said Harriet. 'What can you tell us about the man who was harassing Samanntha?'

'His name was Dave Spalding. Sam looked after his fiancée when she had been injured in a factory accident and she showed this bloke a great deal of sympathy. Trouble was that he mistook Sam's kindness as a "come on" and she couldn't get rid of him.'

'Did she ever date this Spalding?' asked, Ed.

'Absolutely not. Sam didn't even like him, but she was sweet and kind to everyone, and it wasn't the first time her sweetness had been misinterpreted by men.'

'What do you mean?' Ed looked up from writing in his notebook.

Fiona put her hands on her hips and leaned against the wall. 'Oh, patients fancied her – and so did some of the doctors. But she wasn't having any of it. She would never go out with patients or anyone to do with where she worked. Even one of the injured men from the factory fire tried it on with her and she became quite anxious about it. She thought he was becoming obsessed by her. He kept trying to give her presents and she kept refusing them. Sam decided to leave the hospital altogether and move away so that neither this patient or Dave Spalding could find her.'

'Do you know the name of the patient from the factory accident who was keen on her?' Harriet asked.

'Well, I *did*. Let me think, he had an unusual first name.' She placed her fingers to her temple and frowned. 'Murdock! That's it – Murdock.'

Ed was writing furiously. 'Do you know this man's surname?'

''Fraid not. Sam must have mentioned it, but honestly I just can't remember. I might if you said it, though.'

'It doesn't matter,' said Harriet. 'We have a list of all the men injured in the accident and the name Murdock won't crop up very often.'

Ed asked the next question. 'Could we have the address of Samanntha, please?' Fiona nodded and went to a drawer in a small desk by the window. She took out an address book and opened it. 'Here you are, Inspector. Samanntha – with two "n"s – Farndon, Two Railway Cottages, Station Road, Amchurch, Northants.' She added the postcode, but Ed had enough. At last they now had the name of the missing nurse.

As Ed drove the Saab back to Leicester he went over the information they had been given. 'Seems June McFarland was mistaken about Nurse Farndon running off with her fiancé. She apparently isn't a man-snatcher after all.' He glanced sideways at his companion.

'No,' agreed Harriet.' But it doesn't make June's hurt any the less painful.'

'True.' Ed was quiet for a minute or two. 'I'll ask Jack Fuller to go back through the names of the injured workers to discover who this Murdock chap is.'

'Yes, thanks, Ed. And we had better visit this Samanntha, with two "n"s, tomorrow.'

'Right, Ma'am. Morning or afternoon?'

'Let's go first thing. If she isn't at home we can track her down at work. I wonder which hospital she is now at?'

'I vaguely know Amchurch. Used to have a lovely little railway station, so I can guess where Railway Cottages are. It also has a Cottage Hospital so possibly our next witness works there.'

'Excellent. We'll leave at eight thirty or as soon as possible after briefing. Would you do the honours tomorrow, please, and I'll meet you as soon as I've seen to the Super. We've moved on a bit today, Ed. I think the pieces of the jigsaw will suddenly fall into place.'

'Let's hope so, Ma'am.' Harriet almost winced at the formal, Ma'am, but she said nothing. She had decided not to invite the Inspector to use her first name again. There was a limit as to how long she could continue with her efforts to offer amity. It was now up to, Ed.

They arrived back at Torreston police station and Ed hastened to the Incident Room whilst Harriet went to her office to write up her report. She put a call through to the office of George Hollyoak and arranged to see him at the end of the day. She switched on her PC, and some time later rose from her chair and walked down the corridor to the Incident Room. DI Harrington was busy pinning information on the notice board when she poked her head around the door.

'I shall be off the premises for about an hour, Ed. I need to catch the shops before they close and then I will have to nip home to feed Toastie as I propose to work late. I'll be back before six thirty.'

'Right, Ma'am.'

Harriet left the building and climbed into her red Lotus to drive up to town. There was something she wished to purchase and now was as good a time as any. She was going to work late tonight so an hour off was not out of order.

Harriet returned to the Station at 6.20, having made her purchase and visited her house to make a fuss of her pet and give him food. She went to the kitchen where she made a large pot of strong coffee to set her up for a long stint of work. On returning to her office she placed the tray on her desk and left the coffee to infuse. She gathered up her report for Superintendent Hollyoak and left the room to keep her appointment with him.

George Hollyoak was always delighted to see his goddaughter. She was like a breath of fresh air whenever she floated in. He greeted her warmly.

'Right, m'dear, what have you to tell me today?'

'We've had a good day, George, and collected a few more names that could be relevant to our enquiries.'

'Good, good. We need a result, don't we.'

'We will get him, George. That I do promise. Because we have had no real leads it has been jolly difficult but now that we have uncovered connections between some of the people involved, we are beginning to see some sort of pattern emerging. At least it now makes a bit more sense as to what is happening, and why.'

'Does that mean you have a suspect?' George Hollyoak sounded hopeful.

'Several in the pipeline, George. But we are narrowing it down.'

'I have every faith in you, Harry. I know you won't jump in until you are absolutely sure you have the right person. The local and national papers have been pestering us for a statement. I said you would oblige tomorrow; is that all right with you?'

'It will have to be in the afternoon. In the morning I'm going with Ed to speak to a nurse who looked after one of the factory victims and was also hounded by another victim's fiancé. It's all in the report. It makes quite complicated reading, but somewhere in there, lies the answer to these killings.'

'I'll take it home with me, Harry. Your reports are always written so beautifully and are explicit in every detail. They make interesting reading. Perhaps you should have been a journalist.' George Hollyoak laughed.

'Had I chosen journalism I would have found it difficult to elaborate on the factual evidence George. I only believe in the truth.'

'That I do know,' smiled the Superintendent.

'I'll ring the Press Office and arrange a time for the interview sometime after lunch,' said Harriet. 'Now, George, I have a slight dilemma and would appreciate your advice.' She proceeded to relate the story of the two wives of Bill Caldwell and how she felt suspicious about the circumstances surrounding their deaths. 'Would I be out of order in requesting an exhumation on the body of Sarah Caldwell?' she concluded.

George Hollyoak had listened in silence as Harriet explained her intuitive feelings about Bill Caldwell and now, looking thoughtful, he considered her proposal of requesting an exhumation order. 'I think you have every reason for being suspicious, Harry. I will certainly back your request to the Coroner.'

Harriet sighed with relief. 'I can't explain how strongly I feel about this situation, George. Thank you for your trust in me. I shall write to the Coroner immediately and bring the letter to you in the morning to sign.'

She left the Superintendent's office with a spring in her step. Once back at her desk she poured herself a mug of strong coffee before sitting down at her computer, where she wrote her request for an exhumation of Sarah Caldwell. Having completed the letter, Harriet turned her attention to the case of the murdered nurses. Again and again she read through all the evidence in front of her, trying to make sense of the various pieces of the puzzle and the people involved. She worked late into the night, finally realising that she had not eaten for hours. She decided to remedy that fact. It was already nine. She would call at the Red Lion for something to eat, as she had no desire to rush around at home at this hour to prepare a meal. As she closed down her computer there came a light knock on the door. It opened to reveal DI Harrington. 'I saw the light under your door, Ma'am,' he said.

'I wondered if you were still in the building, Ed,' smiled Harriet. 'I didn't think you would leave without saying you were going.'

'I'm going now. My head is beginning to go round. It's so full of information and my stomach tells me I'm starving.'

'Mine too. Will you join me for a bite at the Red Lion?'

Ed hesitated. He was cautious about becoming too friendly with the new DCI, but on the other hand they were colleagues and colleagues did eat together from time to time to discuss a case. He nodded. 'Good idea. I don't fancy preparing food at home at this hour. I'll meet you there in ten minutes.'

He withdrew from the room and Harriet smiled to herself. What did she have to do to make this man unwind? Never mind, it was still early days, barely two weeks, and they were getting on well enough when working together. She picked up her briefcase and turned off the light, closing the door quietly behind her.

Harriet drove to the Red Lion and found a table for two tucked away in a quiet corner. It was already quite smoky, but she was too tired to bother about such trivialities even though she usually disliked the smarting of her eyes and the odour that was left clinging to her hair and clothes the following day. She had barely sat down when Ed arrived. He stood beside the table, his tall form towering above her. 'What would you like to drink?' he asked.

'Oh, just a grapefruit juice – without ice, please.'

Ed nodded in his usual solemn manner and vanished towards the bar. He returned carrying the drinks and a bar menu, which he handed to Harriet. 'At least you can always rely on the food being decent here,' he said. 'I don't need to look at the menu, I've already decided on the home-made steak and kidney pie.'

'Is it that good?'

'It's excellent, I can most certainly recommend it.'

Harriet closed the menu. 'Then I shall join you, Ed.' She took a twenty-pound note from her purse and handed it to, Ed. 'And no arguing. It's my treat, we agreed last time.'

Ed took the note and said, 'Right, thank you,' and returned to the bar.

At least he wasn't calling her Ma'am away from the Station... Thank goodness, thought Harriet as she sat casting her mind back over the last few days. Ed returned and sat down, handing Harriet her change. 'How do you feel the case is going?' he asked.

'I'm beginning to feel a great deal happier now that we have established some sort of link between the Perfect factory fire, the hospitals and the nurses. Somewhere in all of this lies the solution to the murders. We just have to sort it through and get the right man.'

'You don't think it was Bill Caldwell, do you?' said Ed quietly.

'No, I don't. I'm not mad about the man and I certainly wouldn't trust him any further than I could throw him, but no, I don't think he's our nurse killer. Now a wife killer, that's a different matter.' She wrinkled her nose in the manner that was becoming familiar to, Ed.

'Are you going to request an exhumation of Sarah Caldwell?' he said.

'Yes. I had a long discussion about it with Superintendent Hollyoak and he has agreed to back me. I've already written the letter and first thing tomorrow I shall present it to him for his signature.'

Ed nodded. 'You have to follow a gut feeling. I discovered that a long time ago. I failed to follow my instincts a few years back because I had no sound evidence about this chap I was investigating. I just knew he was running a stolen car racket. I searched his garage and found nothing. I even brought him in for questioning but still couldn't break him. Months into the investigation we followed him because of a stupid driving offence and found he had a second place on the other side of Northampton that was chock-a-block with stolen vehicles. So I think you're right to be guided by your instincts in this case.'

'Thank you, Ed, that's a great help.' The food arrived at that moment which was to Ed's relief, as he had no desire get deeply involved in showing over enthusiastic support for the DCI.

The time at the Red Lion was pleasant, the steak and kidney pie living up to its reputation. They had a lively discussing about the on-going investigation and the plans for the following day. Nothing personal was broached by either of them and just before closing time they left the pub and parted company. As Harriet entered her cottage she felt a little more relaxed. Toastie flung himself at her legs and she picked him up and stroked him affectionately. 'You're my friend aren't you Toastie,' she murmured into his long fur. 'You'd smile and call me Harry if you could, wouldn't you?' She carried her pet into the kitchen to give him his supper. She yawned. A hot bath and bed she thought. Tomorrow her letter to the Coroner would be delivered and hopefully the wheels would commence turning.

Chapter Twelve

Harriet arrived at the Station early the next morning. She was eager for Superintendent Hollyoak to countersign her request for the exhumation of Sarah Caldwell and wanted the letter to catch the first post. Her instincts were telling her that Bill Caldwell's wives had died in suspicious circumstances, and although it was now impossible to prove anything in the case of the death of his first wife, she felt strongly that a post-mortem on Sarah might turn up some incriminating evidence against the husband. The letter clasped in her hand, she took it to the Superintendent's office and handed it to George Hollyoak for him to approve and sign.

DI Harrington took briefing that morning; he was to meet with DCI Love later when they had arranged to visit the home of Samanntha Farndon at Railway Cottages in Amchurch. Charlie and Sally Pringle were to revisit Mrs Charteris in Leicester to verify Dave Spalding's story that he had returned home at eight thirty on the night of Friday the twenty-fourth and Bob Finch and Narinder Pancholi had been given the task of speaking to all the participants of the stag party that Garry Hobbs had been to on the night of Monica's murder. Eliminating the various suspects would narrow the field considerably and hopefully expose the real killer. As Ed gave details of the day's investigations to the team, he secretly wondered how much of a suspect these men he was referring to really were. However, confirming their alibis would cross them off the suspect list completely, or if the alibis were unsubstantiated then the suspect would be subject to further investigation. Either way all this had to be done.

Ed left the room and made his way to the staff kitchen; just time for a coffee before he met DCI Love. He switched on the kettle before noticing the large, new, gleaming cafetière standing on the work surface. Leaning against the pot was a card with the message, ENJOY SOME REAL COFFEE! – YOU'VE EARNED IT.

HARRIET LOVE. A tin of ground coffee stood next to the coffee pot. So this was what the DCI had dashed into town to buy last night! As Ed picked up the tin of coffee and removed the lid, Sally Pringle appeared at his side.

'The boss does think of the team doesn't she, Sir?'

'She does indeed, Sally. I'll leave you to christen the cafetière and bring the coffee along to the Incident Room.'

'You bet.' Sally tipped three large scoops of the strong-smelling granules into the glass pot and poured the hot water over them. The wonderful aroma filled the small kitchen and Sally swiftly placed several mugs on a tray. She found a milk jug at the back of the cupboard that as far as she could remember had never been used and she washed it under the tap and wiped it dry. She filled the jug from the bottle of milk in the refrigerator. It seemed that the days of the milk bottle on the tray, and one sticky teaspoon between six or seven of them, were over. She carried the tray triumphantly into the Incident Room.

Harriet walked down the corridor to deposit her letter with the Duty Sergeant downstairs. Superintendent Hollyoak had commented favourably on the wording of her request, and all she had to hope now was that the Coroner would add his approval. She handed the letter to Sergeant Yates. 'Pete, I was going to put this in the post, but do you think you could arrange for someone to deliver this by hand immediately? It's most important and I'd like the Coroner to receive it this morning otherwise it won't reach him until Monday.'

Sergeant Yates took the letter. 'No problem, Ma'am, the men are about to go out in the cars. I'll catch someone straight away.' Harriet smiled her thanks and turned to return to her office. As she passed the kitchen she recognised the pungent smell of real coffee. She poked her head round the door and noticed that her gift to the team was missing. She smiled. Good, may they enjoy their coffee as much as she did.

DCI Love and DI Harrington set off for Amchurch soon after eight forty. 'Are you sure you don't mind me driving all the time?' asked Ed, as he drove smoothly down narrow country lanes that would take them across country to their destination.

'Not at all, Ed,' lied Harriet, who missed her little Lotus

dreadfully. 'Anyway you know the way so it does make sense.'

Ed nodded. 'The team appreciated your gift,' he said in a stiff voice. He found being beholden to his senior officer very difficult.

Harriet chipped in swiftly, recognising Ed's uneasiness in appearing grateful. 'Good. They're a great bunch and as most of us have to survive on regular infusions of coffee throughout the day, I thought it would be nice to show my appreciation by supplying them with the real stuff.' She laughed her musical laugh and Ed wished she were not so charming all the time.

Soon they arrived at Amchurch. It was a small, old-fashioned village that still supported a quaint little village shop and a public house. The houses were mostly made of Colly Weston stone, and in the main street the buildings were of varying shapes and sizes and all very individual. Ed turned off down a narrow lane that bore the name Station Road, passing a disused and sad-looking railway station, a victim of the Beaching cuts of the late sixties. At the end of the lane was a row of red brick cottages. 'Railway Cottages,' announced Harriet, as she looked up at the plaque on the wall of the end cottage.

'And here's Number 2,' said Ed pulling up outside a blue door that bore a large white 2.

'It's very quiet,' muttered Harriet as she walked from the car to the front door. She pressed the doorbell and they both waited. She rang again. 'She must be at work, Ed. Do we try the local hospital?'

'I can't think where else she would be employed, unless it's at the local surgery.'

They began walking back down the path when the door of the house next door opened. 'Can I help you?' enquired a brusque female voice.

On turning Harriet and Ed saw a large imposing figure standing on the step of Number 1 Railway Cottages. The big woman had her arms folded across her ample bosom and her sharp eyes were looking them up and down. Harriet quickly produced her warrant card and Ed did likewise. They held them up for the woman to scrutinise over the low fence that divided the two houses. 'Hmm,' said the large woman, remaining stiff and forbidding on the doorstep. 'And what exactly do you want with Samanntha?'

'We need to ask her a few questions about an investigation that we are conducting at present,' said Harriet. 'Could you tell us where we might find her?'

'She's on holiday. Been away one week already and should be back this weekend but I'm not sure when.'

The voice was still somewhat aggressive. People with unhelpful attitudes always annoyed Ed. He couldn't understand how DCI Love always kept her cool and didn't just put these people in their place. After all, they were here on official business and questions needed to be answered. He stepped forward and spoke in a cold voice.

'Could you give us your name, please?'

'What for?' The big woman glared at Ed.

'We wish to ask *you* some questions, as we are unable to contact Miss Farndon until the weekend.'

The big woman sniffed. 'Martha Wilks. What do you want to know?'

'Might we come in?' came Harriet's gentle voice. 'We can hardly conduct a discussion across a fence, can we?'

'If you must,' replied Martha unfolding her arms. The two officers left Samanntha's pathway and walked through the gateway next door. Martha Wilks held open the front door and stood to one side allowing them to enter. 'Wipe your feet. This lane is always muddy whether it's rained or not. You can't keep the place clean for a moment. Go in the front room – and you'd better sit down, I suppose.' She followed Harriet and Ed into the room and stood in front of them with her hands on her broad hips. 'Right! what do you want to know?'

Harriet opened the questioning, 'We are investigating an incident that occurred three years ago when Miss Farndon was a nurse in Leicester, and we hoped that she might be able to throw some light on the whereabouts of a patient that she nursed at that time.'

'Hmm,' Martha narrowed her eyes. 'She left that place because she was being pestered and now here she is being bothered again.'

'We are not exactly pestering her,' said Ed, still feeling

annoyed that they were having to be wary of this woman. 'Miss Farndon might hold the answer to a very serious crime that we are investigating.'

The formidable woman focused her eyes on the DI. 'I wasn't referring to you so much,' she said in a less aggressive tone, 'but some months ago a man came round asking questions about Sam and I lied and said she had moved away. I don't know that he believed me, because I saw him hanging around in the lane a few weeks later. I told Sam about it and she was not very happy, I can tell you – scared, even; but she refused to inform the police like I advised her.'

'Can you describe the man?' asked Harriet.

'Average height, quiet voice, reasonably well-spoken, can't really tell you much more about him. He asked where Sam worked and I said in Bedford. That's not true, of course, she works at the Cottage Hospital here in Amchurch; but I felt very uneasy about him asking questions about the poor lass. She had been harassed at her last working place. She told me all about it, and that's why I try and protect her a bit.'

'Very commendable,' said Ed dryly. 'Did this chap walk with a limp?'

'Can't say that I noticed. He was standing on my doorstep when I opened the door to his knock and I closed the door before he walked away. Now you've got me really worried. What's this all about?'

Harriet decided that it might be beneficial to the investigation if they gave this woman a few details of their concern about the man they were trying to trace. She was obviously at home most of the time and her eagle eyes probably missed very little. She smiled at Martha Wilks. 'I can see that you are an intelligent woman and keen to protect Samanntha. Our concern in finding this man, who might have been a patient in the hospital where she worked, is that we think he might have a connection to the two murdered nurses. You may have read about them in the paper.'

Martha Wilks gasped and her hand flew to her mouth. 'Oh my God!'

'We don't wish to alarm you,' added Harriet hastily, 'but any help you can give us in tracing this man would be appreciated.'

Mrs Wilks had certainly softened in her attitude to the two police officers. 'I'll do anything I possibly can,' she whispered hoarsely.

'In that case,' said Ed, 'think really hard and try and give us a few more details about the man who was asking questions about Miss Farndon. Colour of hair, eyes, anything that might help.'

Martha screwed up her face. 'He wore a woolly hat so I couldn't see the colour of his hair. His eyes were light, probably pale blue or grey. That's about all I can remember. I'm sorry.'

'You've done well,' said Ed in a much more kindly voice. 'But should anyone call again asking about Samanntha, please telephone myself or Chief Inspector Love immediately.' He handed his card to the woman.

Harriet touched Martha's arm. 'We should be grateful if you could ring us the minute Miss Farndon returns from holiday. If neither of us is available at the station please use my mobile number or even my home number.' She too handed Martha Wilks her card.

Mrs Wilks stood with the two cards in her hand. 'Samanntha is very vulnerable, you know. Men appear to want to own her. I can't explain what it is, but she's had hassle all her life with men trying to possess her. She gets very upset and her answer is to move away. She can't do that all her life though, can she?' She looked up at Harriet and Ed and there were tears in her eyes. Gone was the fierce expression she'd worn when she confronted strangers she thought had come to stir up mischief for the gentle young lady who lived next door. Now the lined face showed only concern. She had never had children of her own but had she, she would have wanted a daughter just like the delicate Samanntha. 'And by the way,' she said softly, 'I'm expecting Samanntha back Sunday evening.'

'Thank you,' said Ed, writing in his notebook.

'What about Samanntha's parents?' asked Harriet as she and Ed moved towards the front door.

'Both dead. She doesn't seem to have any relatives who she can turn to, but she has plenty of very loyal friends, including myself and my husband Bert.'

Harriet thanked Mrs Wilks for her time and help and she and

Ed left. Once in the car Harriet turned to the Detective Inspector. 'What do you think, Ed?'

'Well, the description of the chap asking questions about Samanntha Farndon matches the man who was at the place where Monica worked, apart from the limp, that is; but then Mrs Wilks didn't actually see him walking.'

Harriet nodded. 'She mentioned pale eyes, and that immediately made me think of Dave Spalding. He has the palest eyes I've ever seen.'

'His alibis are being checked out by Charlie today,' said Ed. 'We'll have to see if he's still in the frame by this evening.'

'We need to speak to Samanntha urgently,' said Harriet, 'she seems to hold the key to the whole mystery. We'll just have to hang on a day or so until she returns from holiday. We need to determine if the man in the woolly hat who was seen at Monica's workplace, is in fact the man who worked at the factory in Leicester and was nursed by Samanntha after the fire.'

'Yes, until we know this we can't be sure if we are chasing one man or two,' said Ed as he started the engine of the Saab. 'Where to now?'

'The Cottage Hospital, I think. It won't do any harm to ask a few questions there.'

DI Harrington drove back up the lane and headed for the town centre.

'Look, there's the police station,' said Harriet, pointing as she spotted the sign. 'There aren't many of these small police stations left. I hadn't realised that Amchurch had held onto theirs.'

Ed grunted. 'They don't know for how long they will be able to keep it, but personally I think these small stations are invaluable.'

'I agree. It might make sense to call in and alert the men here to our suspicions about "Mr Woolly Hat" and Samanntha Farndon.'

'Good idea,' agreed Ed and he quickly pulled into the Station car park.

They entered the building and approached the enquiry desk. Ed rang the bell and immediately the window of the enquiry office opened.

'Yes Sir?' came the brisk, matter-of-fact voice.

'How can I help you?'

The Duty Sergeant was a young, rather cocky individual, and Ed in his usual dour manner looked him in the eye before stating, 'Detective Inspector Harrington. Could I speak to the senior officer in CID, please?'

'Certainly Sir, if you would wait one moment.'

'Don't you want to see my warrant card, Sergeant?' asked Ed as the sergeant picked up the telephone with a flourish.

Unflustered by this obvious reprimand the younger man simply held up his hand to Ed as the telephone was answered at the other end, saying 'All in good time, Sir.' He spoke into the mouthpiece. 'Hello Andy, is DI Howarth still there? Oh good. I have a Detective Inspector Harrington with me who would like a word with him please. Right! Thanks, Andy.' He replaced the receiver and turned his attention to, Ed. 'Now Sir! could I see your identification, please?'

Harriet had been standing a little way off and she hid a smile as she witnessed the way in which the sergeant had coped with, Ed. Anyone else would have been extremely uncomfortable by now, but this young man had the confidence of a strutting peacock and was obviously quite capable of talking his way out of any precarious situation. He studied Ed's warrant card with deliberation. 'Thank you, Inspector, and the young lady?' He eyed Harriet up and down giving a knowing smile to, Ed. 'I presume she is with you?'

Harriet walked forward and produced her own warrant card. 'I am indeed, Sergeant.'

'Ah yes, Ma'am.' He swallowed hard as he read her card. Undaunted, he flashed a smile. 'Chief Inspector Love, I'm Sergeant Johnson and I'm delighted to make your…'

Harriet's green eyes stopped the officer in full flow, 'Cut the waffle, Sergeant, and let us through please. We are on a very tight schedule and don't have time to spend on niceties.'

'Yes of course, Ma'am.' At last Neil Johnson showed a modicum of decorum, He unlocked the doorway to the main entrance hall allowing Harriet and Ed to enter the police station.

'He'd soon drive you mad if you worked with him,' muttered Ed as he looked around the building they were in.

Harriet chuckled. 'You must admit he's a master at covering up his faux pas.'

'Perhaps he should have been a barrister, then,' replied Ed sourly.

'He may well become just that, I should think,' laughed Harriet, unperturbed by the encounter with Sergeant Neil Johnson.

A tall man came towards them. 'I'm DI Paul Howarth, how can I help you?'

'DCI Love,' said Harriet, 'and DI Harrington.'

Harriet and Ed spent twenty minutes at Amchurch police station. They explained the situation to Paul Howarth, telling him of their need to interview Samanntha Farndon and about the man she nursed at the Leicester Infirmary three years ago. Harriet asked if the Amchurch police would be on the lookout for a man wearing a woolly hat and walking with some sort of limp. 'If a patrol car could make the occasional trip down Station Lane it might be reassuring for Mrs Wilks and Miss Farndon,' said Harriet. 'Also if you would inform your officers to be aware that this man is still at large, and could they keep an eye on the hospital. All nursing staff have been alerted to the dangers and we can only hope that they don't put themselves in any avoidable danger by walking home alone.'

Inspector Howarth had been in the force for some time and he was a shrewd, conscientious officer. He was well aware of all that was going on in his area and made a point of studying all incoming notices from the other forces around the country. He had read with some disquiet the information about the deaths of the nurses around the country and the fact that the latest killing was so close to home. His youngest daughter was a nurse at the Cottage Hospital and he had already made a point of visiting that establishment to ensure that the warning posters sent by Chief Inspector Love were clearly displayed on all available notice boards. He looked at Harriet and she noticed the anxious look on his face. He spoke in a quiet, solemn voice.

'The men have been briefed about the nurse killer, Ma'am. I have read all your briefings and have personally checked that your posters are clearly displayed at the Cottage Hospital and both old people's homes in the area. We have also placed the posters on various notice boards in the town. Apart from that we do extra patrols in the hospital area and the men have been advised to check anyone looking the slightest bit suspicious anywhere near nursing establishments.' Paul Howarth did not add that he was personally sick with worry and was prepared to do anything he could to assist in catching the murderer.

'Thank you, Inspector. There's not a great deal more that we can do.'

'Mind you,' added, Ed. 'We have to stress that we're not sure that this character has anything to do with the nurse murders. At the moment we just know that he has been harassing Miss Farndon, who happened to be at the hospital where the workers were treated after the factory fire.'

'We are still trying to trace him,' added Harriet, 'and it would be helpful if we could find him so that we can eliminate him from our enquiries.'

'I wish you luck,' said Paul Howarth. 'The sooner we discover who this madman is the better. I'll be in touch if I have anything to report, Ma'am.'

Harriet handed the Inspector her card. 'My mobile number is on there as well,' she said, 'should you need me urgently.'

DCI Love and DI Harrington left Amchurch police station. As they passed through the outer door and by the enquiries window, Harriet glanced briefly at Neil Johnson. 'Thank you, Sergeant,' she said. Ed gave his customary nod and was convinced that the arrogant Sergeant all but bowed to Harriet as she went by. *Upstart*, thought, Ed, following his boss out to the car park.

Once in the car, Harriet spoke. 'Shall we try the local pub, Ed? It's well past lunchtime and I don't think there is any need to visit the Cottage Hospital. It seems that Inspector Howarth is well aware of the situation and is keeping a keen eye on things.'

'He's certainly on the ball,' agreed, Ed. 'I shouldn't think much escapes his notice.'

'Right,' said Harriet. 'Shall we find the pub?'

'If you like, Ma'am. I could certainly eat something.' He started the car and drove back down the road they had come in on, remembering that he had seen the Hare and Hounds as they approached from Station Lane. The public house was small and quaint, with oak beams and numerous horse brasses hanging from the low woodwork. Ed had to bow his head as he moved through the bar area but he was able to stand upright when he reached the bar. 'Coffee, Ma'am? Or will you risk something stronger, as I'm driving?' He turned to Harriet as he spoke. As he looked at her, he was once again struck by her handsome face. Again he felt that twinge of guilt, unable to explain why he felt jealous and why he was uneasy in her presence.

Harriet smiled, making her green eyes sparkle. 'Are we being humorous, Inspector?'

Ed fidgeted and wished he hadn't made the reference to 'something stronger'. Harriet put him out of his misery. 'Coffee will be fine, thanks, as I see it's Kenco.'

Ed ordered two coffees and a plate of sandwiches and they retired to a corner table. 'Are we making headway, Ed?' asked Harriet as she sat down with a sigh.

'I think things might be clearer when we finally catch up with Samanntha Farndon and track down this Murdock chap.'

'His name will be on the lists that Jack gave us. We'll check them as soon as we get back to the Station. You can be sure that there will only be one Murdock. Let's hope that Jack has now been able to trace the whereabouts of all the patients from the fire, especially this Murdock.'

'Let's hope so.'

'It's nearly two weeks since the first murder on our patch, Ed, and the powers that be will soon be getting nasty if we don't come up with something. That means my head will be on the block.'

Ed wanted to reassure DCI Love, but words failed him. He could not bring himself to show her compassion or concern for her predicament. He again felt that anxiety about getting too friendly with this woman and he was grateful that their lunch arrived at that moment and the necessity to respond was overtaken by events.

While DCI Love and DI Harrington were travelling to Amchurch, Sergeant Marlow and Sally Pringle were on their way to Leicester. They were relieved to find Mrs Charteris at home. She remembered Charlie, and invited him and Sally into her front room. 'More questions, I suppose,' she said. 'What would you like to know?'

'Simply confirmation that Dave Spalding arrived home at 8.30 from Nottingham on the night of Friday 24th. You informed me on my last visit that you always care for his cat whenever he is away or expected to be late home, so I'm sure that you will remember what the arrangements were on this particular Friday.'

'I can see what you are getting at, Sergeant, Friday the twenty-fourth was the night that that nurse was murdered, wasn't it? And yes, I can remember it well. Dave was home by eight thirty, no doubt about that; I popped round and told him not to go out to get food as I had made a lasagne specially for him and would bring it round if he wished.'

'And?' Charlie waited for the remainder of the tale.

'He said he would be very grateful for the food and I took it round about twenty minutes later. This means he was at his house next door at nine that night, and I could hear him moving about until very late, eleven-ish at least.'

'Thank you once again, Mrs Charteris.' Charlie closed his notebook. 'That's all we need to know for the time being.'

'You're barking up the wrong tree, you know, if you think Dave Spalding killed anyone. He may appear a bit intense at times, even a little strange, but he wouldn't harm a fly, I promise you.' Mrs Charteris stood on the doorstep and watched as the two officers left.

'Let's hope you're right, Mrs Charteris,' said Sally as she followed DS Marlow from the house, disappointed that she had not met the man herself.

As Charlie started the car he turned to, Sally. 'The DCI has asked us to call on June McFarland to ask her for a photograph of Spalding. Prepare yourself for a shock, Sally, she isn't a pretty sight.'

Charlie was in high spirits as he drove back to Torreston, although Sally was somewhat subdued having witnessed the horrific disfigurement of June MacFarland. Charlie was thinking of his date with Liz that evening. His feelings towards the pretty Sister at the Cottage Hospital were beginning to take over his every thought. Whenever possible he met her at the front of the hospital when she came off duty and walked her home. He was anxious that the killer might still be in the vicinity, and having made Liz promise that she would never walk home alone, he made it his business to be around to do the escorting if she came off duty when he was free.

'You've really got it bad, haven't you, Sarge?' said Sally, forcing a smile, as she listened to Charlie chatting on about the wonderful woman he was dating.

'She's amazing, Sally. I never thought I could feel like this. I've always been a bit of a fly-by-night as far as women are concerned, and having been crucified by Claudia, I was determined not to get involved again for a very long time and now—'

'Along comes Liz,' interrupted, Sally.

'Yes! Along comes Liz.' Charlie grinned, keeping his eyes on the road. A feeling of warmth crept over him and he breathed in deeply.

'I'm happy for you, Sarge.' Sally really meant what she said. Sergeant Marlow was very popular in the police force, and for all his chauvinistic ways there was not a female at the Station who did not have a sneaking admiration for him.

'Thanks, Sally. I shall be taking her to the Gala Dinner tomorrow night. Can't wait to show her off.'

'I expect DCI Love will be going. Do you know if she had a partner?'

'Haven't the foggiest.' Charlie wondered about Sir Richard Fitzwilliam but he knew when not to gossip to subordinates and he said nothing to the young DC at his side. 'Are you going, Sally?'

'Hardly! The tickets cost an arm and a leg, and I don't think lowly constables would be welcome.'

'It's open to all ranks,' replied, Charlie, 'but I agree it is expensive. Still, I'm sure you'll hear all about it.'

'I'm sure I shall. I shall be spending most of Saturday at the athletics track. The Club has an important meeting coming up and I need to be fit.'

'You seem to spend a great deal of time training, Sally. Is it all worthwhile?'

'Certainly, if you enjoy athletics as much as I do.'

'Rather you than me. I don't think I could be disciplined enough to keep up the training. While you are aching in a hot bath, Sally, just think of me enjoying myself at the Gala Dinner!'

'I will,' smiled, Sally. 'But just see that you behave, Sarge.'

'My days of misbehaving are over,' replied Charlie. And for the first time in his life he knew that he meant it.

Chapter Thirteen

Harriet and Ed arrived back at Torreston police station at two thirty. Harriet had arranged her meeting with the press for four that afternoon which left her enough time to write up her report. First she needed to look at the lists of patients that Sergeant Jack Fuller had presented to her the other day. She took them from her drawer and ran her eyes down the names. Murdock Pollard. Here was the man they were looking for. Now all that was needed was for Jack to discover where he was living at present.

Charlie and Sally had already returned to the Station and were reporting to DI Harrington in the Incident Room. Charlie was speaking: 'I know this Dave Spalding is a creep, but his alibis do stand up. Mrs Charteris is adamant that he was at home all evening on the twenty-fourth. We have telephoned the Red Dragon in South Wales, where as we know he received a receipt for his stay there, and the manager remembers him from my description. He agrees that Dave Spalding was in the bar most of the evening. There's no way he could have nipped back here to kill someone.'

'Right,' said Ed. Turning to Bob Finch, he asked, 'What did you turn up in the case of Garry Hobbs and his stag party?'

'We spoke to six of the blokes who attended the party,' answered Bob. 'They can all vouch for Garry and agreed that he was with them the whole time.'

'Except for the time that he passed out and had to be put on a bed upstairs to recover,' added Narinder. 'We checked the room he was put in, and to leave the pub he would have had to come through the bar area to get outside. He couldn't have done that without being seen.'

'How long was he indisposed?' asked Ed.

'Just over an hour,' replied DC Finch. 'Barely time to get to the murder scene and back again and in the state he was in, pretty difficult, I would say.'

'We seem to be eliminating all our suspects at a rate of knots,' said Charlie. 'Who have we left in the frame, Sir?' Although they had been close friends for many years Charlie always addressed Ed as "Sir", or "Inspector" when they were in the presence of the other officers. Ed answered Charlie in his usual sombre fashion.

'We're checking out the victims of the factory fire in Leicester who were nursed at the Royal Infirmary. I have the list of names here and I see that there *is* a chap called Murdock. Now, he was the one who was interested in Nurse Farndon, and as yet we have not eliminated him from the enquiries. Jack will be here in a moment and hopefully he will have some information as to where he lives at present.'

'Why is this Murdock in the frame, Inspector?' asked Sally Pringle.

'We don't know that he is in the frame, but we do have to account for all the men who were nursed in the hospital after the fire. They are the only connection with nurses that we have left.'

Sergeant Fuller arrived at that moment. 'I've traced all the patients from the factory fire, Sir, with the exception of a man called Murdock Pollard. He seems to have vanished from the face of the earth.' He handed a piece of paper to DI Harrington. 'As you can see,' he added, 'all but one still live locally, but this last one, Murdock Pollard, seems to have disappeared. I've checked the records on deaths etc. – with no luck.'

'Interesting, very interesting,' murmured, Ed. 'Perhaps he is someone we need to look at more closely.' He left the Incident Room with Charlie and headed for DCI Love's office.

'Good morning, Ed, Charlie. I expect you have read the list of patients that Jack gave us and spotted the name Murdock Pollard.'

'We have indeed, Ma'am, but the interesting thing is that Jack can find no trace of him since he left the hospital.'

'I suppose he's still alive?' Harriet raised an eyebrow.

Jack has been through the records of deaths, Ma'am,' answered, Charlie. 'His name doesn't appear, so we can only presume that this Murdock chap doesn't wish to be found.'

'This seems to be the break we need, Ed. Let's see what his injuries were.' Harriet returned her attention to the paper she held. 'Severe burns to his back and legs, crushed pelvis and both legs broken.'

'Would account for the limp on the chap we are interested in.'
Ed too was beginning to feel hopeful.

'But why has he vanished?' asked Harriet.

'He has no criminal record according to the files,' said Ed. 'Well, that is, in the name of Murdock Pollard.'

'You think he's changed his name, then?' Charlie peered at the information on the desk in front of him. 'So he must have a very good reason for wishing to disappear.'

'Like murder,' suggested, Ed.

'Because he's our killer?' Harriet wrinkled her nose. 'Perhaps. Are there any photographs of the men from the factory? It would certainly help if we knew what he looked like.'

'I'll get someone on to that,' said Ed. 'Our best bet of course is Samanntha Farndon. When she returns from holiday we'll set up a photofit session with her.'

'In the meantime,' said DCI Love, 'I think perhaps I should like to visit Amchurch Hospital after all. 'If this Murdock *has* traced Samanntha, then he will have discovered where she works as well. I know Mrs Wilks said she thought she had put him off by saying she worked at Bedford, but this chap is no fool. If he knows where she lives then he knows where she works and I *do* think she is in danger.'

'It's a good job that she's away on holiday, then,' said, Charlie.

'But she's back on Sunday,' Ed reminded him.

'We'll go to Amchurch tomorrow morning,' said Harriet. And as Charlie glanced across at Ed she added with a smile, 'I know it's the Gala Dinner, Charlie, you'll be back in plenty of time, I promise.'

Charlie grinned. 'Thank you, Ma'am. I take it you will be there too?'

'I shall. I was informed that it would be bad form for me to miss such an occasion, so I hastily purchased a ticket. You'll be going won't you, Ed?'

'I shall, Ma'am. I always escort my mother, who has a special invitation being the wife of a police officer who won the George Medal.'

'Of course, Ed. How very proud you must feel.'

Ed nodded, but as usual did not elaborate on the subject. 'What time would you like us here tomorrow?'

'Well, I shall be in early as I have quite a bit to do. But shall we leave for Amchurch at nine – and if you don't mind, could we go in two cars. I would like to dash off after our visit to the hospital as I have a few calls to make.'

'That suits me fine,' replied Ed. 'Charlie and I have things to do as well before we leave, so nine will be about right.' He turned to, Charlie. 'I'll pick you up at the usual time tomorrow, Charlie. I won't say don't be late, as I think your timekeeping of late has been exemplary.'

'Good grief, praise from Harrington,' quipped, Charlie.

'Must be the new woman in your life,' said Ed with the semblance of a smile. 'You'll be showing her off tomorrow night, I don't doubt.'

Harriet noted the banter between the two friends and wished that Ed would respond similarly towards her. She had a keen sense of humour and enjoyed a laugh with colleagues, but at present felt obliged to curb her temptations to be amusing when with the DI, as usually her jokes fell on deaf ears.

Ed and Charlie left her office and Harriet prepared herself for the visit from the press. She dislike intensely facing reporters; not because she was in any way nervous or intimidated by their presence but because she felt that they were always determined to find fault with the work the police were doing or criticised what they had already done. The police never appeared to be doing the correct thing in the eyes of the press. Harriet gathered some papers together and put them in a folder, just in case she wished to refer to them. She knew she needed to be careful. She had no intention of letting anything slip that might let Murdock guess that they were looking for him.

At four on the dot Sergeant Yates telephoned from downstairs to inform Harriet that the press had arrived.

'Would you show them to the interview room, please, Pete. I am ready for them. How many are there?'

'Fourteen or fifteen, Ma'am.'

'Right, I can probably handle them,' laughed Harriet. 'See you in five minutes.'

The group of journalists were from the local papers as well as the nationals and all but three of them were men. They eyed the DCI up and down as she entered the room.

'So you're the new broom,' said a tall thin man with wispy fair hair and piggy eyes.

In return Harriet looked at him with steady green eyes. 'If you mean am I the new Detective Chief Inspector, then yes I am. The name is Harriet Love, and you are?'

'Colin Bragg of the Northampton *Tribune*.'

A large chubby man whose appearance was decidedly scruffy, stepped forward. 'Tom Cavendish, *The Mail*, Ma'am. Most people call me Beefy.' He grinned, exposing very yellow teeth and Harriet wondered whether he was called Beefy because of his size or because he consumed an enormous amount of beef. A third member of the group who made a point of stepping forward to introduce himself was Michael Dellaware of the *Herald*, another local paper. He was younger than the other two who had presented themselves to Harriet. He was tall with dark hair and keen brown eyes. He was smartly dressed in a suit with a tie and spoke in a quiet, well-educated voice. He smiled a warm smile as he introduced himself.

'Please sit down,' said Harriet, indicating the chairs that had been arranged in readiness for the interview. 'Now, I think it would make more sense if you introduced yourselves as you asked your question. I can't promise to remember all your names, but I shall do my best. Who would like to go first?'

Colin Bragg peered at her through his small eyes. 'No one told us you were a beauty queen.' He giggled at his joke and Beefy sniggered.

'I can do without any smart-alec remarks,' snapped Harriet. 'I am far too busy to be able to waste time on your sad humour. Now, either you wish to ask sensible questions or please leave; I have a great deal to attend to and most certainly can't afford the time that I have put aside for you.'

'Sorry,' muttered Bragg. 'I was just breaking the ice.'

'Consider the ice broken. Now! Ask your questions.' Harriet's green eyes gleamed and she looked around the group in anticipation.

A tall young woman rose from her chair. 'Rosemary Ware, the *Independent*. First off, Detective Chief Inspector, I should like to congratulate you on you post here in Torreston. We women are more than pleased to see top jobs being held by females.' Harriet smiled and nodded her thanks as Rosemary continued. 'My question is, do you think this killer is likely to strike again in this area?'

'We have no idea as to where he might strike again. Up until these local murders he had never struck twice in the same place. This change in his pattern is somewhat disconcerting but we have alerted all hospitals and have not ruled out the possibility of another attack close to home.'

Michael Dellaware spoke quickly. 'How close are you to an arrest, Ma'am? I understand that several men have been questioned about the murdered nurses, but no one appears to have been charged as yet.'

'That is so,' agreed Harriet. 'Until we are absolutely sure of our facts we shall not be charging anyone. We have eliminated several suspects and I am confident that the net is closing in on the real killer.'

'What can you tell us about this "real killer"?' Tom Cavendish licked his stubby little pencil and prepared to write in his notebook with equally stubby fingers. 'We haven't been told much.'

'I am hesitant to tell you anything,' answered Harriet. 'It would be irresponsible of me to give away confidential information at this stage. But I can assure you that we do have a suspect and as soon as we have our man you will all be informed.'

Colin Bragg, still smarting from the sharpness of DCI Love's tongue, snapped his next question. 'Don't you think two weeks is long enough for this killer to go undetected? It doesn't appear that the Police have done a great deal towards catching him.'

'That is of course the sort of response one would expect from someone ignorant of police procedure.' Harriet smiled sweetly at Bragg, who felt himself going red. 'Elimination of suspects can be a slow, tedious task, but to ensure that the right person is charged, then that is the route that we have to follow.'

Bragg was persistent. 'The total of dead women across the country is now...er...seven, or is it eight? And they started months ago. Not very good, as far as I can see,' he smirked. 'Puts the police in a very bad light.'

Harriet voice remained calm. 'There was little to link these killings initially, but finally, through hard and dedicated police work, we think we have discovered a connection. However, at this stage of the investigation I have no desire to impede our inquiries, which I am happy to inform you are going to plan, by disclosing details of our suspects at this time.' Harriet cast her eyes over the group. Beefy was writing furiously, licking his little pencil at regular intervals, while Bragg looked decidedly gleeful as he jotted down one or two notes. Michael Dellaware smiled to himself as he wrote. He was thinking what an amazing woman this Harriet Love was. No one would get the better of her very easily, and most certainly not the slimy Bragg or the scruffy Beefy. He looked up and caught Harriet looking at him. They both smiled. 'Something else, Mr Dellaware?' she asked.

'Just one thing, Ma'am. I take it you are convinced that the killer of the two local nurses *is* the same person who has killed nurses in other parts of Britain?'

'Yes, I'm afraid so.' Harriet's face clouded. 'We are dealing with a serial killer, and no one knows better than I that we need to apprehend this person as quickly as possible before he strikes again.'

'You say there is a possibility of him striking again,' snapped Beefy. 'So what exactly are the police doing to prevent this happening?'

'All the hospitals have been alerted as I told you and we have put up posters advising nurses on ways to safeguard themselves. A close watch is being put on all these establishments.' Harriet cast her eyes around the room. 'But let's hope we apprehend him before he can strike again.'

A few more questions were asked by the journalists before Harriet was obliged to ask them to leave as she was inundated with paperwork which urgently needed her attention. Bragg and Beefy left her office with the rest of the journalists but Michael Dellaware loitered for a moment. 'I wish to apologise for the behaviour of some of my colleagues,' he said to Harriet. 'We're not all as rude as they are.'

Harriet laughed. 'There is no need to apologise. I meet all sorts in this job and some of them are pretty grim, I can assure you. I take it all in my stride and accept it as part of my workload.'

'I wish you luck in the case,' said Michael, 'and I hope I have the pleasure of meeting you again.'

'Thank you.' Harriet shook the hand that was offered. 'Let's hope that next time we meet I have some better news for you.'

Michael Dellaware left the police station in somewhat of a daze. He felt intoxicated by the auburn-haired woman who had been standing in front of him for the past half-hour. He had to see her again. Her perfume still lingered in his nostrils and her beauty was trapped inside his mind. He could hear her calm, voice. It was pure music, and her laugh was like the gentle tinkling of bells. Yes! He had to see her again, had to convince himself that she was real. He strode towards his car with a spring in his step. Perhaps his new job here in Northampton was going to be more interesting than he had anticipated. He jumped into his car to return to his office to do justice to his report on this serial killer who was hunting nurses.

Harriet sighed and stretched her long arms above her head. It was barely five and yet she felt that she had been on duty for an interminable length of time. She took her coffee beans and cafetière from the cupboard in her desk and went to the kitchen. She could survive without food but she needed her infusion of coffee at regular intervals. As she waited for the water to boil Charlie entered. 'Snap!' he said with a grin. 'I'm coffee boy.'

'There's plenty of water for us both,' smiled Harriet. She poured water into her own pot and held out the kettle waiting for Charlie to put forward his cafetière, the one she had recently bought the team.

'Oh, thanks.' Charlie held the pot while Harriet poured in the water. 'Coffee never tasted so good before you gave us this.' He stirred the coffee grounds vigorously before resting the filter lid gently on the top of the glass jug.

Harriet's eyes twinkled as she looked at the Detective Sergeant. 'Tell me about the new lady friend, Charlie.'

Charlie shuffled his feet. 'Oh well, Ma'am, she really is something special.' For once Charlie looked almost sheepish. 'I met her at the Cottage Hospital when we were carrying out our investigations after the murder of Carol Young. She's a Sister there.'

'Well, at least something pleasant has come out of this dreadful case,' said Harriet, her smile fading. 'What motive has this beast got for killing young innocent nurses, Charlie?'

'God knows, Ma'am, but it certainly gives you the creeps, specially when you're involved yourself with someone in the nursing profession.'

'How are the nurses coping with the situation?'

Charlie frowned. 'They're all pretty nervous about being out on their own but they're doing as our posters suggest. Moving about in groups and staying away from quiet roads. I collect Liz from the hospital myself whenever her duty allows, but when she's doing a difficult shift she makes sure she goes to and from work with friends.'

'We must get him, Charlie, and soon.'

'We will, Ma'am, I'm convinced of that.' Charlie left the kitchen to return to the Incident Room leaving the smell of coffee floating down the corridor.

Harriet returned to her office. She liked Charlie and his enthusiasm, and was more than pleased to hear him speak in such a positive manner about catching the killer. Of course they would catch this madman. The net was closing in all the time. Once they could determine who this Murdock fellow was, then the rest of the jigsaw would fall into place. But who was Murdock Pollard? Where was he at this moment?

In the Incident Room, Ed was leaning over the shoulder of Jack Fuller as he scanned through the various files on births, deaths, convicted murderers and men known to inflict bodily harm on women. 'Nowhere does the name Murdock Pollard crop up, Sir,' said Jack. 'I'll keep hunting through files, you never know, but as far as I can see this bloke has vanished.'

'Then he has to have changed his name.' Ed spoke in a hard voice. 'And if he has changed his name, then it's for devious reasons, you can be sure of that.' He turned and walked over to the notice board just as Charlie returned with the coffee. 'Thanks Charlie, pour me a black one.'

Charlie handed out mugs of coffee before joining the DI at the board. 'What's new?' he asked.

'Just that this Murdock fellow vanished as soon as he left the

Infirmary. I'd like you and Sally to go back to the hospital and check his files and see if there is any clue as to where he might have gone. They will have his old address; check it out and see if the neighbours know where he went.'

'I can do that now if Sally is happy to work late. Liz is on the late shift so that she can have tomorrow night off for the Gala Dinner, so I'm free to work as late as you like.'

'Good! Finish your coffee and go and find, Sally.'

Sally as always was eager to get involved. The Chief Inspector had taken the time to tell her personally that an application for an exhumation order on Mrs Caldwell had been sent to the Coroner's Office and she was really feeling part of the team. In fact she decided, everyone was feeling involved and all regarded themselves as an important spoke in the wheel. She was over the moon when Sergeant Marlow asked her to accompany him to the Royal Infirmary in Leicester.

'Of course I'll come, Sarge. Unlike you, I have no love life at present so all my nights are free.'

'How sad, Sally,' grinned Charlie knowing full well that the pretty DC had plenty of young men falling at her feet to date her. Together they left the police station and headed for the car pool.

DCI Love entered the Incident Room and joined Ed at the notice board. 'No luck in finding Murdock Pollard then?' she said.

''Fraid not. I've sent Charlie and Sally back to Leicester to see if neighbours at his last address might know where he went when he came out of hospital.'

'Good! He can't have vanished into thin air, even if he has changed his name.'

'What we need of course is a photograph.' Ed wiped his brow with the back of his hand. 'Phew! It's hot today. I doubt if our killer would dare go out in his woolly hat and anorak in this weather.'

'I suppose at night it's not so conspicuous. And in the dark people don't really take any notice, do they?'

'It doesn't get dark that early,' said Ed. 'It must have been reasonably light when he killed Monica. She was going on duty for nine.'

'Has anyone come forward to say they saw someone on the park that night, who fits our suspect's description?'

Ed shook his head. 'No such luck. People either don't wish to be involved or they walk around with their eyes closed.'

'Do you think we should put out the description of this man and appeal for any sightings of him?'

'Anything is worth a try, I suppose,' agreed, Ed.

'Of course we need to tread carefully, as at the present time his only crime is being seen at the nursing home and possibly near Samanntha's house.'

'It's the old story,' said Ed. 'We need him to come forward so that we can eliminate him from our enquiries.'

Harriet smiled. 'I should think that the public get fed up with hearing that statement.'

Ed nodded. 'Trouble is, it's the truth. Perhaps this chap is totally innocent, in which case he will come forward.'

Harriet was thoughtful. 'I'll get in touch with Central TV News. They're always helpful in cases like this. I'll say just that Ed. That we need to eliminate this man in an anorak and woolly hat from our enquiries. If he has nothing to hide he will contact us.'

'That sounds sensible to me, Ma'am.'

Harriet left the Incident Room and returned to her office to telephone Central Television.

Detective Sergeant Charlie Marlow and Detective Constable Sally Pringle arrived at the Leicester Royal Infirmary late that Friday afternoon. Charlie had telephoned the hospital to request seeing the files on Murdock Pollard, and Mahar Jellad had agreed to stay in the records department and await their arrival. 'I normally finish at five,' she explained to Charlie, 'but as you explained that it was urgent and tomorrow being Saturday, when I don't work, I thought I ought to oblige and stay on.'

'That's really good of you,' replied, Charlie. 'As I said on the phone, we are desperate to track down this killer and we have very few leads. This Murdock Pollard is one chap that we so far have been unable to cross off the suspect list.'

Mahar had shown them into the room where all the hospital records were kept. 'We have to store them for ten years after the patient has been discharged, and as you can see we are running short of space. Now here is the year that you are interested in and the Ps are the next row. Here we are!' She stopped and began peering closely at the filing cabinet drawers. Swiftly she pulled one of them open and quickly riffled through the folders. She took one from the drawer. 'Pollard,' she read. 'Murdock James.' She handed the folder to, Charlie. 'I'll leave you to read through it. I'll be at my desk when you've got what you want.'

Charlie took the folder and went over to one of the tables at the side of the room. He and Sally sat down and began searching through the file inside the folder.

'According to this Sarge,' said Sally, 'this Murdock was discharged to his home here in Leicester. Forty-nine Newbold Road.'

Charlie wrote the address down. 'It says here that his next of kin is his mother, Mrs Mary Pollard, and her address is Stirling, Scotland. Crikey, Sally, that's where the first murder of a nurse was reported.'

'Yes it was,' said Sally in an excited voice.

Charlie wrote this address down as well. Sally took some photographs from the folder. 'Look at these, Sarge. Not a pretty sight, are they?' She placed the prints in front of Charlie and he found himself looking at horrendous burns to someone's back and legs. He read the report of the injuries that Murdock Pollard had suffered in the factory disaster. He wrote for several minutes before finally looking up.

'Right I think we have enough information, Sally. Time to move.'

They thanked Mahar for waiting for them and left the hospital to visit 56 Newbold Road.

It was after midnight before Harriet finally crawled into bed. Her brain was still in a whirl and she was unable to stop images of a man in a woolly hat, chasing young nurses down dark lanes, flashing through her mind. She tossed and turned in her bed until finally she rose and put on her dressing gown to go downstairs. There was no sign of Toastie. He was obviously out on the prowl. Harriet would have liked a cup of coffee but knew that this would only aggravate her insomnia. She picked up the cafetière and reluctantly put it down again before pouring herself a glass of cold milk and taking it with her into the sitting room. She picked up her folder on the 'nurse murders' and curled up on the settee. Harriet spread all the information she had on all the dead women on the coffee table in front of her and read through the names again and again. There had to be a connection. Why had the killer moved across the country killing. Or rather *down* the country. The first murder had been in Scotland, in Stirling... She went over the names and places once more. Suddenly Harriet gasped. She grabbed her pen and started writing furiously. After a few moments she leaped to her feet and went to the telephone where she dialled Ed's number. Ed's alert voice answered on the second ring. He was used to calls in the middle of the night and his brain clicked into action automatically. He heard the DCI's excited voice. 'Ed, I've got something, I've found a real clue – can you come over?'

Ed glanced across at his bedside clock. It was one thirty. 'Give me twenty minutes.' He shot out of bed and dashed to the bathroom. He cleaned his teeth before pulling on jeans and a T-shirt. DCI Love had sounded jubilant on the telephone, and he was eager to discover just what she had uncovered. He arrived at Magnolia Cottage, where many of the rooms were lit up, and walking swiftly up the drive he knocked lightly on the front door. Harriet opened the door immediately. She was now dressed, and her face, which was scrubbed clean and without make-up, was alive with excitement.

'Come in, Ed, come in. I've made coffee. I wasn't going to because it doesn't exactly help me sleep, but I think we are going to need it at this moment.' She pushed open the sitting room door. 'Go and sit down and I'll bring the coffee.'

She vanished down the hall to the kitchen and Ed entered the room where the large Maine Coon sidled up to him and rubbed against his legs. Toastie had appeared through the cat-flap the moment he heard his mistress moving about, and his return had paid dividends as he had been rewarded with an extra plate of food. Ed bent down and stroked the long fur, which made Toastie purr immediately. The big cat tuned his head and sniffed the stranger's hand. He would know this man next time he called.

Harriet arrived with a tray of coffee and biscuits. 'I couldn't sleep Ed so I got up and went over all the information we had on the murders. I changed tack and instead of going over the names of the victims I concentrated on the names of the places where they were murdered.' She began pouring the coffee. 'See what turned up?'

Ed leaned forward to see what Harriet had written. 'What did you discover?'

'Just look.'

Ed picked up the sheet of paper and read the list.

1.	Scotland	Stirling
2.	Scotland	Airdrie
3.	Scotland	Motherwell
4.	Scotland	Annan
5.	England	Newcastle
6.	England	Northallerton
7.	England	Sheffield (Nurcroft)
8.	England	Northampton (Torreston)
9.	England	Northampton (Harbourne)

Ed looked up into the bright green eyes and the face which although devoid of make-up, was as beautiful as ever.

'You see?'

'You can spell SAMANNTHA from the murder scenes.'

'Exactly. There are three Ns and he needed only two, but he was never successful. Two of the nurses survived: June Pawlett in Northallerton and Sheila Werrington in Nurcroft. But he did manage one of the Ns, the nurse in Newcastle, so he gave up on the second N and moved on to the T, which was Torreston.'

'My God!' Ed leaned back. 'So the real target *is* Samanntha and, the A is Amchurch.'

'That's what it looks like.' Harriet stirred her coffee vigorously. 'Only people who know Sam would spell her name with two Ns. It has to be someone who knows her well. We must put her under protection when she returns from holiday, Ed.'

'Well done, Ma'am. So much for too much coffee and

sleepless nights!' Ed actually smiled and his praise sounded sincere.

Harriet felt herself flush. 'I'm sorry I woke you up, Ed, but I just couldn't wait until morning. I suddenly saw the spelling as I sat here gazing at my list. It hit me like a bombshell.'

'No problem. I'm as delighted as you are to know that there is, after all, a connection. At least we can now understand what we are up against. If Samanntha is the next on the hit list then our deduction that Murdock Pollard is our man becomes decidedly more realistic.' He finished his coffee and rose, putting a hand over his mouth to cover a yawn. He smiled again and Harriet thought what a transformation. 'Sorry,' he said. 'But don't worry, I'm always able to get back to sleep after a disruption.'

Harriet showed him to the door and placed a hand on his arm. 'Thanks for coming, Ed. I'll see you in the morning.' She gave one of her disarming smiles, which made her eyes sparkle and her whole face come alive.

Ed turned quickly and walked down the drive. He raised a hand as he went 'Till tomorrow.'

Harriet stood on the doorstep for a few moments and watched the car move away. Perhaps there had been a small breakthrough tonight, and she did not mean only in the murder case.

Chapter Fourteen

The sun was already breaking through when Harriet rose the next day, Saturday, and she hummed to herself as she busied herself in the kitchen. She fed Toastie, having given him his customary hug and fondle, then she switched on the kettle to make her first pot of coffee before running up the stairs to turn off the taps of her bath, the water of which was perilously close to the top. It was Harriet's idea of heaven to lie in a hot bath with a mug of coffee within arm's reach, and this morning as she lay there, she once again mulled over what she had discovered in the early hours of the morning. She was surprised that she did not feel tired after the long night but she was stimulated by her discovery and knew that this would keep her going for hours to come. There was still another day to wait before the return of Samanntha Farndon. Would this young woman be able to help them solve the mystery of the missing Murdock? Or was he really no more than a frustrated admirer of the young nurse? The ringing of her telephone broke into her thoughts and grabbing her bathrobe, Harriet hurried downstairs. She lifted the receiver and heard the voice of Charlie Marlow.

'Sorry to call you so early, Ma'am but I thought I ought to inform you about something that Liz – you know, my nursing friend from the Cottage Hospital – told me last night.'

'Go on, Charlie, what happened?'

'This chap, a Mr Skinner, caused quite a rumpus in A and E. He came in demanding morphine or stronger painkillers and went for the nurses when they asked him to sit down and wait his turn.'

'That's not totally unusual, is it, Charlie?'

'No, Ma'am but he shouted that all nurses were trash and they should watch out for themselves. Liz was on the late shift, and as I was working late at the Station I had arranged to collect her from the hospital. When she told me the story I recognised the name

Preston Skinner. He lives over the shops in Osborne Road where the body of Carol Young was found and he was subsequently interviewed by us after her murder.'

'Now that is interesting, Charlie. Why was he requesting painkillers from the hospital?'

'He's an outpatient there. Broke both his legs when he fell down the stairs at the flats and he attends the hospital for physiotherapy. Says he's had poor treatment from the hospital, especially from the nurses, who he insists show him no sympathy.'

'Right, Charlie. Put all this in your report and I'll get someone over to re-interview him this morning. I'll see you later as planned. Well done, and thank Liz for her help.'

Charlie hung up and turned to look at Liz, who lay in the bed beside him. 'Don't know what the DCI would say if she knew I had enticed you back here last night.'

Liz smiled. 'Not a lot, I should think. From what I have heard of your new boss, I should think she would most probably approve.'

'You're probably right.' Charlie kissed the woman who had turned his life around. He couldn't remember having ever felt like this before. What he had had with Claudia, he now realised, was not love but some sort of adoration of a beautiful woman who had infatuated him. Beauty, he decided, could sometimes be only skin deep and in his ex-wife's case that had certainly been true. He ruffled Liz's hair as he slid from the bed.

'Sorry I have to go on duty this morning, but you have a lie-in. I'll be back soon after lunch and then we can look forward to the Gala Dinner tonight. I think there will be one or two people very interested in seeing you. Will you cope with that?'

Liz laughed. 'I have to cope with far worse at the hospital. Don't worry, Charlie, I won't let you down.' The dark brown eyes of the twenty-nine-year-old sparkled as she gazed fondly at the tall muscular figure bending over her. Charlie kissed her forehead before heading for the bathroom.

Liz Jaques had always wanted to be a nurse and on leaving school had attended Birmingham University where she gained a BNs degree. Her first post as a Staff Nurse had been at Kettering

General, and two years ago she had accepted promotion here in Torreston at the Cottage Hospital, where she was now a junior Sister on Nightingale Ward. Liz loved nursing and could not imagine herself doing anything else. She had had one serious relationship in her life with a surgical registrar, Ben Cavendish, who was also on the staff at Kettering Hospital; but two years on, she had discovered that he was married. She was devastated by the discovery, and although he had told her that his marriage had been over for some time and that he had feelings only for her, Liz felt betrayed. It was the fact that he omitted to inform her that he was married that had damaged any trust that they might have had in their relationship. From then on, whatever she had felt for him diminished until finally she decided their life together was over. It was this break with Ben that had prompted her to apply for promotion, and now, having moved on, she was once again contented with life and greatly involved with her work. Having met gregarious Charlie Marlow, she was beginning to realise that there was more to life than just work. She knew that the feelings she was experiencing for this man were real and she had no intention of letting anything interfere with what the two of them were sharing.

Charlie appeared at the bedroom door. 'I'm off, Liz. I should be back by two. Have a good day.' He held her slender body in his strong arms and kissed her goodbye tenderly. He left the house to wait for the arrival of Ed.

DI Harrington and Charlie arrived at the police station at the same time as DCI Love. 'Lovely day,' called Harriet as she climbed from the red Lotus.

'Certainly is,' responded Charlie, feeling elated this morning after his first 'all night' with Liz.

Ed glanced across at his friend. He could see that Charlie was glowing, and half guessed that his relationship with Sister Jaques was more than just casual. He held up a hand in a near friendly manner to Harriet. 'Good Morning, Ma'am, it's going to be another scorcher.'

'Not a good day to be stuck in a car, then,' said Harriet. She addressed Charlie. 'Explain to Ed about Preston Skinner, Charlie and the incident at the hospital last night, and when you've done that bring your report to my office, will you; we have something to tell you as well. She looked across at Ed, who nodded briefly. 'We'll also sort out a plan of action before we leave for Amchurch.'

'Right, Ma'am. What's this about an incident at the hospital then, Charlie?' Ed asked as they walked across the car park together. Charlie related the story that he had told DCI Love earlier.

'I'll sit in the office and put it all in writing, Ed, if you'll call me when you're ready to visit the DCI. By the way, what's this news you two have to disclose.'

'Wait and see, Charlie. How long do you need to write your report?'

'Fifteen minutes. Twenty max.'

The two men went their separate ways. On entering the Incident Room, Ed discovered that Sally and Narinder had already arrived. 'My word,' smiled DI Harrington. 'Early birds this morning, aren't we? And it's Saturday too.'

'This case is really bugging us,' said, Sally. 'We thought we would quietly go over all the evidence on display and see if between us we might spot something.'

'Good idea. Tell me, which one of you carried out the interviews with the residents of Osborne Road after the murder of Carol Young.'

'I did Sir, with Bob Finch.' Narinder looked round from her scrutiny of the notice board.

Ed asked, 'Do you remember a character by the name of Preston Skinner? Lives above the shops where the body was found.'

Narinder thought for only a brief moment. 'I do,' she answered. 'He was hateful and vindictive, especially about the treatment he was receiving from the nurses at the Cottage Hospital. We put in our report that he was aggressive towards the staff there and perhaps needed a second interview.'

'I'll re-read your report,' said Ed. 'How mobile was he, Narinder?'

'He was able to walk slowly with sticks, but when he visits the hospital for physio he's taken and brought back by Garry Hobbs in the hospital car.'

'Seems he made it to the hospital under his own steam last night,' frowned, Ed. 'Caused something of a riot down in A and E when he demanded painkillers from the nurses. Security had to be called and he was escorted out of the building.'

'Is he a suspect in our murder?' asked, Sally.

'Well, he wasn't, but he goes on the list now. Perhaps one of you would go to the Cottage Hospital with Bob when he arrives and speak to the security people who were involved with the incident last night. I should like to know just how aggressive this Preston Skinner was and just how well he copes on his own two feet unaided.'

Narinder looked across at her friend. 'As I was the one who questioned him with Bob last time, I'll do the return visit, if that's all right with you, Sal. Here's Bob now.'

DC Bob Finch entered the room with Duncan McAllister. 'Are we late?' he enquired seeing the group standing in front of the notice board.

'Not at all,' said Ed. 'I've got a job for you, Bob.'

Ed explained to the officers what he wanted them to do that morning and then he left the room to collect, Charlie.

'Just finished,' said Charlie as Ed entered the CID room. 'Luckily I wrote up the report on our visit to Leicester yesterday afternoon as soon as I got back. Thank heaven for personal computers and a spell-check. Makes life so much easier.'

Together they went to Harriet's office and neither was surprised to smell the familiar aroma of freshly made coffee in the corridor. Charlie chuckled. 'I'm never quite sure which smell is the stronger when DCI Love is around. Her perfume or her coffee.'

Ed grunted but made no comment. He knocked lightly on the door and he and Charlie entered. Harriet looked up and smiled. 'Coffee's ready,' she said. She poured coffee into the three mugs and accepted the report handed to her by, Charlie. She read through it quickly. It was just as Charlie had explained to her over the telephone. Preston Skinner had arrived in Accident and Emergency at nine the previous night quite the worse for drink and demanded to be given an injection of morphine or an extra strong painkiller because, as he stated, 'The pain in my bloody legs is killing me – why don't you sods do something about it.'

The doctor on duty had been called, but as he was already engaged in an earlier emergency there had been a wait of some minutes. Skinner became more and more abusive and when the Duty Nurse had asked him to sit quietly he had physically given her a shove. It was at this point that Security had been alerted, and on arrival in A and E they had forcefully taken him by the arms and escorted him from the building. As he was being removed he began shouting abuse again. It was directed towards the nurses, and in one such outburst he had said, 'Just watch out, you bloody nurses! Think you are little angels, don't you, but I know different and you'll get yours, and sooner than you think!'

'Thank you, Charlie,' said Harriet, as she put down the report. 'I don't suppose you've had time to speak to Liz this morning, but when you do, please ask her if there has ever been an incident like this before, will you?'

Charlie did not meet the sharp eyes of the DCI but made a point of stirring his coffee vigorously.

He swallowed hard. 'Certainly I will,' he said. He was cross with himself. Why shouldn't he spend the night with the woman he loved, anyway. They were both adults and had every right to a private life, but somehow Charlie felt that he did not want details of his new relationship broadcast just yet. This romance was different, and he had no intention of being frivolous about what was going on in his life at present.

Harriet then read the second report that Charlie had given her. 'So Murdock Pollard's mother lives in Stirling.' She raised an eyebrow and looked at Ed. 'Stirling! the first murder scene.' She wrinkled her nose before adding, 'His neighbours in Newbold Street think he went to live at his mother's after his discharge from hospital.'

'They can't be absolutely sure,' said Charlie, 'but the chap immediately next to Number 56 saw the car that collected him and said it had *Ecosse* on the back window and the chap helping him into the car spoke with a strong Scottish accent. The driver had to assist Pollard because of his crutches. He guessed Pollard was going to his mother's in Scotland.'

'Did Pollard take everything with him?' asked Harriet. 'I presume someone else now lives in the house?'

'Yes, a young couple. Pollard rented the place fully furnished so the furniture and everything else came with it. He obviously had very little to move out when he left.'

Harriet closed the folder. 'Well done, Charlie, we will have to look into the Stirling link. But now we have something very significant to tell you.' She explained what she had discovered the previous night, or rather early this morning, and how she had called Ed from his bed to check her findings. She informed Charlie that they now realised that it was Samanntha who was the real target and that she must be kept under close guard.

'Wow! Who would have thought this crank would go to all this trouble and killing, just to murder on person!'

'Murderers move in strange ways, Charlie, as you should know,' said Ed. 'But in any event Samanntha is our main concern once she returns from holiday.'

Harriet rose from her chair. 'We will keep this bit of information under our hats for the time being. We don't want to alert the killer. For now we have a date at Amchurch. Are we ready to leave, gentlemen?'

It was five minutes to nine as the three officers left the police station together and minutes later the black Saab, followed closely followed by the red Lotus drove out of the car park.

At Amchurch Cottage Hospital they all met in the foyer. 'We'll report in and collect our Visitor badges,' said Harriet, 'then I think it might be an idea if we split up and talk to as many people as possible. Nurses, doctors, porters et cetera.'

'Right, where do you want to start?' Ed waited for Harriet to decide and he noticed the now familiar wrinkling of her nose as she thought.

'If neither of you have any objections, I should like to begin on the ward where Samanntha works. Shall we meet back here in an hour to compare notes?'

'Sounds like a good idea to me,' grinned, Charlie. 'Let's get those badges and start the ball rolling.'

At the security desk they showed their warrant cards and explained why they were visiting the hospital. They were handed their badges which they clipped on their jackets. Harriet lead the way to Reception where she asked the woman on the desk which ward Samanntha Farndon worked on. The woman manning the department flicked through a large folder and told her, 'Nurse Farndon is attached to Pitsworth, but she's away on holiday at the present time.'

'That's fine,' replied Harriet. 'It's her colleagues I wish to speak with.' She turned to Ed. 'I think it might be beneficial if you ask some searching questions here, about visitors and strangers asking questions about Samanntha. I'll head off to Pitsworth Ward.' She turned to leave. 'See you both in an hour.' The tall, slender figure walked gracefully up the corridor and momentarily Ed kept his eyes on the vanishing redhead.

Charlie chuckled. 'Does she look as glamorous when she's just got out of bed?'

Ed glared at his friend. 'That's not funny, Charlie. Last night was business and I couldn't even tell you what she was wearing, let alone what she looked like.'

Charlie coughed. 'Okay, Ed, shall we get started? Where do you want me to go?'

'I'll hang around here and speak to people in Reception. You wander off and grab anyone who may have any information that might help us.'

Charlie nodded and moved away to search for likely customers.

Harriet arrived on Pitsworth Ward and spoke to the Sister. 'I'm Harriet Love from the Torreston Police, could you spare me a few moments?'

The Sister was a small, thin woman in her mid-forties. She had sharp eyes and an equally sharp nose set in her narrow features. 'We're very busy, but if you tell me what you want to know, I'll do my best.'

Harriet explained the situation about the man they were looking for and asked if Nurse Farndon had ever mentioned being harassed since she had been working at Amchurch.

'Not as far as I know,' replied the Sister, 'but her close friend, Diane Willarby, is on duty this morning so you might be in luck. I'll call her over, but I really would be grateful if you didn't keep her too long. You can talk to her in my office.' She smiled at Harriet, making her severe face less intimidating. She moved away up the ward and seconds later a young nurse came towards Harriet.

'I'm Diane Willarby, a friend of Sam's. I believe you wish to speak to me.'

Harriet put out her hand in friendship. 'I'm Chief Inspector Love,' she smiled, 'shall we go to the office?' Once in the room Harriet sat down and Diane followed suit. 'Has Samanntha ever told you about a man who has been bothering her?' asked Harriet.

'There was a man when she was in Leicester, but since she moved here I don't think she has been harassed at all.' The solemn face looked anxious. 'Is something wrong?'

'Not that we are sure of,' replied Harriet, 'but we do need to be certain that there is no connection between the man annoying Samanntha and the maniac who is killing nurses.'

A light gasp escaped from Diane's lips. 'Sam was very bothered about the chap in Leicester but I don't think for one moment she linked him with any murders. She was upset at being hounded. Upset rather than frightened, if you see what I mean.'

Harriet nodded. 'I see. She's back from holiday tomorrow, I understand. When is she actually on duty again?'

Diane's hazel eyes looked at Harriet earnestly. 'Not until Tuesday morning. She's not in any danger, is she?'

'Let's hope not,' replied Harriet, 'but we nevertheless need to take precautions. Can she stay with you on her return? Just until we can flush out this character we would like to speak to.'

'Of course she can,' said Diane. 'We often stay at each others places anyway, so that's no problem. I have a house over in Torreston that I share with a colleague called Heather Howarth, and Sam's welcome to stay, there's plenty of room.'

'Good.' Harriet rose and placed a gentle hand on the arm of the young nurse in front of her. 'Just take care – and this applies to you all. Don't go out alone and most certainly not at night. Move about in groups until we have this man out of circulation. Hopefully that won't take too long.'

A few minutes later Harriet left Pitsworth Ward wishing she felt as confident as she sounded about catching the murderer.

It was eleven by the time the three colleagues met up in the entrance foyer. 'It has to be coffee time,' said Harriet, as she came up to Ed and Charlie. 'I can feel the withdrawal symptoms setting in.'

Charlie grinned. 'Wonder what sort of coffee they serve here…?'

'Hospital catering has improved by leaps and bounds, so I'm told, Charlie, so I shall expect the real thing. Come on, we'll find the restaurant and share what information we have discovered before going back.'

They followed the signs to the restaurant and Harriet was pleased to see that ground coffee was available. 'My turn,' said Harriet, briskly collecting a tray from the pile, not sure whether or not in fact it was. 'Coffee for you both?'

As Ed and Charlie both thanked her she went to the counter. Ed made his way to a corner table and he and Charlie sat down. Charlie stretched out his long legs.

'I'm becoming a coffee addict like our boss,' he grinned. 'Was never that keen until she introduced us to the real stuff.'

Ed gave his usual grunt.

Charlie carried on. 'Who do you think the DCI will bring to the Gala Dinner tonight?'

'How on earth should I know, Charlie? For heaven's sake, does it matter? You'll know soon enough anyway, but she'll most probably come on her own. A lot of us do, you know.'

'There's that tone again,' gibed Charlie. 'You could find a woman any time you choose, Ed. You've just got a chip on your shoulder and you're now being stubborn.'

'Put a sock in it, Charlie. When I meet someone I feel something for, I'll ask your advice – okay?' Luckily at that moment Harriet returned to the table carrying a tray with three coffees and three large Danish pastries on it. She placed the tray on the table and her face broke into one of her wide smiles, making her look very young.

'Couldn't resist the pastries,' she said. 'Hope you'll join me.'

'My pleasure,' replied, Charlie. 'I always have room for food and I'll only be having something light at lunchtime as I shall be gorging myself tonight.'

'Is the food good at these functions then?' asked Harriet.

'Top class, hence the cost of the tickets.' Ed had no qualms about paying out the exorbitant price for the Gala Dinner as the proceeds went to the Police Benevolent Fund, which was more than generous to the widows of policemen and the wives of those whose husbands were injured in the line of duty. His mother had already been a beneficiary and he was grateful.

Harriet sipped her coffee. 'Mmm, a life-saver. Now what have you two found out?'

'Not a great deal, I'm afraid,' said Ed. 'Security has been stepped up since we sent out our posters and warning notices, but no strangers have been spotted loitering in or even near the place.'

'Head of Security is an ex-copper,' added Charlie, 'and he really is on the ball. He considers himself guardian to all the nurses and God help anyone who attempts to harm one of them.'

'Well, that's reassuring news anyway,' smiled Harriet as she delicately wiped crumbs from her mouth. Seeing Charlie looking at her, she added, 'You can't east these things with any speck of elegance.'

Charlie grinned. 'No, but they're pretty good. Thanks for the treat, Ma'am.'

Even Ed agreed. 'Yes, thanks. I certainly feel better for that. You sometimes forget that you haven't eaten when you get involved with the job, and then you wonder why you feel light-headed.'

Harriet explained about the nurse who was Samanntha's friend and informed her colleagues how on Samanntha's return from holiday, Diane was going to invite her to stay at her house until the man they were looking for was found.

'That sound sensible,' agreed, Ed. 'By the way, did you know that one of the Staff Nurses at this hospital is the daughter of Inspector Paul Howarth who we spoke to at Amchurch police station the other day?'

'Really?' Harriet raised an eyebrow. 'The nurse that Diane Willarby shares with is called Heather Howarth; she must be his daughter. No wonder the poor chap is so concerned about the safety of the nurses here. He must be worried sick.'

'Is there anything else we can do before we return to Torreston?' asked Ed, packing away the plates and cups.

Harriet shook her head. 'No, I don't think so.' Looking at

Charlie, she added. 'I did promise we'd be back by lunchtime, didn't I.'

They left Amchurch Hospital and parted company at the car park. 'I'll see you both tonight,' called Harriet as she got into her car and drove smoothly away. Ed and Charlie followed in the Saab but by the time they had reached the main road the red Lotus was out of sight. 'The DCI has put her foot down,' commented, Charlie, 'perhaps she's got a date.'

'Now don't start again, Charlie. I really don't want to discuss Ms Love's personal life with you, or anyone else for that matter.' He picked up speed and headed for Torreston.

DC Bob Finch knocked on the door of Preston Skinner's flat. He looked at DC Narinder Pancholi and pulled a face. 'Let's hope he's not still feeling aggressive,' he said ruefully.

'He'll have slept it off by now,' replied Narinder. 'It was most probably the drink talking last night. I don't know why men drink to that level if they know they're going to change into monsters.' Before Bob could answer, the door was opened. Preston Skinner stood on the threshold looking decidedly seedy.

'What d'yer want?'

'Police,' said Bob, holding up his warrant card. 'Can we come in, please?'

Skinner stood to one side. 'If you must. I suppose this is about the trouble at the hospital last night. If they'd just given me some bloody drugs I'd have been away from there, no problem. But no, it's, "Wait your turn, Mr Skinner" … "We won't be long, Mr Skinner" … "Just a few more before you, Mr Skinner" … and so it went on until I blew me top.'

'You made some pretty dreadful threats towards the nurses,' said Narinder quietly.

'They don't care about me,' growled Skinner. 'Why should I be nice towards them?'

'You can't be abusive and throw your weight around in a public place like that,' said Bob, 'no matter what sort of raw deal you feel you might have had.'

'It were partly the drink,' muttered the somewhat subdued man in front of them. 'And the pain in me legs. Sometimes I can hardly bear it.'

'Have you seen your GP?' asked Narinder. 'I'm sure he will see to it that you are prescribed stronger painkillers.'

'It's a bloody long way to the surgery,' complained Skinner.

'You made it to the hospital well enough,' pointed out Bob. 'Perhaps next time you go for your physio you'd be as well to ask them for a prescription, or at least ask Garry Hobbs to take you round to the surgery in the hospital car.'

'When is your next appointment?' asked Narinder.

'Monday. I always go on Monday.'

'Before we leave,' said Bob, looking the man directly in the eye. 'Could you tell us where you were on the nights of Monday the twentieth and Friday the twenty-fourth?'

'Oh, now I see what all this is about.' Preston Skinner's voice became raised and instinctively Narinder took a step back. 'You think I'm that bloody killer, don't you? Just because I said a few offensive words about our angels of mercy, you think I go around killing them. Well, I ain't killed anyone, so bugger off!'

Bob stood his ground. 'Please answer the question, Mr Skinner, or perhaps you would prefer to come with us back to the Station to be interviewed.'

'Are you arresting me?' sneered the man.

'Not at the moment,' answered Bob. 'But I should be obliged if you would tell us where you were on the two nights I have mentioned.'

Preston Skinner sat down. 'I was nowhere. I don't go out at night. Where do you think I would go with these legs?'

'You were out last night,' said Narinder still a little wary of this man.

'So I went out last night. I've told you I were in pain and went to Casualty for help. Not that I got any.'

'So you have no alibi for the twentieth and the twenty-fourth,' persisted Bob Finch writing in his notebook.

'No,' came the sullen reply. 'And I never killed anyone neither.'

Bob and Narinder left the flat and returned to the car. 'You wouldn't like to meet him on a dark night, would you,' said Narinder, shivering.

'Certainly wouldn't,' agreed Bob. 'Let's get back and write up our report. Then it's up to the DCI to decide if she wants it taken any further.'

Ed and Charlie arrived back at Torreston police station and Ed told Charlie to go home. 'I'll finish up here, Charlie, you get off home. I'm sure you're meeting Liz before tonight.'

Charlie grinned. 'I promised her lunch out if I made it back in time. Thanks, Ed, I owe you one. See you tonight then.' And he was gone.

Ed went to the Incident Room. He hadn't a great deal to write up, just the name of the Head of Security at Amchurch Hospital and the fact that all there were on red alert. He would leave it to DCI Love to write up about Samanntha being the next target and the fact that she was going to stay with her friend Diane on her return from holiday. At least he could add all of this to the equation. Were they making headway? he wondered, as he read through the lists on the notice board. Life could certainly be made a great deal easier if Samanntha Farndon was back from her holiday and she were able to give them a description of this man Murdock. He had still not been found. Now that was suspicious, his disappearing like that. He was out there somewhere; people didn't just vanish. Unless they were dead, of course. Ed stuck a few more papers on the board and then retreated to his office to tidy his desk. He decided to wait for the return of DC Finch and DC Pancholi to see what they had to report on their interview with Preston Skinner, before he too would go home. DCI Love had decided to inform the team of their discovery of the murder places and the spelling of the name SAMANNTHA tomorrow at briefing, so he had no need to worry about that at present. He was not over-enthusiastic about attending the Gala Dinner tonight, but his mother always enjoyed the outing and he felt it his duty to attend.

He sat back in the chair and stretched his arms above his head. Would the DCI be attending tonight's function alone? he mused. He wondered why a woman such as Harriet Love was unattached, or had she a secret admirer tucked away somewhere? Of course, there was Mr Justice Fitzwilliam; he and Charlie had seen them together and looking extremely cosy. That would certainly be a scandal.

He jumped to his feet as he heard the voices of Bob and Narinder coming down the corridor. He must put DCI Love out of his mind. He was behaving in an irrational manner. If the woman did have an admirer then it was none of his business anyway, but all the same he was intrigued. Tonight all would be revealed no doubt. He went to the office door to greet the two DCs.

Chapter Fifteen

Harriet had dashed from Amchurch back to Torreston where she had booked a hair appointment. She now left the hairdressers and drove over to see her parents. They were always delighted to see their bright daughter and were eager to hear how the murder case was going.

'Slowly, I'm afraid,' was Harriet's reply. 'But I know we're going to crack it. I just have this very positive feeling about the way the case is unfolding.'

'Just be sure you get the right man, m'dear,' said her father, placing an affectionate arm about her slender shoulders. 'Don't be bullied into a decision you might regret later. We all know about the press and the bigwigs at the top who are desperate for a result. They insist you make an arrest, then the case gets to court and the chap is acquitted on some trivial omission of solid evidence by the prosecuting team, and that's him off the hook, guilty or not.'

'We know you'll do the right thing, dear,' smiled her mother. 'You're a chip off the old block, you know.' She slipped her arm through her husbands and looked up at the big man towering over her. 'Oh yes! Harriet's your daughter, all right.'

'And proud of it.' Harriet kissed them both fondly. She declined the invitation to join them for lunch, and left twenty minutes later to return home, where she prepared herself a light meal of tuna salad. She would spend the rest of the afternoon reading quietly in the garden, if it were at all possible to keep her mind off the murder case. She was now quite looking forward to the forthcoming Gala Dinner. It was some time since she had enjoyed a social evening among real friends and it would be a pleasant change to eat decent food. It was a hot afternoon, as predicted by Ed that morning. She sat down in the garden chair beneath a large colourful umbrella. Ed! What about the Chief Inspector? She was unable to fathom him out. He was always polite and respectful towards her, but somehow she had the feeling that he had something against her. Was it just because she was a woman? Harriet didn't think this was the case; Ed Harrington was not like that. She sighed as she opened her book. They had been working together on this case for two weeks and she felt that he was as cool towards her now as he had been on their first encounter, which now seemed like a life time ago. She turned her attention to *Faceless in the Fog* – a version of the Jack the Ripper story, but with a difference as it was from the point of view of the prostitutes in London in the 1880s. She smiled to herself as she began reading. Jack Fuller was probably correct in his assumption that this serial killer would have been caught had the police of the time had had access to modem techniques such as DNA profiling.

Harriet read for over an hour before deciding that she was too hot in the garden, even under the umbrella. Toastie had long since retreated to the coolness of the house and she followed his example. She would have her bath and then think about getting ready for the Gala Dinner. George and Nancy Hollyoak were picking her up at seven fifteen. Harriet was known for her punctuality and tonight would be no exception. She would be ready and waiting.

Ed arrived at the Guildhall with his mother and was greeted warmly by the Chief Constable, Brian Nattrass. 'Good evening, Harrington. Lovely to see you again, Mrs Harrington. May I get you some wine, or would you prefer sherry?'

'White wine would be lovely,' smiled Ellen Harrington.

'Red or white, Harrington?' asked Brian Nattrass. 'Or are you driving?'

'Red please, Sir, and no, I'm not driving, we came by taxi.' Their host departed to collect the drinks.

'Charming man,' said Mrs Harrington. 'He always makes a point of paying me some attention whenever we meet.'

'A small gesture in the circumstances,' replied her son dryly.

The Chief Constable returned with the wine and after a few more words he left to join his party at the top table. Ed looked around for Charlie, hoping he wouldn't be late, and was relieved to see him enter the room at that very moment. Holding onto his arm as if she never wanted to lose him was Liz, looking beautiful in a salmon pink gown, her dark brown hair framing her pretty face and her dark eyes sparkling. She looked almost frail against the tall, broad Charlie and barely came up to his shoulder. They came across the room and joined Ed and his mother. As they exchanged greetings, Ed glanced over Charlie's shoulder and caught sight of Harriet Love entering the room with George Hollyoak and his wife. Harriet was wearing an emerald green evening dress, which even from this distance made her eyes shine even greener. The silk gown accentuated the smooth, olive skin of her bare shoulders and her auburn hair was the crowning glory to a beautiful picture. Ed was transfixed, and it was Charlie who broke into his thoughts.

'Looks stunning, doesn't she?'

Ed pulled himself together. 'She's quite something, I have to admit. But come on, let's find our table. Number 3, I believe.' He turned abruptly and moved away.

Harriet and the Hollyoaks were assigned to the top table and as they were escorted across the room by Brian Nattrass, Harriet walked over to table Number 3.

'Good evening, everyone,' she smiled.

Ed rose to his feet quickly and introduced his mother.

'Mother, this is Harriet Love, our new Chief Inspector.'

'I'm delighted to meet you,' replied Ellen Harrington, gazing with admiration at the handsome woman in front of her.

'I'd far rather sit here with all of you, but I'm afraid I shall have to go, as top table is waiting for me. I should love to speak to you after the dinner, if I may.'

'I should like that very much,' agreed Mrs Harrington graciously.

Harriet floated away to join the main party, realising that for the first time Ed had used her first name. He'd introduced her to his mother as Harriet. It had sounded wonderful hearing him use her name and she wished that he could be as informal towards her during their working hours together.

Sir Richard Fitzwilliam and his wife arrived. Charlie caught Ed's eye.

'Sir Richard and Lady Fitzwilliam,' muttered, Charlie. 'This could be interesting.'

The Chief Constable hurried back across the room to shake hands with Sir Richard and his wife. The judge was all of six feet three tall with grey hair and a bushy RAF-type moustache. He was sixty-nine years of age and very distinguished looking. His wife, by contrast, was five feet four, petite and in her early sixties. Her short brown hair was expensively cut and her black silk dress was worn with great elegance. Ed watched as Harriet too turned and then hurried back towards the Fitzwilliams. The judge openly kissed her on both cheeks, his wife doing likewise, and again Charlie glanced across at Ed. He raised an eyebrow but Ed looked away without responding. It was none of his business.

The meal was excellent and Ed was pleased to see his mother enjoying herself. From time to time he cast his eyes in the direction of the top table and watched as Harriet chatted happily to her neighbour, the judge, with Lady Fitzwilliam sitting on her husband's right. George Hollyoak sat on Harriet's other side and Ed noticed how the striking woman was the centre of attention. The music was playing and the small dancing area was immediately taken to by many of the guests. Charlie grabbed Liz.

'Come on, Liz, let's see how good you are.'

'Be very careful about challenging me,' laughed Liz. 'The one thing I am an expert at is dancing, so you may have bitten off more than you can chew!'

'Oh Lord! Trust me,' grinned Charlie, pulling Liz onto the dance floor and sweeping her into his arms.

Mrs Harrington smiled. 'They make a lovely couple. It's good to see Charlie happy again.'

'It certainly is. He's very taken with Liz, as you can tell.'

'Chief Inspector Love is beautiful,' said Ellen Harrington. 'I had no idea she was so striking. And how clever to wear that green, it makes her even more attractive don't you think?'

Ed did not want this conversation, and after muttering some sort of reply he invited his mother to dance.

Michael Dellaware arrived at the Guildhall. He had persuaded his editor to give him the job of reporting on the Police Gala Dinner. He had been unable to rid his mind of the vision of the Chief Inspector since he had interviewed her and had decided that covering the Dinner would give him an opportunity of seeing her again. He stood in the doorway and cast his eyes around the room. The slender figure in green was dancing with the man he knew to be Mr Justice Fitzwilliam. He made his way across the floor and swiftly aimed his camera at the couple. Harriet turned her head as the camera flashed. She blinked and then smiled as she recognised the man she had spoken to recently.

'Sorry if I startled you,' grinned Michael, 'but the natural shots always turn out the best.'

'I'll forgive you, but only because I'm hoping for a generous report about our current case in your newspaper next week.' The couple had stopped dancing.

The judge looked down at his partner, his arm still around the slender waist. 'That sounds horribly like blackmail to me, young lady.'

Harriet smiled at the big man. 'Depends how you look at it. I call it diplomacy. What do you think, Michael?'

Michael Dellaware thought what a magnificent picture Harriet made, but said out loud, 'I think I'll agree with you, Chief Inspector, and call it diplomacy.'

'For heaven's sake call me Harry when I'm off duty. I'm an ordinary person outside the Station.' She turned back to face the judge and they began dancing again, moving away with a flourish. Michael stood watching the couple for a few moments before he moved off to do his duty in photographing the Chief Constable, Deputy Chief Constable Martin Cotton, and other guests.

From across the room Ed too was watching Harriet as she danced with the tall, distinguished figure of Sir Richard Fitzwilliam. What could a young attractive woman like Harriet Love see in a man old enough to be her father? He sighed and picked up his glass of wine. Charlie and Liz sat down beside him, Charlie openly puffing.

'Whew! I'm not as fit as I thought I was. I'll have to start back at the gym again if I'm to keep up with Liz. She's dancing me off my feet.'

Liz rose. 'Come on, Ed, show Charlie how it's done.' She placed a light hand on Ed's shoulder, and with one of his rare smiles, he stood, took her elbow and guided her onto the floor.

Charlie turned to Mrs Harrington. 'May I have the pleasure?'

Ellen took the arm that was offered. 'Charmed, young man, but don't expect me to be as lively as Liz.'

Charlie laughed out loud. 'I was hoping that would be the case! Liz has about killed me off.'

As the music faded, indicating the end of the dance, Harriet came over to table three. 'I thought I would never manage to get across to you.' She sat at the table next to, Ed. 'Are you all having a good time?'

'Best Gala Dinner ever,' said Charlie pulling an extra chair over. 'But of course, I'm biased. I've never had such a wonderful partner before.'

'It's always a pleasant evening,' said Mrs Harrington. 'I used to be very apprehensive about coming, but now I quite look forward to the occasion.'

'And you, Ed?' The green eyes looked straight at him.

'Oh, er, it's all right. The food is always very good and it pleases me to see Mother enjoying herself.'

'And you're an excellent dancer,' Liz laughed. 'After Charlie you are Fred Astaire.'

'Hey, come on, that's not fair!' Charlie defended himself vigorously. 'I didn't tread on your toes once.'

Liz was still laughing. 'That's because I'm pretty quick on my feet and kept out of your way.'

Ellen Harrington joined in the laughter and even Ed had to smile. 'I always said you had two left feet, Charlie,' he said.

A flash of a camera made them look up. 'Just a happy group photo,' said Michael Dellaware, 'you all seem to be having such a good time.' His smile was directed at Harriet. 'I have been asked by the Chief Constable to invite you to come to the top table for an official photograph. Sorry to drag you away, this table seems far more fun.'

Harriet wrinkled her nose. 'Sorry. I thought it was too good to be true that I might be able to get away from the senior members of the party.' She flashed a smile and walked away with Michael Dellaware to where the guests of honour were gathered in expectation of having their photographs taken.

Charlie was quick to notice that the judge took Chief Inspector Love by the arm and firmly placed her at his side. She turned and smiled at him and took her place without dissension. Lady Fitzwilliam stood on the other side of her husband with the Chief Constable and his wife beside her. The remainder of the group gathered and were duly placed in position by the businesslike reporter. The photograph was taken and Michael stood by George Hollyoak, writing down the names of the guest and putting them in the correct order to coincide with his photograph. Charlie turned his attention to Liz, who was talking to Ed. Ed had obviously not watched the group picture being taken so had not seen the possessiveness of Sir Richard Fitzwilliam towards DCI Love. Charlie shrugged his shoulders slightly and joined Liz and Ed. So the old boy fancied Ms Love! It happened all the time, what was new?

'My turn to dance with this beautiful woman,' grinned Charlie as he took hold of Liz's arm. 'Now why don't you ask DCI Love to dance, Ed?'

Ed made no reply but the look he gave his friend said everything. Liz glanced across at the top table. 'I should think she would far rather be over here with us than with all the dignitaries she is obliged to be pleasant to. They're all pretty ancient, after all. She looks like a fish out of water.'

Charlie looked at Ed but said nothing. He moved onto the dance floor with his partner.

Ed and his mother left the Gala Dinner at eleven thirty when the taxi that Ed had ordered arrived. Mrs Harrington was feeling tired and Ed was glad of an excuse to leave. He could not remember enjoying a Gala Dinner less than he had done tonight. He could not explain the hollow feeling in the pit of his stomach, nor the loneliness he was experiencing.

Charlie was happier than he could ever remember him being, even in those early days when he was first married to Claudia. Ed had a sneaking feeling of envy, although he was more than pleased for his friend. Charlie had been through some dreadful times and Ed would not wish that on anyone. Charlie had been correct when he had told him that he could have the companionship of a number of women if he wanted to. There were many with whom he was well acquainted who would leap at the chance of accompanying him to a function such as this. He had no reason not to date. He had done so in the past, so why not now? He did not look back across the room as he guided his mother through the door. He did not see the wistful look on the face of Harriet Love as she saw him leave without so much as a friendly wave.

Ed sat beside his mother in silence. Mrs Harrington understood her son well and gathered that he was under some kind of pressure, perhaps from work, and said little as the taxi wended its way through the traffic. They had never had secrets from each other, and since the death of her husband they had grown even closer, but this was not the time or place for her to interrogate her son. The taxi pulled up at Mrs Harrington's house and Ed walked his mother up the path to the front door, making sure she was inside with the door firmly closed and bolted before he returned to the waiting car to continue the journey to his own address. Next year he would take a partner. He had been stupid not to have done so this year. Now that Charlie was besotted with Liz and all his spare time devoted to her, it was time that he too made the effort to find himself a female friend. He had to move on. Everyone else seemed to be doing just that, and now so must he. He paid the taxi driver on arrival at his house and briskly walked up the path. He yawned. He had not realised how tired he was but then the week had been pretty hectic, and with no day off as yet, he was looking forward to a relaxing day tomorrow.

Sunday morning. The sun streamed in through the bedroom window as Harriet lay in bed thinking of the Gala Dinner and the strained behaviour of Ed Harrington. She wondered if perhaps she should have it out with him. If they were to be close colleagues, then this was no way to be behaving. They should be on first name terms and feel at ease with each other, but Ed was certainly not at ease with her and she had no idea why. Had she upset him in some way? Had she trodden on his toes over this murder enquiry? She did not think so; she was always very careful to include him in all her decisions and to seek his advice even if she did not really need it. Did Charlie know what the problem was? She could not ask Charlie's opinion, though. Ed was his superior and that would be unprofessional. But I bet he knows, thought Harriet, as she jumped out of bed. She had agreed to lunch with George Hollyoak and his wife Nancy today so at least she would have no need to cook. It was a beautiful morning and heavens, it was already nine thirty. She would dismiss all thoughts of DI Harrington. She went to the kitchen to make her first pot of coffee, gathering up her cat on the way and nestling her face in his thick fur. 'Are we hungry then, Toastie?' she murmured. 'Have you had to wait for me this morning?'

What would Mrs Harrington be able to tell her about her son? she wondered, as she placed the plate of cat food on the kitchen floor and then switched on the kettle. Just supposing if one day she somehow found herself in close proximity to Mrs Harrington's home and popped in on a courtesy call? A secret smile crossed her face. Women talked to each other; perhaps this was the way for her to discover what made Ed Harrington tick. She poured the hot water onto the ground coffee beans and sniffed the strong aroma with pleasure. Taking her tray of coffee into the sitting room, she placed it on the small table before collecting a file from her briefcase and taking it with her to her big armchair where she curled up. She made sure she was within easy reach of her coffee before opening the file.

Harriet began flicking through the pages. It was her personal file on the 'nurse murders' and she wished to remind herself of every detail.

It was two hours later that Harriet closed the file and placed it on the table beside her. She leaned back and closed her eyes, going over and over again in her head the names of the people connected with the hospital and those who were involved in the factory in Leicester. There had to be a connection here. They were on the right track, she was sure of it. The telephone rang shrilly in her ear and she picked up the receiver.

'Is that the Chief Inspector?' The voice was slow and hesitant.

'This is she,' replied Harriet.

'This is Mrs Wilks – you remember, I'm looking after Samanntha's house while she's on holiday.'

Harriet sat bolt upright. 'Of course I remember you, Mrs Wilks. Is anything wrong?'

'No. But I thought I ought to let you know that Sam has just telephoned to say her flight has been delayed and she won't be home until the early hours of Monday morning.'

'Thank you for letting me know, Mrs Wilks. Which airport exactly does she arrive at?'

'The East Midlands. It's the flight from Cyprus and should be landing around three a.m.'

'Thank you for ringing me, Mrs Wilks. Don't hesitate to call again if you feel there is anything I ought to be told, however insignificant it might appear to you.'

'I will. Thank you, Chief Inspector.' Mrs Wilks hung up, satisfied that she had done her duty. Her husband had insisted that she was making a fuss but she remembered what the young policewoman had said to her and she was determined to do her bit to help protect Samanntha and to catch this dreadful killer who was still at large.

Having spoken with Mrs Wilks, Harriet then telephoned the police station and spoke to Sergeant Yates. 'Pete, it's DCI Love, could you do something for me?'

'Certainly, Ma'am.'

Harriet explained what she needed doing and thanked the sergeant for his help. 'I *am* concerned about this young woman, Pete, and I would be most upset if anything happened to her whilst we are in possession of facts indicating that she might be in danger.'

'I agree with you, Ma'am. Now don't worry, I'll do as you ask, no problem.'

Next, Harriet dialled the number of Diane Willarby. Diane already knew of the delayed flight. Samanntha had called her after speaking with Mrs Wilks. Harriet explained to the young nurse what she would like to happen on her friend's return. Having obtained the agreement that she had hoped from Diane, and feeling greatly relieved that she had taken the steps that she had, she sat down and poured herself another cup of coffee. She would telephone Mrs Wilks in a moment and tell her what she had arranged. She didn't want the older woman to become anxious unnecessarily. Harriet felt satisfied that she was doing the right thing. They were now convinced that Samanntha Farndon was in danger and she felt it her duty to protect her. What had Ed Harrington said to her some days ago? – 'Always follow your gut feeling, Ma'am, because you will be right.' That was exactly what she was doing. The morning had flown. It was time she began to get ready for her visit to the Hollyoaks.

Ed arrived at his mother's house for Sunday lunch as promised. He could still feel the results of the enormous amount of food that he had consumed the night before and wondered if he could possibly find a space to take the roast that he knew his mother would present to him. Ellen Harrington hugged her son.

'What a splendid evening it was at the Gala Dinner last night. I'm sure they get better every year. Come in, Ed dear, and sit down. Didn't Charlie look happy? And what a lovely young woman Liz is. So much better suited to him than Claudia. I never did like Claudia as you know, but of course I never said anything detrimental about her to Charlie. You can't say anything to people about their choice of partner, can you? They wouldn't listen anyway, would they?' Mrs Harrington chatted on, barely giving her son a chance to agree or disagree, so he just nodded or shook his head where appropriate and occasionally gave one of his grunts.

'Did you have a nice time, Ed?'

'Yes, thank you, Mother. I ate too much though, so please don't pile my plate high this lunchtime.'

'Very well, dear. I think I over ate as well, so we'll both be a little conservative in our diet to day.' Mrs Harrington bustled about, insisting that Ed sat down whilst she opened a bottle of wine. 'You can drive on one glass, can't you, Ed?'

'Yes, Mother, but let me do that.' He jumped to his feet and took the bottle of wine from his mother, deftly pulling the cork in one swift movement.

'My fingers don't seem to have the grip they used to,' smiled Ellen Harrington, 'but then again I don't open a bottle of wine every day.'

'Perhaps you should.' Ed looked at his mother with affection. 'Come and sit down and stop flitting around like a moth.'

She did as she was bid and sat opposite her son. 'What did you think of Detective Chief Inspector Love, then? Didn't she look exquisite?'

'I suppose so, but then so did Liz – and so did you, Mother.

Now, no more chatting on about last night, let's change the subject.'

Ellen Harrington realised that the subject was now closed. Nothing would draw her son into conversation about the Gala Dinner and certainly not about Harriet Love. She rose from her chair. 'I've done roast lamb, but I promise I won't overfill your plate.' She left the room to go to the kitchen and Ed leaned back in his chair and sighed.

After lunch Ed lingered over his coffee. He smiled as he watched his mother pour her own. 'I see you've dug out the cafetière and produced ground beans.'

His mother laughed. 'I'm not to be outdone by your new boss. I prefer ground coffee anyway, it's just that the instant is so convenient, especially when you are on your own.'

Ed nodded in agreement. 'When my lunch has settled I'll cut the lawn for you. I still need to chop down that old elm at the end of the garden but I'm going to wait until Charlie can help me, if that's all right with you?'

'Of course, Ed. Why don't you invite Charlie and Liz to lunch next Sunday? We ladies can sit in the garden and watch you two at work on the tree.'

'That would be a good idea. I'll have a word with Charlie tomorrow and see what he and Liz have planned for next weekend.' Ed finished his coffee and went into the garden to cut the lawn.

It was late afternoon when Ed finally left his mother's house. He had declined the offer of afternoon tea, reminding her that they had agreed to watch what they consumed today.

'You're quite right, Ed, we've done nothing but eat of late. We'll just have a cup of tea before you leave.'

She vanished into the kitchen to make the tea and an hour later Ed was on his way home. It was a clear evening and not quite six. He turned into Waverley Road and drove round to the other side of the park. The houses here were older than most of the buildings in the town and as he circled the park he realised that he was close to where Harriet Love lived. He had not driven here deliberately but he suddenly recognised Butt Lane. Her cottage was only metres away, less than halfway down the lane. In God's name, what was he doing! Mooching around like a teenager... What was Harriet Love to him, anyway? Just a colleague and nothing more. He was being stupid and unprofessional. Ed put his foot down hard on the accelerator and sped away around the perimeter of the park, heading for home.

Harriet had only just returned to her cottage and at that very moment was preparing a light meal for herself and her guest, who was due to arrive at any time. She had had a pleasant lunch with the Hollyoaks, and although she was extremely fond of them both she had been quite pleased to make her excuses and leave. Harriet was quite unaware that Ed Harrington was at the end of the lane, but had she known, she might well have invited him in to join herself and another colleague for supper. The doorbell rang and Harriet opened the door to admit Stacey Boston.

'This is marvellous,' smiled Stacey. 'I can't tell you what a delight it is to have someone to visit and talk to in the evening. I was only sorry that I was unable to attend the Gale Dinner last night.'

'So am I,' replied Harriet. 'But is there no man in your life at present?'

'Well, sort of.' Stacey frowned. 'There are problems, however. He insists he is separated from his wife, but I'm not so sure and I really have no desire to break up a marriage or to be involved with a married man.'

'I don't blame you. What makes you think he's still with his wife?'

The frown returned to Stacey's face. 'Oh, you know, the usual things. He's not always available or he has to suddenly rush off when we are out to dinner and we always dine in discreet restaurants. And that old gut feeling, Harriet.'

'I know all about gut feelings, but have you asked him outright?'

'Yes – once – and he snapped at me saying I didn't trust him. But in my heart I don't think I do.'

'So what does the future hold for this romance?'

'Heaven knows!' Stacey sighed. 'I'll just go along with things for the time being and see what develops. Anyway, Harry, what about you? Any romance in your life?'

Harriet laughed. 'Not at the moment, I seem to be far too busy on this murder case and I really do want to crack it or the top brass will be putting me on the spot very soon.' They discussed the murders for a time and then moved on to the possible exhumation of Sarah Caldwell. 'We should have the answer from the Coroner very soon,' said Harriet. 'With luck the reply will give us the all clear to go ahead with the lifting of the body.'

'I haven't met this Caldwell man but I understand that he and his brother are nasty pieces of work.'

'They are indeed,' replied Harriet. 'Unfortunately I don't think they are involved with the murders of the nurses. But something isn't right about the deaths of Bill Caldwell's wives.'

'Well, if there is anything to discover from the body of Sarah, I promise to discover it for you, Harry.'

Harriet rose to serve supper. 'I knew we'd end up talking shop,' she smiled. 'I thought we could eat on the patio, it's a perfect evening.' She vanished into the kitchen to serve the fresh salmon salad that she had prepared. Harriet enjoyed the company of Stacey Boston and found that the two of them had a great deal in common, not just work, but the theatre and music and by all accounts their men friends or lack of them.

Stacey entered the kitchen behind her. 'What needs taking onto the patio?' she asked.

'All this,' said Harriet, indicating the various plates and bowls laid out on the table.

'Looks wonderful, Harry, we must do this more often. My place next time, although I warn you my house is not as elegant as this.'

They carried the laden trays out to the garden and setting the table they sat down to eat and to continue their conversation.

Chapter Sixteen

Flight ECA 859 from Cyprus touched down at Donnington Airport at exactly 0300 hours. Samanntha Farndon was tired after her long wait in Lamaka Airport but she was feeling much more relaxed after her two-week holiday away from the hectic life of nursing. She was barely suntanned. She, or rather her very sensitive skin, was highly allergic to extreme sunrays and although this did not deter her from going to warm countries, she refrained from lying outside in the heat of the day and spent her time reading or visiting museums and other sites of interest. She swam in the evening when it was cooler and enjoyed the solitude of her table for one at mealtimes. Samanntha had always been something of a loner and frequently went on holiday by herself from choice. The friends she did have were devoted to her and she to them and she enjoyed their company when they were all working together. She was happy staying over at Diane's house from time to time and returned the compliment frequently. But somehow she looked forward to time on her own and every so often this holiday by herself was needed.

At this hour of the morning there was no hold-up with collection or passing through customs. As she entered the arrival lounge she was amazed to see two police officers in uniform standing at the barrier, the younger of the two men holding up a board clearly displaying her name. Samanntha moved across to the two policemen.

'I'm Samanntha Farndon. Is anything wrong?'

'Not that we know of, Miss,' said the older man, who had three stripes on his arm, 'but we have instructions to escort you to your friend's house, Miss Diane Willarby of Twelve Kelmarsh Road.'

'But whatever for? Has my house burned down or something?' Samanntha was now beginning to feel anxious.

The young officer spoke. 'The instructions are from Detective

Chief Inspector Love of the Torreston Police. She has asked us to collect you and deliver you safely to this address. It's something to do with a man who has been killing nurses.'

Sergeant Jim Mirams chipped in, glancing sharply at the young PC. 'There's no need to be alarmed, Miss, this is just a precaution but apparently you have been having trouble with a chap pestering you at the hospital, and DCI Love is concerned about your safety.'

Samanntha's heart was pounding in her chest. Surely she was not in danger from a lunatic who was attacking nurses. She *had* been bothered by someone asking after her prior to her going to Cyprus, but she had put this down to an over enthusiastic ex-patient. It sometimes happened that patients took a fancy to a nurse, but you just had to ignore them and eventually they became bored and vanished from the scene. It had happened to her in Leicester, and that *had* been rather scary because the man had been so persistent. In fact it was because of Murdock Pollard that she had left the Infirmary and moved to Amchurch to work. She looked up at the two officers. 'Has a nurse been killed while I've been away?'

'Two in this area, I'm afraid, Miss,' replied the sergeant. 'And it turns out that there have been other murders in different parts of the country that appear to match the pattern.'

Samanntha's stomach turned over and her hand flew to her mouth. 'Were the murdered nurses from my hospital?'

'No, miss,' said PC Luke Stockwell quickly, 'They were from the Cottage Hospital at Torreston and an old peoples' home there.'

'We've got a car waiting,' said Jim Mirams, 'and your friend is expecting you.' He picked up her case and Samanntha made to follow him.

'What a welcome home,' she whispered, 'I feel quite sick.'

Diane Willarby heard the police car pull up outside her house and she leaped out of bed. She had lain awake for hours quite unable to sleep. Who would be able to sleep having received a telephone call from a senior police officer informing you that she thought your friend might be in danger, and could she stay at your house the minute she arrives back from holiday? She peered through the curtains and saw the police car. At the top of the stairs she met Heather Howarth coming from her bedroom. 'You heard the car?' said Heather. Diane nodded, dashed down the stairs and opened the front door. Samanntha fell into her arms.

'It's okay Sam! You'll be safe here with us.'

'What on earth is going on, Diane?'

Diane put her arm around her friend and guided her inside. Heather vanished into the kitchen to put the kettle on. Diane turned to look at the two policemen. 'Would you like a coffee?'

Luke looked questioningly at his Sergeant, who half smiled as he nodded. 'That would be very nice, thank you. We've got a long stretch ahead of us and I have my radio on should they need us.' He and Luke followed Diane into the small sitting room where she indicated the settee.

'Do sit down, I'll just let Heather know how many want coffee. We can explain to poor Sam just what has been going on while she's been away on holiday, as we drink.'

The three friends finally retired to their beds at five a.m. Sergeant Mirams and PC Stockwell had left at about four, having reassured the three women that the police were keeping the hospital under close surveillance and they were not to worry, although the advice to all nurses was to move about in groups, especially at night. Diane had telephoned the hospital to explain to them that Samanntha's return flight had been delayed and could she therefore work the late shift next day, rather than reporting for duty at seven a.m.

'They didn't mind you changing shifts,' said Diane to Samanntha once the two policemen had left. 'In fact, Lucy Clark was pleased to swap with you as she had half promised her boyfriend she would be able to go out with him this evening, and now she can.'

'Thanks for everything, you two. What a shock to return to this! You don't really think Murdock Pollard could have anything to do with the murders, do you?'

'I've never met him, Sam,' said Diane, 'you're the only one who might be able to answer that question.'

'He was certainly intense and he became very possessive, even when I explained to him that I never went out with patients. He was quite rude to one of the doctors who stood talking to me in the ward one day; in fact the more I think about it the more I realise that he became most strange if there was ever another male anywhere near me.'

Heather placed a gentle hand on her friend's arm. 'Don't think about it any more, Sam. Detective Chief Inspector Love is going to interview you tomorrow when you come off duty. I've told her she is welcome to come here, so you can tell her everything that you can remember about this Murdock fellow when you see her. Now come on let's get to bed.'

On Monday morning Ed Harrington collected Charlie from his house as usual and once again Charlie was ready and waiting. He leaped into the Saab and grinned up at Ed. 'I've decided to sell the motorbike and buy a car,' he exclaimed.

'I don't believe what I'm hearing,' said Ed. 'That bike has been the centre of your life for as long as I've known you.'

'True, but my life has changed, Ed. I'm moving on now and I really do know what I want.'

'Be very certain that you know what you're undertaking, Charlie. You've only known Liz a couple of weeks.'

'And I feel as if I've known her for ever, Ed. Weird, isn't it? I just can't remember my life when I didn't have Liz beside me.'

Ed glanced across at his friend. Charlie was glowing. His eyes shone and his back was straight. Ed was happy for him.

Harriet was already at her desk when Ed knocked on her door. 'Good morning, Ed. Did you enjoy the Gala Dinner on Saturday?'

'Yes, thank you. I get pleasure out of seeing my mother enjoying herself, and she always seems to enjoy those gatherings.'

Harriet decided not to pursue the topic of the Gala Dinner and changed the subject.

'I arranged for Samanntha to be collected from the airport last night, or rather the early hours of this morning. She has been taken to Diane Willarby's house and I have arranged a twenty-four hour police surveillance on the house and on Samanntha, until we are sure she is in no danger.'

Ed nodded. 'That's a good idea. When do we interview her?'

'When she comes off duty this evening. Diane has invited us

to talk to her at her house at about nine thirty. Is that all right with you, Ed?'

A slight smile crossed the DI's face. 'No problem. I wasn't going anywhere. Shall I meet you there?'

'Fine! Nine thirty at Twelve Kelmarsh Road. Now, what's happening today?' Harriet briskly picked up a sheaf of papers that she had been reading on Ed's arrival. 'I'm hoping for a reply from the Coroner today giving us permission to exhume Sarah Caldwell's body.'

Ed grunted. 'I'll carry out briefing, shall I? We'll inform the rest of the team about your discovery of the name SAMANNTHA in connection to the murder places when you next come to briefing. Later I shall be carefully checking the report on this chap Preston Skinner who caused a rumpus in casualty the other night.'

'Right, carry on, Ed, but tell them not to let too much information about the investigation leak out. Harriet stretched her long arms above her head as she often did when sitting in her office. 'I'm dreading this interview with Midlands Television this morning. I've never been on television before. I always do my best to stay hidden when I see cameras.'

'You appeared to be caught a few times Saturday evening.' Ed moved towards the door, wishing he had not just said that.

Was that a pointed remark, or was Ed joking? Harriet flushed. She felt the comment was sour and she bit her tongue without responding. She knew she had to transcend from any snide remarks her colleague made and refuse to be drawn into petty squabbles. She was determined to bide her time and hope that this tension between herself and DI Harrington would sort itself out. As Ed left the room she turned back to her paper work. She had to write her report for George Hollyoak before leaving for the television studio. At least the filming was scheduled for the morning, which was a blessing. Once over she could concentrate on the matter in hand. The actual showing of the interview would be on the news at various times throughout the day.

In the Incident Room Ed went over the meeting of Preston Skinner with Bob Finch and Narinder Pancholi.

'He certainly is a nasty piece of work, Sir,' said Bob.

Narinder spoke with feeling. 'I was actually scared of him. If I was ever on my own and met him, I would most definitely be afraid.'

'You say he normally has transport to the hospital outpatients. How come, if he is able to walk?' Ed looked from Bob to Narinder waiting for a reply.

Bob answered, 'He has great difficulty in walking and it isn't put on, that's for sure. He said he struggled to the hospital for painkillers in desperation. He asked for morphine or something just as strong.'

Ed nodded as he jotted down a few notes 'Right – thanks, you two. Carry on.'

After briefing, Ed decided to pay a visit to Torreston Hospital. He felt he would like to speak to Garry Hobbs as he appeared to be closely involved with many of the patients, including Preston Skinner. He called Charlie over.

'You're coming with me to the hospital, Charlie. I'd like to speak to Garry Hobbs, the hospital car driver. Somewhere in all of this, someone knows something even if at the moment it means nothing to them.' The two men left the police station.

At the Nottingham television studios Harriet was feeling nervous as the make-up lady put the finishing touches to her appearance. She had conducted many interviews at press conferences in her time, but had never appeared before television cameras. She was directed to the studio where the interview was to take place. The heat from the lights was unbearable and the glare made her want to squint but she held her head high and sat in the chair she was shown to. Jon Rawlins, the journalist interviewing her, sat in the chair opposite her and he gave her a smile of support. The countdown commenced and they were on air.

At Torreston Cottage Hospital Ed and Charlie collected their Visitor badges and proceeded to the transport area looking for Garry Hobbs. 'Out on a trip mate,' they were told by a young man leaning on the bonnet of an estate car.

'And you are?' asked Ed.

'Wayne Barnes.'

'Do you drive for the hospital as well?' Ed eyed the tall, thin, willowy figure in front of them.

'Yep! Me and Garry do most of the runs to and from this place. We work Monday to Friday and take it in turns to be on hand at the weekends. We only get called out then if it's an emergency, otherwise they use the ambulance service. They reckon we save the Trust thousands using cars and small vans. Saves calling out the ambulances all the time.'

Charlie stepped closer. 'What do you know about Preston Skinner? I believe he uses your cars quite frequently.'

Wayne Barnes wiped his hand across his face. 'That old bugger – pardon the language – he really is a case of real garbage! Don't think I've ever heard him say please or thank you in his life, and as for his attitude to the staff here, well! He don't deserve the help and attention that he gets from them. They bend over backwards to humour him and all they get is abuse. I'd make him walk home. He can walk 'cos I've seen him. I live in the same street and I've seen him at the shops buying fags. Okay so he limps a bit. So do lots of folk, but I bet they don't get fetched and carried like that old sod.'

'Thank you for that vivid response,' said Ed. 'What do you know of his violence that sometimes flares up towards the nurses?'

Wayne pulled a face. 'I've never actually witnessed the incidents but I've certainly heard about them. Good job I wasn't around when it happened or I'd probably have given him one.'

'Apart from patients who are too ill to walk, do you have many who have leg injuries requiring transport to and from the hospital?' asked, Charlie.

'Quite a few.'

'Could you get us a list of names?'

'No problem.' Wayne Barnes pulled himself up from his lounging position displaying the fact that he was taller than either of the two officers in front of him. He must have been at least six feet six, thought, Ed. The tall thin figure shot of at a high speed and disappeared into a small room at the side of the main building. He returned minutes later with a sheaf of papers in his hand. 'Here you are. A list of all our "customers" for the last six months. Some have, er, moved on, but many of them are still with us and using the cars regularly.'

Ed took the papers. 'Can I keep these?'

'Sure, they're copies. I don't want them back. Here, give them back a tick and I'll mark all the ones who have leg problems.' He took the papers from Ed and, leaning on the bonnet of his car, swiftly went down the list of names marking some of them with a tick. He pushed the papers back towards Ed who took them from him.

'Thanks. This could be very helpful.'

Ed and Charlie left the hospital and returned to the police station. As they entered the Incident Room, Ed turned to, Charlie. 'How about looking through these lists over coffee? I'm gasping for one.'

'Now where have I heard that before?' grinned, Charlie, 'I'll go and put the kettle on.'

Fifteen minutes later DI Harrington and Sergeant Marlow were sitting together at a table, with a pot of coffee and two mugs and the lists of names from Wayne Barnes spread in front of them.

'I recognise some of the names,' said, Charlie, 'they were interviewed after the murder of Carol Young and live in the vicinity.'

'Well, we'll eliminate all the females for the time being,' said Ed. 'That doesn't leave too many.'

'It's pretty helpful having their ailments on the list, and in many cases what actually happened to them.' Charlie picked up one of the pages. 'These three for example are all MS sufferers. Hardly likely that they would be able to commit a murder, don't you think?'

'Depends on how advanced the symptoms are at present,' replied Ed.

'We can cross this chap off, surely; he broke his back in a climbing accident according to this and is totally dependent on his wheelchair.'

'Name?' asked, Ed.

'Ramsay Donaldson. Only twenty-seven poor devil; lives with his parents over on Park Side.'

'Put his name on our list and we'll check him out with the hospital just to make sure his injuries are as severe as stated.'

Charlie wrote the name down. 'I'll do the same with this guy, Mark Ainsley. He's confined to a wheelchair as well. Pelvis and both legs crushed in a car accident, lives in the house of flats where that creep Vince Caldwell lives.'

'How many names are we left with?' asked Ed as they came to the end of the list.

'Only eight, four of whom we have already interviewed when we did the routine visits to the murder area: Preston Skinner and three others. Two of the others who use the cars regularly are over seventy and riddled with arthritis.'

'Leave them on the list, Charlie. No one must slip through the net.'

'They're down. The list is complete.'

'Fine,' said Ed, finishing off the last of the coffee 'Now we need to consider each one in depth, including a re-check of both hospital drivers. Garry Hobbs and Wayne Barnes – although at six feet six inches I don't think Wayne fits the description of our attacker.'

'Why the interest in this particular group of people?' asked, Charlie.

'DCI Love feels that the answer to the killings is here somewhere, and I'm inclined to agree with her. We have not as yet found this chap in the woolly hat who skulks about, and the fact that he has this limp makes me wonder if he does have a connection with the hospital. We need to know if these outpatients are genuinely disabled or is one of them pulling the wool over our eyes.'

Charlie ran his eye over the list of names. 'If they're as injured as they are reported to be here, then there's no way that they could move about and attack people. Even Skinner would find it impossible. I know he *can* walk, but heaven knows, to be able to grab his victim, who would surely struggle, and then to vanish so speedily after the crime would be beyond his capabilities, I'm sure.'

'Perhaps you're right, Charlie, but someone is at large and a threat to the nursing population and we still have to find this guy with the gammy leg, whether he's involved or not.'

'Perhaps he'll come forward after the DCI's appearance on TV tonight.'

At that moment the door opened to admit DCI Love. 'I'm back,' she smiled. 'How's it going?'

Ed stood up. 'We went back to the hospital and collected a list of all those who attend Outpatients and use, or drive, the hospital transport. Having been through all the names carefully we're left with just eight patients and the two drivers. This group requires a second and possibly a more thorough check.'

'Good. Well done.' Harriet moved over to the table and picked up the empty cafetière. 'Too late, I see.'

Charlie took the pot with a grin. 'I'll make some more, Ma'am, but how about your morning? What's it like being on television?' He could not resist a chuckle.

'It was dreadful, Charlie.' Harriet sat down and stretched her long legs in front of her. 'How anyone could choose to be filmed from choice and sit under those hot lights in front of cameras and dozens of people, I just can't imagine. I only hope my shaking legs didn't show, I was terribly nervous.'

'I'm sure you will come out very well, Ma'am.' Ed picked up the list of names from the table and placed them in front of the DCI. 'When do we re-interview these people?'

'Tomorrow, Ed. We'll do it together. As neither of us have spoken to any of them before, we will be fresh and unbiased in our opinion.'

Charlie slipped away to make fresh coffee and Harriet picked up the list of names. 'For those we have already interviewed, Ed, we had better take their original statements with us.'

'I'll see to that. Do we leave after briefing?'

Harriet rose and moved over to the notice board that was covered with all the information they had gathered so far. 'Yes, we'll leave as soon as possible.' Photographs of the dead nurses as they had appeared in life looked back at her from the board together with the gruesome pictures of them in death. She sighed. 'Why do people kill for no apparent reason Ed? This killer couldn't have known all his victims personally, could he? This is a definite vengeance attack on nurses.'

'So it seems,' replied Ed joining his boss at the notice board. 'The earring theory is strange though, and you're right, all the women had pierced ears and wore earrings which appear to have been taken after they were murdered. There has to be a reason for him doing that.'

'Wonder what he does with them...?'

'Incriminating evidence, if he's caught with them in his possession.'

Charlie returned with a fresh pot of coffee and an extra mug. He was followed into the room by Sergeant Yates, who was holding a large white envelope in his hand.

'I think this is what you are waiting for, Ma'am,' he said, handing Harriet the envelope. 'It was delivered by hand a few minutes ago.'

Eagerly, Harriet took the letter. 'Thank you, Pete.' She saw the stamp of the Coroner's Office and hastily tore open the envelope. There was silence from the waiting group as the green eyes swiftly scanned what was written on the single sheet of white paper. The DCI looked up, the sagacious face composed, the eyes bright.

'We've got permission to exhume the body of Caldwell's second wife. I'll take my coffee with me to my office, if I may. I need to set the wheels in motion for this exhumation and I don't want to waste any time.'

Charlie poured a mug of coffee and handed it to Harriet. 'Thanks, Charlie,' she said. 'You know where I am if you need me, Ed.' Then she left the room followed by Pete Yates.

Back in her office Harriet put a call through to Stacey Boston. The pathologist was the most important person in this procedure and needed to be contacted first before the other members of the team were involved. Harriet then paid a visit to Superintendent Hollyoak, who immediately wanted to chat on about the Charity Dinner and how wonderful it had been and how beautiful she had looked and... Harriet hastily interrupted, putting a friendly hand on his arm. 'George, I don't wish to appear rude, but I really do need to get in touch with several people so that we can get this exhumation under way as quickly as possible. You know how difficult it is organising something like this when everyone is so busy all the time.'

George Hollyoak patted the slender hand on his arm. 'Of course, my dear, of course. I'm sorry to gabble on but I'm always so pleased to see you, and we don't seem to get a chance to talk.'

'Now, George, we chatted yesterday at lunch.'

'Only briefly. Nancy always insists we don't talk shop in the house.'

Harriet laughed. 'As soon as this case is over we'll nip to the Red Lion for lunch together. How's that?'

'That would be splendid.'

'But for now, George, I do need to go over these details with you.' Reluctantly the big man sat behind his desk and took the papers that Harriet placed in front of him. It was some twenty minutes later that Harriet left his office and returned to her own. She put a call through to the Incident Room where she spoke briefly with Ed to arrange the details for the following day. First thing in the morning they would have to supervise the opening of Sarah Caldwell's grave at Torreston Cemetery. This had been arranged for eight in the hope that there would be few spectators. Hopefully the press would not have latched on to the news as yet, and they could at least lift the body before anyone spread the word. The interviewing of the patients on the list that Ed and Charlie had compiled would have to take place later that same morning. It appeared that tomorrow was to be another busy day.

That evening Harriet settled down to watch the early evening news, with a glass of wine and a plate of poached salmon and new potatoes. She dreaded seeing herself on television but knew that she had to watch it just the same.

In his house in Claymore Drive, Ed Harrington too was sitting in front of the television awaiting the news. The newscaster introduced the Detective Chief Inspector, and there was Harriet Love on the screen. The handsome face looked out at him and the clear green eyes did not falter as she described the horrific killing of young nurses. Detective Chief Inspector Love appealed to anyone with any information to get in touch with her at the police station. She described the man with the limp and the woolly hat whom they were eager to interview, and explained that the car he used was of a pale colour and of the old fashioned square type, probably a Ford. She stated that this man most probably had nothing to do with the murders but asked that he call in to the Station himself so that he might be eliminated from the investigation. Ed felt that the appeal was genuine and came from the heart. DCI Love certainly came across in a very cool and calm manner and spoke like a true professional. She was obviously very concerned that a killer was still at large but promised the public that this maniac would be caught and that the net was closing in on him.

Ed sighed and hoped that she was right. The days were slipping by, but were they really any closer to catching this man?

At nine thirty exactly, Harriet parked her red Lotus outside Diane Willarby's house. There was no sign of Ed's car so she sat and waited, but not for very long. Soon she saw in her rear-view mirror the black Saab pull up behind her. It was a warm evening and still light. She climbed out of her car, to be joined by Ed. 'Good evening, Ed.'

'Evening, Ma'am.'

'What did you think of the news item?' Harriet waited with apprehension.'

'It was fine. You mentioned everything of importance and hopefully there will be a response from the public about this chap with the limp.'

'He may of course come forward himself, Ed, and prove that he has nothing at all to do with our investigation.'

Ed nodded. 'True, but one way or another we need to know what he's up to.' They arrived at the front door, which opened without them having to knock. Diane Willarby stood on the doorstep. 'Please come in – Sam's ready to see you.'

Diane showed them into the sitting room where Samanntha Farndon was standing by the window. As she turned to greet them, both officers were stunned by her appearance. She stood at no more than five feet tall and looked like a china doll with her fair hair and blue eyes. Her pale skin had an opaque gleam to it, giving it the appearance of porcelain, and her cheeks were devoid of any colour. No wonder men had the desire to own her, thought Harriet, she looked so fragile and in need of protection. She held out her hand to Samanntha. 'Hello, Samanntha, I'm Harriet Love and this is Ed Harrington. I know that Diane has told you that we are the officers investigating this dreadful spate of nurse murders and we wondered if you could help us in any way.'

Ed moved across the room towards Samanntha. He was always aware that DCI Love never pulled rank when they were interviewing together, in fact on most occasions she did not bother to give her full title. Ed took the slim, pale hand that was offered and gripped the cold fingers.

In a brisk, matter-of-fact way, Diane invited them all to sit down. 'I'll make coffee while you start chatting,' she said. 'Heather is on duty.'

The group sat down and in a gentle voice Harriet asked Samanntha to tell them all that she could about the man she had nursed in Leicester who had then begun to harass her.

Samanntha spoke in a quiet, well-educated voice. 'His name was Murdock Pollard and he had been dreadfully injured in the factory fire. He had been crushed by falling beams and had multiple bone fractures and severe burns to his lower back. Initially we thought he would die but over the weeks we nursed him, he gradually pulled through. I felt very sorry for him and as we do to all patients we show them as much sympathy as we can and encourage them in their recovery.'

'But Murdock Pollard wouldn't let go.' Harriet leaned forward.

'Exactly,' sighed Samanntha. 'He kept trying to give me presents and...' she picked up a box that was at her feet and handed it to Harriet... 'I think this might be the clue that you are looking for.'

Harriet lifted the lid of the box and then handed it to Ed. Ed removed the lid altogether and folded back the tissue paper to take out a red woollen scarf, which he laid on the table in front of them.

'This was left at the hospital after I left and it was posted on to me. I certainly would not have accepted a gift. On my birthday he gave me a small box and said: 'This is for you.' When I said I was sorry I couldn't accept presents he became quite nasty. He raised his voice and just said: 'Open it.' I took the lid off and was amazed at the pair of beautiful earrings inside. They must have cost a fortune. I shut the box and handed them back. He went white with anger and I was really frightened. He accused me of leading him on, which I promise you I never did, and I reported the incident to my Ward Manager who got me moved to another area. I have no idea how he discovered the date of my birthday. He must have asked someone. I left the hospital soon after that. It was when I was at my new address down here that the scarf came through the post. The hospital had sent it on. I made me feel quite sick really, as if I was being stalked.'

'Was there a letter in the box?' asked Ed.

'Just a small card that said something weird and was unsigned.'

'What did you do with the card?' Harriet was now convinced that at last they had established the missing link.

'I think I threw it away. I was going to dispose of the scarf as well but thought it was such a waste of a lovely article so decided to give it to a charity shop. I stuck it in a drawer and somehow I forgot all about it.'

Harriet had been writing notes in her pad. 'Can you remember what was written on the card, Samanntha?'

'It started with "Dearest"...' she gave a shudder... 'and then said something about being ever in his thoughts.'

Harriet spoke in a soft coaxing voice. 'Try and remember the exact words if you can.'

Samanntha closed her eyes. '"Dearest,"' she began '"ever in" ...no, it was "amid my thoughts".' She stopped again '"hereafter."' She opened her eyes. 'Yes, that is it exactly. "Dearest, ever amid my thoughts hereafter!" I remember thinking how ominous the "hereafter" bit was. Not exactly affectionate, was it?'

Harriet looked up from writing down the words. 'No, quite chilling really. But put it out of your mind for now. We will deal with it.'

Diane returned carrying a tray of coffee and biscuits. 'It was when I told Sam about the red scarves used in the murders that she remembered the one she had been sent.'

'Does that mean you've been back to Railway Cottages?' Ed frowned.

'Well, yes,' said Samanntha, 'but we went on our way to the hospital at about twelve thirty rather than at night. I wanted to speak to Mrs Wilks to let her know I'm okay.'

'Please don't return to Railway Cottages until we have this man.' Harriet spoke in earnest and Samanntha shivered.

'Do you really think I'm in danger?'

Harriet was not one for frightening people but on this occasion she felt it necessary. This young woman needed to be fully aware that somewhere out there, a madman, was intent on killing nurses, and if her deduction of the name places was correct, then she was next on his list. 'I think you may well be in danger,' she answered. 'Please stay here with Diane until further notice.' She handed Samanntha a sheet of paper and a ballpoint pen. 'Write down a description of Murdock Pollard and anything at all that you can remember about him,' she said. 'We should like you to come to the police station and construct a likeness of this Murdock with the help of the photofit.'

Harriet and Ed finished their coffee and waited for Samanntha to complete her task. The young woman stopped writing and handed Harriet the paper. 'That's everything that I can think of.'

'That's excellent,' smiled Harriet rising from her chair. 'Just one more thing. Do you remember Dave Spalding? His fiancée was also burned in the fire and was a patient at the same hospital.'

Samanntha nodded. 'Yes, I remember him. He visited his fiancée regularly to begin with but eventually he couldn't face her any more. We were all terribly upset for both of them but quite honestly, I understood how Dave Spalding felt. The woman he was visiting was not the same woman he had become engaged to. I talked to him a lot and tried to help but it was no good, he had to break with her. I actually wept for them, it was all so sad. I left the hospital soon after he stopped visiting so I'm not sure of the outcome.'

Harriet produced the photograph that Charlie had obtained from June MacFarland and handed it to Samanntha. 'Is this Dave Spalding?'

'Yes, it is.'

'But it's definitely not Murdock Pollard?'

'No,' answered Samanntha. 'Although strangely, they both have those very pale eyes.'

Harriet had no need to ask Samanntha if she had had an affair with Dave Spalding. June, in her misery, had simply put two and two together and come up with an incorrect answer. She spoke to the young woman in front of her, 'Now, there is a plainclothes policeman outside at all times. I will get him to come over and introduce himself before we go.'

Harriet and Ed prepared to leave. 'Would you fetch whoever is on duty please, Ed.' The Inspector disappeared to return minutes later with a stocky young man dressed in jeans and an anorak. 'This is Greg Henderson.'

'Good evening, Ma'am.' He acknowledged Harriet and then turned to the two young women. 'Don't be anxious, ladies, I shall be outside all night. If you are at all worried flash the front room lights on and off and I'll come running. Have you got a spare front door key? Just in case,' he added, as he saw the fear in Samanntha's eyes.

Five minutes later Ed and Harriet left the house. It was now quite dark and spitting with rain. Harriet turned the collar of her jacket up and pulled it round her neck. 'Well, at last we have the missing piece, Ed. And I feel a great deal happier knowing that Samanntha is under guard.'

'Absolutely. We now understand the reason for the stolen earrings. He's certainly a very dangerous person to go around killing nurses just because one returned his gift and didn't wish to have anything to do with him. By the way, why were you so curious about the precise wording on the gift card?'

Harriet held her notebook in front of Ed's face and he read what she had written. 'Whew! I see what you mean, this chap really is a dangerous character.'

'Can we ever understand a twisted mind, Ed.' Harriet's mobile telephone rang and they stopped at the side of her car as she answered it. Her words were short. 'Where? Right, we're on our way.' She turned to, Ed. 'A young woman has been attacked but she's still alive, thank God.'

'A nurse?'

'Yes, but more to the point it happened at Railway Cottages.' She opened the door of her car. 'Give Charlie a ring, Ed, and I'll see you both there.' The engine of the Lotus fired up and she shot off at speed.

Ed dialled Charlie's number on his mobile and spoke briefly to his friend, then moving swiftly to his own car he followed DCI Love down the road heading for Charlie's house.

Chapter Seventeen

It was just after eleven thirty when the red Lotus drove into Station Lane in Amchurch. It was followed minutes later by the black Saab. The two vehicles pulled up behind the police car with its blue light flashing. Harriet walked over to Ed and Charlie as they climbed from their car. 'Thanks for coming, Charlie. Sorry to call you out at this hour.'

Charlie grinned. 'I'm used to it, Ma'am, don't worry.' He could never remember being thanked for turning out to do his duty before and he found it quite pleasing.

The three walked over to the group standing by the patrol car. It was now raining quite hard and Harriet was glad that she had her large umbrella with her. Figures clad in white could be seen in the garden of Number 2 Railway Cottages; some on their hands and knees others with sticks searching the bushes. The SOCO Team was always quick off the mark on theses occasions. Two young women were sitting in the back seat of the patrol car. Both were very distressed and holding on to each other. A sergeant from the Amchurch Station came towards Harriet. 'You must be DCI Love.'

'I am. Thank you for calling us.' She indicated Ed and, Charlie. 'DI Harrington and DS Marlow.'

Ed and Charlie nodded greetings.

'Inspector Howarth told us to call you, Ma'am,' continued the sergeant. 'Said this attack was part of your ongoing investigation.'

'We think it is,' agreed Harriet.

Jim Mirams came over to the group. 'Evening, Ma'am, Sir. We got the call from Amchurch and came straight over. They were lucky,' he added, holding up something red in a plastic bag.

'What were they doing here at this time of night?' asked Ed, amazement showing in his voice.

'Came to see their friend, Nurse Farndon, as they haven't seen her for over two weeks. The neighbour heard the screams and rang the police before going for the bloke with her broom, would you believe.' He nodded to where Mrs Wilks was hovering a short distance away still clutching her weapon.

'Ed, you and Charlie take Mrs Wilks in out of the rain and get her statement, would you, while I interview these ladies.'

Ed nodded and the two men moved away. Harriet bent down to the two women in the car. 'Is there room for one more?' She shut her umbrella and squeezed into the car, smiling reassuringly to the two frightened women. 'I'm Detective Chief Inspector Love, please tell me exactly what happened.'

The first woman spoke. 'Our friend Sam has been on holiday and we knew she was back today, or rather yesterday, and we decided to drop in to see if she was okay. We were both day off today and stayed over at my mother's in Leicester. As we were on our way back we decided to drop in on Sam.'

'Haven't you heard about the warning to all of you informing you that a man is at large and murdering nurses?' Harriet spoke in a quiet voice.

'Yes, we have,' said the second woman, 'but we felt safe as we came in the car and together.'

Harriet took out her note pad. 'Give me your names… and try to stop crying, you're safe now.'

The first nurse spoke. 'I'm Clare Jennings and this is Becky Selby. We both work with Sam and had heard about the killer thought to be in the area and decided we should warn her because she has been away and probably not heard the news. We thought it would be okay as there were two of us, and anyway why would this man be out here at Station Lane? We parked the car outside Sam's house and I got out and went to her door to see if she was in because there was no light on. I had just reached the front door when I felt something soft go round my neck. I couldn't scream or shout as it was so tight but I did manage to get my fingers underneath it.' She began to cry and put her face in her hands remembering her fear. Becky put her arm around her friend's shoulders and continued the story.

'Luckily I had got out of the car to follow and saw what happened. To begin with I was frozen to the spot and no sound would come from my throat. It was dreadful, I couldn't believe what was happening. I could see Clare struggling and it was all like a nightmare, just not real. Suddenly I came to life and screamed like heck. The door of the next house opened and light flooded out and I think this frightened the attacker because he suddenly let go of Clare. As he turned to come back down the path the woman from next door rushed out and went for him with her broom over the low fence. If it hadn't been so terrifying it would have been funny.'

Clare was now able to speak again. 'He swore as his grip weakened and he ran off. I collapsed in a heap on the ground, my legs were unable to hold me up. I was still holding the scarf. I thought I was going to die. Thank God Becky got out of the car.'

'Thank God you didn't come on your own.' Harriet patted Clare's arm. 'It was definitely a male who attacked you, then, Clare? When he swore the voice was definitely male?'

Clare nodded. 'I'm absolutely certain he was a man.'

'Is there anything else you can tell us about the attacker?'

Clare wiped her eyes before answering, 'He wasn't terribly big, but he was behind me so I didn't really get a look at him. One thing though, he smelled of antiseptic. It was probably on his hands because they were close to my face and the smell was very strong.'

'Good! That's something.' Harriet wrote quickly.

'And what about you, Becky, what did you see when he was caught in the light from next door?'

'I was so petrified it all seemed unreal.'

'Just think hard. There's no need to rush.' Harriet waited patiently.

'Clare's right, he wasn't very tall. His head was only slightly above hers. I didn't see his face.'

Harriet climbed out of the police car. 'I'll get an officer to drive you both home but I'd like you, Clare, to get examined by a doctor first.'

'I'm all right, honestly. Bit of a painful throat but otherwise fine.'

'I still need you to be examined, please. The Police Surgeon has been informed and will see you at the Station.' Harriet walked over to the constable standing with Jim Mirams. 'Good evening,

Luke. I'd like you to do something for me if Sergeant Mirams can spare you.'

Luke Stockwell leaped to attention. The DCI always remembered his name. He was most impressed. 'Yes, Ma'am.'

'I'd like you to drive the nurses to the police station in their car. Dr Coates is on his way to the Station and will give Clare a check over, after which I should like you to drive them both home, please. Is that all right with you?' she asked, turning to Jim Mirams.

'Certainly, Ma'am. If PC Stockwell tells me the last address he will be calling at, I'll pick him up from there when the ladies are safely delivered.'

'Thank you, Jim.' Harriet moved to meet Ed who was returning from his interview with Martha Wilks. Charlie was talking to other neighbours who were now appearing from their homes.

'What have you got, Ed?' She held her large umbrella so that they were both covered.

'Mrs Wilks and her husband were getting ready to go to bed when they heard a woman screaming. Mrs Wilks told her husband to dial 999 and she grabbed her broom and went outside. She saw a young woman struggling with her attacker and as he let go of his victim she had a go at him with her broom. Said she hit him several times around the head.'

'Can she describe him?'

'Not really, but she says he was wearing a woolly hat and an anorak and she noticed that he ran off with a very peculiar gait.'

Harriet was thoughtful. 'Do you think he thought it was Samanntha?'

Ed nodded. 'It looks like it. She *is* the target, that's for sure.'

One of the SOCO team came over to Harriet and Ed and they recognised the owl-like features of Phillip Hewitt. He held up a plastic bag containing something bluey-green. 'The attacker's woolly hat.' he said triumphantly. 'Just what we need for some excellent DNA samples.'

'Brilliant, Phillip! This is a big break for us. He must have lost his hat during the onslaught from Mrs Wilks.'

Ed gave a slight smile. 'She's a formidable lady – I wouldn't like to be in her bad books.'

Harriet too smiled at the thought of the big woman wielding a broom. 'I'll just go and thank her, Ed, she may have saved Clare Jennings' life.' She moved away to where Martha Wilks was still standing defiantly on her doorstep, her broom firmly placed between her feet and grasped in both hands. Martha recognised the handsome female officer who had interviewed her not so very long ago.

'Good evening, Inspector,' Her face was grim and she shook her head, 'What in the world was that young woman doing here at this time of night? My heart sank when I heard the screams, I thought it was Sam.'

'You were very brave, Mrs Wilks. You scared off the attacker and have given us a break in the investigation.'

'How's that then?'

'When you struck the man you knocked his hat off and we shall now be able to obtain some DNA, which will certainly help in nailing the guilty person.' Harriet, at five feet ten, was considered tall for a woman, but as she stood on the path outside the Wilks' household she felt decidedly small. She looked up at the big woman standing on the step above her. 'Thank you for your help tonight, Mrs Wilks, but do take care yourself.'

At that moment a small balding man joined his wife on the doorstep. He grinned at Harriet. 'She certainly puts the fear of God into me sometimes.' He stuck out a hand, 'I'm Bert Wilks, You can see who wears the trousers in this house.'

Martha picked up the broom and poked her husband with it. 'Go on, Bert, you make me sound like a tyrant!' There was a gleam in her eye and affection in her voice and she looked almost coy as the small man beside her put an arm around her ample waist.

'Only joking, me duck.' He turned to Harriet. 'She's a good woman Inspector. Nobody will get the better of my Martha and nobody need try and frighten her, 'cos she won't back off.'

'I can see that, Mr Wilks. My congratulations anyway to you both on your prompt action. The nurses are safe and we are going to drive them both home.' She left the couple on their doorstep and returned to the police car. PC Luke Stockwell had already driven the two nurses off in their car to call in at the police station for Clare to be examined by Dr Coates. Luke would then continue the journey to where the two women shared a house in Amchurch.

Harriet and Ed were joined by Charlie and together they walked over to where the SOCO Team was still scouring the path and garden of Samanntha's house. They kept back from the immediate area so as to prevent any contamination of the crime scene.

Phillip Hewitt came over to them. 'There are footprints of a not very unusual pattern that we found in the garden and several tyre tracks in the lane, thanks to the rain. We have taken prints of them all and will match the tyre prints against the vehicles of the inhabitants of the cottages and see what we have left. Tonight might be this chap's undoing, Ma'am, what with his hat and now footprints and car tracks. Perhaps your prediction on television tonight is coming true and the net is closing in on the killer.'

'Let's hope so, Phillip. I'll leave you to carry on. Thank you for your indispensable work and I look forward in having your report.'

Harriet turned to Charlie. 'Anything from the neighbours, Charlie?'

'Not a great deal, Ma'am. Some of them heard a car earlier on and then a bit later a second car, which was obviously the two nurses, but thought nothing of it. Having spoken to all the occupants of the cottages no one has used a car in the last hour so it looks as if our attacker arrived before the nurses and lay in waiting. Besides Mr and Mrs Wilks, only one other couple heard the screams, but by the time they had decided it was someone in difficulty and gone to the front door, the perpetrator had vanished.'

'You may well be correct about the cars, Charlie,' said Harriet. 'The first one must have been the attacker and the second one the victim.'

The rain was quite steady now and Ed had water running down his face. 'Let's hope that Hewitt gets a tyre print that doesn't belong to one of the residents of Railway Cottages then.'

Harriet smiled. 'If there is a print to be found that belongs to our attacker, then you can guarantee that Sergeant Hewitt will find it. Now come on, let's get home before we drown.'

The trio eventually left the crime scene at twenty to one on Tuesday morning. Under the protection of her enormous umbrella, Harriet and Ed walked together to where they had parked their cars. Charlie appeared to have found an umbrella of his own and like Harriet sported a pair of wellington boots.

'To think I was going to have an early night as we have a heavy day tomorrow.' Harriet stopped at the Saab. 'Shall we meet at the cemetery in the morning, Ed?'

'That makes sense. About a quarter to eight?'

'Fine. Goodnight, Ed, goodnight, Charlie.' As Harriet turned to walk away she realised that Ed was still beside her.

'We'll play safe. I'll see you to your car.'

'Thank you, Ed, that's thoughtful of you.' Harriet flashed a smile that Ed could see by the gleam of her white teeth in the half-light. She closed the umbrella and gracefully slid into her car. Then with a wave of her hand she was gone.

Ed returned to his own car where Charlie was waiting for him a huge grin on his face. 'Quite the gentleman,' he said.

'Come off it, Charlie,' said Ed, getting into his car. 'You know I'd do the same for any female.'

The rain was still running down his face and he wiped his hair from his eyes as he started the engine. He sat for a moment in thought. The DCI hadn't shot him down like some senior female officers did when they were offered help from a male office, insisting that they were quite capable of looking after themselves, thank you! She was never like that. She was so feminine, so gracious, so... *beautiful*... He slammed the car into gear aggressively, and without looking at Charlie, set off for Torreston.

It was still raining the next morning and Harriet grimaced as she looked out of her bedroom window. Not the weather you would choose for digging up a coffin. Having grabbed a cup of coffee she collected her boots and umbrella from the back porch where she had placed them the night before and left the house. It was just seven thirty. On arrival at the cemetery she discovered that Ed and Charlie were already there. They were both wearing boots, and like Harriet, Ed had produced a large colourful umbrella. They greeted each other and made their way together to the graveside. A canopy was in place over the grave. A mechanical digger stood nearby and two police officers were ready and waiting with spades to complete the task in hand. They acknowledged the three officers as they approached. Stacey Boston arrived clad in her protective gear and wearing over-sized green boots. 'Good morning,' Harry, she said. 'Trust the rain to arrive today.' She pushed a stray lock of hair back under her white headgear. 'Right, I'm ready when you are.'

Harriet smiled at her new friend. 'Good morning, Stacey. Yes, let's get started.'

Ed felt a twinge of jealousy as he heard the two women chatting in this familiar manner. He could be part of this friendship himself if he had not been so stubborn. The DCI had frequently invited him to call her Harry but the name always seemed to stick in his throat. It was all his own fault, but he was unable, at the present time, to see a way out of the predicament.

The solemn group stood under the canopy and watched as the digger began its task. The ground at the top of the grave was wet and heavy due to the rain, but once down thirty or so centimetres the soil was dry. There had been no rain in the area for weeks, so this was not surprising. The coffin was suddenly visible and minutes later was raised and carried reverently into a waiting hearse. Stacey Boston turned to Harriet. 'I'll let you have the report on my findings as soon as possible, Harry. I shall start the PM as soon as I get back to the morgue.' She followed the coffin and climbed into the front seat of the hearse to be driven away. Bill Caldwell had been notified about the exhumation of his wife but his protestations were to no avail. The Coroner had signed the application and that made it law. Harriet turned to Ed.

'All we can do now is wait. Let's get back to the Station and have coffee before we brief the team on the happenings of last night. Have you heard how the young nurse is by the way?'

'Liz told Charlie that apparently they took her to the hospital last night because she was in such a state and her throat was very bruised. She had all but lost her voice by the time she reached the police station after she left us. They kept her in, by all accounts.'

'Poor soul.' Harriet was genuine in her concern. 'I'll see you back at the Station, Ed.'

'Right, Ma'am. I'll just speak to the men here and then I'll follow… Can you hang on a sec, Charlie?' he called, walking across to where Sergeant Marlow was strolling away from the graveside.

Harriet moved from the canopied area. Several people had gathered in the rain, including one or two reporters. The group of police officers was keeping them well back. A camera flashed and Harriet blinked. Beefy Cavendish shouted out, 'What can you tell about this then, Chief Inspector? Has it got anything to do with the nurse murders, or are we still fumbling in the dark?'

Harriet could do without these sententious remarks but answered in a calm voice. 'This has nothing to do with the case as far as we can tell. When the post-mortem has been carried out you will all be informed as to what is going on.'

There was another flash from a camera. Harriet tilted her umbrella deliberately and moved swiftly away towards her car. She spotted Michael Dellaware and smiled across at him. He was never intrusive like most of the others. She actually enjoyed his company. Michael raised a hand in acknowledgement but did not speak.

Back at Torreston Police Station Harriet made the coffee and awaited the arrival of her colleagues.

Over coffee with Ed and Charlie, she discussed the attack on Clare Jennings the previous night. Charlie stirred his coffee vigorously. 'I spoke to Liz at the hospital on my mobile this morning. She says Clare is feeling a bit better but has totally lost her voice. She's bloody lucky, Oh! Sorry, Ma'am – to be alive, I mean. We send out all these warnings and then these two do something as daft as visiting Railway Cottages late at night.'

Harriet realised that Charlie, with his relationship with Sister Jaques now progressing, was feeling the attacks were too close to home and it had obviously shaken him.

'Sometimes young people don't always consider what they are doing, Charlie,' she said quietly. 'They thought they would be safe together and after all we are the only ones who know that it is specifically Samanntha that he's after, so they were unaware that Station Road in fact held potential danger.'

Charlie drank noisily. 'Huh! They need to get the message that this bloke is dangerous.'

'This Clare could look rather like Samanntha in the dark,' interrupted Ed. 'About the same height and size, I'd say.'

'That's true. We can now be certain that he's determined to get Samanntha. 'Harriet placed a sheet of paper on her desk. 'This is the description of Murdock Pollard that Samanntha wrote for us. She read what was written, *Not very tall, slight in stature, sandy hair with very pale grey eyes, wears glasses.* Harriet rose. 'We'll carry out briefing.' She yawned. 'Sorry. I don't know about you, but I feel as if I have already done a full day's work.' She left the room followed by her colleagues.

At briefing in the Incident Room, Harriet explained the connection of Samanntha Farndon to the other murders. She wrote on the board the names of all the places where a nurse had been murdered. 'If you take the first letter of each place,' she explained. 'You will see that spelled out is the name SAMANNTHA. He slipped up in Northallerton and again in Nurcroft, when both women survived, and so he obviously gave up on the second *N*. He then moved on to Torreston, where he killed Carol Young, and for the *H* he killed Monica Meyers in Harbourne. The last letter to complete the name is *A*. Amchurch where Samanntha is now living.'

The group of officers standing in front of herself and DI Harrington were open-mouthed. Harriet continued telling the story of how Samanntha had nursed this man Murdock Pollard, and how she had rejected his advances and his presents, before finally leaving the Royal Infirmary in Leicester, to move away to Amchurch.

'This man Murdock Pollard sent Samanntha a red wool scarf,' Harriet told the team. 'It has been checked out and it is identical to the ones used in all the murders. Pollard was a sales rep at the factory and was therefore in possession of a good supply of the scarves. The one Samanntha received was accompanied by a note.' She wrote the words from the note on the whiteboard using capital letters in the appropriate places.

Dearest Ever Amid my Thoughts Hereafter.

Harriet spoke again. 'You will see where I have written in capitals the word spelled out is DEATH. This man is dangerous! Pull the stops out, everyone, we need to catch him. His description is on the board. Take note of it and keep your eyes peeled. All men on the beat will be given this description also.'

There was a buzz in the room as the officers discussed the situation. Jack Fuller spoke. 'I still can't find this chap Murdock, Ma'am. I've tried every trick in the book to trace him but he seems to have vanished into thin air.'

'Unfortunately no one has a photograph of Murdock Pollard, and the description given to us by Samanntha is simply, not very tall, of slight build, light coloured hair, pale eyes and glasses, and a slight accent which she was unable to recognise. But we are now convinced that he is our killer and he will have changed his name and appearance. He's out there somewhere and short of marching Samanntha to confront all the suspects we just have to be on the alert.'

'Samanntha is being brought to the Station by Greg Henderson sometime today,' announced Ed. 'He'll assist her in doing a photofit picture of Murdock Pollard which may be of some assistance to us. In the meantime we have a possible DNA profile, which really is good news. The SOCO team has taken away a woolly hat which we are pretty certain belongs to our man and is bound to have hair in it that we can use.'

'Good old Toowitt!' said someone in the room.

'We may also have tyre prints,' added Harriet. 'Once Sergeant Hewitt brings photographs of the prints in, there is checking to be done and we still have to continue our search for this Murdock Pollard. He is out there somewhere. Probably right under our noses.'

'And his car,' suggested Charlie. 'We need to remember that our suspect appears to have a car.'

'And if the nurse at the residential home who we spoke to after Monica's murder is correct, then we are looking for an old-fashioned, square-shaped car, pale in colour and possibly a Ford.' Harriet cast her eyes around the room. 'You will be issued with photographs of the tyre prints as soon as they arrive, so you all have plenty to do. I will leave DI Harrington to go over your duties for the day.' She turned to, Ed. 'Come to my office when you're finished, Ed. I'll be ready to leave for our session with the patients who use the hospital transport.' She flashed her disarming smile and left the room.

Fifteen minutes later Ed had concluded his briefing with the team and, gathering a handful of papers from the desk, he carried them down to the main office to deposit them with the Duty Sergeant. On entering the main foyer her saw the tall reporter he had met at the Gala Dinner. The young man had numerous photographs spread over the table beside him and he was sorting through them before busily pinning them on to the display board. On hearing footsteps behind him he turned. 'Oh, hi! Detective Inspector Harrington, isn't it? I do have permission to be doing this,' he added hastily as he saw the somewhat sombre expression on Ed's face.

'I'm sure you do,' replied Ed. 'I can't see Pete Yates letting you through the door without a formal pass.'

Michael Dellaware continued carefully choosing and then placing the photographs on the board. 'I'm pretty pleased with these. There's a good one of your group somewhere and an excellent one of DCI Love. She's very photogenic – I don't think there's a single bad one of her.'

'And there seem to be plenty of them,' remarked Ed almost sourly as he sifted through the pile on the table.

Michael looked across at his companion, not sure of his tone of voice. Perhaps he was just imagining it. Ed looked at the various photographs and his eyes lighted on a large one of a radiant Harriet Love on the arm of the very distinguished-looking Sir Richard Fitzwilliam, who was gazing at her with more than just friendliness. He picked it up. Michael looked over his shoulder.

'That's a beauty, isn't it. A very proud man showing off his beautiful daughter.'

Ed swung round. 'What do you mean, *daughter*?'

Michael Dellaware pulled a face. 'Don't think I should have said that, it's supposed to be kept secret! Ah well, too late now. Apparently DCI Love doesn't want anyone to know her father is Sir Richard. She was determined to climb the promotion ladder under her own steam and without using her influential father, he being a judge and pretty well-known in the area. She thought people might think there was a hint of nepotism if she were promoted to DCI, so she decided to use her mother's maiden name of Love when she applied for this position.'

'Well, I'm damned!' Ed let out the exclamation. 'So how do you know all this?'

'Superintendent Hollyoak let it slip when he was gathering people together to have pictures taken. He said to the judge, and I quote, "you must have a photograph taken with your beautiful daughter." When he realised what he had said and that I had overheard, he took me aside and explained the situation. Made me promise not to repeat what I had discovered. But now I've done the same thing, so for God's sake don't let on, will you.'

Ed picked up another photograph. He looked at the smiling DCI Love standing between her parents, her father gazing at her with admiration in his eyes. Yes, that's what it was, sheer admiration. It was the look that any proud father would give his successful daughter. How stupid he had been! It was all so obvious to him now. How could he have even thought that this charming woman could be having a seedy affair with a senior judge? He almost laughed out loud.

Michael Dellaware was speaking, 'This is the one I thought you would like.' He handed Ed the group photograph that had been taken at his table. His mother looked very happy, as did Charlie and Liz. Harriet Love was standing just behind himself, looking for all the world as if she were his partner, her smile as radiant as ever. Ed noticed his own face and felt suddenly guilty. He was almost scowling. He was not giving the impression that he was enjoying himself at all. Then of course that had indeed been the case. He placed the photograph back on the table with distinctly uneasy feelings regarding his behaviour at the Gala Dinner.

'They're very good! And don't worry, I won't mention what you have disclosed to me until the news eventually breaks out – and of course, it will. News like that can't stay a secret for very long.'

He walked away feeling strangely as if a load had been lifted from his shoulders. He puzzled as to why in heaven's name this revelation should make the slightest difference to him or the relationship between himself and his boss. But he knew that it did. He suddenly felt decidedly cheerful. Having handed the papers he was carrying to Pete Yates, he turned to leave. 'Hang on a tic, Ed,' said Pete. 'Paddy Lynch telephoned a few moments ago and asked me to tell you to give him a ring at the garage. He has some information that might help this murder case you're on.'

'Thanks, Pete. Can I use one of your phones?' As Sergeant Yates nodded, Ed picked up the telephone and dialled his friend.

Chapter Eighteen

Before leaving for Torreston Hospital where they were to interview people in the Physiotherapy Department, Ed explained to Harriet what Paddy Lynch had told him only minutes earlier.

'Paddy saw you on TV the other night and rang to tell me that he had an old car brought to his garage some months ago. It was late and Paddy was about to shut the garage when this car drove into the yard. He remembers it well because he told the owner that he thought the only place you would see a car like this was at a breaker's yard. It was a pale blue, square Ford Cortina Mark Three.'

'Fantastic, Ed. And is he able to describe the man?'

'He fits the other descriptions we've had. Not very tall, sandy hair, no woolly hat, but pale eyes. Paddy didn't notice a limp, but the bloke insisted he hung around the garage till the problem was fixed and then paid cash.'

'So he and his car are in the area, Ed. Someone must spot him soon. All the beat officers and patrol cars are on the alert and as Paddy said, you don't see many old cars like that on the road. Come on, Ed, let's get to the hospital and get these interviews over.'

Harriet and Ed Harrington arrived at Torreston Hospital. As always when working together, they had travelled in Ed's Saab. Harriet was surprised as to how talkative Ed was during the journey. Usually it was she who made all the conversation but on this occasion her companion chatted on in a most relaxed manner… a manner that had not been obvious during the other excursions they had made together.

'Right! Here we are,' said Ed brightly as he parked in the visitors' space. He jumped from the car and all but ran round to the passenger side of the car to open the door for Harriet. 'At least it's stopped raining.'

Harriet tried not to show her amazement. There had not been

a single 'ma'am' so far and she was unsure, but was that a semblance of a smile from the DI as he held the door for her?

'Thank you, Ed.' Harriet climbed from the car, and side by side the two officers entered the main entrance of the hospital. They collected their badges and explained why they needed to speak to various personnel in the hospital.

'We'll conduct these interviews together, Ed,' said Harriet, as they followed the signs to the Physiotherapy Department. 'Let's hope that the people we speak to are able to clear up a few of the cloudy areas.'

They reported to the receptionist and asked to see the Senior Physiotherapist. After only a matter of minutes they were directed into a large room which had the appearance of a well-equipped gymnasium. A woman in her early forties approached them.

'I'm Gloria Gardiner. What can I do to help you?'

'We are making enquiries about some of your patients who require physiotherapy,' said Harriet, with her usual charm. 'Could we speak to the person who takes care of these gentlemen?' She handed a piece of paper to the woman in front of them.

Gloria Gardiner pulled a face as she read the name Preston Skinner. 'He's mine. I could think of nicer people to treat than him, but there you are. Mark Ainsley, Mike Epsom and Ramsay Donaldson belong to Zoe Piper.' She pointed across the room. 'Zoe is working with Mike now, look, over there.'

On the far side of the room a tall young woman was assisting a large, solid-looking man in his early thirties to walk between parallel bars. His legs were heavily encased in straps and his expression was one of almost anger as he struggled to put one leg before the other. The patient was less than cooperative with his instructor and he could be heard grumbling and cursing as she gently tried to coax him to attempt the movement.

Ed indicated the other two names on the list. 'And these?' he asked.

'Both are MS sufferers and are cared for by Bella in another room, just down the passage. Their regime is slightly different from the patients in here, therefore they are attended to separately. The patients in this gym are involved in muscular and nerve repair and most have suffered trauma from accidents. Severe accidents,' she added.

Ed nodded. 'We'll start with Preston Skinner, then, as he is your responsibility.'

Gloria shook her head. 'I expect you are aware of his aggressive manner. I understand that the police were called to A & E the other night when he arrived demanding painkillers.'

'Yes, we were informed of the incident,' replied Harriet. 'As you know, we are investigating the murders of two nurses in the area and should like to know just how able Mr Preston is. He is one of the people we need to eliminate from our enquiries.'

'He *can* walk,' replied Gloria. 'But quite frankly he's not too steady on his feet and he does need arm crutches. You say you are investigating the nurse murders,' she went on. 'We don't have nurses down here in the Physio Department, as you will see. So whoever you are investigating would not have contact with nursing staff through this area.'

'Yes, that's interesting,' said Ed, 'but to get back to Mr Skinner. He managed to get to the hospital the other night, and from his flat to here must be all of a mile.'

'True,' agreed the physiotherapist, shaking her head. 'I was amazed that he had come so far on his own. If you had asked me last week if it were possible, I would most certainly have said no. But then, as I am sure you know, fear and anger give people new strength.'

'Thank you,' said Harriet. 'We'll have a word with Zoe if we may? But before we move on, do nurses ever have occasion to help out here?'

'Very rarely. If a patient collapses or becomes ill in any way, then of course we summon medical help.'

'Has there been such an incident in the last few weeks?' asked Harriet.

Gloria moved to the desk. 'I can soon tell you. All medical alerts are recorded.' She took a large red book from a drawer and flicked through the pages. 'Two scares in the last month,' she said.

'Which nurses came to assist?' asked Harriet hardly daring to hear the response.

Gloria was reading the entries. 'On the first occasion old Mr

Hammersley became very short of breath and Nurse Waterford attended and on the second Ramsay Donaldson had a violent nose bleed and Nurse Young attended. The same medical ward is on call for us.'

Harriet looked across at Ed and her eyes widened. Ed raised an eyebrow and then turned to Gloria Gardiner. 'May we speak to the rest of your staff please?'

'Of course. Speak to whoever you wish. Anything that we can do to help, just ask.' Harriet and Ed moved away. 'Well, there's your link with Carol Young and the Physiotherapy Department,' muttered Ed as they crossed the room.

'Indeed,' replied Harriet. 'Carol Young attended Ramsay Donaldson but she could have been seen by the other patients. Preston Skinner was there at the time – but isn't he a big man?'

'Biggish,' replied Ed.

'All the witnesses insist the attacker was slight. In fact the women who survived all say the man was not much bigger than themselves. Surely this rules out Skinner, however nasty he is.'

'Possibly.'

Harriet and Ed made their way across the room to where the tall, muscular figure of Zoe Piper was speaking gently to the large, stocky young man hanging on to the parallel bars. He was cursing and seemed less than willing to attempt to move. 'I don't want to bloody do this! I'll never play rugby again, so why bother to try and make me walk?'

Zoe was as patient as ever. 'You don't want to spend the rest of your life sitting in a chair, Mike. You're better than that. If you stick at it there's no reason why one day you won't be able to walk on your own.'

'Huh! Maybe I'd rather sit in a chair all day if I can't play rugby.'

'That's a poor attitude,' replied Zoe her voice remaining calm. 'I've had young men in here far more disabled than yourself and they have been determined to recover the use of their legs and most certainly have not given up.'

Mike Epsom ducked his head still grumbling and slowly dragged one leg forward.

'There you are, one whole bloody step!'

Harriet and Ed came up to Zoe. 'Could we speak to you for a few moments please?' said Harriet, showing her card. 'We are investigating the nurse murders.'

'Of course. Mike, you can have a rest while I speak with these people.' She wheeled a chair to the end of the parallel bars and assisted Mike into it. Go and get yourself a drink,' she said kindly. 'You've earned it.'

Ed spoke. 'Don't know how you have the patients with people like him. Don't you just want to fly off the handle sometimes?'

Zoe smiled a sad smile. 'I look at them and think how lucky I am to have two sound legs, and all my impatience vanishes. I'd rather put up with twenty hostile men during the morning than be in their position. Now, what can I do to help you?' She led the way to a corner of the room where there were some chairs and asked them to sit down.

Ed set the ball rolling. 'What can you tell us about Mike Epsom, Mark Ainsley and Ramsay Donaldson? Are any of them able to walk unaided and could they drive a car?'

'Mike broke his back in a rugby match. It could have been far worse. He could have been paralysed from the waist down, but in fact his paralyses are temporary and some feeling is returning to his legs. He will never be as mobile as he was before the accident but one day I hope he will be able to walk on his own.' Zoe sighed. 'At the present time he would be unable to drive a car.'

'You're saying he can't walk unaided at the moment?' suggested, Ed.

Zoe shook her head. 'You saw him on the bars. He can only just drag one leg before the other.'

'There's no chance he could be faking his disability?' suggested Harriet.

'No chance. His spinal injury is genuine; he was transferred here from the Royal Infirmary in Leicester soon after it happened and I have read all his notes. Anyway, for another thing, he's not the type; he couldn't cheat about something like that. He may be bitter about what has happened to him but he wouldn't hurt anybody.'

'We'd like the dates of the time he spent at the Royal Infirmary, please,' said Harriet.

'No problem, I'll get his notes when I have a spare moment and let you have the information.'

'What about Mark Ainsley?' asked, Ed.

'Lovely man, rarely complains. Pelvis and both legs smashed in a car accident. He is unable to walk at all. His legs were virtually rebuilt by the orthopaedic surgeon.'

'Will he ever walk?' Ed pursued.

'Doubt it; his back was damaged as well. He has great difficulty putting any pressure on his legs as yet. His therapy was slow getting started because of the horrendous burns when the car caught fire. He had to have skin grafts and they took some months to heal as you can imagine.'

'Was that done here?' enquired Harriet.

'No, Mark came to us less than a year ago. I'm not sure where he came from, but I can find out.'

'Thank you,' smiled Harriet handing Zoe her card. 'Give me a call when you have time to delve into these patients' notes. I can see you are very busy here.'

'And what about Ramsay Donaldson?' asked Ed.

'Totally paralysed from the chest downwards. Broke his neck in a climbing accident and he is quite immobile I can assure you.'

'Thank you for your help,' smiled Harriet, 'and we'd be grateful for that information about Mark Ainsley and Mike Epsom as soon as you can manage it.'

Harriet and Ed left the room. 'Wonder if Mike Epsom was nursed by Samanntha while he was at Leicester?' whispered Harriet as they headed for the room where the muscular sclerosis patients were having their therapy.

'Yet another line to follow up,' replied Ed.

They entered the next room, which was smaller than the first. Six men and four women were sitting in chairs and using frames to pull themselves to their feet. The movements were slow and laboured. A middle-aged woman standing in front of them like a conductor of an orchestra was encouraging them. On seeing the two officers she came towards them, calling over her shoulder to the group. 'Take a rest.'

Harriet and Ed showed their warrant cards and explained the reason for their visit. Bella Landsdown shook her head. 'I can categorically say that not one of my patients is capable of walking, let alone running, and as for strangling someone, absolutely impossible.' She waved her hand toward the group sitting quietly in their chairs. 'This is the more able of my groups, and there's not one of them who could manage to do what you suggest.'

Harriet and Ed were inclined to agree and minutes later they left the hospital. 'Perhaps we're on the wrong track after all, Ed,' said Harriet, as they made for his car.

'Early days yet,' replied Ed. 'We'll check out the two drivers again, just in case we've missed something.' Ed held the car door for Harriet and she smiled as she gracefully slid into the passenger seat.

'Good idea, but we still have to visit Mark Ainsley and Ramsay Donaldson.'

'Right, we'll do that first.' Ed drove off towards Osborne Road. 'Number 113, bottom flat, I believe.'

The front door of the house opened just as the two officers were about to ring the doorbell. A woman stood on the top step her face a mass of bruises and with a cut above her left eye that was still oozing blood.

'Good heavens, what has happened?' asked Harriet, stepping forward instinctively.

'Fell down the stairs,' muttered the woman, her eyes filling with tears. Ed was reading his notebook.

'Are you Veronica Caldwell?'

'Yes, and I suppose you're the police?'

'Why do you supposes that?' asked Harriet eyeing the woman's injuries.

The woman shrugged. 'You look like police.'

Ed closed his notebook. 'Has your husband been hitting you again?'

Veronica Caldwell burst into tears and Harriet took her arm and guided her back inside. 'Come along, tell us what really happened.' They followed Veronica up the stairs.

Once inside the top flat Harriet took a closer look at the cut above Veronica's eye. 'I'm no medical expert but I think that needs a stitch or two.'

'I was just on my way to the hospital,' wept the distraught woman.

'Why do you put up with it?' growled Ed. 'According to information I have from your neighbours this has been going on for some time.'

Veronica shivered. 'He doesn't mean it, I know he doesn't. But he just can't help himself when he's in a temper. He'll come home afterwards and be very sorry for what he's done and then everything will be fine again.'

'Until the next time,' said Ed who could never understand men who handed out violence to women.

'Do you wish to bring charges against your husband?' asked Harriet quietly.

Veronica shook her head. 'No.'

Harriet turned to Ed. 'Would you run Mrs Caldwell to casualty and I'll call on Mr Ainsley downstairs. Join me at his flat when you return, the hospital is only minutes down the road.'

Ed nodded. 'Come along, Mrs Caldwell.' The tearful woman rose to her feet and followed the tall figure of DI Harrington from the flat. Harriet followed closing the door behind her. On the ground floor she rang the bell of the only door on that level. She waited for a response. The sound of movement could be heard from inside the flat, and after what seemed to Harriet to be an inordinately long time, the door was opened by a pale-faced young man in a wheelchair.

'Sorry to keep you waiting, these things are not that easy to manipulate in a confined space. What can I do for you?' He dabbed his eyes with a handkerchief. 'Got an eye infection, have to be careful.'

Harriet produced her warrant card. 'Mark Ainsley?' and when the young man nodded. 'I'm making enquiries about the murders that have taken place in the area recently and wondered if you would mind answering a few questions.'

'Two officers have already been round asking questions,' replied Mark Ainsley his expressionless face looking up at Harriet.

'Yes and I'm sorry to disturb you again, but since this second murder we are retracing our steps to make sure we haven't missed anything. Sometimes people remember something that had escaped them on our first visit.'

The pale face smiled. 'Please come in. Anything that I can do to assist the police in these despicable murders would give me great pleasure. How anyone can kill young women just for the sake of killing amazes me.'

'There will be a reason, however bizarre it might appear to us,' said Harriet, following the wheelchair as the young man moved back into the flat. He bumped into the coffee table as he turned his chair around to face his visitor and promptly backed into the standard lamp, which was deftly caught by Harriet as it started to topple over.

Mark Ainsley smiled sheepishly. 'Thanks, I'm always doing that. There's not a lot of room in here.'

The room they were in was not that small but to someone in a wheelchair it must have appeared like an obstacle course. Harriet wrinkled her nose as the smell of incense reached her nostrils.

'Sit down, do,' said Mark Ainsley, nodding towards an armchair. 'I hope my joss sticks don't offend you?'

Harriet sat down and opened her notebook. 'Not at all,' she answered, 'but they are rather strong.'

'They give me such pleasure,' came the reply.

Harriet looked up from her notebook. 'I understand that you have been attending the Physiotherapy Department at the Cottage Hospital for about a year. At which hospital were you having your treatment before that?'

The young man frowned. 'Surely I'm not a suspect?'

'No one is a suspect at present, Mr Ainsley, but we do have to clear everyone who has contact with the hospital and who is unable to account for his movements on the nights of the murders.'

'Even if they're unable to walk?' The pale face had become quite sullen and the dark blue eyes that at this moment were red-rimmed, blinked rapidly to clear his vision.

'I'm afraid so.' Harriet remained cool and composed. 'We are treating everyone exactly the same, Mr Ainsley.' The doorbell rang at that moment. 'That will be my colleague, do you mind if I let him in?'

'Be my guest.' The voice was quite miserable but Harriet ignored the tone and went to the door to admit Ed. They returned to the room. 'This is the big interrogation now, is it?' asked the man in the wheelchair with a sardonic laugh.

'Not at all,' said Harriet. 'This is Detective Inspector Harrington, now where were we… You were about to give me the name of your previous hospital.'

Ed nodded to Mark Ainsley before sitting down. The man in the wheelchair seemed to pull himself together. 'I'm sorry. It's just that I get so depressed with my inability to do anything that sometimes I get a bit annoyed. I'm sure you can understand how I feel.'

'Of course,' replied Harriet. 'I can't begin to imagine how I would behave in your predicament.'

'Nor me.' Ed shook his head. 'Must be grim having to go everywhere in a wheelchair.'

'And relying on other people most of the time,' added Mark. He turned to Harriet. 'I was attending the Newcastle Infirmary before Torreston. Anything else?'

'Just one thing,' said Ed. 'I understand you were in a car accident some years ago, which resulted in your present condition. Could you tell me exactly where and when this occurred?'

'So this *is* an interrogation.' Mark Ainsley gripped the arms of his wheelchair his knuckles showing white and Ed thought he was about to burst into tears.

'Not at all, Mr Ainsley. We are just filling in a few gaps in our information.' Ed's voice remained calm as he looked at the young man, momentarily feeling mean.

'I crashed my car in the early hours of the morning in early February about three years ago.'

'I don't suppose you can remember the date?' Ed did not look up from his notebook.

'For God's sake!' Mark Ainsley wheeled his chair across the room angrily. He hit the coffee table again and stopped, swinging the chair around to face Harriet. 'Do I have to put up with this?'

'Sorry,' replied Harriet. 'But they are only routine questions so please answer Inspector Harrington.'

'Can't remember the exact date.' The voice was now sullen again. 'But it was a Saturday and early in the month.'

'In Newcastle?' Ed was not deterred.

'Yes.'

Ed rose to his feet. 'I think that will be all for now. Thank you, Mr Ainsley.'

Harriet and Ed left 113 Osborne Road and returned to the car. 'What do you think, Ed?' Harriet leaned on the Saab and turned to her colleague.

'Can't imagine he could commit a murder from his wheelchair, and the physio did say he hadn't even attempted steps as yet.'

'True, but something about him bothers me.'

'Probably the smell of those joss sticks.'

Harriet wrinkled her nose. 'Yes, they were pretty sickly, weren't they. But something is niggling at the back of my mind and I can't put a finger on it.'

Ed unlocked the car and opened the door for Harriet. 'It'll come,' he said.

On their way to Ramsay Donaldson's house Harriet enquired about Veronica Caldwell.

'I left her in casualty,' said Ed. 'But you're right, I should think she'll have a couple of stitches in that wound.'

Harriet sighed. 'Why is it some women put up with violence in the home without ever complaining?'

'Can't imagine.' Ed pondered over this and decided that he could not visualise his boss putting up with such treatment, but on the other hand he could not imagine that any man would wish to raise a fist to her. He pulled up outside a large detached Georgian house. 'This is the address.'

Ramsay Donaldson lived with his parents and it was his mother who opened the front door to them. Having explained the reason for their visit, Mrs Donaldson invited them in. 'I only wish my son did have the strength to commit a murder, not that he ever would. But you know what I mean, don't you.' She smiled a sad smile at the two officers and opened a door in the hallway. 'Here's Ramsay. We have fitted this room out for him to give him as much assistance as possible.'

She showed them into a room that was equipped with rails and pulleys where a young man was sitting in a wheelchair. On the table in front of him was a computer. Ramsay Donaldson was holding his right wrist with his left hand and laboriously tapping on the keys. He looked up as Harriet and Ed approached.

He stopped typing and allowed his right hand to drop into his lap. 'Hi. What can I do for you?'

He was almost cheerful and Harriet had the desire to turn and leave. This man had been seriously injured in a climbing accident and she felt guilty that they were disputing it. 'Just a couple of questions, Mr Donaldson. We're sorry to disturb you.'

'No problem. It's nice to have visitors. What can I tell you?'

Ed too realised that in no way was this man faking his disability and quickly spoke. 'We know that you visit the hospital for physiotherapy and wondered if you had ever seen anything or anyone suspicious that could be linked to the nurse murders?'

'I don't go that often because it's such a palaver getting me to and from the place. Mostly the physiotherapists come here to me. But I look forward to going to the hospital because for one thing it's an outing, and for another I meet people in the same mess as myself.'

Harriet nodded sympathetically. 'So there is nothing that comes to mind that might appear unusual or suspicious?'

'Sorry, nothing.'

Harriet turned to Ed. 'I don't think we need stay any longer do you, Inspector?'

'No, no. This is just routine, Mr Donaldson, we are obliged to speak to everyone.'

'No problem. Here, let me see you out. I'm not totally useless. I am able to use my fingers which control this chair by these buttons under the arm.' He gave a wistful smile. 'I just have difficulty in lifting my right arm, but once I have it in position I can usually manage.' He deftly manipulated his chair across the room. At the door his fingers moved again, finding the correct button under the wheelchair's arm, and the door opened. 'There! All done by remote control.'

Harriet and Ed thanked the man and left the house.

Once back in the car Harriet let out a big sigh. 'That was dreadful, Ed! That poor man is completely disabled, apart from being able to move his fingers. Thanks for helping out with the questions, I felt such a heel when I saw him like that.'

Ed nodded. 'Makes you grateful for good health and sound limbs, doesn't it?'

'It certainly does. At least having wealthy parents enables Ramsay Donaldson to have the best of everything at home, but I bet he'd swap all the money just to be able to use his own two legs again.'

'You can bet on it. What now?'

'Back to the Station. It must be time for coffee.'

A group of police officers was gathered in the reception area looking with interest at the photographs that Michael Dellaware had pinned to the notice board.

'Good one of you, Sir,' chirped Sally Pringle as Harriet and Ed arrived.

'Yes, you really look as if you're enjoying yourself,' laughed Duncan, noting the scowl on the Inspector's face.

Ed felt embarrassed and started to move away.

'Oh, come and have a look, Ed,' said Harriet.

'I've already seen them. I was down here when that reporter was putting them up.' He carried on upstairs.

Harriet thought the photographs were very good and she smiled as she watched Charlie gazing at the one of himself and Liz.

'You make a handsome pair, Charlie,' she said.

'Thanks, Ma'am. Liz is pretty special.'

They returned to the Incident Room together to find that Ed had already made the coffee.

'What a wonderful reception,' laughed Harriet as she sat down. 'I'm gasping for a cup, Ed.' Ed poured the coffee and handed Harriet a mug.

'Thank you. Now I might survive the rest of the afternoon. Right! We have several lines of enquiry to follow. Inspector Harrington will delegate these duties in a moment. I'd like Sally and Bob to re-interview June Pawlett in Northallerton. She was attacked in March and managed to survive. Her attacker left behind the red scarf that we have now matched to the ones used here in Torreston. Check the CCTVs in the car park, if there are any. June told us she didn't hear a car after her attack, but we now think our killer does indeed drive a car. You've got the details of the suspected vehicle. Old-fashioned, square shaped and a pale colour. Probably a Ford. Ask the local police what, if any clues were turned up at the scene. Were there tyre tracks, for instance? Anything that might match what we have found here.'

Ed turned to the two officers. 'It's already two, and it takes a good three hours to Northallerton. Would you rather leave it until tomorrow?'

Bob looked at his colleague. 'I'm game to go now if you are, Sally. I haven't anything planned for this evening anyway.'

'That's fine with me. I should have been at training tonight.' She took out her mobile telephone. 'But I'll just give my coach a ring to let him know I won't be there. I don't often miss sessions so I'm sure he'll let me off.'

DCs Sally Pringle and Bob Finch left the room. They would have to set off immediately if they were to be back at a decent hour this evening. Bob turned to Sally as they set off for Northallerton. 'Sorry about that, Sally, but I'm sure you would rather spend the time with me than go training.'

Bob Finch grinned as he sensed his partner pulling a face at him. He knew Sally to be a talented athlete and how dedicated she was to her training. When she was competing in big events, especially Nationals, those of her workmates who were off duty made a point of turning up to support her.

They arrived in Northallerton in good time and were lucky to discover June Pawlett at home.

'Come in,' she said on opening the door to them. 'Last visit I had from your Police Force was from that glamorous Chief Inspector. Couldn't believe she was a police woman!'

'She certainly is,' smiled, Sally. 'She has put all the men on their toes I can tell you. Even Bob here wears aftershave these days.'

'Don't be daft, of course I don't!' Bob was indignant but he felt himself go hot around the collar.

They asked June about the possibility of a car driving off after the attack on her, but as she had told the Chief Inspector, she couldn't remember having heard one. 'The only thing that really sticks in my mind is the smell, and you're not going to believe this, but I can smell it now.'

'What sort of smell?' asked Bob.

'I described it as antiseptic, but I'm not sure that's the correct description.'

'And you're a nurse!' laughed, Sally. She moved over to June Pawlett and sat beside her on the settee.

June sat upright. 'I *can* smell that smell. It's on you.' She looked at Sally in amazement.

Sally stood up and looked across at Bob who grinned at her. 'I know what that is. It's that stuff you rub your legs with when you're doing athletics. I get so used to the smell that I really don't notice it any more.'

'Oh gosh! Is it really that overpowering? I'm so sorry, but yes, I do use a strong embrocation on my leg muscles.'

'Well, that's what I smelt the night I was attacked,' said June Pawlett jubilantly.

'That's very interesting,' said Bob as he wrote in his notebook. 'Thank you for your help, Miss Pawlett, that bit of information could be quite significant.'

The two officers left the nurse's house to make their way to the police station where they met Sergeant Remshore. Bob produced his warrant card and introduced himself and Sally at the enquiries window. He informed the sergeant why they had come, and explained what information they required. The minute Gordon Remshore recognised from which force the two officers came, he was on his guard. 'Is that dragon with you?' he asked Bob, grinning slyly.

'I beg your pardon?'

'That Detective Chief Inspector Love.'

'She's certainly no dragon.' Sally leaped to their boss's defence.

Bob too felt obliged to defend Harriet. 'DCI Love is one of the best senior officers I've ever worked with.'

'Well, you haven't worked with many, sonny, have you,' sneered Sergeant Remshore. He still smarted when he remembered how Harriet had reprimanded him and he was in no mood to hide his hostility. 'Throwing her weight around as if she owned the place. Glad she doesn't work here.'

'She's probably glad too,' chipped in Sally. 'DCI Love doesn't tolerate fools gladly.'

'What d'you mean by that?' Sergeant Remshore glared at the young DC in front of him. These women coming into the force were nothing but a nuisance, whether they were young impudent constables or high and mighty senior officers. What was the force coming to? He pressed the button vigorously to allow the pair through the door, scowling as they passed by him.

Bob Finch and Sally Pringle spent nearly two hours at Durston police station. They read and re-read the files on the attack on June Pawlett and jotted down the information they considered relevant. There had been no CCTV cameras in the hospital car park at the time of the attack, but a footnote on one of the pages indicated that this was being rectified immediately. 'We always close the stable door when the horse has bolted, don't we,' said Sally as they closed the files. They left the Records Office and returned to reception to be allowed out.

Sally turned to Gordon Remshore at the exit. 'Thank you so much, Sergeant.' She smiled at the disgruntled figure sitting in the small office. 'Wonder what DCI Love did to upset him?' she whispered to Bob as they went down the steps.

'Can't imagine, but you're right when you say she doesn't tolerate fools. I should think she probably put him in his place at some point during her visit.' They returned to the car. It was just after seven.

They had completed the enquiries that they had been instructed to do and now it was time to return to Torreston. They would report their findings at the briefing tomorrow morning.

As they got in the car Bob Finch said, 'We'll consider ourselves off duty, Sally, fancy a bite to eat at a pub?'

'That would be great. I can't remember when I last ate anything. But we go Dutch, if you don't mind.'

'Okay. Keep your eyes peeled for a decent pub and that's what we'll do. I've just realised that I'm starving.' He put the car into gear and headed for the road.

Chapter Nineteen

Harriet had been home barely ten minutes when the telephone rang. Stacey Boston could hardly contain herself as she delivered the news that excessive amounts of barbiturates had been discovered in the body of Sarah Caldwell. 'I've just arrived home Harry and couldn't wait to call you with this result. You were right to be suspicious about the cause of death.'

Harriet took a deep breath. 'Well, what a revelation! I know I was suspicious about Bill Caldwell having two wives die in surprising circumstances, but when the results actually turn up positive, it's still difficult to comprehend.'

Stacey laughed. 'Well, I can assure you, the results are very conclusive. I discovered massive amounts of barbiturates at Mrs Caldwell's autopsy so the rest is up to you. I'll call at the Station in the morning to give you my full report.'

'Thank you, Stacey. Come for coffee, will you?'

'Will do. See you tomorrow.'

Harriet sat and digested the piece of news that Dr Boston had just given her. She did not think that either of the Caldwell brothers had anything to do with the murders they were investigating, but she had always considered them dangerous characters. She remembered Veronica's face when she had called at 113 Osborne Road with Ed that very morning. She dialled Ed's number. It rang several times before the answerphone cut in. Harriet left a brief message asking him to call her back if it was not in too late when he returned home. By ten thirty Harriet was yawning, and with Toastie doing his best to trip her up she climbed the stairs and went to bed. The large Maine Coon jumped up beside her and nestled down.

Harriet slept soundly and awoke with her alarm ringing in her ears. Toastie did not appear to have moved at all and she stroked his long fur affectionately, saying, 'Come on, you lazy thing, breakfast time.'

Harriet arrived at the Station at ten to eight. Ed and Charlie appeared on the hour and went immediately to Harriet's office. 'Sorry I didn't call you back last night,' said Ed, 'but it was after eleven when I got in and I didn't think you would appreciate me calling at that hour.'

'Out somewhere interesting?' asked Harriet.

'Went to the pub with Paddy Lynch.'

'Paddy might well be interested with the news I have as he was the officer in charge of Mrs Caldwell accident.'

'You've got the result of the autopsy, then?' chipped in Charlie excitedly.

Harriet nodded. 'Dr Boston telephoned me at home last night; that's why I called you, Ed. Massive amounts of barbiturates were found in Sarah Caldwell's body.'

'Well I'm blowed!' Ed puffed out his cheeks. 'Do we arrest him this morning?'

'Indeed we do.' Harriet took her coffee and cafetière from the cupboard. 'After coffee.'

'My turn, Ma'am,' grinned, Charlie. He took the coffee-pot and tin of coffee from Harriet and left the room.

'You were right, then,' said Ed. 'But are you still convinced he's not involved with the nurse murders?'

'You can never be totally sure until the case is closed, Ed. But quite honestly, no, I don't think he or his brother are involved with killing the nurses. What we will do before we make the arrest is check all the despatch notes at Garratts warehouse. The files must show discrepancies somewhere, if Caldwell has been helping himself to drugs.'

Ed nodded. 'I'll get a search warrant so that we can check his house before we go to the warehouse. It would help to have some sound evidence against him.'

'Absolutely. I'll leave you to obtain the warrant, Ed. We'll leave as soon as Dr Boston delivers her written report. That will give us time to carry out briefing before we set off.'

Charlie returned with the coffee and Harriet explained to him what they had decided to do.

At briefing Harriet explained the situation to the team. 'Sally, I know you will be interested to hear that the second Mrs Caldwell died from a huge dose of barbiturates and must have been unconscious before she went over the cliff in the car. We will be searching Bill Caldwell's house before checking the warehouse records for missing drugs and then hopefully we shall be arresting him.'

'Pity his first wife was cremated,' said, Sally. 'She was probably drugged as well.'

'We shall never know the answer to that one, Sally, but with luck we shall get him for murdering Sarah.' Harriet turned to Bob Finch as he asked the next question.

'How does he fit in with the nurses murders, Ma'am?'

'At the moment we have no evidence to show a connection between Bill Caldwell and the other murders,' she answered.

'And his nasty brother Vincent?' Sally was delighted that they were getting one Caldwell but Vincent Caldwell needed removing as well, as far as she was concerned.

'I know how you feel, Sally,' answered Harriet. 'I only wish his wife would make charges against him, but you know as well as I, that we cannot force her to come forward.'

Harriet looked across at Ed and he stepped forward. 'We still have a great deal to do. Now, would Sally and Bob like to enlighten us about their visit to Northallerton yesterday.'

Bob Finch took over. 'It was quite interesting. As June Pawlett stated, she heard no car at all the night she was attacked, and there are no CCTV cameras in the car park. Not that we think a killer would oblige us by parking in an official car park. But she did give us a lead.' He looked at Sally, who stood up to continue the story.

'June recognised the smell she smelt the night she was attacked.' The young DC smiled. 'She smelled it on me. It was embrocation. The stuff that I rub my legs when I've been training.'

'The stuff that someone with leg muscle weakness might use,' said Charlie triumphantly.

'Interesting,' mused Harriet. 'Perhaps you and Bob should pay Sheila Werrington a visit. She's the other nurse who was attacked and survived. She too said she smelt antiseptic. See if she agrees with June Pawlett. Oh and Sally. Remember to treat your legs before you go.' Harriet smiled as she spoke.

Sally giggled. 'I hadn't realised that I was going around the place smelling.'

'We're all used to it,' said Narinder. 'I live with you and the house smells like a chemist shop.' In a whisper she added, 'I'm not sure which smell is the stronger, your embrocation or the DCI's perfume.'

Ed interrupted. 'Right let's move on, there's a lot to get through today.' The group dispersed.

Stacey Bolton arrived with the post-mortem report and was shown into Harriet's office. Ed and Charlie had left to apply for the search warrant. Harriet made more coffee before she and Stacey sat down to go over the results.

'It's all quite conclusive. Massive amounts of barbiturates, and she was certainly dead before she went in the water. There *is* no evidence of drowning and no other injuries. The car simply slid over the side into the water.'

'Thanks, Stacey, this is just what we need.'

Stacey Boston rose to leave. 'We must make a date for dinner at my place, Harry.'

'As soon as this case is closed. I really do feel that the net is closing in on the killer, so we will arrange our get-together as a celebration.' Harriet walked to the door with the young pathologist.

Stacey nodded. 'Let's hope it's soon. I'll be in touch,' she said, and left.

The telephone rang. The voice of Michael Dellaware came on the line. 'Did you like the photographs, Chief Inspector?'

'Oh, Michael, hello… Yes, they were very good. Thank you so much for a wonderful display and I shall be ordering some, as will my colleagues.'

'That's fine,' replied Michael. 'I was using the photos as an excuse to call you, Harry. I wondered if you would have dinner with me tonight.'

'Under normal circumstances I would love to, Michael, but until this case is solved I'm going nowhere socially. In fact, I've just turned down another invitation, so could we put dinner on hold?'

'Of course. I'm disappointed but I do understand.'

'Thank you, Michael. I'll keep the press informed of progress, and with luck the case will be closed in a matter of days. But don't print that will you,' Harriet added hastily.

'Of course I won't. I'll ring you soon. Goodbye.'

Harriet replaced the receiver with a smile. A date for the future. Michael Dellaware was certainly charming. She would look forward to having dinner with him.

George Hollyoak poked his head round the door. 'Harry, can you spare a moment?'

'Of course what is it? You look so serious?'

Superintendent Hollyoak frowned. 'I've got the Deputy Chief Constable in my office asking how the case is getting on. He would like a word with you. He doesn't appear to be in a very good frame of mind, Harry, so tread carefully.'

Harriet had butterflies in her stomach as she followed George Hollyoak from the room. Martin Cotton was known to have reservations about women in senior positions and she had learned, after her successful application for promotion to Chief Inspector, that the one person on the interviewing panel who had opposed her appointment had been him. She held her head high and entered the Superintendent's office. Martin Cotton was a tall, corpulent man with thinning grey hair, an aquiline nose and sharp, hard eyes. He rose as they entered.

'Ah, Chief Inspector.' He held out his podgy hand which Harriet grasped firmly, determined to show no sign of her nerves. 'What can you tell me about this murder case? It seems to be dragging on…'

'Hardly dragging,' replied Harriet meeting his eyes with a steady gaze. 'Dragging implies moving tediously and slowly. The investigation into the nurse murders is neither of those. We are moving in a positive manner but confirming each new disclosure as we go along. No stone has been left unturned and I honestly feel we are all but there.'

'But not actually there.' Martin Cotton's eyes narrowed as he reseated himself. 'Do sit down,' he said to Harriet.

Harriet obliged and waited for the next question.

'Look, I wondered if it might be a good idea to bring DCI Westwood in to assist you?'

Harriet sat up straight. 'Is that because I'm a woman, Sir?' she asked in a cold voice.

'No, no, certainly not. I just thought you might need some help.'

Harriet rose to her feet and faced him. 'When I need help I will ask for it, Sir. I keep Superintendent Hollyoak fully informed about how the case is progressing and he is aware of all that I and the team are doing. So far I have received no complaints from him.'

George Hollyoak intervened. 'The case has been a puzzling one, Sir. There has been no motive to these murders, which in turn makes it very difficult to find a lead. Chief Inspector Love has been most diligent in her investigations and I am convinced that she is close to making an arrest.'

'Thank you, Superintendent,' said Harriet. She sat down again and returned her attention to the pompous man sitting at the desk in front of her. 'These murders started a year ago in Scotland,' she continued. 'They moved down the country to the Midlands and it was my team who recognised that there was a link, instigating the enquiries that uncovered the possible connection. I now know why the murders took place in the manner they did and I also know the name of the man we are looking for. It is only a matter of time before we have him and all this has happened in just over a week. I don't think anyone would call that an excessive amount of time, Sir. However, if you choose take your complaint about me to the Chief Constable I shall be happy to enlighten him on the matter.' Harriet's green eyes flashed and Martin Cotton shifted uncomfortably in his chair. He did not want the Chief Constable involved. He knew Brian Nattrass was very keen on promoting strong women into senior positions and this woman in front of him was certainly that. She was not going to crumble under his pressure so better let her get on with it. He coughed.

'Well, so long as you are happy with the way things are moving, Chief Inspector, and you Superintendent also, we'll let you continue.'

'How kind of you, Sir.' Harriet was still on a roll. She tossed her head. 'I sincerely hope that I shall be continuing with the case because I am doing a satisfactory job and making excellent progress with the investigation. I have done nothing incorrectly therefore no one has the right to remove me from the case other than the Chief Constable if he feels I am incompetent. Do you consider me incompetent, Mr Cotton?'

Martin Cotton rose to his feet. He felt decidedly shaky. 'Now, young lady…'

'Do not patronise me, Sir. Please answer my question. Do you consider me to be incompetent?'

'No, no I never said you were incompetent, I only asked if you needed some help with the case.' He wished he had never started this conversation; why hadn't he just let well alone? Hollyoak had told him the case was moving satisfactorily, but he had thrown his oar in and disturbed still waters. He coughed. 'Chief Inspector, all I can say is that I am sorry. I had no intention of upsetting you and I most certainly do not consider you incompetent.'

Harriet had forced the Deputy Chief Constable to admit that she was not incompetent and she was pleased. Martin Cotton was speaking again. 'I am more than happy that you continue with this case, Chief Inspector, and may I wish you good luck in a satisfactory and speedy conclusion.'

Superintendent Hollyoak stepped forward hastily and took Harriet's elbow. He had no desire for Harriet to push her luck too far. 'Er, if that's all, Sir,' he said, looking from the DCC to Harriet. He guided her towards the door and as he opened it he whispered in her ear, 'Well done, Harry.'

Harriet returned to her office to find Ed and Charlie waiting for her. Her face was flushed and was still fuming. This was noted by her two companions.

'Anything wrong Ma'am?' asked Ed.

'Martin Cotton.' Harriet sat down behind her desk. 'He is only implying that I'm not up to the task of solving this case. He suggests he brings in DCI Westwood to assist me. What a cheek.'

'Wally Westwood,' sneered, Charlie. 'He *would* want him on the case, they're as thick as thieves. Westwood is a real creep. Sucks up to all the senior officers and some of them are taken in. He'd just love to muscle in on our patch.'

'What was the outcome of all this?' asked Ed in a subdued voice. He too had little respect for Westwood and dreaded the thought of him taking over from DCI Love.

Harriet looked up, her cheeks pink and her eyes glinting. 'Don't worry – I gave as good as I got and Cotton backed off. We are back on the case, gentlemen.' She grinned and her face lit up.

Ed wondered if the Deputy Chief Constable knew that the woman he had challenged was the daughter of Mr Justice Fitzwilliam. Probably not, if he had dared to try and undermine her. He looked at the woman sitting at the desk in front of him. She was alive and eager to get on. He showed her the search warrant. 'Shall we go?' he asked.

Bill Caldwell lived in a large house on one of the new estates. The three officers walked up to the front door and Ed knocked. They heard movement inside and waited.

The door was opened by a young woman in her twenties who eyed them up and down cautiously. 'Yes?' she enquired.

'Police,' said Ed, holding out his warrant card. 'We have a search warrant for these premises. May we come in?'

'Don't suppose I can stop you.' The woman held the door open for them to enter.

Ed and Charlie vanished into the house and Harriet turned to the woman. 'What is your name?' she asked.

'Tracie Tocane.'

'Do you live here with Mr Caldwell.'

'Yes. I'm his partner.'

'How long have you been his partner, Miss Tocane?'

'About ten months.'

'Did you know Mrs Caldwell? She died barely twelve months ago.'

'I sort of knew her,' replied Tracie Tocane. 'But not really as a friend.'

'I'm sure not.' Harriet walked past the woman and joined Charlie in the front room. Tracie Tocane followed.

'What are you looking for?' The woman now appeared agitated. It was Charlie who answered her.

'We'll know when we find it.'

Ed came from upstairs. 'I think this is what we are after.' He was carrying a cardboard box containing an assortment of boxes and containers. He took out a few cartons. 'Antibiotics, barbiturates and heaven knows what else – all the evidence we need, I think.'

'I know nothing about any of this,' shouted Miss Tocane. 'What Bill does is his own business and nothing to do with me.'

Ed nodded to Charlie. 'There's another couple of boxes at the bottom of the wardrobe in the back room if you'd like to go and get them.' Charlie left the room and Harriet moved across to Ed and spoke in a whisper.

'We'd better take her with us Ed or she will contact Caldwell before we can get to the warehouse.'

'Right.' He turned to Tracie Tocane. 'We should like you to accompany us, if you don't mind, as we need to ask you a few more questions.'

'Are you arresting me?'

'No, you're simply helping us with our enquiries. Please get your coat.'

Charlie returned with two more cardboard boxes. 'He must have been filching this stuff for a very long time to have accumulated so much.'

'Put the boxes in the car, Charlie,' said Harriet, 'and let's get over to the warehouse.'

On arriving at Garratts warehouse Charlie was left in the car with Tracie Tocane while Harriet and Ed made their way to the manager's office. On introducing themselves they asked to see the delivery books. 'Do many items go astray?' asked Harriet.

'There's always a certain amount of damage and breakage,' replied Granville Smith, 'and as you will see in the book everything is clearly recorded and signed by the member of staff involved, and myself.'

Ed flicked through the pages. 'An awful lot of stuff appears to have been destroyed by the Caldwells.'

'When packaging is damaged causing contamination, the drug is destroyed and I always witness that procedure myself, I can assure you.'

Harriet looked over Ed's shoulder. 'How are the damaged drugs disposed of?'

'They are burned in the furnace in the basement.'

'May we see the furnace, please?' asked Ed.

'Of course.' Granville Smith removed his spectacles and polished them vigorously. He hated scenes like this. He just wanted to do his job as well as he could and collect his pay at the end of each month. 'If you'll follow me I'll lead the way.'

Down in the basement a furnace was roaring in the corner of the large, brick, cellar-like room. Cardboard boxes and other rubbish lay around. Smith turned to the officers. 'Can you tell me what all this is about?'

'Eventually,' replied Harriet. She looked at the furnace, which was like a large oven with a glass front showing a glowing red through it. The heat was easily felt from some distance away. She turned to the manager. 'You say you supervise any destruction of drugs. Can you demonstrate how exactly you do that?'

Granville Smith coughed. He was now becoming nervous. There had never been any trouble at the warehouse in all the time he had been in charge and he did not want any now. 'The person filling in the damaged goods book brings the box down here and I stand beside him as he puts the packages in the fire. I then sign the book to confirm they have been destroyed.'

'Do you actually handle the drugs before they go in the incinerator?' asked Harriet.

'Well, not exactly. I read the box to check the name of the drug and I record the lot number in the book. I stand and observe as each package goes into the flames.'

'In other words,' said Ed dryly. 'The items going into the flames could be anything. Packets of flour or boxes of Smarties.'

Smith sat down on a wooded box and mopped his brow with a large handkerchief. 'Oh my God, what has happened?'

Harriet answered him in a quiet voice. 'We have reason to believe that two of your drivers have been helping themselves to barbiturates and other drugs. Certain names turn up all too frequently in this book and I'm surprised that alarm bells did not ring, Mr Smith, seeing the number of times the Caldwell brothers declared damaged or even lost drugs. I thought Vincent Caldwell only helped out when you were desperate? He seem to be here a great deal lately.' She turned to Ed. 'We need another search warrant, this time for Vincent Caldwell's flat.'

Mr Smith coughed nervously. 'Vincent Caldwell is legally on the books. He now works here part-time.'

'Indeed.' Harriet frowned. The two brothers working together formed an undesirable combination, in her mind.

'I'll see to the search warrant,' said Ed and left the basement room.

Harriet turned to Smith. 'Where are the Caldwells at the moment?'

'Both out on deliveries.'

'When will they return?'

'Late afternoon.'

'Very well,' said Harriet. 'The moment they drive into the yard you call me on this number and we shall be over. And not a word to anyone, please.' She handed him her card. 'I should like to borrow this as well,' she said picking up the 'destroyed drugs' book. 'We have some drugs in the car that we should like to match with drugs from this warehouse.' Clutching the book, she left to join Ed.

Back at Torreston police station Harriet sent for Narinder Pancholi. She explained who Tracie Tocane was. 'We need to keep her here until we have arrested the Caldwell brothers, Narinder. Give her lunch and a cup of tea and make her comfortable. After her lunch take her to an interview room and do the usual questioning, but nothing too heavy. It's the boyfriend we're after. She might know something, but I doubt it; we just need to make keeping her here look official until we bring in the Caldwells. Convince her she is not under arrest, and as soon as we return with the two men we can let her go.'

'Right, Ma'am, I understand.' Narinder smiled at the DCI and left the office.

Harriet had remembered to bring sandwiches with her and having made a pot of coffee she took them from her desk drawer. She had just taken the first bite when the internal telephone rang. It was Pete Yates at the main desk.

'Sergeant Hewitt is on his way up, Ma'am. I said you were in, I hope that's all right.'

'Of course, Pete. Thank you.' As she replaced the receiver there came a knock at the door. 'Come in, Phillip.'

Sergeant Hewitt entered the room. 'Are you psychic, Ma'am, or are you able to see through doors?' The serious face broke into a smile.

'Pete Yates called me. No one gets by Sergeant Yates unannounced. Sit down, Phillip, you obviously have information for me.'

'I do indeed, Ma'am.' He sat down at the desk and produced some photographs. 'Some excellent shots of tyre tracks, none of which belong to any of the cars belonging to the residents of Railway Cottages. As they were made on the evening of the attack they can only belong to the attacker's car.'

'For once we must be grateful for rain,' said Harriet, taking the photographs. 'These are certainly clear, Phillip.'

'And distinctive, Ma'am. You will see that the treads are of an unusual pattern and on one of the tyres there is a deep, jagged cut across the pattern. There would be little difficulty in matching this tyre with the attacker's car, if we could just find it.'

'Thank you for these,' smiled Harriet. 'We'll distribute them to all units and hope that some sharp-eyed officer spots the car we're after.'

Phillip Hewitt stood to leave. 'Any news on the DNA from the hat, Ma'am?' he asked.

'Not yet, but it shouldn't be long now.'

After the departure of Phillip Hewitt, Harriet called Jack Fuller to her office and handed him the photographs of the tyre prints. 'We need copies of these distributed to the men in uniform, on car patrol and to all CID officers, Jack. We just need one stroke of luck in this car being found and then perhaps we can trap him. Explain that we think the car is of the old-fashioned square type and pale in colour. There *is* such a car in the area Jack, it was taken to Paddy Lynch's garage recently. He rang Ed to say that a pale blue Ford Cortina Mark Three had been brought to him for repairs. We need to find it. The nurse describing the vehicle she had seen was not exactly au fait with cars, but thought it could be a Ford, so with Paddy's information it looks as if she could be correct.'

Jack puffed out his chest. 'Leave it to me, Ma'am, I'll see that the photographs are distributed immediately.' Clutching the precious pictures he hurried away.

Harriet finished off her sandwiches and awaited the return of Ed with the second search warrant. It was mid-afternoon when the three officers set out to search the house in Osborne Road. When Veronica Caldwell answered the door Harriet was most apologetic. 'I'm sorry to have to ask you to allow us to search your house Mrs Caldwell.'

Veronica Caldwell still looked the worse for wear, with her bruised face and steri-strip stitches over her cut eye. She looked tired and forlorn and made no comment as she held open the door. Harriet with her two colleagues entered the flat. As Ed and Charlie commenced the search, Harriet turned to Veronica and asked, 'How do you feel?'

The injured woman shook her head. 'Pretty awful,' she replied. 'But it's not just my cuts and bruises. I feel so depressed at what keeps happening to me, and now this! What has Vince been up to now?'

At that moment Ed reappeared carrying a cardboard box. 'Same as in his brother's house,' he said. 'Charlie has another couple of boxes of the same.'

'What is it?' asked Veronica sounding genuinely surprised.

'Drugs, I'm afraid,' answered, Ed.

'Oh God.' Veronica Caldwell held her aching head in her hands. 'It's his brother, I swear it. People think Bill's the quiet, decent one but he's not, I tell you that. He's bloody not. He has a real hold over Vince and Vince like a fool does everything he's told to do.'

'Does that include hitting you?' said Ed, bitterly.

Harriet looked at the pitiful figure in front of her. 'Do you know anything about these drugs, Mrs Caldwell?'

'No, nothing! I had no idea Vince was into drugs. I'm sure he never takes any. I'd know if he did.'

Harriet spoke again. 'We shall be taking your husband to the police station when he arrives back from his deliveries, so don't expect him home on time. If you wish to come to the station to be with him, you may, of course.'

'No, I won't bother,' replied Veronica. 'He'll be home soon enough for me.' Carrying the three cardboard boxes containing the drugs, the officers left the flat on Osborne Road.

As Ed and Charlie placed them in the boot of the Saab, Harriet's mobile phone rang. She said only two words. 'Thank you.' She turned to Ed and Charlie as she pressed a series of numbers into her phone. 'The Caldwell brothers are back at the depot. I'll just call the station for cars to meet us there and then we're off.'

Harriet and her two colleagues arrived at Garratts warehouse to be greeted by the manager, Granville Smith, who was hovering nervously in the car park. 'I haven't said a word to them,' he said as they approached.

'Thank you,' replied Harriet. 'Where are they?'

'In the large warehouse round the back. They're unloading and finishing up for the day. You don't need me with you, do you?'

'That won't be necessary,' said Ed. 'I'm sure the Caldwells will be in touch with you at a later date. When the police cars arrive, ask the officers to wait here for us, please.'

They set off for the warehouse. Bill and Vincent were sitting on a box by the side of a large covered lorry when the three officers entered the building. They were sharing a laugh about something and Harriet thought to herself that they would not be laughing for very much longer. She stepped back allowing Ed to take over. He produced his warrant card and faced Bill Caldwell. 'Bill Caldwell, I am arresting you for the murder of your wife, Sarah Caldwell, you do not have to say anything but anything you do say…' He continued reading the arrested man his rights.

Charlie likewise faced Vincent Caldwell. 'Vincent Caldwell, I am arresting you on the suspicion of stealing drugs from your employer, Garratts Warehouses.' Vincent too was read his rights.

Bill Caldwell let out a hoarse laugh. 'What a bloody joke! Sarah was killed in a car crash and nobody suggested murder. You're making one hell of a mistake.'

'I think the mistake was yours, Mr Caldwell,' said Harriet. 'Your wife's body has been shown to have an inordinate amount of barbiturates in it and you too are being charged with obtaining drugs by stealing. We have searched both your houses and removed large quantities of drugs that bear corresponding batch numbers to drugs from this warehouse. All of which, I may add, were supposedly legally destroyed by one or other of you.'

As the group walked back to the main entrance of the

warehouse company two police cars were waiting. The brothers were placed in separate cars and driven away.

Harriet sighed. 'Well, that's one matter dealt with, but now back to the Station and the other matter of murder still to be resolved. Charlie can I leave you to the details of charging the Caldwells?'

'Certainly, Ma'am, it will give me great pleasure.'

They climbed into the black Saab to return to Headquarters.

Chapter Twenty

Bill Vincent was remanded in custody and charged with the murder of his second wife, Sarah. Vincent Caldwell was charged with stealing drugs from his employers, Garratts warehouses, and released on bail. Charlie explained the situation to Harriet in her office.

'Thanks for that, Charlie. Let's hope that we can put at least one nasty piece of work away for a while. I wonder if Sarah Caldwell was disposed of to accommodate Tracie Tocane?'

'Probably,' said Charlie 'and I wonder how long Tracie would have lasted before she was tired of and eliminated.'

'Heaven forbid, Charlie.'

Charlie pulled a face. 'There are certainly some strange people about, Ma'am. Take this creep we're looking for at the moment. Who in their right mind goes around killing nurses for no apparent reason?'

'You're right, Charlie, although in his own twisted mind he will have a reason. Let's just hope his days are numbered and we will get him before he is able to do any further harm.'

'It was a pity Samanntha was not too confident about the photofit she did of Murdock Pollard. She said her memory of him had faded and the only thing that stuck in her mind were his pale eyes. I left a copy of the photofit on your desk, Ma'am.'

'Yes, thank you, Charlie, I have it here.' Harriet picked up the picture and looked at it. 'It doesn't really resemble anyone who we have on our list does it?'

''Fraid not.' Charlie pulled a face. 'At least we know Samanntha is under protection. I'm going over there this evening to speak to Greg Henderson. He's been sleeping on the settee at night so that the nurses feel safer.'

'That's good, Charlie. If Greg does the night shift, who is with her during the day?'

'The squad car takes Samanntha to the hospital and leaves her.

It collects her when she comes off duty and returns her home. There is a rota of officers covering the rest of the time until Greg takes over, and of course on his day off.'

'That sounds fine. Just make sure she is never on her own when away from the hospital, Charlie.'

'Sure thing, Ma'am. See you tomorrow.'

Charlie left the Station. Liz was working the late shift tonight and he had agreed to pick her up from the hospital when she finished her duty. Charlie felt so much happier having Liz at his house. He could keep an eye on her and make sure she came to no harm. Not that it was such a big issue any more as it was now obvious that the killer's target was Samanntha. He would go home and have something to eat before calling at Diane Willarby's house to see how things were progressing.

It was nine thirty when Charlie pulled up in Kelmarsh Road. It was raining very slightly. A storm had been forecast, which was not surprising as the last couple of days had been hot and humid. The lights were on at Number 12 and music could be heard coming from the front room. As Charlie rang the doorbell he heard laughter and he smiled. Not a bad job for a bobby, spending his evenings with three young ladies… Diane Willarby opened the door a few inches keeping the chain securely in place.

'Oh hello, Sergeant,' she smiled, releasing the chain and opening the door fully. 'Come in, we're just having coffee.'

Charlie entered the front room where PC Greg Henderson was sitting between Samanntha and Heather on the settee, the three of them obviously getting on like a house on fire. Greg jumped to his feet as Sergeant Marlow appeared. 'Evening, Sarge.'

'Hi Greg. All's well, I see.'

'Absolutely fine. No strangers about the place and no callers.'

Charlie nodded. 'That's good. But in future make sure it's you who opens the door and not one of the ladies, Greg. Let's be absolutely on our guard.'

'Of course, sorry,' Greg replied.

Dianne jumped to his defence. 'That was my fault, Sergeant. I was in the kitchen making the coffee and got to the door first. Will you join us for a cup? Please sit down.'

'Thanks, I will,' said Charlie sitting down in the chair that

Diane indicated. He turned to Samanntha. 'So no problems, Samanntha?'

'None at all and please call me Sam.'

Charlie grinned. 'Thanks.' He accepted the cup of coffee handed him by Diane and took a sip. 'Glad to see you serve the real thing,' he said. 'Our new boss won't drink anything else and now has us all following suit.'

Greg Henderson chuckled. 'She's a smasher, though, Sarge. How do the men cope in CID? Especially Jack Fuller, who is known as anti-women senior officers.'

'You'd be amazed,' replied, Charlie. 'He thinks she's the bee's knees and won't hear a word against her.'

'Wow! That's a turn up for the book. Never thought I'd live to see the day that old Jack was happy working under a female officer.'

'Well, there you are,' said Charlie, rising. 'We're all so wrapped up in this case that quite honestly no one has the time to discuss the new boss. We just want to catch this blighter before...' Charlie quickly changed what he was about to say when he noticed the fear creep into Samanntha' s eyes... 'before he leads us much more of a dance.' He moved to the door. 'Now don't you ladies worry, you're in safe hands. Come and see me out, Greg.'

At the front door Charlie spoke in a whisper. 'If there is any sign of trouble or anything that makes you suspicious – however stupid it may seem, call me. It doesn't matter if it's a false alarm, we just can't afford to have anything happen to Sam. You have my mobile number don't you?'

'Yes, and the DCI's and Ed Harrington's.'

'Good. Keep alert, Greg and I'll see you tomorrow.'

He left the house and heard the door being locked behind him. It was quite dark now and the rain was much heavier. There was a distinct rumble of thunder above his head and just as he reached his car a vivid flash of lightning split the sky in half. Charlie quickly unlocked the car and jumped inside. He drove off in the direction of the hospital where he had arranged to collect Liz.

Diane Willarby cleared away the coffee cups. 'I hate storms,' she said. 'I know we're safe and sound in here, but I'm always terrified when there's a loud clap of thunder.'

Greg stood up. 'Now there's no need to worry, nothing will harm you while I'm around. Off to bed all of you, I'll wash these up.' He took the tray from Diane and vanished into the kitchen. As he started the washing up he heard the women going up the stairs to bed. In unison they called out, 'Goodnight, Greg.'

'Goodnight, ladies.' He deftly washed the crockery. Being single and living alone he was a dab hand at the everyday chores. He looked up sharply as a flash of lightning lit up the garden. Was it his imagination, or had he seen a figure dash into the shrubbery? It was too dark outside to see clearly and he waited for another flash of lightning. When it came he strained his eyes into the night but there was nothing to be seen. Should he ring Charlie? He pondered this question. If there *was* anyone out there then they would have seen him at the window. This at least would scare an intruder off, knowing that there was a male on the premises. Greg finished the washing up before walking round the house checking that all the doors and windows were securely fastened. He settled down in an armchair to watch the late film. He would not be sleeping tonight.

The following day, after briefing, Sally Pringle and Bob Finch set off to visit Sheila Werrington to see if she, like June Pawlett, could recognise the smell of embrocation oil. Sally had made a deliberate point of oiling her legs that morning and she laughed as Bob turned up his nose. 'It's not that bad, Bob. I've been rubbing this stuff into my muscles ever since we've been duty partners and you've never complained before.'

'Strange,' replied Bob. 'I'd never really noticed it until all this talk of the attacker smelling of antiseptic and then June Pawlett recognising the smell to be your embrocation.'

'You get used to something that's around all the time,' agreed, Sally. 'Well, let's find out if Sheila spots the smell. I never thought that I would be the centre of a smell analyses.'

Ed and Charlie joined Harriet in her office. As usual the pot of coffee was steaming on her desk. The telephone rang and Harriet picked up the receiver. 'It's for you, Charlie. Greg Henderson.'

Charlie quickly took the handset offered to him. 'Yes, Greg?'

He spoke for a few minutes mainly saying 'yes' or 'fine' and then, 'Why didn't you call me, Greg?' There followed a pause while Greg obviously answered Charlie's last question and then came, 'Okay, I'll be over later. Bye.' Charlie replaced the receiver. 'Greg thought he saw someone in the garden at Diane Willarby's house last night. Just a glimpse in a flash of lightning, and this morning he checked the garden and found broken shrubs and footprints in the wet soil. He has informed Phillip Hewitt, who is on his way to the house at this moment.'

'Why didn't he call in for assistance?' asked Harriet, wrinkling her nose.

'That's what I asked. He insists he wasn't sure if it was just his imagination. It was only in a flash of lightning and he felt he could have been mistaken.'

Harriet frowned. 'He was not that unsure Charlie if he had to search the garden this morning to look for prints.'

Ed chipped in. 'Charlie, you must insist that any incident however small must be reported at the time. We can't afford to allow anything to happen to Samanntha.'

Charlie nodded. 'I'll visit again this evening and stress the point.' He felt a little annoyed, knowing that he had told Greg to call him if there was any incident during the night. Anyway no harm done. If there had been a prowler last night, he had obviously been scared away on seeing a man at the kitchen window.

'We had better double the guard on Samanntha,' said Harriet. 'I'm very concerned that our man has discovered where she is living.'

'I'll see to that, Ma'am.' Charlie rose to his feet. 'I'll do it now, if you don't mind, and then I'm going over to the hospital to speak to Sam herself.'

'All right, Charlie.' Harriet nodded as the sergeant left the room and then she turned to Ed.

'What else should we be doing, Ed? It's pretty worrying if this man has discovered where Samanntha is living.'

'We'll certainly double the guard. Greg can stay in the house with the women and we'll put a patrol car outside just to be safe.'

'That's a start, Ed. I'd like to go and see this garden where the prowler was spotted. Can you be ready in about an hour?'

Ed nodded. 'I'll meet you at the front. My car?'

'That'll be fine, Ed.' As Ed left her office Harriet wondered what had happened to instigate the Inspector's change in attitude towards her. He was certainly most civil of late and there were hardly any 'Ma'am's, which used to be added at the end of virtually every sentence when he addressed her. Harriet leaned back in her chair and stretched, as she often did when alone. Perhaps her colleague was getting to know her better and was realising that she was not as intimidating as he had thought she might be. Ah well! Only time would tell if Ed had accepted her fully. She rose to her feet and left the room. Harriet visited George Hollyoak to bring him up to date with the investigation. She was feeling confident that things were coming to a head and the killer they were after was being pushed into a corner. He was close at hand, she was convinced of that. He lived in the area, she was sure. He was on one of their lists, she believed. Having spent half an hour or so with the Superintendent, Harriet returned to her office. Gloria Gardiner, the Senior Physiotherapist, telephoned with some information that Harriet had requested and minutes later Stacey Boston telephoned to report that they now had a DNA profile of the attacker of Clare Jennings on file. This had been obtained from hairs inside the woolly hat they had found at the scene. Phillip Hewitt called in to tell Harriet that the footprints found in Diane Willarby's garden matched those found at Samanntha's house the night Clare was attacked. Harriet felt excited. At last things were coming together.

'Thank you, Phillip, suddenly I'm beginning to feel hopeful.' Phillip Hewitt smiled one of his rare smiles. 'I'm pleased to have been able to help, Ma'am. The pattern on the trainer is quite common but on the print in question a small part of the tread is missing on the left shoe.'

'That's terrific, Phillip. Just as long as we can confirm this chap who was in the area where the attack on Clare took place has now shown up at Diane Willarby's house. If we can get him, then the DNA will do the rest.'

When Sergeant Hewitt had left, Harriet grabbed her jacket and set off to meet up with Ed. The storm had cleared and once again the day was bright and warm. At Kelmarsh Road they discovered a patrol car parked outside Number 12. There was no officer present. Ed knocked on the front door. It was opened by a young PC who immediately stood erect and said, 'Good morning, Sir, Ma'am.'

Ed responded similarly and Harriet smiled as they entered.

'Are you on your own, Marsh?' asked Ed.

'Yes Sir. Sergeant Marlow has told us to have someone on the premises at all times until the nurses return from the hospital and PC Henderson takes over.'

'Good idea,' replied Harriet. 'All we need is for someone to ensconce himself in the house during the day when it's unguarded.'

'Charlie's being positive,' agreed, Ed.

They went into the garden and walked around the small area until they discovered the patch in the bushes that had been flattened by someone who had stood there. The clear prints could be seen, and a shiver when through Harriet's body as she thought of the young women lying in bed last night whilst a prowler lurked in their garden. Thank goodness Greg had been in the house. The two officers left Kelmarsh Road and drove to Amchurch where they called at the hospital and asked to speak to Samanntha. The slight figure of Nurse Farndon hurried down the ward towards them her pale face and blue eyes accentuated by the blue of her uniform. She certainly resembled a china doll thought Harriet. Out loud she said, 'Sorry to interrupt your work, Samanntha, we can see how busy you are.'

'Nothing new,' smiled Samanntha. 'It's always pretty hectic on the medical wards. Is anything wrong? Sergeant Marlow has only just left.'

'No, no we were just checking to see that you are safe and nothing untoward has happened. I take it that Sergeant Marlow explained to you about the guard being doubled. Officer Henderson will remain in the house whilst you are there and a patrol car will be outside.' Harriet was not sure if the young woman was aware of what Greg had reported from the previous night and did not want to alarm her any further.

'This all sounds rather dramatic, Inspector,' said Samanntha.

'Do you really consider it necessary? With Greg in the house we feel totally secure.'

'We're just being careful,' said Ed. 'By the way thank you for visiting the Station and completing the photofit picture of Murdock Pollard that we asked for.'

Samanntha nodded. 'I did, but I'm afraid I wasn't terribly helpful.'

'I'm sure it will help us,' said Ed. 'By the way, Samanntha, did you ever nurse a patient by the name of Mark Epsom? He was in the Royal Infirmary about the same time as Murdock Pollard.'

'The name doesn't ring a bell. What ward was he on?'

'We are waiting to learn that bit of information but he was admitted with a broken back sustained in a rugby match.'

'I wouldn't have nursed him, then. He would have been taken to an orthopaedic ward not a medical one.'

'Fair enough,' said Ed, 'but if we learn at a later date that in fact he was taken to a medical ward we might get back to you.'

Samanntha nodded. 'Okay, but I think I would remember a rugby player with a broken spine.'

Harriet thanked Samanntha for her time. 'And do take care, Samanntha,' she added. 'Go nowhere on your own until this maniac is caught.'

Samanntha smiled weakly. 'I'm on night duty for the next five nights.'

'You should be safe on the ward,' said Ed, 'but even so I'll have a word with hospital security.'

Harriet and Ed left the ward, and true to his word Ed visited the Security Office where he spoke to the man in charge. He rejoined Harriet at the front door some twenty minutes later. Their next visit was to the local police station and Ed was pleased to see that the cocky Sergeant Neil Johnson was not on duty. A much older Sergeant eyed them up and down and immediately requested their warrant cards before unlocking the inner door. They were ushered through to the reception area where they were greeted by Paul Howarth, eager to know how the investigation was progressing.

'Have you got someone in the frame?' he asked Harriet. 'I read in the paper that the net was closing in and you were hopeful of an arrest soon.'

'We certainly have a suspect, Paul,' she replied, 'but as he has changed his name and temporarily vanished we are finding it difficult to nail him.'

Ed chipped in. 'We now have a DNA profile of the man who attacked Claire the other night, and we're convinced he's the man we're after. He's still in the area, that's for sure. His time is short-lived, I can assure you.'

Paul Howarth nodded. 'I shall be relieved when he's caught I can tell you, Ed. I'm worried sick every time my daughter goes on duty.'

Harriet put a gentle hand on Inspectors Howarth's arm. 'The one thing I can tell you is that he is after one particular nurse and we have her under a twenty-four-hour surveillance. We honestly don't think any other nurse is in danger but we shall continue to keep all nurses on high alert until we get our man.'

'That's some small reassurance,' conceded Paul Howarth, 'but I know that I, and my wife, will not feel at ease until this maniac is behind bars.'

'Let's hope that's soon,' said Harriet. Ed nodded in agreement and together they left Amchurch police station to return to Torreston.

Jack Fuller was hovering outside Harriet's office when she and Ed arrived back at the station. 'Ah, Ma'am, you're back. I have some information about Murdock Pollard.'

'Excellent, Jack, come in.' Harriet opened her office door and the three of them entered.

'Shall I make coffee, Ma'am?' said Ed with a solemn face.

Harriet suspected there was a hint of amusement in his voice, but she simply smiled and agreed that that would be a life-saver. Ed collected the necessary equipment and left the room. Harriet turned to the portly Sergeant. 'Now Jack what have you got for me?'

'I've traced Pollard's mother in Scotland. She lived in Stirling and the neighbours have told the local police, who carried out the enquiries for us, that her son did return home over a year ago, on crutches, but vanished soon after his mother died. The house where they lived is empty and boarded up.'

'I don't suppose that anyone knows where the son went?'

'That's correct, Ma'am but here's the trump card. The son drove a pale blue square-shaped Ford.'

'Well done, Jack!' Harriet clasped her hands together in delight just as Ed returned with the coffee.

'Obviously good news,' he said placing the tray on the desk.

Harriet told Ed of Jack's discovery. 'We are now certain that Pollard is the man we're after. All we have to do now is unmask him, and as quickly as possible. Sit down, Jack, and have coffee before you return to your computer files and folders. And once again, well done.'

Jack Fuller beamed. He decided to accept the offer of coffee, even though it was uncharacteristic of him to mingle too closely with senior officers. Somehow this occasion felt right, and with only slight hesitation he sat down and grasped the mug of coffee handed to him by Detective Chief Inspector Love. He turned to Inspector Harrington. 'I've nearly completed the search on that other enquiry you gave me, Sir. I should be able to have the answer for you by the time of the meeting.'

'Good, Jack, that will be very helpful.'

A working lunch had been arranged in the Incident Room and at noon Harriet and Ed joined the team. Harriet addressed the group.

'Please eat your lunches whilst I'm talking,' she said with her usual smile. 'Inspector Harrington and I will go over all the evidence that we have and we shall endeavour, between us, to eliminate some of the suspects and so narrow the field.' She walked to the large board that held all the pictures and other relevant information on the case. 'This is what we have so far. The murders of nurses starting in Scotland and moving down the country seemingly paused here in Northamptonshire. The last murder being in Torreston. The first letter of each murder place spells out the name SAMANTH. One N missing because he failed to kill his victim in Northallerton and again missed out in Nurcroft. We presume he gave up and moved on to the T and then the H. Now that we are sure his victim is Samanntha Farndon and she is in Amchurch, the pattern is obvious.'

Ed took over, 'We have the connection between Samanntha and Murdock Pollard inasmuch as he was besotted by her when she nursed him at the Infirmary in Leicester after he was badly injured in the factory fire where he worked. The scarves were made at this factory and as he was a rep there, he was in possession of a case full of samples. He sent Samanntha a scarf which was posted on to her after she had left Leicester and the cryptic message which is here on the board spells out DEATH.'

Harriet again, 'Samanntha had already rejected the pair of earrings that Murdock tried to give her and this we think is the reason for him taking earrings from his victims.'

'Sad bastard,' said Duncan with his mouth full.

'Sad indeed,' replied Harriet, 'but also deadly dangerous. This whole campaign has been carefully planned, so he is also clever. He left Leicester to convalesce with his mother in Scotland and that presumably is where he plotted his whole regime of terror.'

Ed took over the discussion and Harriet hastily picked up a mug of coffee.

'The first murder took place in Stirling not far from where his mother lived. She died after Murdock had been there for about a year. The house is all boarded up and although neighbours said they had seen him at her house on and off for months, no one was able to tell us where he went. The one bit of news we do have, thanks to Jack, is that he drives a pale blue, square-shaped Ford.'

'Wow!' Exclaimed Narinder. 'He *is* our man then.'

'We did think Murdock Pollard is who we're after for some time now,' answered Harriet. 'It's finding him that's the problem. We have no photograph of him, just a vague description. Not very tall, sandy haired and very pale eyes. We know he is on our patch but under an assumed name, our priority is to suss him out.'

Sally put up her hand. 'Ma'am, Dave Spalding fits that description, and apart from the pale eyes so does Garry Hobbs.'

'True, Sally,' replied Harriet, 'but we have shown Samanntha a photograph of Spalding and it isn't him. She knew Spalding when she was at the Leicester Royal Infirmary and she assures us that he and Murdock are two different people.'

'What about Garry Hobbs?' Sally persisted. 'He dated Carol Young but when questioned denied having anything to do with her.'

'And he was at the Royal Infirmary at the same time as Samanntha Farndon,' added Narinder.

'His alibi for Monica's murder holds up,' interjected, Charlie, 'and I challenged him about his statement where he said he didn't know Carol Young very well. His reason, according to him, was because of his lack of an alibi on the night of her murder. He felt that because he had told a lie to Mark Ainsley, so as not to have to spend the evening with him, he thought he might be in trouble if we knew he had dated one of the victims. In fact, these so-called dates – and I checked this with Carol's friends – were in fact two meetings at the local pub after work for a drink.'

'You would hardly call Garry Hobbs' eyes pale, though, would you,' stated Bob Finch.

'Ever heard of contact lenses, Bob?' asked Sally.

'Thank you, thank you.' Harriet brought the group back on line. 'To continue with the evidence we have. This pale blue square Ford has to be in a garage somewhere near here.' She turned to Ed and nodded and the Inspector took over once again.

'Paddy Lynch – you all remember Paddy – informed me that a man brought a pale blue Cortina Mark Three into his garage a few months ago and hung around until the repairs were done. He paid in cash and vanished. This man was slight in stature and had very pale eyes. We need to find this car. DVLA have no record of a car taxed in the name of Murdock Pollard so it is either taxed in another name or not taxed at all.'

Charlie stood up wiping crumbs from his mouth. 'The description of the car, together with photos of the tyre marks found outside Railway Cottages, have been circulated to all mobile units and beat bobbies. There can't be another such car in the area, it's too distinctive.'

'It appears that Murdock only goes out at night,' said Harriet.

'If as you suspect he is one of the men visiting Outpatients for physiotherapy and is in a wheelchair or on crutches,' suggested Duncan, 'then I suppose he would have to be very careful about being seen walking, especially if he lives near the hospital.'

'Our man has definite leg abnormalities,' answered Harriet 'and I do believe he attends or works at the hospital.'

Ed finished his mug of coffee and continued. 'We have

Samanntha under a 24-hour surveillance, and to play safe Charlie has an officer in the house when she is on duty whether or not her two friends are at home. This chap is devious enough to get into the house during the day and wait. We can't afford any slip-ups at this stage. Diane Willarby is also in danger as she is protecting Sam.'

Harriet pointed to the board. 'Other information here is the smell of antiseptic reported by two of the victims who survived attacks. Sally?'

Sally stood up. 'It turns out that the smell the two nurses who were attacked smelt was in fact embrocation. They both recognised the smell on me. Sorry if I have been stinking the place out but none of you ever said anything…'

Narinder giggled. 'I'm used to it. I live with her.'

'We're all used to it,' grinned Bob. 'Funny how you don't notice it after a while.'

'Several of the physio patients smell of embrocation,' interrupted Harriet.

'Ramsay Donaldson and Mark Epsom certainly did,' agreed Ed.

'The staff in physio do as well,' pointed out Sally.

'As do some police officers,' smiled Harriet. 'But to be serious, both victims were adamant that they smelt this embrocation when they were attacked.'

'Perhaps it was on his hands, then,' suggested, Charlie.

'It's possible,' agreed Harriet. 'But it does convince us that our man has need of some form of liniment because of the type of aches and pains that he suffers.'

'We, or rather Jack, is still tracking down some information for us,' said Ed. 'Hopefully you will have the results for us soon, Jack.'

'Indeed I will, Sir,' replied Sergeant Fuller. 'I'm having difficulty with one of the investigations and if you could spare me some time after briefing, I'd like to show you exactly what I have found out.'

'I'll do that, Jack.'

Briefing over, the team dispersed to continue with their various tasks. Ed joined Jack Fuller at the computer. Jack brought the screen back to life and pointed to the information shown on the screen. 'You see, Sir! There's absolutely nothing on record on the date, or even close to the date that you gave me. I've even checked on nearby counties just to be sure and I can assure you that the information you gave me does not hold water. Someone is telling porkies.'

Ed stroked his chin. 'Very interesting, Jack; this is one of the suspects we can't cross off the list at the moment. I'd better tell the DCI about this immediately.' He turned quickly and left the Incident Room to join Harriet in her office.

Chapter Twenty-One

Ed explained to Harriet what Jack Fuller had just told him. 'This chap is either muddled about dates, Ma'am, or he is lying.'

Harriet noted that the 'Ma'am' had returned but her expression remained unchanged. She wrinkled her nose as she looked at the information in front of her. 'He's lying, I should think, Ed. Strange, but he's the one person I was never sure about and yet could never quite fathom what it was. I still can't really, but there *is* something that I can't put my finger on. But it will come as you pointed out, I'm sure of that.'

'You did mention your doubts about him when we visited him. But it really is hard to imagine that he is able to carry out the murders and attacks that we have witnessed.'

'He's clever, Ed, very, very clever. No smell of embrocation in his home, and we know why. Confined to a wheelchair, true, and we know he doesn't have pale eyes – but remember what Sally said: "Ever heard of contact lenses?" Everything falls into place, Ed. What you have just told me convinces me that he could well be Murdock Pollard.' Harriet stabbed her finger at the list in front of them.

'Do you really think it's him?'

'I do, Ed.'

'What do you want me to do, then?' Ed was alert as he waited for instructions.

'We need a search warrant, Ed, and quickly, but as yet we haven't enough on him to ask for one. Get Charlie to put a watch on his place. We need something concrete in order to get the search warrant. He'll slip up, Ed. He has to, and then we'll get him.'

'Right. I'll get onto it straight away.' Ed jumped to his feet and left.

Harriet sat at her desk and pondered over the revelations about the man she had wondered about for some time. It wasn't surprising they had been unable to find Murdock Pollard. He had been hiding under their very noses the whole time. Sally had been spot on when she mentioned contact lenses. The man they were after no longer had pale eyes because of just that. Pale eyes were such a giveaway and he had had to cover them up. The smell of embrocation that was evident in the houses of the other invalids was never present in this man's home. Oh yes, he was certainly clever. She closed her eyes and visualised the men that she and Ed had interviewed together: Mike Epsom, Preston Skinner, Mark Ainsley and Ramsay Donaldson. The four main suspects. She could see them all clearly. Suddenly Harriet clasped her hands to her head. Of course! That was what had bothered her during their visits to these men's homes. She sat up and opened her eyes shaking her head with a smile. It was just a small thing but to her it was most significant. She would explain it to Ed later, but for now, while the Inspector was off arranging for a check to be put on their suspect's abode she would quickly write up her report for Superintendent Hollyoak.

Harriet felt a sudden thrill run through her body. This would be one in the eye for the Deputy Chief Constable if only she could get a positive result on this case. She felt jubilant as she sat down in front of her computer. Thank heavens for a supportive team! Not just the CID department for whom she was responsible, but all the officers, and that included Paddy Lynch. Everyone had done their part. Without them all pulling their weight there was never going to be a successful conclusion to these murders, but now she was feeling hopeful at last. Harriet truly believed that they could see the light at the end of the tunnel. They were going to get this killer, and very soon.

It was early evening by the time Harriet had cleared her desk of all her paperwork and delivered her report to George Hollyoak. The big man was delighted with the news that his goddaughter had to give him. He put an arm across her shoulders. 'This is brilliant news, Harry. I knew you'd crack the case and without any interference from outsiders.' He smiled knowingly, looking positively gleeful, and Harriet understood how relieved he was. She knew how anxious he had been over the insinuations made by Martin Cotton only days before, and now with an arrest in sight the pressure was off.

Harriet returned to her office just as Ed arrived accompanied by, Charlie. Ed actually smiled as he spoke: 'I've done some fast talking and the powers that be have agreed to give us a search warrant.' He held up the white paper.

'Great! Well done, Ed. Let's get going. Oh, and by the way, the thing that was bothering me about our suspect has just clicked in my head. Remind me to tell you about it later.' They left the room.

The black Saab pulled up outside 113 Osborne Road and Harriet rang the doorbell of the ground-floor flat. There was no reply. She pressed the bell again and they waited. No movement could be heard from inside the flat. Charlie pressed his ear against the door.

'Not a murmur,' he said. 'Do we break in, Ma'am?'

'Not yet,' replied Harriet. 'Our evidence against him is very slim at present and I would rather it was he who allowed us into his flat rather than us smashing down the door and then finding nothing.'

'It's surprising that he has gone out before it's totally dark,' said Charlie.

'He's getting cocky,' said Ed.

'Or desperate,' added Harriet. She turned to Ed. 'What time will the surveillance get here?'

'Any time now,' replied Ed. 'I told Bob Finch and Narinder Pancholi to have supper before taking over the watch on this place, as it could be a long night.'

'Talk of the devil, here they are,' said, Charlie.

Bob and Narinder left the CID car and came over to the group standing on the steps of 113. 'Has something happened?' asked Bob.

'It appears that our suspect has left,' said Harriet.

'Is this man really our suspect?' asked Narinder. 'He seemed so quiet and inoffensive when we interviewed him, and totally unable to walk.'

'Killers often appear like that, Narinder,' replied Harriet. 'But we have yet to prove a case against this man, so we have to be careful.'

'Do we still stay and keep watch, then?' asked Narinder.

'You do indeed,' answered, Ed. 'He has to return sometime.'

'Do we nab him if he does?' Bob Finch hoped that this would be the case.

'Yes!' stated Harriet, firmly. 'Ask him to come to the Station to answer some questions and don't let him get inside his flat. We need to search it before he is able to hide any evidence.'

Bob Finch nodded. 'Right, Ma'am. We'll go and hide the car somewhere discreet and start the surveillance.'

'Call me on my mobile the minute there is any development,' added Harriet handing Bob her card. 'And good luck.'

'Thank you, Ma'am. We've brought plenty of coffee to keep us awake.'

Harriet smiled as she, Ed and Charlie returned to the Saab. 'Back to the Station, I think, Ed,' she said, 'so that we can reassess what has happened and decide what to do next. I'm concerned that this man is out and about, and I'd dearly like to know where he is and what he's up to.'

Ed started the engine of his car. 'When we get back, I'll telephone the hospital and make sure Samanntha's all right.'

'Good idea, Ed,' replied Harriet. 'We'll go across ourselves later.'

'It's pretty dark now,' said Charlie. 'I'd like to know just what that bastard's up to at the moment.'

Back in Harriet's office Ed telephoned Amchurch Hospital. Samanntha was safely on duty. There appeared to be no problems there. Ed then asked to speak to security and he put the officer in the picture as to what had occurred and what it was they were concerned about. The Head of Security promised to keep a special eye on the medical ward where Samanntha was on duty. Feeling a little more at ease, Ed hung up.

'It's getting late,' said Harriet. 'Shall we pay our visit to Amchurch now?'

'Ready when you are, Ma'am,' answered Ed.

'I thought we had dispensed with the "Ma'am",' said Harriet, without thinking, and then wished she had remained silent. She had vowed to herself that she would not try and persuade the Inspector to be more relaxed with her, but of late he had been decidedly more friendly and now that the 'Ma'am' had reappeared she was disappointed.

'Sorry, force of habit.' Ed was abashed. He had been determined to be more relaxed when with his boss and indeed he had been, up until tonight. Why he had suddenly reverted to his old stubborn self he didn't know. He really did intend to make an effort and he wished fervently that he could bring himself to call her Harry, but the name just stuck in his throat. Somehow it was always 'Ma'am' that sprang forth when he addressed her.

They left Harriet's office and began to head down the corridor.

'Your telephone's ringing, Ma'am,' said Charlie.

Harriet hesitated and then turned. 'I'd better answer it. You can guarantee that if you ignore a call it turns out to be of vital importance and you kick yourself for ever for being so stupid.' She re-entered her office and picked up the telephone receiver. The voice of Sergeant Jim Mirams came on the line.

'Glad you're still in you're office, Ma'am, something positive has come to light. I'm on patrol with PC Stockwell and we have been checking all lock-up garages for the blue Ford you're looking for. Our luck's in. We've found tyre tracks that match the photographs of the attacker's car.'

Harriet could not hide the excitement in her voice. 'Where Jim?'

'At the lock-up garages at the back of the shops in Osborne Close.'

'Where Carol Young was murdered. Oh, well done, Jim, well done!'

Jim Mirams smiled as he listened to the Chief Inspector. Charlie Marlow was correct when he had said the new boss was full of enthusiasm and acted absolutely naturally to all news whether good or bad. This one being good news was bringing out DCI Love's pure delight. 'It was young Stockwell who spotted the prints, Ma'am. He's got eyes like a hawk. Even in this failing light he found what he was looking for.'

'Give him my congratulations then, Jim. Now, can you hang on there until I join you?'

'Certainly, Ma'am. We'll wait for you at the back of the shops.'

Harriet replaced the receiver and turned to Ed and Charlie, her eyes alight. 'That was Jim Mirams, he's on patrol with Luke

Stockwell and Luke spotted tyre tracks that match the ones we circulated.'

'Well done, Stockwell!' said, Charlie. 'That young man will go far.'

'I think you may well be correct, Charlie. But let's get moving. The tracks are at the lock-up garages at the back of the Osborne Road shops.'

'Not far from the first murder,' said Ed.

The three officers hurried from the Station and headed for the car park. 'Both cars, I think Ed,' said Harriet, making for her little red Lotus. Ed raised a hand in acknowledgement and minutes later the two cars set off in the direction of Osborne Road.

Sergeant Jim Mirams and PC Luke Stockwell were sitting in their patrol car by the row of garages behind the shops as the Saab and Lotus swept into the enclosed area. The row of eight garages was well sheltered with trees and high hedges and it was quiet, dark and dismal here behind the shops. Litter was everywhere and there was evidence that bonfires had been lit recently as piles of ash were visible in several places. Harriet stopped close to the patrol car and Jim Mirams and Luke Stockwell hastily climbed from it as she approached. Ed and Charlie were close behind.

'Good evening, Ma'am.' Jim and Luke spoke together.

'Good evening to you both – and well done.' Harriet beamed at the young PC. 'A special congratulations to you, I understand.'

Luke Stockwell stood up straight. 'I just happened to be the lucky one, Ma'am. I'll show you where the prints are.' He eagerly led the way over to the garages.

The group followed PC Stockwell, and at the very last garage, close to the overgrown hedge, he bent down and pointed the beam of his torch onto the ground. Clearly seen in the damp soil were tyre prints. Ed stepped forward holding the photograph of the incriminating print and placed it beside the imprint on the ground. 'An exact match, Ma'am,' he said.

There was absolutely no doubt about the match. The pattern was identical and clearly seen across it was the jagged cut.

Harriet spoke to Sergeant Mirams. 'Is the garage locked?'

'Yes, Ma'am, we tried the up-and-over door.'

Ed nodded to Charlie and the two of them tried forcing the door without success.

'We need a crowbar or something,' said Harriet.

'How about this?' Luke offered a large iron bar that he had picked up from the ground 'It's something of a rubbish tip here,' he said. 'There's all sorts of things lying around.'

'Including hypodermics,' growled Charlie, gingerly stepping away from the long grass where he too had been searching for a suitable instrument to assist in the breaking open of the garage door. 'Be careful, all of you. This place is a den of iniquity.'

Ed took the piece of iron from Luke and with the help of Jim Mirams he forced it into the gap at the top of the door and heaved.

'Something's giving,' grunted Jim. 'One move, heave.'

Suddenly there was a crunching sound followed by a snap and the garage door began to pull downwards. As the entrance opened all eyes were on the interior. It was empty.

'Where's the blighter gone?' asked Charlie bitterly.

The bleak garage contained nothing more than a few old paint tins, a length of rope and a ladder. It smelt stale and mouldy. There was a pool of oil on the floor with an old piece of sacking half covering it.

Harriet frowned. 'That's worrying. Is he just out and about on the prowl or is he out looking specifically for Samanntha?'

'If it was him at Diane Willarby's house the other night, then he already knows where she lives,' said Ed. 'But with a double guard at her house she should be safe.'

'Except that she's on night duty at the moment,' interrupted, Charlie. He looked at his watch. 'If the night staff go on duty at the same time as they do here at Torreston General, then she will already be at the hospital.'

'She is,' replied Ed. 'But I've alerted Security, so she should be safe on the ward.' Harriet straitened up. 'Jim could you and Luke remain here in case our man returns in the car,' and as Sergeant Mirams nodded she added, 'Ed and Charlie, I think it's time we entered that flat in Osborne Road after all.' She hurried towards her car followed by her colleagues.

At Number 113 they were joined by Bob Finch and Narinder Pancholi, who reported that all was quiet. 'Change of plan,' stated Harriet. 'We're going to enter the flat. Stay as you were, Bob, and should our man return, do as we had arranged – head him off and don't let him in.'

'Right, Ma'am.'

Ed and Charlie put their shoulders to the door and at the second attempt the door flew open. A strong smell of incense greeted them. 'The reason we never smelt embrocation,' pointed out Harriet, switching on the light.

'What was the other clue that suddenly came to mind?' asked Ed.

'This,' said Harriet, walking over to the wheelchair standing in the corner of the living room. She put her hand on the arm of the chair. 'Think about all the patients in wheelchairs we visited, Ramsay Donaldson in particular. They all manoeuvred their chairs like racing drivers. The exception was Mark Ainsley. He hit everything in sight and collided with all the furniture in this room. Anyone confined to a wheelchair for any length of time becomes an expert and they're able to move about without hitting anything, especially in their own home. It was this that was at the back of my mind. I thought it so strange when we were here in this room with him, Ed. He knocked everything flying. That's because he isn't in his wheelchair when he's at home, he damn well walks about.'

'Like now,' agreed Charlie leaving the room to forage around.

'His eyes were red and sore on that day as well,' said Ed. 'Contact lens trouble I presume.'

'Absolutely,' agreed Harriet. 'And he told us he had an eye infection, didn't he? He took ages to open the door on that occasion. I presume he had to whip in the lenses before he appeared at the door.'

Ed nodded. 'When you think about it, those dark blue eyes looked quite out of place in his pasty face. Foolish of him to pick such a vibrant colour.'

'Vanity,' replied Harriet.

Charlie appeared in the room. 'Well, here's the evidence you require regarding the contact lenses.' He held out a box of coloured lenses and the various bottles and sprays used for cleansing purposes. 'Found them in the bathroom cabinet.'

'Dark blue contacts,' said Harriet, sardonically. 'What a surprise!'

In a cupboard in the living room they discovered several pairs of trainers and three pairs of shoes. 'Not exactly what you'd need if you never walk anywhere,' remarked, Charlie.

'It's the red scarves and earrings we want,' said Harriet, as they entered a small box-room. In one corner there was a cross-trainer. A piece of equipment used for strengthening leg muscles was against one wall and at the other side of the room there was a bench and several weights, obviously all designed for use on the legs. A shelf housed an assortment of creams and oils. The strong smell of liniments was now hanging in the air.

'No need to disguise the smell of embrocation in here,' said Ed. 'This is his secret workout room, hidden from everyone's eyes.'

'He must have been building himself up for months.' Harriet walked round the small room. 'His evil little mind must have been planning and plotting his revenge ever since Samanntha turned him down.'

They moved into the main bedroom. The naked light bulb above their heads threw out a stark white light, illuminating the untidy room. The large double bed was unmade and clothes were strewed across the floor. Empty coffee mugs were sitting on many of the surfaces and the smell of joss sticks was strong and overpowering. The three officers set about their search and it was not long before Charlie triumphantly cried out, 'Bingo!' He took a cardboard box from the top of the wardrobe and placed it on the bed. 'Look at this.' From the box he took a large folder which he opened as Harriet and Ed came across to him. 'News cuttings of the murdered nurses,' said, Charlie. 'They're all here, including the two killed on our patch.'

'Put the folder back in the box, Charlie,' said Harriet. 'We'll take it with us when we leave. What we desperately need to find are the red scarves and the earrings he took from his victims.'

They searched the flat from top to bottom but there was no sign of the earrings or the scarves. 'In his car perhaps?' Suggested, Ed.

'Risky,' replied Harriet.

'Would he keep them with him?' asked, Charlie.

'Again, very risky.' Harriet wrinkled her nose. 'Where might he keep something as precious, and as dangerous, as the earrings from his victims and the murder weapons?'

'We didn't search the garage in any great depth,' said Ed. 'I'll rectify that immediately.'

'Good thinking, Ed,' acknowledged Harriet. 'He probably stashed them away from where he lived just to be safe. They really are very incriminating if found on him.'

Ed called into Headquarters on his mobile phone and spoke briefly to the duty officer. He instructed him to recall all the CID team working on the case. 'Ask Jack Fuller to call me back on this number when everyone has reported in,' he ended. He turned to Harriet 'I've recalled the team. I think they would appreciate being in at the kill, and apart from that, they know the case inside out. As soon as Jack calls in I'll get him to organise the search of the garage. I know it's getting dark but with laser torches they should be able to make a reasonably detailed search.'

'Excellent, Ed. And that's good of you to think of everyone else who's been working on this case.' She smiled, but on this occasion there was an anxious look in her eye. The usual sparkle was absent. Her mind was on the whereabouts of Mark Ainsley, or as they now knew him to be, Murdock Pollard. 'Get Phillip Hewitt and his SOCO men over here, Ed,' she added. 'He may well do better than us.' She cast her eyes around the scruffy bedroom. 'There's nothing more we can do. We'll check Diane Willarby's house and if there's nothing happening there, we'll make our way over to Amchurch. Everyone is on high alert, especially at the hospital; heaven forbid anything could happen to Samanntha tonight. I think we will get him, Ed, and very soon.'

Ed nodded. 'I hope your right Ma... er... yes, I hope you're right. The garage is staked out and so is his flat, so he's unable to put his car away or indeed return to his house without being spotted.'

Harriet pretended not to notice the Inspector's hesitation and deliberate avoidance of calling her ma'am. Things were looking up if he was consciously making the effort. Charlie on the other hand smirked at his friend's embarrassment and Ed hastily strode from the room. 'Come on then, Charlie, if you're coming with me. See you at Kelmarsh Road,' he added to Harriet over his shoulder.

Charlie followed Ed from the flat. 'I'll just organise the sealing of this place,' he said. 'Be with you in a tick.'

It was now quite dark and the rain clouds that had been threatening for the last couple of days added to the density of the night. Harriet looked up at the sky. Not a star in sight, just blackness. She shuddered, a feeling of impending danger gripping her. Where was Mark Ainsley at this moment? What had he planned for tonight? Had they done enough to protect Samanntha Farndon? Surely she was safe on the ward at the hospital.

Samanntha Farndon put the finishing touches to her appearance and waited for Heather at the bottom of the stairs. The two women made for the front door. Samanntha called goodbye to her protector of the moment. 'Goodbye, Greg! Give my regards to Diane when she gets home and I'll see you in the morning.'

'Hang on, Miss, I have to escort you to the car.' The young Constable appeared from the kitchen. 'Don't want anything happening to you on my shift,' he grinned.

Samanntha smiled back. 'I really don't think anything is going to happen to me. I do feel a fraud, all this attention just because some crank took a shine to me and I rejected him.'

'You're not a fraud, Sam,' retorted Heather Howarth. 'This chap is a real nutcase.'

'He's more than a nutcase if you ask me,' said Greg Henderson, 'If he's killing nurses just to get to Sam.'

Samanntha's face saddened. 'You're right. People have died because of me, and that's unforgivable.'

The Constable led the way outside and walked beside Samanntha and Heather to the police car that was waiting for them. 'Evening Joe,' he said brightly to the driver. 'Two VIPs.'

He opened the car door for the women and held up a hand in a wave as they were driven away. He then returned to the house. Not a bad tour of duty, he thought as he returned to the kitchen to make himself yet another cup of coffee. The other nurse would be home soon and then he could look forward to a quiet evening of TV.

At Amchurch Hospital, Heather Howarth and Samanntha Farndon parted company in the foyer. Heather headed for her own ward and Samanntha with her escort, went up the stairs to Harrowden Ward. She was greeted by her colleagues who thought the whole incident was a bit of a joke and more than a little exciting. They looked forward to the police arriving on the ward with Sam and whenever possible were happy to make them coffee.

'Not tonight, thanks, ladies,' said the Constable in answer to the offer of coffee. 'There appears to be something big on at the moment and we're all needed out and about.'

'Nothing to do with me, I hope?' said an anxious Samanntha.

'Haven't been told exactly what's happening,' he replied. 'All I know is we have to be at the end of the radio in case we're needed.' He said goodnight and left.

Head of Hospital security came up to the ward. Doug Wendel had been at the hospital since leaving the police force almost fifteen years ago. He had worked his way up from an ordinary security officer to being appointed the man in charge. Samanntha knew him by sight, but had never had occasion to speak to him other than to say good morning or goodnight when coming or going off duty. At this moment the big man's face registered concern as he asked the young nurse in front of him if all was well.

'I'm fine, thank you, Mr Wendel I'm so sorry to be causing all this trouble.'

'Not your fault, m'dear. We can't have maniacs entering the premises and causing problems. You have my bleep number if you're at all anxious about anything, however silly it may seem. Now don't hesitate to call, will you?'

'Thank you. I promise I'll call you if I see or hear anything suspicious.'

The day nurses completed the handover to the night staff and left to go home. There were two trained nurses on duty, Samanntha and Jessica Underwood, and three health care assistants. Five staff for thirty patients situated in five bays of six beds. Samanntha was responsible for the first three bays. Being a medical ward, it was mainly elderly patients occupying the beds, and Samanntha, assisted by care assistant Anne Dores, set about making the patients comfortable for the night. Old Mrs

Hargreaves in bay two was as difficult as ever and complained that she never slept at night and that the ward was far too noisy. Samanntha gave her the Temazepam that she was prescribed and coaxed her into lying quietly until she fell asleep.

'I had this stuff last night,' complained Doris Hargreaves 'and it did bugger all then. Why should it work tonight?'

'Let's try it once more, Mrs Hargreaves,' said Samanntha in her quiet voice. 'If it really has no effect this time, then I'll ask the doctor to write you up for something else.' Reluctantly the old lady took the tablet and the two nurses left the bay.

Once the hot drinks had been given out the nurses had time to have a drink themselves. Anne went to the ward kitchen and filled the kettle with water. The bright lights were dimmed and the ward became quiet. A figure in uniform appeared at the end of the corridor. 'Security again,' said Jessica. 'What's it like being a celebrity, Sam?'

'Terrifying! No one in their right mind would want to be guarded because some madman was out to kill you.'

'True,' replied Jessica. 'I'm beginning to feel nervy just being with you.'

The young security officer came up to the nurses' station. 'Everything quiet?' he asked.

Neither nurse recognised the man and Jessica deliberately took hold of his hospital identity badge and carefully checked the photograph and read his name. 'Sorry, John, but we don't know you.'

'You're right to be careful Mr Wendell has instructed us to walk through this ward every half-hour, so don't be alarmed.' He in turn peered at the nurse's badges. 'So you're Nurse Farndon,' he said looking at Sam.

'I'm afraid so,' she said weakly. 'Can I get you a coffee.'

'Not at the moment, thanks, I have to patrol all these top corridors before I can stop. Perhaps later, on another of my visits. I have to make a point of speaking to you each time I come.' He smiled amiably and continued through the ward to the other end, where he vanished through the double doors.

A light flashed on the board by the desk and Jessica rose to her feet. 'Come on, Mary, that will be Gordon. He'll be wet again and messed up to his eyeballs.'

Mary Allen, a care assistant, followed Nurse Underwood to bay five. A second light flashed indicating bay two and Samanntha rose.

'We'll go, Sam,' said Anne and she and Fay Peach left to sort out the problem. Another wet bed, thought Samanntha, as she sat down again picking up a pile of case notes. She set about reading the medical histories of her patients.

By midnight all was quiet on the ward once again. More coffee had been consumed and the five women were again sitting at the nurses' station quietly talking. The now expected figure of a security officer came down the corridor. 'Hi John,' said Jessica in a loud whisper. 'Ready for that coffee now?'

'As it's ready, I will. Thanks.' He accepted the mug of coffee handed to him and leaned on the desk to drink it.

'You're very regular,' said Samanntha. 'On the half-hour exactly, one of you appears in the corridor.'

'That's what it's all about. Timekeeping. I'm sure you ladies don't have to be reminded how important timekeeping is.' He looked at his watch. 'Talking of which, I have to be somewhere else in ten minutes. Thanks for the coffee. Might see you later.' He left Harrowden and once again the ward fell silent.

The quiet was broken by Samanntha, 'My turn to wash up,' she insisted gathering the mugs together. 'You're all wrapping me in cotton wool but I must do my share of the work.'

She carried the tray to the kitchen. Having washed the mugs she walked to the end of the corridor to do the rounds of her three bays. It was almost twelve twenty. As she came from bay one she saw a shadowy figure in a peaked cap in the main corridor. He was standing peering back towards the stairway. Security again, and early this time. She entered bay two. All the patients appeared to be asleep; even Mrs Hargreaves, who usually rang her bell more than any other patient in her three bays put together. Samanntha checked the IV fluids of Pauline Bostock in bed six and noted that the saline would be through in about ten minutes. She would go and collect the new bag and have it ready. She left the bay and headed down the corridor, informing Fay where she was going as she passed the nurse's desk. The store cupboards where the supplies were kept were outside the ward in the top corridor. Ahead of her the security officer was vanishing through the end doors of the ward. He had not, after all, stopped to speak to her on this visit, thought Samanntha. Actually, the figure ahead of her was shorter than John, so perhaps this officer had not been instructed to see her personally on each visit. She followed the uniformed figure through the double doors and went to the cupboard.

It was dark in the corridor. Only a single night light set in the ceiling lit the whole area. Samanntha knelt at the cupboard, straining her eyes to read the labels on the boxes. Without warning something soft was flung around her neck and she was pulled backwards. Caught off guard, Samanntha fell to the floor. Struggling for breath she forced her fingers under the cloth that was choking her. Lying on her back she looked up into the cold, pale eyes that she recognised. She was unable to speak but managed to squirm, around and lifting her leg she kicked out frantically, making contact as she heard her assailant grunt with pain. She kicked out again and again, panic creeping over her as she realised that the threatening nightmare was now a reality. Her heart was pounding in her chest and she thought it must burst. She was being dragged down the corridor towards the end bathroom, which was in darkness. She had to stop him. Samanntha kicked out desperately but made no contact this time. Her senses were becoming blurred but she desperately hung on to the scarf, for surely it was a scarf, around her neck. She had to keep her fingers beneath it or she would die. They had reached the bathroom now and Samanntha pushed her feet up against the door jam to prevent her attacker dragging her inside the isolated room. She heard Murdock Pollard swear, and just for a moment he relaxed his hold on her throat as he grabbed for the back of her tunic to enable him to force her through the doorway. Samanntha tried to scream but no sound came from her throat. Was this it? Was she to be the final victim? She felt the scarf tighten again and, lacking strength, her fingers let go of the ligature around her neck as she began slipping into oblivion.

Chapter Twenty-Two

At Diane Willarby's house in Kelmarsh Road all was quiet. Diane had just arrived home from the hospital and she and Greg Henderson were having coffee together in the sitting room. Heather, who was on night duty, had travelled to the hospital with Sam in the patrol car. PC Henderson was now preparing for the night shift and before accepting the coffee had undertaken a detailed search of the house and gardens. 'We've been ordered to be on extra special alert tonight,' he said. 'Something has come to light about this chap they're after. But there's no need for you to worry,' he added hastily, 'it isn't you he's after. It now appears to be certain that's its Sam.'

'Poor Sam! How terrifying for her.'

'She'll be fine,' said Greg reassuringly. 'The hospital has been alerted and her ward is being kept under surveillance.' He jumped to his feet as there came a knock on the door. 'Stay where you are, Diane,' he said in a somewhat hushed voice. He went to the front door and called out. 'Who is it?'

Charlie's voice answered. 'Me, Greg, with DCI Love and DI Harrington.'

Greg breathed a sigh of relief and slipped back the chain before opening the door.

'Good evening, Greg,' said Harriet, as she entered the house. 'No problems here I take it?'

'None, Ma'am. I did as I was instructed and searched the grounds and the house when I took over and there's nothing to report.'

Diane appeared in the hallway. 'Hello, Chief Inspector. Sam will be all right, won't she? All this cloak-and-dagger stuff is getting to me, but I don't really think that Sam understands the seriousness of it all.'

'The hospital is on full alert, Diane,' answered Ed. 'We are on our way over there now just to make sure Sam is safe, so there's no need for you to worry about her. PC Henderson will stay the night here as before, so there's nothing for you to fear either.'

'Thank you. Would you like a coffee before you head off for Amchurch? It is real coffee,' she added, smiling knowingly at Harriet.

Harriet wondered how her penchant for the real thing had reached the ears of this household, but she did not react. 'No thank you, Diane, we'd better make our way to Amchurch. It's already nearly eleven thirty.'

Greg Henderson showed them to the door, and standing on the doorstep asked Ed just what had happened tonight to put everyone on high alert. Ed spoke in lowered tones.

'We've found the garage, where there are tyre marks that match the ones that we're circulating. We are presuming they belong to this mysterious blue Ford. Trouble is, the garage is empty, so chummy is at large somewhere. No sleeping tonight, Greg, and ring me if anything occurs.'

'Of course. And good luck.' He turned to Harriet 'Are you expecting an arrest tonight, Ma'am?'

Harriet gave an uncustomary weak smile. 'That's what we're hoping.'

Diane called out just as they were leaving. 'Give Sam my regards and wish her happy birthday! It'll be after midnight by the time you see her.'

'It's her birthday?' asked Harriet turning sharply.

'Yes, tomorrow,' replied Diane. 'Sam tried to change her night duty, but due to the shortage of trained staff she was unable to. We shall celebrate at the weekend instead.'

Harriet threw a quick look at Ed and Charlie. 'I think we need to put our foot down, gentlemen. Our killer gave Samanntha those earrings she rejected as a birthday present He is probably hoping to deliver another present to her tonight.' She put a hand to her forehead. 'And how stupid of me! Of course he won't kill her here in Torreston. He needs an *A* to complete the spelling of Samanntha. That means it has to be Amchurch. Why didn't I realise that sooner?' Quickening her pace, she headed for her car, calling over her shoulder. 'We'll meet at the hospital.'

Ed and Charlie broke into a run and made for the Saab. The

two cars left Kelmarsh Road and set off for Amchurch at speed.

It was twelve fifteen as they entered the main doors of the hospital. Not a soul was in sight.

'So much for high security,' growled Ed striding briskly up to the reception desk. There was no one behind the counter and as Ed was joined by Harriet and Charlie, a dim figure came towards them down the main corridor. Doug Wendel stopped in front of them. 'You must be police. Could I see your identification, please?'

'Why is there no security at the main entrance?' Asked Harriet producing her warrant card.

Doug Wendel frowned. 'That's what I should like to know. I left Fred Parsons here with strict instructions to have the entrance manned at all times. All other entrances are locked at night, so apart from A and E, which is a separate wing, all visitors have to come through here.'

Harriet checked the identity badge of the man in front of them.

'I see you are Head of Security here, Mr Wendel. I take it Harrowden Ward is being kept under surveillance.'

'I have a man passing through the ward every half hour, Ma'am. He has been instructed to speak to Nurse Farndon on each visit.'

Harriet nodded then turned to Charlie. 'Get up to Harrowden Ward, Charlie, we'll follow.'

'Right, Ma'am.' Charlie glanced quickly at the directions board before he bounded up the stairs two at a time to the third floor where Harrowden was signposted.

At that moment a grossly overweight individual in security uniform came through the front entrance. He looked horrified on seeing the group of people standing at the main desk. 'Has something happened?' he asked in a strained voice.

'How should we know?' retorted Doug Wendel furiously. 'There's no one on the door.'

Fred Parsons was flustered and ill at ease. 'I just nipped out for a fag,' he said lamely. 'I've only been gone five minutes.'

'A great deal could happen in five minutes!' snapped, Ed. But knowing that these men did not come under police jurisdiction he said no more. He could see by the look on Wendel's face that the matter would be dealt with later. Harriet peered along the deserted corridors. The dimly lit passageways were silent. An almost eerie hush had fallen over the entire building. 'How quiet it is,' she remarked.

'It's unusual, I must say,' replied Doug Wendel 'But there will be more activity up on the wards, and A and E will be heaving, I can assure you.'

Harriet shivered even though the hospital was warm. She suddenly had a feeling of impending danger. She turned to Ed and said, 'Come on.' She headed for the staircase where the sign on the wall named the various wards and the floor where they could be located. With Ed in close pursuit she climbed the stairs.

Charlie arrived at Harrowden Ward at the same time as a young security officer. It was twelve thirty. John Keen held up a hand. 'Excuse me, what are you doing up here at this time of night?' Charlie produced his warrant card and held it close to the young man's face so that he could read it in the dim light. 'Sorry, Sergeant, but you can't be too careful.'

'You're absolutely right to check everyone,' agreed Charlie, as together they walked up the ward to the nurses' station. 'Where's Sam?' he asked Jessica.

It was the care assistant who answered. 'She's just gone to the top corridor to collect IV fluids.' Fay Peach pointed in the direction of the double doors at the end of the ward corridor. 'One of your men was just ahead of her,' she added to John. 'I thought he was you…'

Charlie was already running for the double doors with John at his heels. As he neared the top corridor he could hear a commotion, and flinging open the doors he came across two nurses from the adjoining ward kneeling at the side of an unconscious Samanntha, who was lying on her back on the floor. The small face was drained of any colour, the all too familiar red scarf was lying on the floor beside her. One of the nurses pointed down the other corridor. 'A man!' she gasped. 'He ran down there.'

John ran down the corridor, speaking into his cellphone as he went. Charlie took one look at the lifeless figure on the floor, before chasing after the young security officer. The two nurses continued their resuscitation procedure on Samanntha.

Jessica Underwood and the care assistants arrived on the scene, closely followed by Harriet and Ed. 'How is she?' Harriet's voice was hushed but calm.

The nurses did not look up as one of them spoke: 'We're working on her.' The group waited what seemed to be an eternity before the nurse spoke again. 'Thank God! She's breathing.'

Fay was crying and Jessica put an arm around her shoulders. 'She'll be all right, Fay, she'll be all right.'

Ed spoke in a whisper to Harriet. 'I'll go down and see if they caught Pollard. I'll have a word with Doug Wendel and let you know what's happened.'

'Right, Ed.' As Ed vanished down the corridor, the slight figure on the floor began to cough. 'Thank God!' muttered Harriet. She bent and picked up the red scarf, carefully folding it and placing it in a plastic bag that she took from her pocket.

Samanntha sat up on the floor and held her head in her hands. She began to cry and Harriet stepped forward and knelt beside her. She put a gentle hand on the young woman's arm. 'You're safe, Samanntha. Your attacker has gone and you're coming with me.' She helped Sam to her feet. 'Do you feel up to walking?'

'Yes. I can manage if I can hang onto you. I'm shaky, but alive. It *was* Murdock, Inspector, I'd recognise those eyes anywhere.' She began to cry again. 'He really did want to kill me, didn't he?' She looked up at the two women who had interrupted her attacker. 'Marian – oh and Seema… Was it you who saved me?'

'We needed IV fluids from the cupboard,' said the staff nurse, 'and as we came through the doors from our ward we saw this figure trying to drag you into the bathroom.'

'Oh God! If you hadn't come to the cupboard when you did, I would be dead now.' Samanntha put her slender hands to her throat which felt very bruised and sore.

'Well done, you two,' said Harriet, turning to the two nurses who had revived Samanntha. 'Not just for interrupting the attack on Samanntha but for your skills in resuscitation.'

'That's what we're trained in,' replied Marian.

'And as for frightening off the attacker,' said the Care Assistant

Seema, 'I've never been so terrified in all my life! I'll only come to this cupboard with someone else because I'm so scared in this dark corridor, and when we saw this man fighting with Sam my legs went to jelly.'

'We just threw ourselves at him,' added Marian, 'and he fled.'

'We thought she was dead,' added Seema. 'My fingers wouldn't work as I tried to untie the scarf. Marian had to do it.'

'You are both heroes,' smiled Harriet.

'The bleep-holder – that's the Sister in charge – is on her way,' said Jessica. 'I called her to let her know what has happened.'

'Good,' replied Harriet. 'I can tell her that I'll be taking Samanntha away with me.'

She led the still shaking nurse back down the corridor to Harrowden ward where they were met by an anxious sister.

'Is Sam all right?' she asked fearfully.

'Yes, thanks to these two.' Harriet indicated Marian and Seema. 'I shall be taking Samanntha with me, Sister, if you could cover her duties please.'

'I shall have to,' replied the sister. 'You poor thing, Sam! Doug Wendel told me what had happened. They're still searching the building for the man,' she added, looking at Harriet, 'But no sign of him so far.' The sister turned to Marian and Seema. 'Sorry, you two, but you'll have to get back to your own ward. It's been left understaffed and they're pretty hectic.'

The two women from the adjoining ward reluctantly left Harrowden and returned to their duties. Night duty would never be the same again. What a story they had to tell…

Harriet sat Samanntha in a chair and Jessica went to collect her jacket and handbag. The 'bleep Sister' was on the telephone desperately tying to find a ward that could spare a trained member of staff to cover for Samanntha. She eventually replaced the receiver and turned to the group. 'Intensive Care are sending someone. They appear to be relatively quiet at the moment.'

'Thank you, Sister, I'll just get assistance from my colleague and then I'll leave with Nurse Farndon if you don't mind.' Harriet dialled a number and spoke quietly to Charlie. Then she took Samanntha by the arm. 'Ready?'

Samanntha nodded and together they walked to the end of the

ward where they were met by Charlie. 'I called you because I'm playing safe, Charlie,' said Harriet. 'This Pollard is around somewhere and we can't afford to let him get near Samanntha.'

'Absolutely right, Ma'am. Here, come on, Sam, take my arm.' Together they made for the staircase.

Down in the foyer Ed had telephoned Sergeant Mirams to inform him that the blue Ford might be on the way back to the lock-up garages. 'Stay hidden, Jim, and the minute he drives up to the garage arrest him.' Having spoken to Jim Mirams, Ed then contacted the forensic officers at Mark Ainsley's flat, telling them to leave the premises. 'If he doesn't return the car to the garages, Hewitt, he might just go straight home, in which case we'll nab him there. As far as we understand he has no idea that we now know who he is.'

Phillip Hewitt informed Ed that they had all but completed their search of the flat. 'I need to take away a few items of clothing,' he said, 'but I doubt they will be missed for a while.'

'Okay! If you uncover anything truly incriminating call me tomorrow.' Ed put away his mobile as Harriet and Charlie appeared with Samanntha. Ed told Harriet what he had done.

'Excellent, Ed. I want this maniac tonight.'

Doug Wendel arrived accompanied by Inspector Hathaway and some uniformed officers. 'Doug called us,' said Paul Howarth. 'We've searched the hospital without success, although some of my men are continuing just to make sure.'

'Thank you, Paul. But I have a feeling our suspect has made good his escape.'

'The fire doors can be opened from the inside,' said Doug Wendel, 'so you could be correct.'

Paul Howarth walked over to Samanntha whom he knew. 'Are you all right, Sam?'

'I think so. Have you spoken to Heather?'

'Yes,' replied the Inspector. 'I visited all the wards upstairs, including my daughter's, and I've told her that you are okay.'

'Thank you,' Samanntha gave a weak smile.

'Time to leave,' said Harriet, matter-of-factly. 'Charlie will you let Greg Henderson know what has happened and that Samanntha will not be returning to Kelmarsh Road for the time being.'

'Yes, Ma'am. I presume that Greg is to stay at the house.'

'Absolutely,' replied Harriet. She turned to Doug Wendel and Paul Howarth and thanked them both before she headed for the main exit followed by Ed and Charlie, who was still supporting Samanntha.

Jim Mirams and Luke Stockwell sat in the police car that was discreetly parked behind the bushes at the entrance to the lock-up garages. Sergeant Mirams had received the message from Ed Harrington and they now waited in anticipation. The church clock chimed one and Luke sighed. 'P'raps he won't bring the car back here.'

'He doesn't know we've found the garage,' replied Jim Mirams. 'Be patient. He'll come.'

One fifteen chimed and almost immediately a car engine was heard. Sergeant Mirams braced himself and Luke Stockwell sat bolt upright. A car drove slowly up the narrow road. Only sidelights were visible. It turned into the opening to the garages and pulled up in front of the end building.

'Come on,' whispered Jim as he quietly opened the car door. PC Stockwell did likewise, his heart beating rapidly under his uniform. Action at last! Together they started to move across the open space towards the car that had stopped in front of the garage door. A figure had climbed from the vehicle, but even as they moved forward this figure leaped back into the car and reversed furiously, turning the car to face the two officers. The headlights were switched on, blinding Jim Mirams and his young colleague. The engine revved up and the car headed straight at them. Sergeant Mirams threw himself to one side but the unfortunate Luke was struck a blow as the car sped passed.

Sergeant Mirams picked himself up and hurried over to Luke, who lay unconscious where he had fallen. The older man took out his torch and put the beam on the prone figure. He made no attempt to move the casualty but took out his mobile phone and called for an ambulance. Next he contacted Inspector Harrington, who informed him that he and Charlie were just arriving back at Torreston police station. 'Chief Inspector Love and Samanntha are right behind me,' he told Sergeant Mirams. 'I'll tell the DCI what has happened, Jim, but you stay with Stockwell at the hospital. Keep me informed as to how he is.'

Ed was saddened to learn that young Stockwell had been injured. This chap Murdock had much to answer for. He pulled up outside the police station and in his rear-view mirror he saw the Lotus come to a halt close behind.

Harriet walked over to Ed as he remained sitting in his car. He wound down the window as she approached. 'I'm taking no chances, Ed,' she said. 'I'm leaving Samanntha here at the station. Will you ask Sally to report in and stay with her until she is calm. Do you think that Sally could take her home for the night?'

'I don't see why not. Sally is a good sort and I'm sure she'll help if she can,' replied Ed. 'But look, I've just had Jim Mirams on the phone. Our man returned to the garages as we thought he would, but he must have spotted that the door had been forced. He turned the car round and drove at Jim and PC Stockwell. Jim managed to dive clear but I'm afraid young Luke took a hit.'

'Oh no!' Harriet was genuinely distressed. 'How is he, Ed?'

'Still unconscious. Jim was waiting for the arrival of the ambulance when he called me.'

'Wait here for me, Ed. As soon as I've handed Samanntha over and I know she's safe, we'll all go in your car to Osborne Road.' She turned to, Charlie. 'Here are my car keys, Charlie. Park the Lotus for me, I won't be long.'

Charlie eagerly took the keys. Another chance to drive the Élite, but like that first time, when he had dropped the clanger with the new Chief Inspector, it was only as far as the parking area. He squeezed himself into the driving seat and started the engine. Harriet guided Samanntha up the steps into the police station and nodded to Pete Yates through the enquiry window. 'Evening, Ma'am,' said the sergeant.

'Good evening, Pete, or is it morning?' replied Harriet. 'Pete, this is Samanntha Farndon, and I need you to keep her here until Sally Pringle arrives.'

'Certainly, Ma'am.' Sergeant Yates unlocked the inner door to allow the Chief Inspector and her ward through. So this was the nurse that all the trouble was over! She certainly looked a frail little thing. He opened the office door and Samanntha entered.

She was tired, frightened, her throat hurt and she felt very sick, but for the moment at least she was safe.

Harriet rejoined Ed and Charlie in the Saab. 'What did Sally say, Ed?'

'No problem. She's on her way to collect Sam and will take her home with her for the night.'

'Good. Well this is it then guys. Keep your fingers crossed that Mark Ainsley, or rather Murdock Pollard, is at home.' They set off for Osborne Road.

As they neared their destination they could see a group of people and the flashing light of an ambulance. 'It's outside one hundred and thirteen,' gasped Charlie. 'Now what's happened?'

They soon discovered the cause of the commotion. Approaching the group they were in time to see Veronica Caldwell being carried on a stretcher into the ambulance.

'What happened?' asked Harriet.

'It appears she fell down the stairs,' answered the paramedic. 'Her neighbour found her at the bottom and called for us.'

'Is she able to talk?' asked Ed stepping forward.

'She's unconscious,' replied the paramedic. 'She's taken a hefty blow to the head and one leg is definitely broken.'

Harriet peered at the figure on the stretcher, noting the badly cut and bruised face. 'Where is Mr Caldwell?' she asked.

'Doesn't seem to be at home.'

'I bet he's not,' muttered, Charlie.

'Who was the neighbour who discovered her?' asked Harriet.

A voice at the top of the steps answered. 'I did, Chief Inspector. Good job I'm always at home or she might have lain there for hours.'

Harriet looked up to see Mark Ainsley in his dressing gown, sitting in his wheelchair just inside the doorway. This gave them a good excuse to interview him, she thought. 'May we come in and speak to you?' she asked casually.

The ambulance drove off carrying Mrs Caldwell. Harriet and Ed started to walk up the steps. Charlie remained where he was and used his mobile telephone briefly before following them. 'I've just called Liz and asked her to keep us informed about Mrs Caldwell and young Luke,' he said as he joined them.

'Good thinking, Charlie,' said Ed.

'Wonder where this bloke will say he's been?' whispered, Charlie.

'Don't forget, he doesn't know we have been inside his flat Charlie,' Harriet reminded him. Her mobile phone rang at that moment and she answered it swiftly. 'Really Pete? That *is* interesting. Who is at the scene? Right! Keep me posted, please.' She closed down and turned to Ed and Charlie. 'A blue Ford Cortina Mark Three has been found ablaze on the waste land the other side of the Common.'

'Surprise, surprise,' said Ed. 'He must know we're closing in.'

'But he still doesn't realise we actually know who he is,' added Harriet. 'Come on let's meet him.'

Together they entered the ground floor flat where Mark Ainsley sat facing them in his wheelchair, the pasty face blank and expressionless, the eyes no longer pale, but dark, vibrant blue. They looked so artificial now, so out of place in the sallow face.

'You'll want me to tell you all about the fight I heard upstairs,' he said. 'I couldn't sleep and was just getting a glass of milk when I heard this commotion up above. Caldwell was shouting and swearing and then I heard this almighty crash as someone came down the stairs. I went to the door and found Veronica lying there.'

'And where was Vincent Caldwell?' asked, Ed.

'No sign of him. He must have scarpered. It took me a while to get to the door in this thing so I must have missed him.'

'Do you normally put your trainers on in the middle of the night?' asked Harriet sweetly.

Ainsley looked uncomfortable. 'We all do odd things sometimes,' he muttered. 'So what if I put my trainers on?'

'Have you been out tonight, Mr Ainsley?' asked Ed 'Is that why you needed to be wearing trainers?'

Mark Ainsley exploded. 'What a bloody stupid thing to say to a man confined to a wheelchair.'

Harriet's calm voice interjected. 'Not so stupid when we tell you that we have already paid this flat a visit and you were not at home.'

'I must have been asleep and didn't hear you knock.' The voice was now sullen.

'When you didn't answer the door we took the liberty of letting ourselves in.' Ed found pleasure in dropping this bombshell.

The sallow face was now a shade of purple as the man in the wheelchair gritted his teeth. 'How dare you.'

Harriet held out the search warrant for Ainsley to read. 'It was quite legal.'

'What are you accusing me of? So what if I have been out! Practising using my legs at night is not a crime.'

'No, it isn't,' said Ed. 'But we should like to know about your interest in the nurse murders. Oh yes, we found the file on top of your wardrobe.'

'It's also not a crime to be interested in murders,' snarled Ainsley.

'Indeed not,' agreed Harriet. 'But why change your name from Murdock Pollard, and why lie about your accident at the factory?'

'There are no records of your so-called car accident,' said Ed, 'and the hospital you named has no record of you ever having physiotherapy there. All very strange, don't you think, if you have nothing to hide.'

'And why change the colour of your eyes and tell people that you can't walk?' Charlie chipped in.

'None of these things are crimes.' Pollard was obviously shaken but he remained belligerent. 'So I changed my name. What of it? You can't prove I had anything to do with these murders.'

'Did we say you had?' asked Harriet.

Mark Ainsley shifted uneasily in his wheelchair. 'What do you want?'

Ed stepped forward. 'We should like you to come down to the Station with us to answer some questions.'

'Are you charging me?'

'Not at the moment,' replied Harriet. 'And shall we leave the wheelchair behind, you can practice your walking a little more.'

Mark Ainsley heaved himself from the chair and glared at the three officers in front of him. 'You can't prove anything,' he sneered. 'Nothing I've done is a crime.'

'Shall we go,' snapped Ed, looking down with disdain on the

slight figure in front of him. He took out his mobile and asked for one of the police cars to come and collect the suspect before taking Ainsley's arm and leading him from the house and down the steps. Harriet watched the two figures in front of her, the tall solid Harrington and the thin scrawny Ainsley, who did not even came up to her colleague's shoulder. Ainsley's limp was barely noticeable. As one of the witnesses had suggested, his walking action was a slight dragging of his legs. He must have worked very hard over the months to make such a recovery, thought Harriet.

The police car drew up and Ed handed Ainsley over to one of the constables, telling him: 'Take him to the station and book him in with Sergeant Yates. I'll be in later to interview him.'

Charlie locked up the house and joined Ed and Harriet. 'I've spoken to Liz at the hospital. Veronica Caldwell is still unconscious and in a poor state. That's another bastard who needs putting away,' he added.

'Perhaps this time Mrs Caldwell will press charges,' replied Harriet. 'If she refuses to do so then there is nothing we can do, Charlie.'

Charlie pulled a face. 'I know what I should like to do.'

'What about Stockwell?' interrupted, Ed.

'Liz hasn't managed to find out about him yet. She'll get in touch when she has.'

'Good,' said Harriet. 'Now back to the matter in hand.' She frowned. 'We're still thin on the evidence. We need the scarves and those earrings.' She took the latest scarf from her pocket and handed it to Ed. 'Another one for your collection. I have no doubt that it will match the others.'

Ed took the plastic package and carefully put it in his own pocket. 'I'll see that it undergoes the usual forensic tests.'

Harriet spoke again, 'Ainsley, er, Pollard is correct when he says that the things he has done don't actually constitute a crime. We can't even prove that the blue Ford is his. We need something really substantial.'

'There were no driving documents at the flat,' said Ed, 'and having checked with DVLA there is no car registered in the name of Pollard. I'll get Jack to check under the name of Ainsley but I have feeling we shall draw a blank there as well.'

'He won't have had a licence or been insured,' said Charlie. 'He's not daft, there won't be anything to incriminate him.'

'There's not a great deal more we can do tonight,' said Ed. 'I'll tell the team to go home and then I'll return to the station and sort out Ainsley. Tomorrow we'll pull out all the stops to find the scarves and earring. They must be around somewhere. Don't worry, Ma'am,' his voice softened as he looked at Harriet. 'We'll find them.'

Harriet smiled gratefully. 'Thanks, Ed. I'll keep my fingers crossed.' They returned to the Saab and headed back to the police station.

As Harriet climbed from the car Ed said: 'We'll lock Pollard up for the night and let him sweat, if that's all right with you. We'll interview him tomorrow.'

'Good idea, Ed. I think we've all had enough for tonight.' Harriet gave a weary smile. 'Thank you both for your support,' she said, and was gone.

She did not head for home, instead she drove to the hospital where she paid a visit to Luke Stockwell. The young constable lay unmoving in the hospital bed and Harriet sat down beside him. The nurse who had shown her to the patient stood beside her. 'Are you a relative?' she asked Harriet.

'No we work together.'

'You're a policewoman then?'

'Yes. How is he?'

'Severe concussion and a broken left arm.'

At that moment Luke Stockwell opened his eyes. He gave a weak smile. 'Hello, Ma'am.'

'Hello Luke. How do you feel?'

'I've got a splitting headache.'

The nurse touched his arm. 'I can get you something for that. I won't be a moment.' She left the bedside and hurried away.

Luke looked up at the DCI. 'Sorry I didn't get out of the way, Ma'am. Did you get him?'

'We've taken Mr Ainsley down to the station but we still need evidence that will stick. But you are not to worry about any of this Luke. Just get well.' She rose to leave as the nurse arrived with medication for the patient. 'Goodnight, nurse, and thank you.'

Harriet did not sleep too well that night – not that there was much of the night left. It had been after three when she finally crawled into bed. She tossed and turned, the happenings of the night a turmoil in her mind. Where could Ainsley or rather Pollard have hidden the scarves and the earrings? They had to find them. They needed some concrete evidence against this man. She finally fell asleep to dream of running down long, dark corridors with red scarves hanging from the walls where she was unable to find a door to escape.

The alarm clock shrieked in her ear and Harriet sat bolt upright in her bed. Morning all ready! She remembered what had occurred the night before and hastily rose and headed for the bathroom. An hour later her red Lotus drove into her parking space at the police station.

Chapter Twenty Three

A weary looking group gathered in the Incident Room. Harriet stood at the front of the room and thanked everyone for their efforts of the previous night. 'We still have to nail this man,' she said. 'The news cuttings of the murders that we found in Pollard's flat are not evidence enough to convict him. The blue Ford is a burned-out shell and Forensic are going over it at this very moment but we are unable to connect this car to Pollard at present. One good point is that Forensics have obtained a clear set of fingerprints from the garage door and these are being matched with prints collected at Pollard's flat. We do have Samanntha's word that the man who tried to kill her last night was indeed Murdock Pollard, but in court a good defence barrister would convince a jury that in the dark and very frightened, she may well have been mistaken. The pale eyes alone are again, not sufficient evidence. However we do have DNA from the woolly hat and with luck this should match our suspect. We have DNA samples from Pollard and Doctor Boston has promised to rush the results through.'

'We shall be searching the lock-up garage thoroughly as well,' added, Ed. 'Forensic have completed their check for fingerprints, but we shall be looking for a hiding place for the scarves and earrings. Pollard has hidden them somewhere and we need to find them.'

Sally Pringle entered the room. 'Good morning,' she said brightly. 'I've delivered Samanntha to Kelmarsh Road as instructed. She is with the officer of the day and her two friends.'

'Thank you, Sally,' said Harriet. 'With Pollard in custody she should be in no danger.'

'Right everyone!' Ed looked around the room. 'You all know what to do so let's get to it. Meet back here at one – and let's have a result by then, shall we.' He gave one of his rare smiles. 'Jack, I'll leave you to do another check with DVLA to see if the blue Ford is registered under the name of Ainsley.'

The group dispersed and Ed moved over to Harriet. 'I was about to inform you of the condition of Luke Stockwell but I understand you visited him in hospital last night.'

'I did, Ed. I couldn't go home knowing that young man was injured because of our investigation.'

Ed noted the concern on the handsome face and nodded. 'He's going to be fine. I'm going to interview Pollard after lunch, we should have more evidence by then. Let him sweat a little longer it won't do any harm. I'll see you back here at one.'

'Thank you, Ed.' Harriet went to her office to write up her report. She was not altogether jubilant. She had hoped for an arrest last night, but this Murdock Pollard was devious. It was not going to be that easy to make the evidence stick.

At the garages where the car tracks had been discovered, the CID team was searching the end garage where the tracks had indicated that the blue Ford had been housed. Duncan McAllister was on his hands and knees opening every paint pot. 'Nothing,' he muttered. 'Absolutely nothing.'

Bob Finch walked in having scoured the surrounding area with Narinder. 'Same here. There's nothing and nowhere he could have hidden the scarves and earrings.'

'They have to be somewhere,' said Sally. 'If Phillip Hewitt found nothing at his flat then they're not there, so they have to be somewhere else.'

'Let's just think.' Duncan held up his hand. 'What do we have here in the garage. Old paint pots, empty, a rope and a ladder. Why a ladder out here in this isolated place?'

'The roof?' suggested Narinder.

'Well let's see.' Eagerly Bob ran to the garage and carried out the ladder. He placed it against the side of the building and clambered up.

'Anything?' called Duncan.

'Nothing,' came the reply. 'It's a flat roof with no hiding place.' He came back down the ladder.

'Okay,' Duncan scratched his head. 'So where else would you need a ladder. How about the trees?'

'Come on,' called Narinder, heading for the area of trees.

'Hang on a minute,' Duncan strode forward. 'Let's be

systematic about this. Firstly it has to be a tree with an opening in it somewhere and secondly if this Pollard visits it regularly there may well be evidence of this on the ground.'

'Good thinking, Duncan.' Bob joined his friend. 'Right, now careful everyone and start looking for a trampled area under a tree.' The officers spread out and began the search. It was Duncan who a few moments later gave a shout. He was rapidly joined by his colleagues. Duncan was pointing to the ground. Under a large oak tree the ground was flattened and muddy. Looking up into the green foliage they scanned the branches for evidence of a hideaway.

'I can't see any hole,' said Duncan, 'but the leaves are pretty thick at this time of year. I'll get the ladder and go up and take a closer look.' He hurried back to the garage and returned carrying the ladder, placing it against the tree. Bob stood at the foot and held it securely while his friend climbed up. Duncan reached the fork in the thick trunk. He looked around and felt carefully at the back of the biggest branch. He could see and feel nothing.

'Anything there?' called, Sally.

'Not that I can see.' Duncan was disappointed but not prepared to give up. He looked again. He saw a branch that was hanging down over the fork in the trunk. Duncan leaned forward and lifted it carefully. His heart missed a beat as he saw the small opening in the tree. Excitedly he slipped his hand into the hollow. He felt around inside the cavity tentatively. His fingers rested on something soft. He pulled out his discovery and looked at the bag he held in his hand. Duncan's voice croaked as he called down to his colleagues at the foot of the ladder. 'Got it! My God we've got it. Catch, Bob!' He gently dropped the precious bag, which was caught deftly by Bob Finch standing at the foot of the ladder.

Duncan descended at great speed a big smile on his face. 'This will please the DCI.' The bag was a small canvas haversack and with nervous fingers Bob undid the flap.

They all leaned forwards eagerly. 'We'd better not remove anything,' said Bob, 'but look, you can see something red through the plastic bag inside. Ten to one it's the scarves.' He closed the flap again. 'Come on. Let's get back to the station.'

At one o'clock precisely everyone gathered in the Incident Room. Harriet and Ed stood at the front. Jack Fuller reported that no car was registered under the name of Ainsley so obviously he had been driving the vehicle untaxed and unlicensed. Harriet thanked Jack but said she was not in the least surprised by this revelation. The officers became excited as DI Harrington stepped forward. He turned to Harriet with a wry smile. 'The team did not let you down, Ma'am' he said triumphantly holding up a large plastic bag containing the canvas bag. 'We think this bag contains the red scarves and the earrings. We haven't emptied out the contents as they have yet to be fingerprinted and we don't want to destroy any evidence.'

Harriet clasped her hands together. 'No! Oh, well done all of you. Where was it?'

'Duncan!' Ed looked over at the red-head whose hair was standing on end more than usual today. The constable stood up.

'Well, Ma'am. We searched the garage from top to toe and then I sat and thought about the few items inside the place, one of which was a ladder. Why a ladder I thought? So I suggested to everyone that we searched 'up'. We tried the roof of the garage with no success and then I realised that the obvious place was the trees. The garages are surrounded by trees, Ma'am. We looked for a tree that showed activity beneath it. You know, trampled grass and that sort of thing. Sure enough we found one such tree and a search disclosed a hole containing the bag.'

'Congratulations all of you. And especially you, Duncan.' She beamed at the group in front of her.

'If the earrings are in the bag,' said Ed 'and the backs are missing we are heading in the right direction. As you pointed out, we don't think he made any attempt to collect the tiny backs, that's why we always found them near the victim.'

Harriet's face lost its smile. 'We still have to connect Pollard with these findings.'

'No problem, Ma'am.' A voice behind her made her turn sharply. Phillip Hewitt had entered the room unnoticed. Sergeant Hewitt held up a small plastic envelope. 'One earring back found in the fibres of one of Mr Ainsley's sweaters,' he grinned, holding up another plastic bag containing a sweater. 'And I guarantee that this little piece of gold will match the earring back from Carol Young's earrings. The back that we never found at the crime scene. That always annoyed me,' he added with a slight smile.

A cheer went up. 'Good old Toowitt!'

'Well done Hewitt!'

'Brilliant, Sarge!'

'You're amazing, Phillip,' said Harriet. 'Well done!' She turned to the group in front of her, her face alive. 'We have him. This is all we needed, just one small piece of evidence, and you can't get much smaller than an earring back. The DNA should match Carol Young's so just let him try and explain that away.' She handed the small packet to Ed. 'Dr Boston will be delighted to receive this, Ed.' She took the plastic bag containing the haversack from the tree and gave it to Sergeant Hewitt. 'Something else for you to fingerprint Phillip. Now, Ed, let's go and speak to Murdock Pollard, shall we.'

In the interview room Murdock Pollard sat sullen and resentful, a police officer in uniform was standing just behind him. The pale eyes narrowed as the two senior officers entered the room. 'Come to let me go have you?' he sneered.

'Not exactly,' replied Ed dryly. 'I am here to question you about the murder of Carol Young.' Pollard made no response.

Harriet and Ed sat at the table facing him. Ed held up the plastic bag with the sweater inside obviously visible. 'Do you recognise this sweater, Mr Pollard?'

'What have you got that for? I've done nothing wrong, you can't prove I had anything to do with these murders.'

'Is the sweater yours, Mr Pollard?' Ed persisted.

'Well if you took it from my place then you know damn well it is.'

'Where were you last night?'

'At home except for a few minutes when I went for a walk to use my legs.'

'And what time was that?' Harriet kept her voice low and calm although she certainly did not feel calm. She wanted to shake the man in front of her and tell him just what she thought of a callous killer who murdered just to make a point.

Pollard gave a sickly smile. 'At whatever time you called and found me missing.'

Ed snapped back, 'Not good enough Pollard. I suggest that you were at the Amchurch hospital where you attacked a nurse by the name of Samanntha Farndon.'

'Who?' The smile did not falter. 'Another nurse murdered? What a shame.'

'She's not dead.' Harriet smiled in return. 'She is also able to identify you.'

'The pale eyes glared and the smile on the sallow face faded. 'I want my solicitor.'

Ed rose. 'I thought you might. Give me his name and telephone number and I will contact him for you.'

'I'll do it myself.'

'Very well.' Ed took the man by the arm and led him from the room. No one had mentioned the discovery of the earring back from the suspect's sweater. That would be the ultimate trump card that Harriet was holding on to. She had no doubt in her mind whatsoever that Pollard could not wriggle out of this. They were still awaiting the result of the tests on the woolly hat and Harriet was confident that the DNA from the earring back would match that of Carol Young. Everything else would fall into place. She rose and left the room. Charlie could accompany Ed in the interview, he deserved to be in at the kill.

As yet Pollard had not been charged. Harriet was determined that all the evidence would be positive before the final showdown. There must be no slip-ups at this stage. She would go and complete her final report. Thank God they had caught their man. Not just for her own satisfaction and pride, but to put a stop to any further murders. Sergeant Yates appeared in the corridor and called her name.

'Yes, Pete.'

'A Veronica Caldwell is asking for you, Ma'am. She's at the hospital in a bad way and wants to speak to you.'

'Thank you. I think I know what she wants me for.' Harriet hurried to the Incident Room where everyone had found second wind and were happily writing up their personal reports of the night's happenings. There was an air of excitement in the room.

Harriet stood in the doorway. 'Veronica Caldwell has asked to see me at the hospital. Sally, as you helped nail Bill Caldwell perhaps Narinder would like to accompany me to see Veronica. Hopefully she is going to bring charges against her husband. That would put both Caldwell men behind bars.'

Narinder leaped to her feet.

'Nothing would give me greater pleasure, Ma'am.' Harriet smiled broadly. 'What a twenty four hours we've had. Charlie would you join Ed in the interview room while I go to the hospital with Narinder. We haven't charged Pollard yet, we're saving that for later. Ed is waiting for Pollard's solicitor. When he arrives the questioning can get under way.'

Charlie grinned. 'No need to ask twice, Ma'am. I'm on my way.' He left the room at speed.

Harriet and Narinder followed Charlie and headed for the car park where Narinder's eyes lit up at the sight of the red Lotus. 'Wow! I've always fancied a ride in this.'

'Now's your chance. In you get.'

At Torreston Hospital Harriet asked to visit Veronica Caldwell. The bruised and swollen face looked up at them from the bed. One eye was totally closed and there were stitches across her forehead. She tried to smile as her visitors entered but she obviously felt pain. 'Thank you for coming,' she whispered through clenched teeth. 'You were right about my husband, he will kill me if I don't do something about him.'

'Are you bringing charges?' asked Harriet gently.

With tears running down her face, Veronica nodded.

Harriet turned to the young policewoman at her side. 'Would you take Mrs Caldwell's statement, Narinder.'

'Of course.' Narinder took out her notebook and sat gingerly on the side of the bed. An hour later the two women left the hospital and climbed back into the Lotus.

'When we return to the station, collect Bob and go and arrest Vincent Caldwell,' instructed Harriet.

'That will be my pleasure, Ma'am.' The engine roared and the little car sped away.

Harriet had been in her office for barely five minutes, when a light knock announced the arrival of Superintendent Hollyoak.

'Brilliant news my dear, absolutely brilliant. I knew you could do it, I never doubted you for one moment. Has this man you have in custody actually been charged yet?'

'No, George, but we now have sound evidence against him. With luck we shall have even more when Doctor Boston concludes her tests on the woolly hat. The earring back found in Pollard's sweater is conclusive evidence and that too is being tested for a DNA match with Carol Young.'

'Excellent. I shall look forward to your final report, Harry. Let me know when this man has been charged as I shall need to inform the Chief Constable. I shall then leave it to him to contact the deputy Chief Constable.' He smiled slyly at Harriet and then looking more than a little relieved the big man left the room. Harriet sighed. Poor George, his anxieties over this case had certainly caused him sleepless nights, but now he was like a dog with two tails. Harriet decided to visit Ed before writing up her report and as she walked down the corridor she met Sergeant Hewitt who was on his way to see her.

'Ah, Detective Chief Inspector. Thought you'd be happy to learn that we have a clear set of fingerprints from the garage door and they match perfectly with prints we took from Pollard's flat. We also have a beauty from the leather strap on the haversack, again a perfect match with Pollard. There were six red scarves in the bag and quite a collection of earrings, minus the backs of course. All the evidence you need I would say ma'am.'

'Thank you once again Phillip I shall have great pleasure in sharing this information with the gentleman concerned.' She flashed Sergeant Hewitt a smile and hurried off to join Ed in the interviewing room. As she passed the Incident Room, Sally appeared.

'Doctor Boston is looking for you, Ma'am.'

'Thank you, Sally, where is she?'

'In here, Ma'am.' Sally opened the door to the Incident Room and stepped aside to allow Harriet to enter.

Stacey Boston greeted her friend warmly. 'Good result, Harry. Well done.'

Harriet smiled in return. 'Brilliant teamwork, Stacey. Everyone has been superb I can't praise them enough.'

Stacey held out a piece of paper. 'Here you are, one more piece of the puzzle.'

Harriet took the paper eagerly and read what was written

there. 'That's just what we needed.' The excitement in her voice was obvious. 'DNA from the woolly hat matches Pollard, all we need now is the DNA from the earring back to match Carol Young.' Her eyes shone as she folded the paper. 'I shall now visit our suspect and see what he has to say about this.' She thanked Doctor Boston again before hurrying off to join Ed.

In interview room two, Ed was still questioning Murdock Pollard when Harriet entered. Ed spoke for the tape as she came into the room. 'Two forty-five, Detective Chief Inspector Love has entered the room.' Harriet sat down beside Ed and slipped a note to him. Ed read what was written there and then turned to Harriet and nodded.

Murdock Pollard sat glowering beside his solicitor and now he turned his pale eyes towards Harriet. 'None of this crap will stick,' he growled. 'You might as well let me go.'

Harriet fixed he eyes on the pale face in front of her. 'Do you have a car, Mr Pollard?'

'Of course not, you can check with the DVLA.'

'I didn't ask if you were registered to have a driving license, I simply asked if you had a car.'

'No!'

'So you don't have a garage at the back of the shops on Osborne Road?'

'Course not.'

'Have you ever been to the garages at the back of the shops on Osborne Road?'

'Never.'

'Strange,' said Ed. 'Could you explain how your finger prints come to be on one of the garage doors there.'

Pollard shifted uncomfortably. 'You're lying.'

'I don't think so.' Harriet eyed the man in front of her. 'And just to convince you that our case against you is airtight, I have to inform you that hairs inside a woolly hat found at the scene of one of the crimes have been analysed. The DNA taken from these hairs match your DNA. How do you explain that, Mr Pollard? And how do you explain the earring back found in the fibres of your sweater? An earring back that will most certainly have DNA to match that of Carol Young, one of the murdered nurses.'

'You bitch!' Pollard jumped to his feet. 'You still can't pin any of these murders on me.'

'Oh, I think we can, Mr Pollard, you see we have found the bag hidden in the tree near the garages.'

'Don't know anything about a bag in a tree.'

Ed joined in. 'You don't know anything about a bag containing red scarves and earrings?'

'No.'

Harriet spoke in a quiet, deliberate voice. 'I have to inform you, Mr Pollard, that your fingerprints have been found on this bag which contains several red cashmere scarves manufactured at the Perfect factory where you were a sales rep. Also in the bag are numerous earrings which we believe to have been taken from murder victims across the country.'

Murdock Pollard leaped to his feet. '*Bitch!*' he cried. 'You're just like all the others. *Bitch, bitch, bitch.*' He spat out the words and his solicitor took his arm advising him to sit down and say no more. Pollard was now incensed and did not heed. 'They got what they deserved. Think they're little angels but all they do is lead you on. Bitches all of them especially dear little Nurse Farndon. May she rot in hell.'

'I think we now have enough, Mr Pollard.' Ed stood up. 'Thank you for your frank response, that was most helpful. I am charging you with the murder of Carol Young and I must warn you that anything you say may be taken down and...' Ed read Murdock Pollard his rights before turning to the officer standing at the door. 'Please take Mr Pollard to the cells, Wilson.' The officer stepped forward and took Pollard by the arm. Pollard began to struggle but was immediately grasped on the other side by Charlie. The three men left the room.

Ed recounted what was happening for the benefit of the tape recorder before switching it off. He and Harriet left the interview room with Pollard's solicitor.

Back in her office an hour later, Harriet was informed that several members of the press were clamouring at the front of the police station, demanding information about the arrest. Harriet agreed to give them a statement. She hurried from her office and appeared on the front steps of the station. The local TV cameras were present and numerous reporters. She spotted Beefy at the very front of the group vigorously sucking his pencil, and standing quietly at the side she saw Michael Dellaware. He gave her a 'thumbs up' and she smiled in return. Harriet held up her hand and the group fell silent. She spoke in her clear, precise voice:

'A twenty-nine-year-old man has been arrested in connection with the nurse murders and at present is being questioned here at the police station. I can tell you that this man has now been charged with the murder of Carol Young and other charges of murder may well follow. This man will remain in custody until further notice and will appear in court tomorrow. This is all I can tell you at present.'

'What about the other murders?' shouted Beefy, his podgy face red and shiny.

'At the moment this man has been charged with the murder of one nurse only. Carol Young.'

'Have you enough evidence to charge him with the other nurse murders, Ma'am?' Michael Dellaware looked up at Harriet and smiled as he spoke.

'I'm sorry, Mr Dellaware I can't elaborate on what I have already said but I can assure you that if there is any development you will all be informed immediately.' She turned and vanished back into the station where Pete Yates firmly locked the inner door behind her. Harriet returned to her office and made an attempt at writing up her report, but somehow she was unable to concentrate. She rose from her desk and headed for the CID room. It was five thirty already.

As she entered the room where everyone was clearing up papers and filing away documents the officers looked up. 'What a day,' said Harriet. 'I don't know about all of you, but I feel exhausted.'

Charlie chuckled. 'The last few hours have been rather hectic and we didn't get much sleep last night, did we?'

'No, you're right, Charlie, we didn't.' She looked across the room to Bob Finch and Narinder. 'What happened with Vincent Caldwell?'

'He was pretty abusive, as you can imagine,' replied Bob, 'but arresting him made my day.'

'We've charged him with assault and ABH, Ma'am,' said Narinder, 'and remanded him into custody. He will appear in court tomorrow morning and as Inspector Harrington suggested, we have opposed bail to ensure Mrs Caldwell's safety.'

'Well done.' Harriet nodded. 'He should go down for a while, which will give his poor wife time to draw breath and decide what to do with her life.' She turned to Sally.

'Sally would you go round to Kelmarsh Road and inform Samanntha and her friends about the arrest and charging of Murdock Pollard; and Charlie, if you would discontinue the surveillance of the house I'd be grateful.'

'Will do, Ma'am,' said Charlie.

'Now everyone,' announced Harriet, 'I think we should call it a day and all go home. Tomorrow we can start the closing down of the case and sift through all the evidence that we have, to ensure we have made no mistakes. Pollard will appear in court at some time tomorrow.'

A murmur of approval went round the room and even Ed nodded gratefully. 'Right everybody pack up, we'll start again tomorrow. Thank you,' he said, turning to Harriet. 'I just have a few words to say to the team before we leave, if that's okay.'

Harriet smiled. She looked tired but happy. 'See you all tomorrow, then, and well done all of you.' With a swift glance round the room she left.

Back home, Harriet sat with Toastie on her lap and a glass of red wine close at hand. She had telephoned her father to give him the news that the case looked as if it was over and now, feeling quite drained, she had collapsed onto the sofa. She felt in somewhat of a daze. So much had happened in the last couple of days and the outcome was only just beginning to sink in. She would sleep well tonight knowing that one dangerous creature was out of action.

Next morning Harriet had to sit and think carefully before getting dressed. Had they really cracked the case yesterday? Were the horrors of murdered nurses really at an end? She showered and dressed before feeding Toastie and snatching a piece of toast while the coffee infused. She was a few minutes later than usual as she drove into the police car park and was amazed to see Ed's black Saab and several other cars already parked. Going home early must have inspired them all to making an early start she thought. She smiled at Pete Yates as she arrived at the reception window and the usually serious Sergeant Yates beamed back. 'Lovely morning, Ma'am.'

'Wonderful, Pete, and for more reasons than just the weather. Have we heard how Luke Stockwell is?'

'He's much improved, Ma'am and should be out of hospital in a couple of days.'

'Thank goodness for that.'

'Oh, by the way,' Pete ducked down behind the glass window reappearing holding a large bouquet of flowers. 'These came for you, Ma'am.' Pete held out the bouquet, which Harriet took in amazement.

'Good gracious. Thank you, Pete.'

Harriet climbed the stairs opening the card as she went. Pausing at the top she read what was written inside. MANY CONGRATULATIONS ON SOLVING THE CASE. NOW HOW ABOUT THAT DINNER? It was signed Michael and Harriet smiled as she pushed the card into her pocket and made for the CID Room. It all seemed very quiet and cautiously she opened the door. An immediate cheer went up and 'For she's a jolly good fellow' rang out.

Harriet stood in the doorway overcome with emotion. She looked at the sea of faces in front of her. Everyone appeared to be present. George Hollyoak was a the top of the room with Charlie and Ed and there was Stacey Boston, Phillip Hewitt and all who had been involved with the investigation. She felt she was running the gauntlet as she passed through the line of colleagues. Stacey hugged her and Phillip Hewitt shook her hand, Jack Fuller beamed and stuck out his hand too. 'Congratulations, Ma'am,' he beamed.

At the top of the room Charlie grinned from ear to ear. 'Well done, Ma'am.'

George Hollyoak took her hand in both of his and gripped it warmly. 'Brilliant, Harry, congratulations.'

Now Harriet was facing Ed Harrington. She looked up at the sombre face that suddenly creased into a smile. Ed put out his hand and Harriet placed her slender fingers into it. He grasped her hand enthusiastically, his smile broadening. The usually dour expression had gone and his face was suddenly alive. 'Well done… Harry.'

Harriet caught her breath as she heard 'Harry', an unexpected flutter in her stomach. 'Thank you, Ed.'

Harriet gazed around the room at her colleagues and hastily blinked away tears. She had arrived at last! She had been accepted by Ed and the entire team. She was now part of the establishment. This was just wonderful. She tried to speak to the gathering but found she had a lump in her throat. She swallowed hard before being able to find her voice. 'Thank you. Thank you all so much but none of this would have been possible without all of you. I don't think anyone could wish for a more reliable, loyal and hard working team than the one I have been privileged to work with.' Sally stepped forward with a large bouquet of flowers.

'We feel privileged to be working with you, Ma'am.'

Everyone clapped and Harriet again had to blink away a tear as she stood there holding two bouquets. This was all too much. George Hollyoak hastily took her elbow. 'Coffee is ready, and we all know you can't get down to work without the real stuff.'

Laughter rang in her ears as she was led to the table where the coffee was steaming and two plates of croissants had been placed.

'Allow me, Ma'am,' said Charlie, as he poured the coffee with a flourish.

'Thank you, Charlie.'

'And a croissant?'

Harriet looked up to find Ed standing beside her. She smiled. 'Now, you know I can't eat croissants with any manner of elegance, Ed…'

'I don't think elegance is a thing that need ever concern you.'

'Then I'll risk it.' Harriet took a croissant from the plate that Ed offered. She felt happier than she had felt for many weeks. She was going to enjoy working in Torreston and could hardly wait for their next big case.